Ma...
who knew... ...ly, had som... ...al to say... ...of them

To Francine, who tried to be a female Henry Miller before turning radical feminist:

> *"If you're going to be a woman's libber, lov, you've got to be able to go at least a night without a man."*

To V. Schimmel, the Dutch airline hostess turned professional divorcee:

> *"You ought to get paid for each shot or each night, lov. You're cut from the mold that made the world's best whores."*

To Jeanette, who had a knack for discovering a man's most covert desire and a pathological need for satisfying it:

> *"Your trouble is you're too easy, lov. All a man has to do is rub your neck and you give head. Good head, lov. The best. But it might be more fun if it were a little harder to get."*

To Karen, who went to work for a pornographer to learn what they had never taught her in Connecticut:

> *"You're a liar, lov, a beautiful liar. You were born a liar and you'll die a liar unless you come to the hospital. After I operate you can go back to your Frenchman, his love oils and his water bed."*

THE
Ms.
GIRLS

~~~~~~~~~~~~~~~~~~~~~~~~~~~~~~~~

CHERYL NASH

A DELL BOOK

Published by
Dell Publishing Co., Inc.
750 Third Avenue
New York, New York 10017

Dell ® TM 681510, Dell Publishing Co., Inc.
Printed in the United States of America
First printing—July 1972
Second printing—September 1972

For Kate Millet, affectionately

In the room the women come and go
Talking of Michelangelo.

T. S. ELIOT

Woman, however, if physically and mentally normal,
and properly educated, has but little sensual desire.

RICHARD VON KRAFFT-EBING

The Ms. Girls

PART ONE

Chapter One

Karen was a liar. She was twenty-three years old and she
had been a liar for as long as she could remember. The way
she told it she came from a small town in Connecticut; her
family lived in the center of town in a large white house
with giant pillars in front, a west wing off the dining room
and an east wing off the living room, screened porches off
the west and east wings, a five-acre backyard and quarters
for the servants over the garage which were twice as big as
the apartment she shared with another twenty-three-year-
old girl on Seventy-third Street near First Avenue.

The way she told it her father was head of the local
paper manufacturing company, as his father had been before him, and so on back to the first Thompson who had
come to this country in the late seventeenth century (when
the town's business was charcoal, not paper). The first
Thompson, the way Karen told it, had fought in King Phillip's War and was there when King Phillip himself was cap-
tured. When asked who King Phillip was Karen explained
that he was a traitorous "praying" Indian. When asked
what a "praying" Indian was Karen became extremely sol-
emn and explained that a "praying" Indian was one who

had been converted by the first settlers to Christianity and who had been given complete run of the settlements. She had read about King Phillip's War in a book which she had stumbled upon and she had become so intrigued with it that she wove it into the fabric of her family history.

Karen was also fond of talking about the works of art which her family owned and which hung in the large rooms of their great pillared house in Connecticut. According to Karen they had several Winslow Homer paintings and several Picassos. Karen liked to ask people whether they had ever seen a reproduction of Picasso's mother and child, the woman extremely haggard, drawn out, in a manner reminiscent of El Greco. It was from Picasso's blue period, Karen would explain. When whomever she was talking to confessed to having seen a reproduction of this famous painting Karen would smile demurely, and almost, whispering, explain that the original hung over the marble-topped dressing table in her mother's bedroom. Then she would explain that her mother and father had separate bedrooms, that as far as she could remember, they always had.

I have a fantastic imagination.

Because Karen was a liar she never believed anything Jeanette told her. If Jeanette came home after a date and explained that she had gone down on her boyfriend in the subway on their way out to a Brooklyn beach, that she had made him sit with her in the little engineer's booth that the Brighton trains still had, and then she had done it to him, Karen just smiled. Jeanette came up with the wildest sex stories. According to Jeanette she was always doing fantastic things to her boyfriends in fantastic places, or they were doing them to her. Jeanette's stories were exactly why Karen liked her. They had a kind of silent compact. Karen would never question Jeanette's sex stories, and Jeanette would never question Karen's tales about her old Connecticut family. Even if she were to find out that King Phillip's War happened mostly in Massachusetts.

Karen was also fond of talking about her family's cars. Her father had a Bentley, she said, and her mother a light green four-door Lincoln Continental convertible. There was a Chevrolet half truck to run around town in and a

Porsche that no one ever used since Karen had come to
New York. Sometimes Karen was asked why she hadn't
brought the Porsche with her and she would explain that
she had made a break with her family, that she was on her
own, supporting herself, not taking a penny from them.
She went home for Christmas, she said, and for her grandmother's birthday in April, but that was all.

I never had a grandmother.

Karen would tell these stories to anyone who would listen but she especially liked telling them to men. It gave her
a quiet thrill when she came out with a really fantastic lie,
like the one about the Picasso original. The more likely it
was that she would be found out the more it pleased her to
go on. Then, when whomever she was talking to expressed
doubt of her, she became haughty, and refused to talk any
further. These were the best moments for her. When she
could turn a cold stare on a man and let him know, without
uttering a word, that because he had doubted her she
would never again have anything to do with him. He could
pursue her forever, it would do him no good. As far as she
was concerned he no longer existed.

The apartment Karen shared with Jeanette took up the
entire left half of the third floor which meant that access
to the back bedroom was through the kitchen, that access to
the kitchen was through the living room, and that access to
the entire apartment could be had only through the front
bedroom into which the hall door opened. The girls had
furnished the apartment with inflatable chairs, beds from
the Salvation Army store, and junk that had been given
them by an old boyfriend of Jeanette's who had left town
to teach in a college in Nebraska. That was Barry who,
Jeanette said, liked men more than he liked women, but
who liked Jeanette because Jeanette was built like a boy in
the back, or almost like a boy, and because she liked it
when he entered her anus. Barry had given them dishes and
stainless steel eating utensils for their kitchen, an old couch
with semen stains on both sides of all three pillows, two
small bookcases and a number of glossy photographs of
male statues which he said were from the Louvre. Jeanette
hung these photographs over the kitchen table (which they
also got at the Salvation Army store) so that she could look

at them whenever she ate. Sometimes she said she missed
Barry, and the apartment he had kept on Washington
Square, and the parties he had given there. She told Karen
she had been the only girl at those parties and she explained how you could never call a homosexual a "lady"
but how you always refer to them as "she". But of course
Karen always took Jeanette's stories with a grain of salt.

But Jeanette is a gas, really.

Karen had been living in New York for three years.
When she first arrived she had stayed at a hotel for women
that overlooked the East River Drive. The rent was high
and the other girls were frequently what Karen called
"cases." This meant that they were so involved with themselves that Karen could not jolt them into paying attention
to her even with the story of Picasso's mother and child. Or
it meant that they were attentive to Karen only because
they wanted to dominate her for reasons Karen preferred
not to think about.

They wanted me to get into their pants.

At that time Karen was working for one of the large uptown department stores. She was taking a course and being
paid to take it. The course was given on the top floor of the
department store in a large classroom by a cold, serious
woman named Mrs. White. Mrs. White taught her students
how to fill out sales slips, how to charge customers' ac-
counts, how to close out cash registers, how to change cash
register paper rolls, how to treat "golden account" customers (who carried special gold charge account plates because
of the level of their past purchases) how to deduct tax
from sales to be delivered out of town or made by special
United Nations personnel. Mrs. White taught them how to
dress, how to treat the sales people, how to deal with difficult customers, what to do if they caught anyone shoplift-
ing, how to refer to the special departments of the store
where goods were to be had for less money than in the regular departments, how and when to accept exchanges, how
to handle the store script, and what to do with the money
at the end of each working day.

To date, no one has ever been in Mrs. White's pants!
Mrs. White was not a gas, really.

It was in Mrs. White's class that Karen met Joe. "Joe" was not his real name. His real name was long and impossible to pronounce. He was an Indian, not a red Indian like King Phillip, but an English-speaking Indian from Bengalore. He insisted that Karen call him Joe because she had so much trouble with his real name. He was always insisting that Karen do things which he knew would please her or be easier for her. He was the nicest, most gentle man that she had ever met. He believed everything she told him completely and feelingly.

While she had been seeing him, Karen often thought that if he were to learn there was no family from Connecticut, no house, no cars, no Picasso, he would deny it firmly. He would insist that of course there were, that they existed as surely as anyone's family and possessions, even if they had their first existence in Karen's imagination. He was that sort of person.

Karen never tested this hypothesis, however. She never gave Joe the chance to tell her everything she imagined existed, did exist. She never confessed to him that her stories were lies. Instead, she stopped telling them. For a long while, while she had been seeing Joe, she lied to no one.

Then Joe had to go back to Bengalore to see his wife and child and when he came back Karen refused to see him. She insisted they would never again be lovers. Joe accepted this just as he accepted her stories, fully, happily, just as if that were of course the only thing to be done if that was what she wanted.

It was the only thing to be done.

When Mrs. White's class was over there was a little graduation ceremony. She gave each of the students a flower. The women were given a gardenia and the men a white carnation. They were told which department to go to and were introduced to their section managers. They were told to learn their section manager's code call (the series of tones played on the store's loud speaker) and they were dismissed by Mrs. White.

After eight months in the department store Karen quit. Nearly everyone she had met there had guessed that nothing Karen said about herself could be believed. It was time to move on. She found a job as a receptionist in an uptown automobile salon. She sat in the showroom alongside the expensive foreign sports cars and answered questions put to her by people whom she did not think were really interested in buying. If she spotted anyone who looked as though they were serious she rang for one of the salesmen.

She was also supposed to answer the phone but the phone almost never rang. The salesmen all had phones of their own and the parts and shipping departments were in another building altogether. Karen was there mostly to look attractive and to be nice to people who wandered in off the street.

Although Karen wasn't showy, and although she tried to hide her sexuality, it wasn't difficult for her to look attractive. Her brown-to-blonde hair was long and thick and framed a long face with high cheek-bones, a classic nose, and a wide mouth. She was tall and broad-shouldered and had a way of seeming to be above sensuality that was more effective than she knew. So when people did wander in it was as much to talk to her as to admire the lush interiors and complex dashboards of the little cars.

Karen didn't mind this. A continuing flow of people made it possible for her to stay with that job longer than she had with the one in the department store. She left it finally, not because the people there all knew she was lying about her family, but because she got bored. People wandered into the showroom mostly at lunchtime. For hours on end in the morning and in the afternoon nothing happened. She wasn't permitted to use the phone for personal calls or to read at her desk.

Then she met Jeanette through a salesman she was dating. They decided to room together and Karen quit her job and started looking for places to live. The railroad apartment on Seventy-third Street was far from the subways and in a miserable block (there were fire escapes in front of all the buildings and a frequent odor from the sanitation plant near the river) but one hundred dollars a month apiece was all the girls could afford.

They moved in and for a time Karen did not try to find another job. She had a few hundred dollars saved and she decided to first get the apartment set up and then to look for work. It was she who found all the furniture in the Sal-

vation Army store and she who helped Jeanette's friend
Barry's friend Harvey up the stairs with the semen-stained
couch. Barry himself was already in Nebraska. He'd been
there for six months.

When the apartment was ready to live in properly Karen
drew up a set of rules. Because they expected to entertain
men Karen decided that 1) *all articles of feminine hygiene
are to be kept out of sight.* Diaphragm cases, tubes of vaginal jelly (Jeanette still used the greasy kid stuff) and the
Emko foam (which Jeanette used when she was in too
much of a hurry to put in the diaphragm) had to be hidden
in the medicine cabinet. The douche bags, which were most
difficult of all to hide, were to be kept in the narrow
bathroom closet. 2) *No sex in the apartment when the
other girl was present.* If one of the girls wanted to spend
the night with someone they were to do it only if the other
girl had previously said she would be away. Otherwise, use
the man's bed. 3) *No "birddogging",* as Karen called it. No
dates with any man the other girl had spotted first. That
was the most important rule of all, Karen explained, because to break it would threaten to dissolve the relationship
and all the time and trouble getting and setting up the
apartment would be wasted. 4) *No discussion with men of
the other girl's problems or personal habits.* This was also
important, Karen said, because she was extremely sensitive
and she thought Jeanette probably was too. Jeanette agreed
and Karen explained the last rule, 5) *No drunks,* in or out
of bed. Karen said she despised drunks, that her father
once had a drinking problem which, thank God, he had
learned to control but which had threatened the paper
company which he ran and therefore the entire economy of
the small town from which Karen hailed. Jeanette agreed
to all the rules and Karen happily went through the want
ads that night. It was time to find a new job.

Jeanette sat on the semen-stained couch with her legs
curled under her and Karen sat with the back pages of the
Sunday Times classified section spread out on the floor.
Jeanette was going out with a doctor named Morris Levy.
He was a vascular surgeon with an office on the Upper
West Side. She had met him at the dentist's office in which

she worked. She was a dental technician. She was sitting on the couch waiting for him to call.

"Here's one," Karen said from the floor. She put her index finger under the ad. "Attractive, well-mannered young woman, prefer English, receptionist, gal Friday."

"It's the gal Friday stuff you have to watch," Jeanette said. "I'll bet that means they want to get in your pants."

"Who doesn't?"

"Morris is adorable. He arranged me on his examination table like I was some kind of display for the female sex organs."

"They always want English girls," Karen said. "They want you to be able to pick up the telephone and snow their clients with your accent."

The phone rang and Jeanette threw herself across the couch to answer it. When she found it was Morris she stretched out and turned toward the back of the couch so that her forehead was resting against the upholstery and her head was on the arm.

Karen picked up the want ads and went into the back bedroom. She threw herself on her Salvation Army bed. She underlined all the ads that asked for attractive and very attractive girls for receptionists and gal Fridays.

Jeanette came into her room and leaned against the wall. "I'm going to meet him."

"Now?"

"Uh huh."

"Why doesn't he pick you up?"

Jeanette shrugged. "It doesn't matter."

"You bend over backwards for these guys."

Jeanette snickered. "I sure do. You know he's going to get around to it tonight. He's been holding something back, I just know it."

"What do you mean?"

"I don't know what it is but he's some kind of wonderful freak, you'll see. I'll tell you tomorrow. I mean so far he's been pretty straight, you know?"

Karen nodded.

"I'm going to take my stuff in case I have to go right to work from his apartment so I won't see you until tomorrow night. He probably wants to use me in some sort of experiment. You'll see."

Karen shook her head. "Boy," she said. "You get involved with the weirdest men."

Jeanette laughed and started out of the room. "You'll be looking for a job in the morning anyway." She meant that in the last weeks she had been spending many of her mornings with Karen because she didn't have to be at the dental office until eleven o'clock.

"You'll see. He probably wants to put his stethoscope inside and listen to me lubricate. That's what I thought he wanted to do last time."

"Well, what did he put inside?" Karen asked.

"It was nice," Jeanette said.

Karen wanted to say that it was Jeanette who was the nut but the girl was gone by then. She had stepped into the bathroom for her diaphragm case and her tube of Ortho-Gynol and had just thrown them into her blue canvas bag and left.

Karen sighed and ran her finger down the column of ads, up along the column to the left of it (proceeding backwards, like a Hebrew, like Morris Levy) and finally stopped her finger halfway down the middle of the page.

Cllg grad.   Eng Maj.   Ed Asst. $120/wk.
Corliss Agency   2 Broadway   Bring Resume

"Jesus," Karen said aloud, and sighed again. She would do almost anything to get a decent job like that one, to sit behind a desk, to work with intelligent people.

She shook herself out of the daydream and went back to the ads for which she was qualified.

rcptnst-gal-fri-must be attractv
outgoing, typng, prfrd, no steno,
Eng prfrd, outer office dress
whlslr OX 9 6911 empy dscnt 95/wk

"Oh, Jesus," Karen said again and threw herself suddenly off the bed. She walked into the bathroom, opened the medicine chest and took down her pack of Enovid. She popped one of the tiny pills from the plastic circle and swallowed it with some water. She had almost forgotten again.

She went back to the want ads.

Well, it's hard to remember, with no man to remind you.

Veltraud Schimmel was a willowy blonde girl whose mother was Dutch and whose father was German and dead. "The only good German is a dead German," Veltraud had been taught by her fellow students in Amsterdam when she was five. Her mother had taken her there after divorcing her German husband in 1949. Veltraud was so impressed with every Dutch child's hatred for every German and everything German that she came home, finally, and told her mother what they were saying. "The only good German is a dead German."

Veltraud's mother had laughed and agreed, which set the small girl's mind at rest. Her mother did not tell Veltraud that she had dual citizenship, that she was as German as she was Dutch, that the first years of her life had been spent in Berlin. It was not until she was fifteen that Veltraud realized the truth.

That was one of the things which made her leave home and take up residence with a married man in an attic on Jan van der Heydenstraat when she was just sixteen. She said she could no longer stand the sight of her mother, but the truth was that she could not bear to be reminded that she was half German. Every day there were a thousand reminders of what the Germans had done in Amsterdam. The Jewish quarter, for instance, had been left standing just as it had been when the city was finally liberated by the Canadians, the buildings were barren, the usable wood had been torn from them by a people desperate for heat in the cold winters of '43 and '44. And Veltraud had to pass through the Jewish quarter every morning on her way to the university.

But once a rich girl always a rich girl. When Veltraud's father died in the early Fifties he left his daughter a considerable number of marks in trust with his former wife. Veltraud's mother was still attractive, so she used the money to live high enough to catch a rich husband, a Dutchman this time, a coffee importer with holdings in the Caribbean. Which meant that when Veltraud was old enough to realize there had once been money in her name it was all gone.

What the money had bought was there, but it was her mother's, not hers. It had bought a berth in a modern mansion an hour out of Amsterdam and an allowance of a thousand guilders a month. For her mother. All Veltraud had was a bag full of hate for her dead father, for the half of her that was German, and an appetite for the kind of life she had led since her mother had caught the millionaire Dutchman, a way of life which was exactly opposite to the one her married "friend" could provide her with in the attic on Jan van der Heydenstraat.

So Veltraud left him. In spirit before she moved out in person. She lied about her age and got a job offer from Royal Dutch Airlines. When the personnel manager at Schipol Airport found out about her real age she found she could keep him quiet by entertaining him in the attic while her married "friend" was with his wife. And when the personnel manager brought a friend to watch, Veltraud took it in stride and invited him into bed with them.

By the time she was eighteen she was a stewardess. Her languages were good and her friend in the personnel department saw to it that no one looked very closely at her school certificate. When she was nineteen she found a lonely, gullible American, married him for his money and his citizenship, moved to Bayonne, New Jersey, talked him into an easy divorce two years later, and saw to it that the alimony was enough to pay the rent on a two-bedroom apartment in a high-rise building on Twelfth Street and Avenue of the Americas.

She had been living there ever since, waiting for the right millionaire to come along to lift her back into the bracket she had found so enjoyable as a young girl in the modern mansion outside Amsterdam. But so far the right millionaire had not come along and Veltraud was twenty-four but could pass, of course, for thirty, or for nineteen, depending on what she did with her hair, her eye-liner and her neckline.

While she waited for the right millionaire she tried to recapture the feelings she had last felt in the first weeks in the attic on Jan van der Heydenstraat. There, where she had renounced everything Germanic about her, and had labored for hours over the body of the man she loved, when the romance of poverty had not yet worn off, she had lost something she had been looking for ever since. She had screamed with passion in that attic, screamed so the people in the houseboats in the Amstel a block away could hear her. And she had not screamed like that since. When she had an orgasm now something would catch and hold her back, keep her from releasing everything that had been building in her body. The orgasm would come and go almost quietly, and the harder she tried, the worse it was. She was always left with something hanging, something extra, that she did not want. Sexual lagniappe.

No one in America could pronounce her name so a week after moving to Bayonne Veltraud became Vee, or V, or V., depending upon who was writing to her. Ivan, her husband, wrote it Vee, his mother used the letter alone and his sister, Francine, who hated her with a hate so crystalline pure she could have bottled it to make instant bigots, wrote it with a period after it. Everyone, of course, pronounced it the same way, as did the gentleman with whom V was in bed that morning, trying to recapture the emotions of Jan van der Heydenstraat, Roger Conheim, a tall, balding, stock-broker.

"Roger. Wake up, Roger. Go wash your mouth out and shave, yah. Hurry, yah."

V almost always spoke in the imperative. Most people thought it was cute. They heard her foreign accent which was so difficult for them to place and guessed V didn't have enough English to temper her speech, to couch her desires in the conditional. They thought she hadn't learned yet to say "could you" or "wouldn't you like". But they were wrong. In her native Dutch V spoke in the imperative too. There was only one man to whom she had not spoken that way, the married man who had set her up in the attic on Jan van der Heydenstraat.

"Roger. Roger! Wake up, yah."

Roger Conheim stirred and lifted his knee in an automatic reflex to hide his morning erection.

"I can't," he said.

"What?"

"I have to go to the office."

"Roger, look at the clock, it is only seven-thirty. Go shave, yah?"

Roger Conheim groaned and struggled out of bed. He was naked because V insisted he sleep with her naked. He wasn't comfortable that way. In fact, he wasn't comfortable with V at all, but he hadn't yet found the courage to tell her that.

Roger was unusually successful with very attractive women, more successful, in fact, than he wanted to be. His money was more aphrodisiac than he could handle. The last thing in the world he wanted was to start the day by making slow, obedient love to V. He had an erection only because he had terribly to urinate.

V watched as he crossed the bedroom and disappeared into the bathroom. Except for a slight bulge of fat around his middle he had a body which excited her. But then most bodies excited her, whether they belonged to men or to women. After a day at the beach she was ready to make love for the rest of the week.

"Hurry, Roger, yah?" she called from the bed.

She heard him gargling with her "Scope". She kicked the sheet away from her body and pulled Roger's pillow down to the middle of the bed. In the attic in Amsterdam, when she had been sixteen, Hans had always made love to her with a pillow under her. If she had a pillow under her and got her legs up right she could rub her clitoris against a man's pelvic bone, but without the pillow she hadn't a chance. And with Roger, she needed every edge she could get. Especially in the morning. He was worst in the morning. Hans had always left her dazed and joyful in the morning, so that all she would do all day was sit around and wait for him to get back. Until the romance of poverty had worn thin. Until the personnel manager.

She pushed the pillow under her and smiled at him as he came out.

"Oh, you haven't shaved. Go shave, Roger."

Roger did an about-face and walked back into the bathroom. She had been ready for him. She had her legs

drawn up and apart in the position she had found excited
him most. She heard the water running and brought her
legs together and rolled over on her side to wait.

In the attic in Amsterdam she had slept that way, legs
curled up to her stomach, foetus style, with Hans curled
around her, his knees against her knees, his penis against
her buttocks and his arms enfolding her. When he was
there. Before the poverty got to her.

On Sundays when he could get away from his family
they would walk down to the river and up, away from the
central city. They were already beyond the canals on Jan
van der Heydenstraat so they had few bridges to cross. In a
city which has so many bridges that was unusual. She remembered it now because she had just read Camus' *The
Fall*. The narrator of the book did not like to cross bridges.
They terrified him.

V didn't like *The Fall*. She didn't like existentialists. She
read it because she had bought it and she didn't like to
waste things. She had bought it because she thought it
would be about sex. She was always looking for information which might help her to have the kind of orgasm she
had once had. She read everything anyone ever wrote
about sex, fact and fiction.

"Roger. Hurry. Yah."

She was already moist. If he hadn't been there she would
have spent a half-hour masturbating with her giant-size
tube of Colgate toothpaste.

Hans and she would walk along the river past the Cen-
turbaan until they ran out of city. Sometimes they would
bicycle all the way out and the tires of the bicycles would
make a sweet sound on the wet pavement. They would
stop for a snack at a restaurant with tables on a dock beside the road and sometimes the sun would come out while
they sat there.

Sometimes, in New York, when it rained, or just after it
had rained, something the rain left in the air would remind
her of Amsterdam. It would cut her cruelly. It was worse
than an insult from her husband's sister. Her ex-husband's
sister. It left her with a sore feeling in her lower back.

Roger appeared, shaved and deodorized. He was wearing
a thick blue towel around his waist. It was not to hide his

penis but to hide his fat. She rolled over onto the pillow and yanked the towel away from him.

Hans had never needed encouragement. Hans was a miracle man, he was always ready for sex. In the morning after he went down to the water closet on the floor below he would come up, take off his robe, and before her eyes his penis would grow stiff and swollen. He hadn't been circumcised. All Americans were circumcised. She hated it.

One morning just to test the strength of his penis she had picked up her shoe. She was already working for KLM then, although Hans didn't know what she had had to do to get the job, and she had a blue uniform shoe with a big heel. She hung it from his penis and it didn't drop an inch. She went to the old armoire the landlady had left in the attic for her. She had a pair of wooden shoes, huge farmer's shoes, a souvenir of Holland bought by a French friend of the personnel manager and left behind one night. She hurried back to Hans with one of them, took the KLM shoe from his penis, and hung the wooden farmer's shoe on it. It dropped a bit but still hung well above the perpendicular. Maybe men's penises lost strength if they were circumcised. At the moment Roger's couldn't have held a baby bootie.

"Come, Roger. Come, yah," V said as she grabbed her breasts to look more enticing for him.

"V. I . . ."

"Just climb over me, it will come up. Hurry."

Roger got into position and she reached down, put one hand on his scrotum and the other in the crack of his backside and massaged him gently until he grew stiff. Then she slid him in.

"Don't move. Just stay there, yah."

If he moved she knew he would come too soon. She had learned that she had to get ready first, before she let him set his own pace. It was that way with most of these circumcised men. She had to rub against him awhile first, rub against the hairy bone above his penis.

Perhaps circumcised men were generally more effeminate. She would have to make a study. If she could only find one who hadn't lost it.

At first she had thought it was nice. All that soft, swollen flesh around the smile in a man's penis. It made it seem more able to do its work, more streamlined. At first it had excited her just to look at it even when it wasn't swollen and erect because with no skin to hide the head it was as if the man were already excited. But they were all like Ivan, her ex-husband, these foreskinless men. A girl had to control them, to tell them when to put it in, and when to move, and when to come.

V swerved and pushed, using the pillow as a pivot and twisting her ankles in and out, watching them. They were dancing, twisting in and out over Roger's flabby buttocks. It was always better if you watched a part of your own body, or if you closed your eyes. Except for Hans.

But Roger stayed stiff and steady and he was heavy on her. It was better if they weighed a lot, so that she had something to push herself against.

"All right. Move, Roger, yah."

Roger pushed himself off her and began to pump. His eyes were closed and his mouth was shut tight. His brows were knit as if he were concentrating. V lifted her legs higher and let him set the pace. She was ready.

"All right, Roger. Come. Yah. Come ahead."

Roger came. Like a man afraid of hurting himself, and V went off too, like a woman with arthritis. She shuddered, and shrank, she felt herself tense and relax and knew that she would be more open than she had been a moment ago, that Roger's circumcised penis would have more room to move around in, if it weren't already shrinking and slipping out. But that was all. There was no real relief. Not even the hint of a cry at the back of her throat. Just Roger sliding away.

She turned and looked at the blank wall on the far side of the bed. She shuddered and muttered something to herself in Dutch and Roger asked, "What is it, darling?"

"Nothing."

"Was it good?"

"Oh, yah, yah, it was good."

"I better hurry. I want to get in early."

"Yah. Yah."

What V had muttered translated loosely as: *somewhere in America there must be an uncircumcised rich man who can fuck. What am I doing wrong that I cannot find him?*

V had a ten-step modus operandi for finding rich men. She was ready to try it again.

1. Bathe, brush teeth, gargle
2. Douche with F.D.S.
3. Squirt Feminique
4. Roll on Ban
5. Get into bikini panties
6. Make up breasts
7. Brush and tie up hair
8. Put on face
9. Decide on either the Lord and Taylor outfit, the Bendels, or the Paraphernalia man-hunting outfit.
10. Put it on.

The Lord and Taylor outfit boasted blue-green and white Pucci pants with bell bottoms, and a long tunic (mid-thigh length) with a deep V neck, the material of which was soft, and clung. She wore it with blue or green sandals.

The Paraphernalia gear was a crocheted mini-dress under which she wore her see-thru no-bra and beige bikini underpants. It was off-white, had a low neckline and long, full sleeves.

The Bendels purchase was for occasions when the other outfits had failed or were in danger of failing. It was composed of a lavender mini-dress deeply cut out under the arms exposing both sides of her breasts. It was worn with no bra. It was high in front but plunged below her waist in the back revealing the very top of the crack of her buttocks. She wore it with deep purple medium high shoes and a Gucci bag. It had never failed to get her a bite.

The taxi driver V hailed after getting dressed was instructed to take her to Rockefeller Center, or to Wall Street, at two in the afternoon or at six in the evening, respectively.

V's gambit was very simple. She would arrive at an expensive bar, in an exclusive hotel or restaurant at an hour when the only clients were likely to be people who ran their own lives. She would order a drink and continually look at her watch. She would invariably be approached by a man.

The bartender at a place on Fifty-third Street near Fifth Avenue knew her. His name was Max. He had rings under his eyes, droopy jowls and a bald pate.

The fourth or fifth time she came into his place he had said, "You know, Miss Schimmel, if you didn't turn so many of 'em down I would have taken you for a high-class hooker."

"Max, you should be ashamed," she told him.

"Sure, sure. But what if I do fix you up with Mr. Right? Plenty of bread, good in the sack, all the requirements?"

"Single or divorced," she said.

"Yes, yes, single or divorced. What then?"

"Then I'd never forget you, Max," she had said.

V lay in bed for a half-hour after Roger left her. Finally, she decided to go the whole hog, as they said in America, a country of disgusting expressions. A country in which all the men were circumcised. She would wear the Bendels outfit. She was a knockout in the Bendels outfit.

Jeanette awoke first. God, it was good to be free, to have your own apartment and not have to be back in it until you felt like it, to have a job that paid the rent and the clothes bill and even left enough over to buy the morning coffee and the lunches and even the suppers you had to pay for yourself. God, but the world was a wonderful place.

She rolled over and examined the top of Morris Levy's head. His brown hair was thinning and bits of pink scalp could be seen where the night-matted hair stuck together. She kissed him lightly there and smiled. She felt like kicking off the sheet and shouting but she didn't want to wake him.

Not since Barry. Not since that god-damned, pig-pricked, son-of-a-bitching bi-sexual Barry had she felt this good. Well, who needed the bastard? Let him stay and rot in the Midwest with his fairy friends. He wasn't the only man on the face of the earth who knew how to please a girl.

She sat up and stretched and Levy groaned and curled up tighter. His head was nearly under the sheet. He was in a foetal position, his knees drawn up against his stomach.

His fat stomach. His fat, hairy, cute, lovely stomach. God, it had been good.

Jeanette looked across the dark room to a place where the morning sun came in a thin streak between the venetian blinds and the window wall. An empty, open bottle of V.S.O.P. was on the floor there. She saw it and laughed.

"Wha— What?" Morris groaned.

"Shh."

"No, have to get up. Have to be at the hospital early. What time is it?"

Jeanette looked over Morris' head to the clock on his night table and told him it was seven-thirty.

"Got to get moving," he told her.

He pulled up the sheet, dove down under it, ran his tongue along her thighs and pushed at her. She rolled over and he started again what he had started the night before and Jeanette shrieked and laughed.

"I thought you had to be at the hospital," she managed to say between convulsive laughs.

He bit her. He hurriedly dove his tongue into her rosebud of an anus, jumped up and started walking away.

"Now you're going to leave me like this," Jeanette said.

Morris nodded and opening the bedroom door left to disappear down the hall. A moment later she heard the water running in the shower. She shuddered as she remembered how he had excited her. She had had to egg him on at first, saying things like, "Come on, Morris, come on, do what you want to me, oh Morris what a lovely thing you've got, do whatever you want to me."

Well, he had. Good God, he had.

She rolled back over and threw the sheet clear off the double bed. Then she sat up again and looked down at her legs. She had good legs. Her skin was light (she had never tanned well and even now, in the middle of July, she was as white as ever) and her curves were nice, understated perhaps but nice. She ran her hands down her thighs and brought up her knees so she could hug herself. She was in love with herself again this morning.

The hell with Barry and the thing he loved you to eat.

"Eat me, eat me, eat me, eat me," she sang softly to herself in mocking memory of the man who, until several hours before, had been the focus of all her thoughts and the cause of the great void in her heart. She was free of him at last. For doing that, Morris Levy could paint her with gentian violet if he liked, and scrape it off with sandpaper. Ohhh, the thought made her shake.

She jumped out of bed and hurried to the bathroom.

"I want to watch you shave, and do everything," she shouted into the curtains.

The steam from the shower had already coated everything in the room, she couldn't see herself in the mirror. She plopped down on the toilet and reached for her douche bag. It had been six hours since he had come inside her, so she could douche now, and wash and change her diaphragm. Not that he was likely to use the normal way now that they had established what he really liked, but it paid to be ready. Anything he wanted was O.K. with her.

He popped his head out from between the halves of the shower curtain and looked over at her with a smile.

"Morris, you're adorable," she told him.

He popped his tongue out and licked his lips, which made her shiver, and then he drew his head back in.

Jeanette Emerson, Jeanette hummed to herself as she used to do when she was small, humming a tune she had made up to go along with her name, and singing the name in her head as she hummed. *Jeanette Emerson, Jeanette Emerson.*

It was amazing how good something new and different could make you feel.

Jeanette Emerson . . . Jeanette Emerson . . .

Jeanette Emerson, who had a behind like a boy's and a turned-up nose, had been born in Waterbury, Connecticut. Her father and mother still lived there and for the first three years that she had lived in New York they had insisted she stay with her Aunt Carol in Brooklyn Heights. She already had a degree from the School of Dental Technology, and a job lined up with an East Side dentist.

She spent her first months in New York commuting between Brooklyn Heights and the Upper East Side, and wishing her employer weren't so square. Sometimes they were alone in the office and she would have liked nothing better than to have taken off her clothes, her white uniform

and her underpants and bra, and gotten into position for
him on the waiting room couch or in the dental chair. She
didn't, even at the tender age of nineteen, give a damn
about his wife and kids. She didn't want to marry him, she
wanted to enjoy her working hours. They bored her
thoroughly; they had since her first day on the job.

She used to spend hours daydreaming about him and
wondering what he looked like naked. All men's penises reminded her of fruit, of apples and pears and peaches and
plums, and she decided after her first week as Dr. Abernathy's assistant that his would be the first she had ever
seen which would look like a banana. It would be curved
and yellowish and slick. Every day she tried to find ways to
see it, to get him to show it to her if nothing else, without
losing her job in the process. He was so stuffy, so square, so
wasteful.

She gave up on Dr. Abernathy after meeting Barry. May
he rot in a homosexual hell in his Nebraska college. Barry
was only an inch taller than Jeanette and the first time he
saw her he told her how much he liked her hair. He said he
loved off-blonde blondes, not dark blondes so much
(Karen was a dark blonde) or platinum blondes (V was a
natural platinum blonde) or even regular yellow-haired
American or Northern Italian type blondes (Francine,
Ivan's sister, had hair that color). What he liked, Barry
told her, was off-blonde blondes, dirty blondes he said, rolling his eyes as he said the word "dirty" and making it clear
just what he meant.

He was a patient of Dr. Abernathy's and a moment later
he was in the dental chair having his molars X-rayed. He
asked her for a date on the way out of the office and she
shrugged and said, sure, why not, your hair is kind of off-
color, too.

She didn't know how right she had been.

And she didn't find out for two years.

He took her out off and on. He had a car and he would
pick her up on spring and summer nights and drive her to
the beach. Once there they would strip and make love. He
finally admitted he liked it better in her anus and she wondered why it had taken him so long to say so. It made absolutely no difference to her. What she liked about sex was

the intimacy, the naturalness. She could be herself when she was naked, among naked people, or with at least one naked person. She never felt herself when she was dressed.

Once a friend of hers with whom she was attending the School for Dental Technology had asked her what she thought of rules. How would she behave, her friend wondered, if there were no rules, if sexual morality (her friend hadn't put it that way but that's what she meant) were wide-open.

Jeanette had answered her immediately. She had told the truth. She said she would behave exactly as she already behaved, except that she would do it openly instead of doing it on the sly.

Her friend had giggled and told her about a girl she knew. The girl had been living with a man for months. They used every contraceptive device known. The man wore a condom (Jeanette hated condoms. She hated them!), the woman a diaphragm. Before doing it they squirted foam. He made her take the pill. He watched her swallow it every day (except the five each month when you weren't supposed to take it). Then they practiced anal entry and coitus interruptus.

Jeanette was aghast. Why? she had asked.

Well, her friend told her, because they were afraid. Then the girl got pregnant and had to have an abortion.

Jeanette said she should have used an I.U.D. The girl frowned and told her she didn't get the message. "It's a joke, dummy," her friend had said, "and you don't even get it."

Neither had the girl in the joke, Jeanette replied.

She had gone out with Barry for a year before she realized he was two-timing her. He would take her out once a week, regularly. That was all Aunt Carol would allow. (Jeanette had got into trouble in Waterbury and her father had decided the only answer was to be very strict with her. Until she was twenty-one she could have only one date a week whether she lived in Waterbury or New York.)

So Jeanette found a way to visit Barry once or even twice a week more, at his apartment in Washington Square. She would either go early in the morning or stop on her way home from work in the early evening. She would shop on these occasions, using money Barry had given her for food, come into his apartment with the key she had, put the food in the refrigerator, undress and get into bed with him if he were there, or wait naked for him if he weren't.

He liked best for her to sit on his lap with his penis in her anus. She liked that, too. She was able to hold him that way, to be close to him for long periods of time. She loved to just sit there with her forehead against his forehead looking down past her breasts at their bodies together, just touching him. Sex for her was a way to commune with another person, a way of being close.

She had never suspected she had a rival. She never had any reason to suspect it. She sometimes looked to see if there were any signs of another woman having been at Barry's apartment, but there never were any. Not that it would have bothered her terribly if there had been, not as long as he would see her as often as ever and be with her naked.

Her dream was to live naked with someone, someplace where no one would bother them, someplace in southern France or in Mexico or Spain, someplace where there was water and sun and each other's bodies. If life were like that, well, she could suffer a thousand Dr. Abernathys, if life could be like that for just a little while.

No, she never had reason to suspect a rival because all Barry's friends were men. Until she found out what men sometimes like to do to each other.

In one way at least Jeanette had been a very sheltered little girl. She didn't know what a homosexual really was until she used her key one afternoon and found Barry and a young student of his in her favorite position. Barry was on the desk chair and his student was in his lap, naked, their arms around each other, Barry's penis in his student's anus and his student's penis hard between their bodies.

"Don't go," Barry had said.

She had been about to leave. She had been about to drop the groceries and run but she made the mistake of deciding to drop them smack on Barry's head. To do that she had to approach the lovers. They both grabbed for her and pulled her to them.

After that afternoon she knew what a homosexual was. She was the homosexual's favorite girl in lower Manhattan.

She still came to Barry's apartment twice a week, sometimes even three times a week. She still went out with him every Saturday night. But they never drove to the beach in spring and summer any longer. They always had a party Saturday night where Jeanette was just one of . . . the girls.

Let him rot in Nebraska with his fag friends, Jeanette thought as she hummed her name on the seat in Morris Levy's bathroom.

Morris turned the shower off and stepped out. He patted her head and started to shave at the sink, dripping wet. He used a brush and shaving soap, lathering up, then shaving carefully with the grain, then washing the cream off under the running water. She loved watching him. Men's toilet habits intrigued her.

She had been a sheltered child but hardly a virgin. She had lost her cherry early, in the back seat of an ancient Ford that a local boy had bought for a few hundred dollars and painted to look like something in a circus. It had a huge raccoon tail on the antenna and ribbons tied to the rear bumper. The radio was always on, blasting rock 'n roll music. The muffler had been purposely ruined and the engine souped up. Square. She had lost her cherry to a hick who was still a hick back in Waterbury, Connecticut.

She hadn't put up a fight. She was sixteen and glad to be rid of it. But it hurt. There wasn't any closeness in it. He was in so much of a hurry he kept his clothes on.

They had driven out to the country after nightfall. They had found a dirt road and parked on the shoulder. They started in the front seat, necking for what felt like hours until they were so hot you could have fried an egg on either of their foreheads. He took his penis out and Jeanette grabbed it. It was the first one she had seen out and stiff and she loved it. She loved its head. She could just see it by the light of the moon and stars.

His name was Jerry. Barry. Jerry. There had been a Billy and a Tommy and a Harry. Thank God for Morris. No one was going to call Morris Morry.

A car had suddenly turned up the dirt road and Jerry said, "Down, quick!" They dropped their heads so as not to be seen by the driver of the passing car. The car went on and Jerry straightened out but Jeanette stayed with her head near his lap.

She could remember saying to herself, "I've never done this before."

She took the end of the thing in her mouth and in a minute he had pushed it all the way in so it jammed her throat. She didn't gag. She found if she relaxed he could do anything he liked to her. She could get the whole thing into her mouth and throat if she breathed through her nose and relaxed.

"Oh, no," he had said. "Oh, no."

He pulled her head up and threw himself into the back seat.

"Hurry up," he told her.

She followed him in there, climbing over the seat. He pulled her underpants off and she got ready for him, the way she knew it was supposed to be done. He had no sooner hurt her by breaking through than he had come— and she couldn't stop him from slamming harder and harder. When she thought about it she could still feel how much it had hurt.

"Did you come?" he asked when it was over.

She was crying. She didn't mind not being a virgin. She wasn't crying because of what she had lost, or because she was afraid. She was crying because it hurt.

He slapped her face lightly to make her stop. He thought she was being emotional. "Did you come? Did you?"

That night Jeanette learned two things. It hurt like hell to lose your cherry. And, if a man asks you whether you came, you'd better say you had. She said she had come and they drove back to Waterbury. He in triumph, and she in pain.

She hadn't come then and she hadn't come since. She liked to play with herself. She liked men to play with her clitoris. But she liked screwing much more, because you were as close as you could be to someone who was naked. She had never come and she didn't care. She got her satisfaction in having a man come, either in her mouth or her hand or inside her, it didn't matter. It made her feel great. It made her love whoever had done it.

Morris Levy finished shaving and brushed his teeth. He

took a tube of hair cream from the medicine chest and carefully put a dab on his left palm, rubbed his hands together and, even more carefully, put the cream on his thinning hair.

"I've got to be at the hospital at nine," he said, drying himself.

"I know, you told me."

"Will you be here when I get back?"

"Oh, I can't, Morris."

She was done douching. She was done washing and changing her diaphragm. She stood next to him, naked. Just being close to him was nice. He had a hairy, lovely paunch. She wanted to hold him.

"Why not?" he asked.

"I have to go to work, too. Then I have to go to the apartment. Karen will be expecting me."

"But what if I want you to move in with me?"

"What?"

"I want you to move in here."

"Oh, Morris, I. . . ."

"Well, think about it. I know you just found a place. Think about it."

Jeanette leaned forward and hugged him. Then she ran into the bedroom and started to dress. She didn't have to be at work for hours yet but she wanted to keep busy. She was afraid to answer too quickly. In the corner of the room she saw the empty open bottle of cognac and smiled.

"I'll think about it," she told him softly.

"Well, I'll call after my rounds."

"O.K."

"I'll see you tonight anyway, won't I?"

Jeanette nodded and Morris went out. He wasn't even carrying his little black bag. He didn't even look like a doctor. Jeanette didn't know what he looked like. He looked Jewish. But he was too tweedy to be a lawyer or an executive. His sports coat was English, his tie was the thin kind that had gone out of style. The first time she met him she had even expected to see pleats in his pants. Of course! He looked like a teacher. A short, slightly dumpy, dark man with thinning hair who looked like a teacher.

She finished dressing and started to examine the things in

his apartment. She went from the bedroom to the living room to the kitchen and back again to the living room. She fell into a large reclining leather chair.

"So," she said in an imitation of a Brooklyn-Jewish accent, "a rich doctor wants you should move in with him. So . . ."

She decided she couldn't do it. If Barry has asked her she would have said yes. She would have said yes to anything Barry asked. If he had asked her to move in with one of his boyfriends she would have done that, or with his mother. But Morris Levy had only freed her from Barry, he hadn't supplanted him, not yet, probably never. She liked what he did to her but, well, that wasn't enough.

After a while Jeanette got up and started to get her things together. She took the douche bag from the bathroom, and the diaphragm case and the tube of Ortho-Gynol and threw them into her canvas handbag. She had plenty of time to get back to Seventy-third Street to change and make up before she had to leave there for work.

There was a desk in Morris' living room and on a whim she went to it and opened the top drawer. There probably isn't a woman in the world who can resist looking through a man's things and Jeanette was no exception. Men, she guessed, were probably the same way with women. She pulled the drawer out and stepped back.

There was a picture of a girl staring up at her, a large, glossy, framed photograph of a beautiful blonde girl with the inscription, *To Morris, always, Francine.*

Morris had told her about a woman named Francine who had just been divorced. The girl in the picture looked so young. Perhaps Morris had known her before she had married. But then why did he still have her photograph? Obviously he had hidden it temporarily. Obviously it had been out recently. She shrugged, closed the drawer, and went to the door.

When she left the apartment she made sure the bolt caught behind her. A few minutes later she was in a cab heading across town on Ninety-sixth Street. Morris lived on Riverside Drive near the university and about three blocks from the building in which he had his office. Jeanette saw the cab driver looking at her through the rear view mirror and smiled at him. He looked down immediately.

She probably looked great. She always looked best after a strange adventure. And she had had some strange ones. After Barry things had seemed to pop all at once. She had gone out with a black man who had made her urinate on his face, and with a bartender who could only come if you tickled his testes with a feather and cooed in his ear. She had gone out with a man who insisted they make love in an elevator in his building while it went from the basement to the fourteenth floor, standing, with him holding onto her buttocks to support her and with her legs wrapped around him. At any moment someone could have pushed a button and the elevator would have stopped, the doors would have opened, and they would have been revealed doing it. He had been a bull of a man. He had just leaned back against the elevator wall and, holding her firmly, had moved her back and forth twice or three times and then come. At the eleventh floor. By the time they got to the fourteenth they looked flushed but otherwise O.K.

She had made love on rooftops, in basements, in the back seats of cabs driving slowly through the park, in women's rooms of office buildings, in the offices themselves. She had given head in the subway, in taxis, in automobiles while the man was driving, and she was once under a man's desk with her mouth around his penis when the door opened, his boss came in, talked to him for five minutes, then went out. All the while she had continued. He had almost killed her when they were alone again except that he was so hot he came when he stood up, shooting all over the place and finally jabbing the thing into her mouth to finish it. After that he was too tired to move, and he had to clean up. She had left quickly—and never saw him again.

In the six months since Barry had gone to Nebraska she had said yes to every proposition put to her, and she had encouraged every man who smiled at her to do whatever he wanted to her. Like Morris, to whom she had said, "Come on, Morris, do what you want to me. Oh, Morris, what a lovely thing you've got, do whatever you want to me."

And he had poured cognac from her pelvic area, mash-ing the stuff into her hair, down between her labia majora, and up the other side between her buttocks, and then he had gotten down and lapped it, every ounce of it, every drop, until he was ready for his *coup de grace,* plunging his tongue into her anus, during which he had come in her hand.

Well, whatever turns you on.

"Hey you, where'd you get your license, Mac?! A shoe store?" the cabbie yelled at someone on the corner of Ninety-sixth and Second Avenue.

Jeanette wondered whether Morris had ever done that with the girl in the picture, with Francine whatever-her-name-was.

Francine Nathan married Peter Klein out of desperation. She thought the life of a married woman was what she needed. It would give her stability, psychological stability, it would calm her down, and it would give her a chance to do what she had wanted to do for years, write about sex the way no woman had ever written about sex before. She wanted to be a female Henry Miller. She wanted to free women from the constraints of a puritanical society. The pill itself, Francine held, was far from enough. Women still had the inhibitions of a pleasure-fearing race.

But marriage to Peter Klein had not worked out. She had not written a word. Her only relief was to continue affairs with men who had meant something to her before she married, and, eventually, to belabor Peter in public. She divorced him, finally, for the same reason she had married him—out of desperation.

She joined WITCH.

She renounced men, bras and her prose. She would liberate women just as she had always planned, but not with the typewriter. She would liberate them with force. With bombs if it came to it.

She called Morris Levy to tell him about it. She and Morris had discovered sex at the age of fifteen. They had necked for hours in her parents' bedroom while both her mother and father were at work and her older brother Ivan was away at college. She had played with him and he had played with her. They had a daily orgasm count and Francine always won. She always came at least twice as many times as Morris did. But they had never made real love. At the age of fifteen they didn't quite know how. Theirs was strictly a dry humping arrangement, a mutual, friendly, competitive kind of masturbation.

"I'm coming again," she would say to Morris.

"Four for you, two for me," Morris would say, keeping count.

She called Morris to tell him she had joined WITCH.

"I have a coat of arms for your group," Morris had told her.

"Oh. What is it?"

"Penis envy rampant on a field of red, white and blue."

"Not funny."

"You've lost your sense of humor, Fran."

"This is serious, Morris."

"Oh, sure, women need boosting. What we need is a little more matriarchy in America. Martha Mitchell, and Mrs. Carswell telling J. Harold to go for a Senate seat."

"Morris, you're a male chauvinist of the worst sort; you're blind, your ego is fed by your supposedly superior position in society. If you didn't have women to trample you'd be nothing."

"I only trample them, Fran, if it pleases them."

"I've given up on men entirely, Morris."

"So you said."

"They're bastards. They need liberating as much as women. They need consciousness expanding to understand what society has done to them, and to women. Men are bastards."

"And you'd rather be the bastards, right, Fran?"

"Right, Morris."

"Make it penis envy rampant on a field of red and white and with a bend sinister, Fran, the mark of illegitimacy."

"I know what a bend sinister is, Morris."

"By the way, Francine, I saw your ex-sister-in-law, V, the other day. I bought her a drink in a mid-town bar. She seemed to be waiting for someone so I didn't hang around."

"That bitch. Ivan is still hung up on her," Francine said.

"I remember him describing sex with her. He said there was something about her in bed, something grasping, searching, something imploring. It made me feel sorry for them both."

"He should have tried playing with her. She wouldn't have been so imploring. His sex information is antiquated, like that of most men. There is no such thing as the vaginal orgasm. Read Masters and Johnson."

"There is no such thing as the vaginal orgasm when you are being made love to by a camera, no doubt, Fran. On the other hand I once knew a girl who came from having her back rubbed, lovingly, of course."

"Oh, go fuck yourself, Morris."

"Be yourself, Fran."

Francine hung up the phone.

What made Francine different from the other girls in WITCH was her good looks, especially her full, sensuous lips and her dark brown, bedroom eyes. Especially because of her eyes there was little or nothing Fran could do to keep from being considered a sex object by men, except, perhaps, to work to develop the depth of her personality and to expand the size of her ideas (the way some women worked to develop the size of their breasts and the expansion of their chests). To do that it was not necessary to picket commercialized expressions of male chauvinism or inane feminism like *Playboy* and *Harper's Bazaar,* or to stick her nose into the business and private problems of exploited housewives, but to think deeply and to search her soul honestly.

Francine attempted neither of these courses, however. Her major contribution to the cause was to give up men. She found after two weeks that it became necessary to revert to the practice of her adolescence and to masturbate with increasing frequency. By the fourth week in the movement Francine had reached that peculiarly shallow state of female consciousness that demeans men by considering them purely as sex objects. She called Morris again.

"Morris, this is Fran."

"Hello, Fran."

"Do you still like me, Morris?"

"I still like you, Fran."

"Will you come over to my place tonight?"

"I'm sorry, Fran, I can't."

"You're the only man I can ask this of, Morris."

"What is it, Fran?"

"Oh, Morris, I need a good fuck."

"If you're going to be a woman's libber, love, you've got to be able to go at least a night without a man."

"Morris—"

"Francine, I have to point out that I do not enjoy being treated as a sex object."

"Fuck you, Morris."

"Call again, love."

She hung up the phone and went to the bathroom. She looked at herself in the mirror of the medicine cabinet and bit her lower lip. She stepped away from the mirror to see herself from the breasts up and then turned and went to her bedroom. Now she was sorry that she had not bought a longer mirror, but this was a temporary apartment, it was serving her only for the months immediately following her separation from Peter Klein and it was furnished à la women's lib. (She had even taken down the poster of the Che Guevara in the hall.) There were no frills, none of the little nothings, the trinkets and souvenirs that exploited women collect to help remind them of their important dates. There were just books and functional furniture. Luckily, *luckily,* she had not thrown out some of the things she had given up upon joining WITCH. Because she had decided on a night of heresy. She just had to get laid. It had been months.

She found her make-up where she had hidden it in the bottom of her suitcase (she was still half living out of the suitcase, she would have to find another apartment in two months when the girl who had rented her this place returned from a liberating trip to Reno) and she found her bra. She began to comb her golden hair.

Francine had a problem with her body. It was a great body. Morris Levy was a connoisseur of bodies and he had often said that hers was the best he had ever had the privilege of being with on intimate terms. But its greatness was disguised. No matter what Francine wore she looked better if she wore nothing. She was five five, her breasts and hips were large and her legs were full, so, dressed, she tended to look slightly dumpy.

But dumpy was not the word for her undressed. The word for her undressed was *incredible,* or *amazing,* or, assuming the mind of the man viewing her had calmed down to the point where it could handle descriptive as opposed to ecstatic terminology, the word for her naked was *voluptuous.*

Francine's breasts were firm and just where they had been when she was twenty (though not quite as high as they had been when she was sixteen) and naked, there was no doubt that where they were was where they were supposed to be. But dressed, and braless, they seemed to hang too low. They were the low-slung, melon-shaped, high-nippled kind of breasts that are perhaps the most beautiful, certainly one of the most sensuous sort, but without a bra, and under a layer of cotton or cashmere, it was impossible to know that.

It was necessary to see Francine's shoulders bare, to note the full vein that ran from her neck to her shoulder when she turned her head, to see the line of her shoulder bone and the bumps of her collar bone, to her lineaments of gratified desire. So Francine broke the rules of the movement. She put on the bra.

Above the bra, Francine put on a light green cashmere sweater. She drew her shoulder length hair back and tied it with a single strand of soft green cord. She was still naked from the bottom of her sweater down.

She was so badly in need of a man she stood for a moment with her hand on her blonde bush. Then she put her hand between her thighs and stood that way for a moment. God, what's happening to me? I'll have to give them up in easy doses. How long has it been? Three months and a week? Yes. After tonight I'll go for four months.

She drew on a pair of striped slacks (the stripes running up and down to make her appear taller and thinner) over her nakedness and slipped into a pair of green sandals. She would go down to the Village. She hadn't been down there in years. Not since she had let Peter Klein rescue her from a life which was simply too hectic to allow her to get any-

thing done, and lead her into one which was too boring to
stimulate her to do anything but escape.

Life with Peter had been so boring that Francine had at
one point debated whether to have a child. The debate was
not long lived. She had never pictured herself as a mother
and housewife, chained to the drudgery and mediocrity of
an average existence. She found a job instead. She used her
hard-earned literary abilities to become an assistant copy
writer. In advertising, like brother Ivan. At the Carter Hall
Agency.

She had had the job for over two years and she was
about to be promoted. It was the news of that change
which had finally precipitated the growing dispute with
Peter and had prompted her to get the divorce.

On the corner of Second Avenue and East Eightieth
Street Francine found a cab and told the driver to take her
to Sheridan Square. She fell back against the leather seat
and let the breeze through the open window brush her hair,
and the cobwebs out of her eyes. She caught the odor of
something she could not name but something she almost
recognized, something she had smelled once before, in the
city in which she had spent the summer after her graduation from college. Paris. A hotel room on Rue Monsieur le
Prince. Three boys who had enjoyed her body for the space
of a week.

They were Germans. Their names were Claus and Hans
and Wilhelm. They were all about twenty years old and
finding her had been the best thing that had ever happened
to any of them.

She had been trying to live like Henry Miller. She had
been trying to do everything that Miller had done in years
of living in Paris and she was trying to do it all in the ten
weeks of her summer vacation. She sometimes even pretended she was the countess in *Tropic of Cancer*, the Russian that stayed with Miller during one of the long periods
of his life in Paris.

Pretending she was the countess, she would say to Claus
and Hans and Wilhelm, "Yes, it is so difficult for me to
come. I am sensitive down there, you see. That is why it is
necessary for me to be sometimes sucked out by a lesbian."

She had met them at the Alliance Française. None of

them spoke much English and only Hans spoke enough to finally understand what she had said when she was pretending to be the countess. So at first they had talked in French. In broken, impoverished, student French.

But it had not taken them long to get the idea. She was free. Free and away from constraint for the first time in her life. And she had certain ideas. Ideas she had the courage to put into practice. And Claus and Hans and Wilhelm had been happy to oblige.

The cab driver turned right on Fifty-ninth Street and drove along the bottom of the park. The odor, whatever it had been, was gone, but the memory of the week with the three German men on Rue Monsieur le Prince was strong enough to sustain itself without help, and Francine was starved enough for sex to cling to that memory, which yesterday, or tomorrow, would embarrass her, would recall to her only what a subverted position women have in society, how impossible it is for them to be as free as men, how the good fight for women's liberation had not yet even begun. Meanwhile, however, she remembered the sustained pleasure of that week in Paris.

They would stay in the room for most of the day, going out only in the late mornings for croissants and cafe au lait and so the room maid could get in and change the sheets and put things in order. (She had wondered how much the boys had tipped the concierge. It must have been a fortune.)

They would come back to the hotel and strip and go at it. Sometimes one of the boys would sit on the edge of the bed and watch while another made love to her, but that was as far as they would go toward interrupting one another's pleasure. They would never try to make love to her at the same time, they would alternate, and sometimes, when none of them were feeling like it, they would sit and talk among themselves in German, smiling at her occasionally, for after the third day verbal communication between Francine and the boys had become superfluous and far too difficult. Even Hans' English seemed to fail him and all the meaning of the French words Francine had memorized with such difficulty were driven from her mind. She was a sensuous, animalistic woman, and that was all. Her mind was empty and her memory shut down and locked away. Her concept of the future was lost as well. She had attained, for that short period of time, the blissful condition of the complete bohemian life.

The only moments of reality she knew were when she would get up to go behind the screen and sit on the bidet to douche. She knew that Coke was a good spermicide so she used a full bottle of it whenever one of the boys came inside her. She didn't have to, she was sure. A man's sperm is not potent enough to fertilize an egg after the first time the man comes each day, but she used the Coke every time anyway, just to be careful.

In the evenings Hans would go out (his French was best) and bring back a bread from the *boulangerie* near Boulevard St. Germain and a paté and wine from the *charcuterie* around the corner. And they would spend the night watching the summer sky through the large double doors that led to the balcony which overlooked the street. (It wasn't much of a balcony, only one person could stand on it at a time, it was that narrow.) And they would let the room grow dark and talk to each other in soft voices in German and occasionally one of them would come to her and make love to her.

She had never known the German language could be so pretty as it was on those dark nights as Paris grew so quiet the sounds of the people talking in the street below their window were crystal clear and the occasional car that stopped at the *cave* toward the boulevard sounded as though it were stopping in the hall outside their door.

But Hans and Claus and Wilhelm finally became bored. Hans, who had come to her more than any of the others at first, had lost interest altogether. She asked him why and he showed her that he was too sore to make love to her again. She laughed. She never became sore. She was always moist (and—truthfully—quick to come, too. She had counted the first day. Eighteen. Eighteen times!).

The taxi turned left sharply at Seventh Avenue and Francine gave up her revery. After Paris she remembered the difficult adjustment to working in New York City, and the men whom on home ground she found she preferred to take one at a time, even if it was with a frequency and disdain that would have done Miller proud. And she remembered how she had always been on the verge of writing about it but never quite got it down, never quite failed to run out of steam after the first few pages, or never failed to get sidetracked by a new man or a new kick. Old Harry Carver, the hot-dog man under the West Side Highway who had a wart on his penis the size of a dime but who spent hours with his mouth jammed to her vagina. Zen Buddism. Paul McCarry, who played jazz clarinet at the Five Spot and who liked to smoke three joints with her before making tediously, unbearably slow, meticulous love. Existentialism. Jules Barney, the giant black man who never came and who had started a black nationalist movement the year before but had given it up for white girls with blonde hair like hers. The movement. Peter Klein. Marriage. Working for Carter Hall and getting the promotion. The movement.

"Which side of the street you want, lady?"

"Oh, it doesn't matter."

Lady! Since when was Francine a lady? She must be looking older than she realized. Since when did a cabbie call her lady? Miss, or honey, or babe, but not lady. Maybe all the shit she had put up with Peter and the divorce had taken its toll on her looks.

"Yes, that's all right. In front of the Voice."

The driver pulled up in front of the Village Voice, Francine paid him and stepped out. A moment later she was alone in the Village again, where she had lived for the first year after she had returned from Paris, when she had been working on and off for a marketing research firm downtown, and trying to write like a female Henry Miller.

The breeze came up again and swept down Seventh Avenue, bringing with it the odor that Francine had half recognized. The same one that had made her think of Paris a moment before. What was it? It hardly mattered. But it filled her with the confidence she needed. A man? If she felt like it she would find three men again, or eight. This was the age of Aquarius, the age of revolution and liberation, and New York City felt as good to her as Paris had once felt, when she had pretended to be the Russian countess, who was so sensitive, so sensitive. . . .

Chapter Two

Karen awoke thinking of jobs. She had slept naked because she knew Jeanette would not be coming back to the apartment. She opened her eyes wide and looked at the sunlight creeping in at the edges of the drawn shade. Out there was East Seventy-third Street, a block she sometimes thought had been created by an evil genius expressly to drive her insane, but inside, on this side of the sun-warmed shade, was Karen's imagination and Karen's nudity.

She thought about the advertisements she had looked at the night before. She thought about getting out of bed.

Not yet, girl. Make yourself happy first.

She thought about applying for a job, about the two different kinds of jobs available, one kind for those with a college education, one kind for those without, and she thought that perhaps it was time to turn her talents to advantage.

And why not? I'm the best liar in the entire U. S. of A.

Why not try to get a job in publishing, like the one she had seen advertised? She knew as much as plenty of college graduates. She had always read a lot. She liked books, history books especially. Her fantasy life had always been given dimension by facts from history. Take King Phillip's

War. It was true facts such as the ones about that colonial conflict which made her stories so believable.

She raised up on the pillows (she always slept on two pillows) and pushed away the sheet from her body. She looked down at her flat stomach and long legs and at the freckled, white expanse of skin. She even had freckles between her thighs from Saturdays at the beach with Jeanette and a man Jan had gone out with between Barry-the-homosexual and Morris-the-doctor, a man called Frank who, Jeanette told her, liked to do it in bathtubs with the faucet running. Jeanette . . . and her wild sex stories.

She cocked one leg to the side and touched herself just at the top of the space between her labia majora. Slowly, she moved her hand down an inch and a half until she had made contact with her clitoris. She felt it swell slightly under her finger and she smiled.

Make yourself happy first.

She lay there, immobile, for some time, watching the shade and the sun behind it and thinking about nothing at all. Then expertly, like a practiced story-teller, she chose a fantasy. She had plenty of reason to be good at fantasies.

I never had a grandmother.

She decided to use a cute black boy who delivered the groceries in the neighborhood. He couldn't have been more than eighteen and was always to be seen pedalling one of those bicycle carts. She thought he worked for Gristede's but she wasn't sure.

In the institution in which Karen had been raised she had learned a good deal about sex. She had spent a good many hours enjoying sex. She had spent a good many hours not enjoying it. And, eventually, fantasies had become more practical.

She did not dislike herself for this somewhat unreal approach. According to Karen, if something worked, it was all right. All rules that she made for herself were based on this premise, or so she would have argued.

By the time she had put her finger into her vagina and withdrawn it, moist enough to rub over her clitoral foreskin, to rub it rapidly and still not get sore there, she had the black delivery boy in the apartment, groceries on the table, clothes on the floor, bent over her vagina and licking her clitoris with a long, pink, rough tongue.

She watched (in her mind's eye) the curly hair on the top of his head while he ate her. She saw the color of his tongue. Which she could not have seen in real life. She reached down and touched his buttocks. Which would have been damned difficult had he really been there.

And, eventually, she came, and continued to come for a minute or so, and felt the world better for it.

Nothing beats it for killing tension. Now go get that newspaper again.

She walked naked out into the living room and over to the semen-stained couch. She flung herself down and lifted the folded newspaper from the cushions beside her. The ad which caught her eye first was the one for the gal Friday who had to be attractive and outgoing.

"No," she said aloud.

If she took that job, or even thought of applying for it, she'd be nothing but a girl Friday all her life, waiting for some damn man with money to come along hoping he'd want to get into her pants, hoping he'd be too afraid to actually try it though, because, God knows, if he did get in there he might please her as much as Joe used to, which was more, she had to admit, than she was capable of pleasing herself.

Well, at least you get your rocks off.

If she applied for that job she would be resigning herself to a fate of taking home eighty (or less) bucks every Friday, or sitting at an empty desk, of smiling at jackasses and lying to them anyway. So why not turn the lying to advantage for once?

Just for once.

She curled her legs under her like the caterpillar in *Alice in Wonderland* (the one that sat on the toadstool), tossed her hair back, and started the alphabetical list at the A's. She knew she had to do it right now, today. If she thought too much about it her resolve would fade, just like her fantasies faded when she achieved a climax, just like all the fantasies she had ever had—and she had had plenty. There wasn't much point in being reality-conscious where she'd been brought up.

All right, Karen, just pay attention to the ads.

She found the one she had spotted the night before.

Cllg grad.   Eng maj.   Ed asst. $120/wk.
Corliss Agency   2 Broadway   Bring Resume

She uncurled her legs and got off the couch, took a deep breath and went into Jeanette's room. She found her room-mate's typewriter in the closet and set it up on her bed. There was paper under a clip in the top of the case and Karen extracted a sheet and rolled it into the machine. She had to force her legs further under her to get comfortable. Jan's bedspread tickled the skin of her behind.

I'll say I went to UConn.

She began to type. Teaching her to type was about all the Hartford Home for Orphaned Children had been good for.

RESUME

Karen Thompson
age: 23
education: graduated with honors from the University of
             Connecticut 1965   English Major   American
             History Minor
work experience: none. Until May when I obtained a di-
             vorce I was a housewife.   I have no children.

See, you're a shoo-in. No one. No one in the entire U.S. of A. can lie as well as you can.

Hours later, dressed in her blue mini outfit and wearing granny glasses (plain lenses) to make her look intelligent (both the outfit and the glasses from Paraphernalia) she entered the lobby of an office building on Madison Avenue. She had already been downtown to see the woman at Corliss.

The elevator took her to the seventeenth floor, the metal door slid open and she stepped out onto the linoleum of the lobby of the Hilt Publishing Company. Straight in front of her was a receptionist's desk with a receptionist behind it. If it hadn't been for her little talk to herself that morning she would have been applying for that sort of job instead. And she had made it over the first hurdle. The woman at

Corliss had believed every word she had told her.

Practice makes perfect.

"I have an appointment with Mr. Morelli," Karen told the receptionist.

The girl looked her over very carefully. She spoke with some kind of accent. "Just one moment, please."

The receptionist turned to her switchboard. She put a black plug into a black hole and spoke into her headset. "Mr. Morelli, there's a young lady here to— What?"

The receptionist turned her perky little head toward Karen and said, "Are you from the employment agency?"

Karen nodded and threw the receptionist a saccharine smile.

"Yes, sir, she's the one. All right."

The receptionist pulled the black plug out of the black hole and smiled at Karen again. It was like a boxing match with smiles instead of punches. The receptionist was one up. "I'll show you the way," she said and took off her headset. She had close-cut brown hair and a pert little body. She was a good six inches shorter than Karen who had decided that the girl's accent was Scandinavian. Karen followed her down a narrow corridor.

"This way," the receptionist sang as she threw her backside from side to side just as if it were a man following her and not Karen. The walls, unfortunately, were an institutional green.

"Here we are."

The receptionist stopped at a white door, knocked on it twice, opened it and stepped aside. Karen could see a man in shirt sleeves seated at a large desk in front of two gigantic windows. There were charts on the walls and a bulletin board plastered with the front covers of paperback books. The man was listening to someone speaking to him over the telephone. He had a white receiver against his ear and he was leaning on his elbows. He waved her in and returned his attention to his call.

"What?" His voice was surprisingly gruff. Surprisingly, because he looked very nice, very gentle. He had Irish features and not the Italian ones Karen had expected. He was about thirty-five, and cute, very cute.

"Look, I'll talk to you later."

He hung up the phone and watched Karen enter his office, close the door behind her, and wait.

"Take a seat, take a seat," Mr. Morelli said.

Karen sat on a long red couch and crossed her legs.

"Corliss called. You're the girl from Corliss?"

"That's right," Karen said.

"University of Connecticut?"

"That's right."

"Recently divorced?"

"That's right."

"No work experience."

Karen nodded.

"Well, that's just as well. What I want is someone I can train, not someone who's already been trained. We put out a special product here. I'll tell you about it, and about us, and we'll see what you think."

Karen smiled. The idea, she knew, was to look interested, to evince patience, to look intelligent, to smile once in a while, to look excited as hell when he got to the part that excited him.

Lying is a lot like acting, you get to really understand what it is to have an audience.

"We put out three lines of paperback books here. The Hilt line, the Clubcar line, and the Bedroom line."

Mr. Morelli paused for only a moment but Karen knew he was waiting for her reaction. She looked at the bulletin board and ostentatiously scrutinized the paperback book covers on it.

Mr. Morelli, evidently satisfied, continued, "We're trying to build up the Hilt line, these are your quality paperbacks, espionage, mystery, gothic, romance, modern novel, and educational books. We're especially trying to build up our educational books."

Karen looked back at the bulletin board with evident interest.

"No, those are our Clubcar books. They're doing well, frankly, Miss, uh, Mrs.—"

"Miss Thompson," Karen said, emphasizing the Miss. "I prefer my maiden name."

Mr. Morelli smiled. He had dimples. "Frankly, Miss

Thompson, the money, at the moment anyway, is in the Bedroom line."

At the mention of the word money Karen raised her eyebrows and looked straight into Mr. Morelli's light blue eyes. Then she nodded once, firmly.

You're doing good, girl, stay cool.

"Our Clubcar books are mildly erotic. They sell well, about fifty thousand each, and we put out ten a month. If we put out more we find we hurt our average. If we print more of each book we sell only a few more. It's a stagnant commodity, it makes money but not at the rate I'd like to see."

Karen raised her eyebrows again and looked at him questioningly.

"No, I'm not the boss. Mr. Murray is the president of the company, but I do the hiring, and the firing."

Karen smiled, trying to look confident that he would never fire her.

"Mr. Murray, of course, has final approval on everything, but he defers to me."

Karen nodded. "This is a very exciting business," she said.

"Frankly, Miss Thompson, we were looking for a man. But I've thought about it, and perhaps a woman would work out."

Sure, no competition for you, Mr. Morelli.

Aloud Karen said, "Why a man, Mr. Morelli?"

"I'm looking for someone to start in the Bedroom line. Hilt Bedroom Books, they're called. They can be pretty rough. There isn't enough work for someone in the educational line yet, so I want a steady copyeditor, copywriter in the Bedroom department who will double—when the time arrives and until the educational line can stand on its own—in that department."

Karen nodded solemnly. "You need someone with all-around ability," she said, being careful not to suggest that she was just that kind of person.

"When I say rough, Miss Thompson, I mean rough. That's why I had originally thought a man would be better."

"A good copyeditor shouldn't care what the substance of a book is. Either she can edit or she can't."

"Can you write copy?"

"I never tried it."

Mr. Morelli looked straight at her and spoke solemnly. "And it won't bother you when you come to a passage in which the hero's semen drips down the heroine's thigh?"

Karen smiled to disguise her disquiet, and looked straight back at him. "Men can be just as puritanical as women. I don't happen to be."

"Miss Thompson, I'm going to give you several of our books, our Bedroom books. I want you to take them home and read them. There is a good possibility that you will decide that you don't like them, that you wouldn't want a job that means working with them eight hours a day."

"I'll be glad to read them, Mr. Morelli, but I can assure you now that this is the most exciting job I can think of, that I want to get into publishing and if that meant editing the phone book I'd do it gladly."

"And there *is* the possibility that the educational line will eventually require a full-time editor."

Karen smiled.

"All right, Miss Thompson. Frankly you're the only person I've interviewed since yesterday that hasn't turned me off. Here, take these."

Karen rose and took the paperback books Mr. Morelli handed her across the desk. She was careful to look hard at the covers but not to give away any of the excitement she felt, or any of the shock, when she saw the photographs on them. One of them was of a man pressed against a woman's bottom, another was of a woman kneeling between a man's legs, and the third was of a couple doing it on a chair, the man sitting, the woman riding him. She could see no male sex organs but plenty of breast and pubic hair. All the participants were naked with the exception of the woman kneeling between the man's legs, who was wearing a black garter belt and mesh stockings. They were the kind of pictures Jeanette would love to pose for, Karen thought.

"Thank you, Mr. Morelli," Karen said.

"If you'll leave your number with the receptionist I'll call you tomorrow morning."

Karen nodded and moved in a businesslike fashion to the door where she turned, smiled once more at Mr. Morelli, and said, "I'd very much like this job, Mr. Morelli." Then she left.

After all, she had sworn to go all out and not be just another receptionist, another gal Friday, another typist. If she read the books and decided she didn't want the job, let it be her choice, not Morelli's.

When she got back into the lobby she walked over to the receptionist's desk and wrote her phone number on a pad.

"You're probably just wasting your time," the receptionist told her.

"Oh?"

"He's looking for a man."

"He was, sweetheart, he *was*," Karen said.

The cab let V out about a block away from Max's bar (of course it wasn't really Max's bar, Max was just the bartender) and V started moving gracefully along the street.

She had never adjusted to the filth of New York City streets, any more than she had ever adjusted to the outsize American cars, or the impoliteness of New York City shopkeepers and pedestrians, or the frenetic war of the subway rush hour, or the fact that she never saw the same people twice in New York unless she followed a strict schedule or purposely went where she knew someone would be, or the coldness of New Yorkers to the troubles of other New Yorkers, or the size, the immense, unbalanced, impractical, insane, unmanageable, mind-boggling size of everything, the buildings, the boroughs (she got horribly lost in Queens once), the bridges, and the bugs, especially the cockroaches. She had never seen a cockroach before she had come to New York with her husband Ivan. This was not Amsterdam. Oh, God, this was not Amsterdam.

In Amsterdam the streets were clean, the shopkeepers and pedestrians were cheerful and polite, the rush hours were manageable and orderly, people cared about each other, the automobiles were small and quiet, Dafs and Volkswagens (*Volks fiets* they were called, folk bikes) and BMW's, and they, the automobilists, gave right of way to the cyclists by law and custom and common sense. And in Amsterdam you were always seeing someone you had seen before in another part of town, in the Concertgebouw or at the ballet or in a tram. In Amsterdam most of the buildings were only a few stories high (the soil was too soft to build them higher) and in the old sections of the city the buildings with step and clock and bell roofs leaned against each other like well-dressed, elderly, female spectators of life in the streets. In Amsterdam the bridges were tiny and picturesque. Many of them still worked by hand. A barge would come up one of the canals and the bargeman would get out and climb the canal wall and hoist up the bridge, then the barge would pass under and the bargeman would lower the bridge and jump back aboard. They didn't have cockroaches in Amsterdam. And in Amsterdam, there were still men with uncircumcised penises.

In V's opinion the City of New York ought to build a great monument to itself in Central Park. It ought to erect (pun intended) a huge marble circumcised penis, twice as large as the obelisk, large enough to be seen from the Plaza (V loved the Plaza) and fat enough at the base so that a hundred working girls could lean against it whenever the weather was pleasant and eat their lunches.

"The trouble with Americans," went an old joke around the airport in Amsterdam when she had been a ground hostess "is that they are overweight, oversexed and over here."

Schipol Airport. God, sometimes she wished she were back at Schipol Airport. But it was too late for that, and it wasn't part of the plan.

"Did you ever think about the signs in America, Max?" V asked her favorite bartender when she had made herself comfortable on her favorite stool in Max's bar.

"The signs of the times, Miss Schimmel?" Max had placed a frozen daiquiri in front of her and was wiping off some glasses. The place was quiet. There were only two other customers, a pretty woman and a Chinese gentleman at one of the tables against the street window.

"No, no, Max. The signs on things, on the streets and on the buildings. Like, for instance, you are out with a man and he takes you in his car someplace, yah?"

"If you say so, Miss Schimmel."

"He takes you in his car and he is just driving around figuring out probably how to ask you what you already know he is going to ask you. Yah?"

"Sure."

"You come to the end of a street. There is no place to go except back the way you came. It is too dark to see much but you look carefully and there is a sign. Dead End. Stupid, is it not?"

"Stupid," Max agreed.

V straightened her shoulders and looked down into her bosom. "Max, you don't think my breasts are too small for American millionaires, do you?"

"No, Miss Schimmel."

"You know in Holland there isn't this breast fetish, Max. Yah?"

"Miss Schimmel, don't you worry about it. It's more important that they are firm."

"Oh, they're firm, Max. Anyway, listen, yah? Once I was on the, what do you call it, *de veer, le bac,* in French, the boat, the Staten Island . . ."

"Ferry."

"Right. The ferry. Once I was on the ferry and I saw a sign. Don't Jump. Max, that is a stupid sign."

"Agreed, Miss Schimmel."

"I was just thinking about Schipol."

"What is Schipol?"

"You got to say it at the bottom of your throat. Schipol. It's the airport."

"Schipol."

"On the way to Schipol is a sign. It says, don't look up in the sky, look at the road. That is not a stupid sign, Max."

"That's a funny sign, Miss Schimmel."

V sighed deeply and looked around. There was no point in going into her act, looking at her watch (she wore a large-faced Spiro Agnew watch on a fat red band that Roger had given her) or looking impatient. There was no one in the bar except the Chinese gentleman with the lady.

"You see what I mean, Max, yah? American signs are silly."

"Why don't you go back, Miss Schimmel? Have you ever thought how much further your alimony check would go in Holland?"

V sighed again and looked down at her breasts again. She moved slightly on the stool so she would appear even more fetching from the doorway.

"Yah, sure, Max. But it's not part of the plan."

"What plan, Miss Schimmel? Finding a man with money?"

"With money and . . . never mind."

"What's the matter with Dutch men—are they too poor?"

"Max, you know something—there are more millionaires per square mile in Holland than anywhere else in the world. That's a fact, Max."

"So?"

"So. There are also more pretty blondes per square mile. So here I have a kind of advantage, you know. I am a little different."

Max nodded.

"And I don't want a Dutch millionaire. I want an American one. I want to live somewhere in this country, though not New York. I don't care to see my mother again, Max, you understand?"

"Sure, Miss Schimmel."

"Hah! Now *that* woman had a plan. Max, you know she spent my inheritance finding for herself a man with money."

"I didn't know that, Miss Schimmel."

"It's too quiet in here, Max."

Max smiled sympathetically.

"You know, Max, I like you. You must be a very good bartender . . . you are so easy to talk to. Max, how am I going to find my millionaire, Max?"

Max didn't answer for a moment, which made V look at him closely. Then Max said softly, "Did you notice the people near the window?"

V nodded.

"You know who that guy is?"

"The Oriental?" V whispered.

Max nodded.

"He's a lawyer named Ho Bin. He's pretty well known, Miss Schimmel."

"What for, Max?"

"For. . . . Listen, Miss Schimmel. Did you ever think maybe what you ought to do is what your mother did?"

"What?"

"Maybe you don't spend enough money. If you spent more money you would naturally associate with others who spend more money. If you lived like a millionairess for a year, you'd meet a hundred millionaires."

"Max. Max. I already spend more than I have. You should see my hair bills, Max."

"Hair bills?"

"From Rudi, who does my hair."

"So that's what I'm saying. You make a bundle fast, spend high, snare your man."

V looked down into her half-empty daiquiri glass. "Max, don't suggest what I think you want to suggest, yah."

"Look, Miss Schimmel—"

"I am not going to whore, Max."

"Whore is not a nice word, Miss Schimmel."

"Max, you make me angry. I am going."

Max reached forward and touched V's hand. "You don't understand me, Miss Schimmel. I was not going to suggest that, not at all. Besides, what makes you so up tight? Relax. I'll fix you a new drink, on the house."

V scowled but stayed where she was and Max took her glass and started to fix her another drink.

"That's no lawyer, that's a *souteneur*, a *maquero*, a pimp," V said, looking at the Chinese gentleman.

"Please keep your voice down, Miss Schimmel. And listen to me. Don't use language like that. I happen to have many lady friends who would tear your eyes out if you called them what you said before, or if you called their handlers . . ."

"All right, Max, I'm sorry. I suppose it's just that I am sensitive about that, yah. I'll explain it to you some time."

"And anyway, that Ho Bin there is nothing like that. He represents money, big Chinese money. A lot of rich Chinese people want to come to America, more than the government lets in."

"So? Max, you mean he finds them American wives?"

"Exactly. That lady he's talking to did it twice, and she's got enough bread to live like a millionairess for a couple of years."

"But Max, if I . . ."

"You would lose your alimony if you married again? So who has to know, Miss Schimmel? I'll tell you who, the immigration authorities. That's all. You think they post your name in neon lights on Times Square if you marry again? Come on. You would only see him once. And you better believe it."

"I believe it, Max."

"If you mention this to anyone I could get in bad trouble, Miss Schimmel. Understand?"

"Yah, Max, yah."

"You marry a Chinese, you bring him to America. Six months later you take a vacation in Nevada. If he's curious, you tell your ex-husband you're taking a vacation, you maybe send him a postcard from San Francisco."

"I wouldn't send him the time of day, Max, yah."

"So, even better. You won't lose the alimony you're already getting, that's my point, Miss Schimmel."

"How much, Max?"

"That you got to talk to him about, you want me to call him over?"

"No!"

Max shrugged. "O. K., Miss Schimmel."

"Max, these men, these Chinese who want to get here, they must have lots of money."

Max laughed. "Sure, you want to marry a millionaire, right? Well, so you marry a Chinese one, that'll make the next one all the easier. Like warming up to it."

Max set V's new drink in front of her.

"Max, what if I didn't automatically go to Reno, Nevada, yah? What if I didn't settle so easy?"

"Don't even think about it, Miss Schimmel. You get a flat rate, no alimony from the Chinese, you understand. They don't think much of women, some of the Chinese people. Don't even think about it, Miss Schimmel."

"Women have rights, Max."

"So join a lib group, Miss Schimmel, and stay poor. But

don't even think of making a deal with Ho Bin and then going back on it. You get a flat rate, a quick divorce, and there's a new American citizen who never hears of you or about you again. That way you stay alive."

"Max!"

"So I never said anything. Excuse me a minute."

Max went over to the table where the Chinese gentleman was talking to the attractive woman and V stared down into her new drink. She sipped at it tentatively.

She had remembered once confiding in her sister-in-law, Francine the Bitch, about how she felt about America, about how America was where to come to get money but how, on the other hand, it was a place in which you had to have money to live. That paradox had pleased V. It had not pleased Francine, who had made V feel that she was stupid, obvious and crass while it was really Francine who was those things. V remembered how she had told Francine that if she were alone and had to work in America she would probably have to become a whore, and Francine had looked wide-eyed at her and remained silent. The stupid, puritanical bitch. They ought to call the penis monument in Central Park Plymouth Rock. That would sum up the whole thing. Sex represented by a circumcised marble penis twenty stories high, and the Great American Puritanical Soup Company represented by calling the thing Plymouth Rock. Maybe it ought to be built in Boston instead of in New York.

"Miss Schimmel?"

"Oh, Max."

"Listen, no hard feelings about what I said before, O.K.?"

"Sure, Max." V turned in her seat. The Chinese lawyer and the woman he had been with had left.

"Just forget everything I told you, O.K.?"

"Sure, sure, Max."

"You want another drink?"

"I still got this one."

V always used the word "got" instead of the word "had" or the word "have." It made some people guess that she had learned her English in Brooklyn. She hadn't. She had learned it in school and from hundreds of American

records. She spoke, not like a Britisher, which was the way
they wanted you to speak in school, but like an American
from Hoboken.

It was during one of those long, boring afternoons in
Bayonne, New Jersey, in the large house Ivan's parents
had, while Ivan was away at work (he was a copywriter for
a small advertising firm) and V was going out of her skull
for want of someone interesting to talk to, for want of
hearing her own language, or any language other than English, and for want, of course, of a decent orgasm (something which was even then driving her out of her mind—
although not as much), that she had confided in Francine.

Francine had turned on her, had called her a little gold-
digger, had said that since she was already a whore she
might as well do a few tricks afternoons. And V had begun
to boil. Who was Francine to talk? Francine who had just
been confessing how she wanted to be a female Henry
Miller. Francine who had been living in Greenwich Village
and probably playing the bunny for anything with pants.
Francine who actually smelled of sex half the time. (Sometimes she would come home from a date and she wouldn't
wash, she probably didn't know enough to wash, or else
and more likely, she wanted her mother to smell it on her.)

"It's so quiet, Max. I never seen it so quiet in here before."

"Everyone's on vacation, Miss Schimmel."

"So, it's like Paris or Rome, eh, when in August everyone leaves. Who are you kidding, Max?"

"Well, not everyone, Miss Schimmel. A lot of our customers, though."

"Because they're rich, Max?"

Max shrugged.

"So, where do they go, Max?"

"I won't know that till they come back, Miss Schimmel.
It changes."

"The jet set," V said.

Max shrugged again. He still seemed angry with V, or at
least a little put out with her.

"Max, if I change my mind about this . . . this Chinaman
thing."

"Better say Chinese man, Miss Schimmel. It's O.K. to say Chinaman if they aren't around, otherwise. . . ."

"O. K., Max, I get it. So, if I change my mind about this Chinese gentleman thing what should I do?"

"Frankly, Miss Schimmel, you could do me a great favor by telling me first. That way I could get a commission, don't you see. It wouldn't come out of your share, you understand."

"Sure, Max."

"Have you changed your mind?"

V shrugged, lifting her bare shoulders a few inches and then lowering them. She couldn't help noticing that Max couldn't help looking at them. They were good, sexy shoulders. "If I change my mind, I'll tell you, Max."

"Thank you, Miss Schimmel."

He wasn't drying glasses. He was just standing in front of her so she finally looked up at him. He was watching her intently. "You want to say something, Max?"

"Miss Schimmel. If you have any ideas about . . . about double-crossing Ho Bin, then I'd rather you didn't tell me, I'd also rather you didn't tell Ho Bin who told you about him, either."

"You mean it, Max."

"It's part of the deal, Miss Schimmel. If you don't do exactly as you agree to do, if you don't right away get the divorce, and stay out of the way after that, they kill you. It's part of the deal."

V nodded.

"I guess I'll go home, Max. There isn't anything doing here."

"Have another drink on the house, Miss Schimmel."

"All right."

During those long afternoons like the one when V had confessed to Francine that she would find it acceptable to become a whore if it ever came to that, V would watch television, or read, or, after a while, try to provoke Francine into confessing the details of her sex life. Perhaps if Ivan had not insisted they live with his parents until they could find a suitable apartment, perhaps if Francine hadn't been staying there, too (it was just before she married Peter Klein, from whom she was now divorced), perhaps then the marriage would have lasted longer. Perhaps V would have found Ivan's thirty thousand a year enough to get by on. Perhaps she would have learned to live with his thin, circumcised penis.

But living with his parents in the huge, dead house in Bayonne, and having to spend afternoons either alone or with Fran the Bitch, tore the whole thing wide open. Even with no rent to pay and with only a small contribution demanded by Ivan's mother to help with the food bill, even then V couldn't have the things she wanted, the things her mother took for granted every day of her life, the furs, the sports car (her mother had a new Volvo like the one the Saint drove on television—she had sent V a picture of it), the jewelry and the weekly sessions in Manhattan at Elizabeth Arden. If she wanted to go to Manhattan she had to take one of Ivan's parents' cars. She couldn't even have the money for an MGB. She had fought for hours with Ivan about money for an MGB.

"You're not mad I suggested what I suggested?" Max the bartender asked again.

"No, no, Max. I'm not mad."

Max nodded and wandered down to the other end of the bar to serve a customer who had just come in, a young man who didn't know how to dress and obviously couldn't afford to even if he did know.

"Ivan, Ivan, just an MGB, that's not so much. An MGB is less than four thousand dollars."

"V, you're impossible. Come on, get dressed, Mother is expecting us down to dinner."

"Je moeder is een vuile slet."

"V, I don't want to hear that kind of talk!" Ivan would shout. He didn't fully understand V's native language but he got the general drift.

Then, after a silent supper, (in which the tension, especially the tension between Francine and her father, a fat, cigar-smoking old Jew who still spoke with an East European accent, was so oppressive V could scream), they would all watch television until Ivan felt it was late enough to leave for their bedroom where he would try to fuck her properly with his thin cock, and V would yawn and feel like a whore.

She wanted to ask him why he thought she had married him if she couldn't even have an MGB, if she couldn't spend a day having her body and face and hair cared for properly, if she couldn't compete with her mother on the other side of the Atlantic.

Perhaps it hadn't been like that at first. Perhaps there had been something between them, something more than Ivan's money and his nationality, but by the time V had been living in the house in Bayonne for six months she could no longer remember what it had been. She knew the sex between them had never been great, had never even come close to approximating the sex between V and Hans, her married friend with whom she shared the attic on Jan van der Heydenstraat, but it had been adequate. Once, it must have been adequate. Once, she must have at least liked Ivan.

"*Ivan, Ivan, just a few thousand dollars.*"

"*V, please, not now.*"

"*Ach!*"

"*Shh.*"

"*Me? I should be quiet? You make so much noise when you do that to me the whole house must hear it.*"

"*Oh, for God's sake.*"

"*Now you stopped.*"

"*Yes, I stopped. What's the point?*"

"*Oh, come on, put it back in. I won't talk about money anymore.*"

"*No, thanks.*"

"*So. Whatever pleases you . . . Ivan?*"

"*What?*"

"*At least let's get out of this house.*"

"*A few months, V, and I'll be able to put down a down payment.*"

After nights like that she would sleep late, feeling like a whore even when she awoke, not remembering ever having felt differently, and she would talk to Francine, or watch television, or try to read.

One afternoon she read about what being a whore does to your ability to have orgasms. Even in those days she was trying to find out why she couldn't have decent orgasms.

The book she had found told her that prostitutes lose their ability to come at all.

One afternoon Francine came home after having spent the entire night and morning away from home. That was just before she announced her engagement to Peter Klein. She had a loud, vicious fight with her mother, Queen Bitch, and then ran to her room. V followed her up the carpeted stairs and along the wide hall. (It was an enormous old house.) V had opened the door of her bedroom without knocking and found her sprawled across her bed, smoking a cigarette. She hadn't been crying. V had hoped to find her crying.

"What do you want?" Francine asked with obvious hostility.

"You are going to get fucked out, just like a whore, you are going to get so fucked out you will never come again."

Francine had laughed heartily and stared at her open-mouthed for a moment.

"Is that what's wrong with you, Veltraud? Is that your problem, honey?"

And V had been the one to burst into tears and spend the afternoon bawling.

"Another drink, Miss Schimmel."

"I'll get plastered, Max."

"Let me just refreshen this one."

"No. I'll wobble down the street. I would be a spectacle, Max."

"You are anyway, Miss Schimmel. You make everyone look at you anyway, you are so damn sexy in that outfit."

"Why, thank you, Max."

"You will think about what I said, about Ho Bin?"

V stood and paid Max for two of her drinks and left a heavy tip. Then she nodded and said, "I am thinking about it, Max. I'll let you know."

She left to try her Wall Street spot but she hadn't much hope of finding anyone. Max was apparently right. Most of the rich people had had enough of the heat and had left the city for a while.

"*I am* thinking about it," she said to herself as she stepped out into the street to find a cab.

Two years after Jeanette lost her cherry to a hick, square teenager in the back seat of his souped-up Ford, a scandal involving teachers and students from two of Waterbury's larger high schools had shocked the town. Jeanette Emerson had been very much involved in that scandal.

That was why, while she was attending the School of Dental Technology, her father allowed her only one, chaperoned date a week. It was why, when she finally graduated from the School of Dental Technology, he sent her to live with her Aunt Carol and Uncle Tim in Brooklyn Heights. It was why Aunt Carol allowed her only one date a week (Saturday night with Barry and the girls) and why the afternoon meeting with Barry had always to be lied about.

Uncle Tim knew about the Waterbury scandal. Eventually, he found out about Barry and the apartment in Washington Square. He discovered, in time, what Jeanette really did with her free afternoons.

Jeanette called him Tim Terrific. Sometimes she called him Tim Terrible. These things she called him to his face because Aunt Carol was sympathetic. Carol called Tim things which were much worse than that. The things Carol called him, however, were not worse than the things Jeanette wanted to call him. Tim the Tit-Eater (because of what Carol had told her he liked to do during foreplay). Tim the Shit-Eater (because of what Jeanette felt Tim ought to do before, during, and after foreplay).

He was a salesman. What the hell else would he be? He sold plumbing supplies. Goods, he called them. He looked younger than he was, and he kept in shape by doing deep knee bends and touching his toes fifty times every morning. And by screwing everything he could get in his sights and into bed with.

He just loved having Jeanette around.

"I just love having a teenage girl around the house," he had said to her when she had first moved in. Carol was doing the dishes in the kitchen, out of earshot.

"I'll be a teenage girl for all of two more months," Jeanette had said.

"If you last that long," Tim had replied. Meaning, if she

could possibly resist his fatal charms for that long.

"Somehow, I'll manage," Jeanette had said, letting him know she understood not just what he had said, but just what he had meant.

The trouble was that Tim, not Carol, was the blood relation. Tim was her father's brother. Otherwise . . . well, otherwise she might not have fought him off quite so hard. At least in the months after Barry had left her for Nebraska and the Plain's State fairies, when she had been obliging every man she could, at least then she might not have fought him off so hard. Not that fighting him off had done any good. Of course, Uncle Tim eventually had "his way" with her.

The books Karen had brought home from the Hilt Publishing Company all had characters in them that reminded her of Tim. And one of them was about teenage orgies, which reminded her of Waterbury and the scandal. There was plenty Jeanette could tell Mr. Morelli's writers. They didn't have half of it down the way it might happen, the way it *did* happen, as far as Jeanette was concerned, all the time. The way it had happened to her and the way it was still happening to her.

The names of the paperback books Karen had brought back to the apartment were *A Snatch In Time, Back Seat Bang* and *Gang-Bang Bernard Grows Up.* In the last one, Bernard, the hero, experiences a flashback to his high school days in Brooklyn and a giant orgy in the basement of a church. That was the book which reminded her of Waterbury.

"This is terrible," Jeanette said.

Karen, who had curled up on the couch, nodded her head.

"Imagine a *title* like this. They must be crazy; I mean who would buy this anyway?" Jeanette exclaimed, holding up the book so that Karen could see the glossy photograph on the cover. It was the one with the woman in stockings and a garter belt going down on a man whose head was not in the picture.

Karen shrugged. "Somebody must."

"I mean why buy it, if you can do it? Jesus, I don't think this kind of stuff will last, pornography I mean, not with the sexual revolution. Everybody is doing exactly what they want. Aren't they?"

Karen shrugged again. "Only if they find *you*," she said.

Jeanette paid no attention to the dig, except to silently affirm that Karen needed a man, needed one badly. Aloud, she said, "But the *title*, I can't believe the title."

"Maybe Mr. Morelli is experimenting with funny titles."

"Funny? Is it funny?"

"Sure," Karen said.

It was Jeanette's turn to shrug. "What's the plot anyway? I'm not going to read anymore."

"What are you up to?"

"He just had a flashback to that orgy in the basement of the church."

"Oh, that's the first chapter."

"Uh huh."

"Well, the whole book follows from that. Bernard wonders what happened to all the girls he and his gang used to fool around with."

"Fool around with?" Jeanette exclaimed. *"Fool around with?* You mean gang rape."

"Uh huh. Anyway Bernard looks them up one after another."

"And what does he find?"

"Some of them are married, some divorced, one of them is dead, one is a whore."

"Just a random sampling of high school girls grown up, huh?"

"No. There's the difference that they all wish they were back in the basement of that church again."

"Oh, bullshit."

"That's what he finds."

"That's just stupid. I suppose they all want his body too."

"Uh huh."

"Well, it's just stupid."

"Well, for Christsake, Jeanette, that's the kind of book it is."

"Well, I have a surprise for the jerk who wrote it!" Jeanette said. "I was in an orgy once, in a teacher's house, and it was a lot like this orgy here," Jeanette shook the book at

Karen. "And I don't wish I was back in that house at all, ever. I wish to God I'd never been there."

Karen smiled and said, "There was something like that in the town I grew up in. There was a big dance at the regional high school and about half the kids got drunk and went to this big barn afterwards, right on the outskirts of town, near Dad's paper factory."

Jeanette sighed audibly.

"It would have been in the papers and everything if Dad hadn't hushed it up."

"Were you there?" Jeanette asked.

Karen shook her head.

"Besides," Jeanette said after a moment, "all the characters in these books remind me of Uncle Tim. Tim the Tit-Eater. Oh listen, can I borrow your F.D.S.? I won't have a chance to wash."

"Sure."

Jeanette got to her feet and tossed the books beside Karen on the semen-stained couch. Then she went to her room to change. She wished to God Karen wouldn't lie so much. She could take all the bitchiness she wanted to dish out if only she wouldn't lie all the time. It was because she hadn't had a man. Not since Joe. Not really. She'd gone out a few times with men that Jeanette had set her up with but it takes practice to make love with someone. If you really want to enjoy it, you have to get used to the other person's body and preferences. It's almost like work until it comes off right. At least that's what Morris had said and Jeanette was ready to believe anything Morris said, for the time being. Anyway, it made sense. And Karen had gone out with the men Jeanette found for her only two or three times. For Christsake, maybe Karen wasn't fucking them! Jesus Christ, Jeanette had never thought of that. Why, the stupid jerk!

Jeanette hurriedly dressed for Morris, not forgetting to spray with the can of vaginal deodorant. Not that it would make any difference once Morris poured on the cognac. She found she was thinking again of Tim.

Tim had been drunk or pretending to be drunk on the one night he had found the courage to come into Jeanette's bedroom. Jeanette had been afraid to make a sound, afraid to do what she really wanted to do, which was scream his ears off. She didn't see any point in alerting Aunt Carol. Not really. It just wasn't worth it to cause that lady any pain.

It was too dark in the room to see much; even after she had been awake for a while her eyes never really adjusted to the dark. He must have come into the room, undressed, thrown off her bedclothes, yanked up her nightgown, and climbed aboard, because the first thing she knew was that he had one hand on her mouth and one hand between her thighs, and he had a knee between them, too, so she couldn't close them.

She smelled booze on him. She felt him rubbing her clitoris, or trying to rub it. That had never done much for her and certainly wasn't going to then, not with Tim the Shit-Eater's heavy paw on it. It was like being made love to by a giant chimp. It was the first time she'd been screwed since that first time in the back seat of the beat-up Ford outside of Waterbury that she hadn't been ready to screw, hadn't been moist. Tim kept his hand on her mouth and his weight on his hand until his other one had opened a passage wide enough for him to enter. And enter he did. She was sore for a week afterwards.

He must have mistaken her pain for passion when he finally got in because he came right away. Then he started whispering frantically.

"Oh, Jesus, I must have been drunk."

"You must have been drunk," Jeanette said snidely. She could still remember the scene vividly, although there was nothing to see but his dark shadow on the edge of her bed.

"Jesus, Jesus, Jesus."

"Oh, shut up."

"You won't tell Carol. You can't."

"Just go away, would you?"

"I'm sorry, Jan, really. You really got to me. Say you won't tell Carol."

"Go away or I'll scream."

"She won't hear you . . . I mean—"

"What did you do to her?"

"Nothing, she just sleeps soundly."

"What did you do, drug her or something?"

"No! Promise me you won't say anything."

She could still form her face into the face she had worn in the dark that night. It wasn't a very pretty thing to do to her features.

"Tim?"

"What?"

"Get the fuck out of here, would you? I want to go to sleep."

"You cold little bitch, you didn't come, did you?"

"Ha! Sure I came. I'm still coming. Go back to bed now, big man, or I *will* tell Carol."

She watched his shape move across the room, stoop to pick up something from the floor, stand there, dressing probably, and finally leave, hurling behind him the one word "frigid."

Jeanette didn't hold it against him, not really. In those days, well, in those days she had probably looked like she needed a good fuck. The trouble was she probably still looked that way and Tim, Uncle Tim, was the last man in the world who turned her on. And almost everybody turned her on.

Jeanette found a cab on First Avenue (the whole area stunk worse than usual because of the summer heat, the garbage incinerator near the river must have been working overtime), and she told the driver to take her to Morris' address.

She was thinking about Morris now. Of course she couldn't live with him. He had at least a thousand books in his apartment. He was an intellectual. They would get tired of just pouring cognac over each other, and then what would they do? Jeanette didn't even have the patience to read *Gang-Bang Bernie* past the first chapter. What would they talk about? Morris had been crazy to ask her. At least with Barry there had been mutual interests. There had been rock music to listen to and Barry's "girl friends" to gossip about and there had been being naked together, holding on to each other. There wasn't anything like that with Morris. Jeanette had to face it, her Jewish doctor, cognac or no cognac, was too educated for her, and too normal. Much too normal.

She knew exactly what Karen would say if she knew

Jeanette thought Morris was normal. *"Normal?* A man that pours goo all over you, licks it off and then comes in your hand, is normal? Jeanette, you're too much."

But Karen would have been wrong. There was no grasping desperate need in Morris' lovemaking. As far as Jeanette was concerned, that made him normal. Nuts was when you *had* to have something. Sane was when you could take it or leave it. Morris was sane, Barry wasn't, Jeanette wasn't. It was as simple as that. And there was certainly nothing crazy about coming in a girl's hand. It was about the greatest compliment a man could pay a girl.

Gang-Bang Bernie. Now *there* was a nut.

The cab stopped in front of Morris' apartment building and Jeanette paid the man and got out. She rang the bell in the lobby, pushed the door in when the answering buzzer sounded, and hurried for the elevator. She hurried because the empty lobbies of apartment buildings, like self-service elevators and subways, made her nervous precisely because she was the kind of girl that attracted deviants of all kinds, especially rapists. She always had to hide her hair in subways; if she wore it down she was sure to be accosted, at the very least she would be rubbed up and down against. Being that kind of girl had its advantages. She never had any trouble getting laid, for instance. But perhaps because of the time with Uncle Tim, she had a thing about being raped. She just knew she wouldn't enjoy it.

A man she had dated (the one she had given head to from under his desk while he listened to his boss lecture him) had once told her that the reason she attracted nuts was because she was the typical masochist. She had that sort of all-American hurt-me-please face. It was clear to everyone who had any sexual sensitivity, the man had said, that she was just dying to get laid but that no matter how many times she got it she just wouldn't break, that she just wouldn't come.

Jeanette had denied that her makeup was so simple and obvious but her denial had not stopped her executive friend from continuing his analysis.

He had said there was a certain kind of girl, the kind that twirl batons and win beauty contests, who aren't teases exactly (it would have been a little difficult for him to have said *that* about her) but who are so obviously intended for pleasure and yet so obviously incapable of giving up everything to a man who pleases them, that they provoke violence, they drive rapists up against the wall.

The man had said that it wasn't that Jeanette *was* that kind of girl, it was that she looked like she was. The qualification had not helped. It was mostly because of that unsolicited analysis which her executive friend had offered that Jeanette did to him what she did to him, almost making him lose his job. Luckily, he had lots of self-control. Until he had stood up and come all over the place.

The elevator was on the main level and Jeanette got into it quickly and pushed the button for Morris' floor.

She had been so angry with her executive friend and his analysis because she knew damn well that he was right. It was why she not only had to cover her hair when she took the subway, it was why she had to make every effort to look her worst. Once, before she knew what to expect in the New York City underground, when she had just moved in with Aunt Carol and Uncle Tim and was commuting back and forth between Brooklyn Heights and the dentist's office, a man had stood over her between Thirty-fourth Street and DeKalb Avenue. She had been sitting next to the door, reading. (It was always best to pretend to read in the subway, even if you didn't like to read.) Every once in a while she had felt strange and had looked up to notice the man was staring at her. Then, quite suddenly, as the train pulled into DeKalb Avenue, the man let go of his strap, opened his fly, yanked his penis out, and came all over her book. Then he ran out the doors just as they were opening, and was lost in the crowd.

The elevator came to a stop and Jeanette got out. Morris' apartment was down the hall and she walked gracefully toward it, no longer afraid now that it was within sight.

The time the man had shot all over the subway was long before she had met Barry. (In fact that was the closest thing to sex she had in her first six months in New York.) She had been naive then, despite her experiences in Waterbury. She thought what everybody liked to do was to make love to people of the opposite sex, at the most, she had believed, a girl might give head to a man, or vice versa, or

both at once. Riding the subway twice a day from Brooklyn had disabused her of those simple notions as much as
finding Barry and his boyfriend.

Morris opened the door for her with a drink in his hand
and promptly gave it to her. She took it as he closed the
door behind her.

"What is it?" she asked. "Cognac?"

Morris laughed. "Scotch. Scotch because I have had a
perfectly lousy day. Drink it and I will make myself a new
one."

Jeanette threw her purse down on Morris' couch, sat
down near it, kicked off her shoes, folded her feet under
her and sipped the drink.

"Cognac is for after dinner," Morris was saying. "Scotch
is for always. I like it when your knees wink at me like
that."

He crossed the room and started to make himself a new
drink at his fancy bar. There was still plenty of light in the
sky, which made Jeanette feel funny about drinking.

"Why did you have a perfectly lousy day, Morris?"

"Would you pull your skirt up a bit, please? I cannot see
the white of your thighs."

Jeanette smiled, sipped the scotch again, and pulled her
skirt up.

"Thank you, miss. You are lovely and obliging and I
adore you for being both at once."

"What happened, Morris."

"I lost a patient. The result of that tragedy is this, I want
to get drunk, place my penis in your anus, get drunker, and
like that."

Jeanette smiled again, but less warmly than she had before. "Who was it?"

"A woman. No one special . . . to me. A doctor often
has a patient who dies. There was nothing that could be
done. There is something that can be done about me, however. If, while I sip this scotch whiskey, you will be kind
enough to slip out of your panties. Just your panties."

"Morris, am I a masochist?"

"Do you want me to hurt you?"

"Right now?"

"Yes."

"A little," she said, softly.

"You mean that you would like it a little if I hurt you or that you would like it if I hurt you a little?"

Jeannette shrugged and said, "Both, I guess."

"Then you are a masochist."

Jeanette looked down at Morris' rug.

"Please, Jeanette, humor a terrible man and slip out of your panties."

Jeanette stood, placed the drink Morris had given her on the back of the couch, and slipped out of her panties.

"Please kneel on the couch, Jeanette."

She did as he had asked, making sure that her ass was close enough to the edge for him to reach her. Out of the corner of her eye she saw him slipping out of his pants and cocked her head enough so that she could see his privates. He had more pubic hair than anyone she had ever known. It was the blackest, biggest bush she had ever seen on a man, or a woman. It was so thick it made his penis appear smaller than it was. A minute later she felt him spreading the lobes of her behind and then he was pushing into her anus.

"You realize, of course, that I realize that I am being brutal."

Jeanette said nothing while he pushed her blouse up, revealing the skin of her back. Then she felt something cold. "What's that."

"I have placed my glass on your back, so that I can squeeze your ass, stop, have a drink, squeeze your ass, and like that."

"Stop saying 'and like that.' After all, you are fucking me in the ass. . . ."

"Sorry."

"I'm almost sorry I suggested to you that I was a masochist. You wouldn't be doing this otherwise."

"On the contrary. I am being a brute because it pleases me to be one."

"You are also talking funny."

"I've got something to tell you, Jan. Your trouble is you're too easy, lov. All a man has to do is rub your neck and you give head. Good head, lov. The best. But it might be more fun if it were a little harder to get."

He slammed into her, spilling the scotch down her back and certainly staining her skirt, which was still on, of course. No matter what they seemed to do, she managed to get alcohol all over her. She didn't like this. She didn't like it at all.

She felt him swell inside her and then come. He groaned loudly. He had never come so quickly with her before. He pulled out and she remained exactly as she had been, until she felt him drying her with a towel.

Then he collapsed on the couch in front of her and she lay down with her head in his lap, her hair all over his penis and pubic hair.

"I'm sorry," he said. "I'm really sorry, Jan."

"It's all right. I guess I'm used to men. . . ."

". . . Who think you're a masochist?"

"Uh huh."

"I guess you look the type," he conceded. "You're not, though."

"I guess I must be." She turned so that she could see the ceiling and stretched out. Her glass was still on the back of the couch, near Morris' shoulder, but she left it there.

"No. You're not. Don't you know what you are?"

She shook her head.

"You're whatever a man wants or needs you to be. You're a sexual medium. It's a kind of artistic talent. Any woman, I guess, could do what a man wants her to, but you do much more than that. You know immediately what he wants, and make him want to do it up front, and then you let him have it, or let him do it to you, and you actually enjoy it. That's a hell of a lot more than any woman I've ever met. It's why I asked you to move in here."

"Tell me about the woman who died," Jeanette said.

"I'd rather not," Morris said. "Listen, would you like a paella?"

"Sure."

"The best damn paella in New York."

"Of course I would."

"Good, I'm taking you out tonight. I'm going to spend a bundle on you, baby."

"You don't have to do that."

"I want to. You're my sex artist. You're the best thing

that ever happened to me, or to anyone else for that matter."

"But my skirt is all wet."

"I'll take you back to your place first. I'm going to do something for you, Jan, I really am. I don't know what yet, but that's a promise."

"More than the *paella?*"

"Much more. But food first. Come on. Let's get dressed and get the hell out of here."

The bar Francine had decided to try first was the one she had frequented often when she had been living in the Village, trying to write like a female Henry Miller. She hadn't been there since she had moved to Bayonne for a few months (to get her head straight, she said) and then married Peter Klein (because she couldn't get it straight). The bar was triangular in shape, conforming as it did to the shape of the small block on the corner of which it was located. It had always struck Francine, who was trying to think of things in terms of sexual outrage, that it was pussy-shaped. Symbolically, it was the pussy of Greenwich Village. In one of her many notebooks Francine had written:

> The Sink is the cunt of Manhattan, the deep, mysterious triangular center and aim of Village life, into which and out of which the seminal urges of the new generation of creators flows with unerring accuracy. When God hurt this city in its sex he thrust his thunderbolt smack into the center of the Sink. Here the wound is deepest; there is the vortex of the pain; and from here will spring anything of importance that will rise from the ashes of this plastic world.

She was wrong about the Sink, of course. (The Sink was what she and other regular patrons called the place. The real name was La Plage.) She was dead wrong about it. Not only wasn't there anyone who drank there regularly who could be counted on to write so much as a decent limerick or paint a good Christmas card, it was even a lousy place to pick up a man. She knew that now. She realized, sadly, that she had even known it then. But she had been trying to romanticize things, to follow in the footsteps of Miller, to mix outrage with religion, to free women, most of all to free herself. She had failed. She had failed to write with originality (that selection from her notebook was typically derivative of *Sexus*, and she knew it now). It was nostalgia, more than anything else, that brought her to the Sink first. Later on, she would go across the street to the Lion's Head (the Maiden Head she had called it in her journals) and press into the crowd that was often there, the crowd of men looking for women and women looking for men. Or, better still, she would go to the 55 where sex-hungry folk crowded a tiny area, bought drinks and tried to drag each other off to various bedrooms around the village. (Needless to say, the 55, in the derivative journals of the Great Emancipatress, was the 69. What else?) Meanwhile, until it got to be ten or eleven o'clock, the Sink would do.

She had written about the back room of La Plage:

> If the Sink is the cunt of Manhattan, the red door at the apex of the triangle corresponding to the labia majora, the aisle between the bar and the tables corresponding to the lubricious vaginal canal, then the back room of the Sink corresponds to the womb of this city wherein can be found the small but ever growing foetus of creativity, conceived in an unholy union of alcohol and sweat, and that foetus once spawned will be the savior of New York, the messiah come to lead us out of all this concrete, glass, plastic and air-conditioning.

Lousy writing. Very lousy writing. And the only thing about the back room of La Plage that could be said to be like the back rooms of cafes in which Miller had lusted and written and drunk his fill was the Scopitone machine, a French invention that combined a juke box with a kind of color television screen. If Miller had seen a Scopitone in Paris in the Thirties he probably would have left for Greece a hell of a lot earlier.

Lousy writing. Francine knew it was lousy writing even then because she had committed whole sections of good

writing to memory and she could easily compare them to
her own short, spasmodic efforts. The comparisons were
especially easy because most of them were from the man
himself, from Miller. There was the paragraph from *Tropic
of Cancer* about being an artist, about being the kind of
person Francine wished she could be, tried to be:

> Today I awoke from a sound sleep with curses of
> joy on my lips, with gibberish on my tongue, re-
> peating to myself like a litany—*"Fay ce que voul-
> dras! . . . fay ce que vouldras!"* Do anything, but let it
> produce joy. Do anything, but let it yield ecstasy. So
> much crowds into my head when I say this to myself;
> images, gay ones, terrible ones, maddening ones, the
> wolf and the goat, the spider, the crab, syphillis with
> her wings outstretched and the door of the womb al-
> ways on the latch, always open, ready like the tomb.
> Lust, crime, holiness: the lives of my adored ones, the
> failure of my adored ones, the words they left behind
> them, the words they left unfinished; the good they
> dragged after them and the evil, the sorrows, the dis-
> cord, the rancor, the strife they created. But above all,
> the *ecstasy!*

But thinking about Miller's writing, and thus thinking
about her own failure, distressed her, so she tried to remember other things about the Sink as she pulled open the
red door (the door was still red) and entered the area she
had once said corresponded to the lubricious vaginal canal
of Manhattan.

"Hey, hey, Francine! Baby!"

Two seconds back in Greenwich Village and it was as if
she had never left. The same drunks leaning at the same
places on the bar, the same bartender, good old "Charlie
Em Cee" (his last name was Mc Something) the same sawdust on the floor, tables along the window, odor of beer
and hamburgers and V.O., the same posters on the walls,
the same chill in the air (too much air-conditioning) and
the same shout from John (the Hard-on) Blunt, supposed
friend of dead Dylan Thomas, supposed author of unseen
great manuscripts, supposed lover of unseen beautiful

women, and certain future member of Alcoholics Anonymous. (Assuming he had the sense to join.)

It was a long, L-shaped bar, and the regulars, like John (the Hard-on) Blunt, and E. K. Gare (known as E.K.) usually sat on the short end of the L. The stool at the corner was vacant and Francine took it. Charlie "Em Cee" put a V.O. in front of her and said, "On the house."

It was just as if she had never left. Except, of course, the drink was free.

"Hey, hey, Francine," E. K. said, "no waiting, baby."

"You always talked big, E. K."

"More than talk, Francine baby."

"Since when?"

E. K. made no answer. He was the only black man in the Village (unless there was a new one around) that couldn't get it up. And, of course, he wasn't really black. He wasn't even very brown. He had the complexion of a tanned Italian. He had put it about that he was part Sioux Indian but Francine had never believed that he could spell Sioux, let alone be one.

John (forty-five, mealy faced, small-featured, with a perpetually languid erection the services of which he had never, as far as Francine knew, offered to anyone) smiled broadly and said, "Dirty-Mouth Fran. Long time no see, Fran. Hear you got married."

"Got divorced, too."

"Well, whatever goes up, must come down."

"No waiting, Fran baby, promise," E. K. said again.

"Lay off, E. K.," Charlie told him. "How are you, Francine?"

"So-so. How are you, Charlie?"

"Good. I'm good," Charlie told her. (Irish baby face, thirty years old, looking like twenty-one. A mean man with the bat he kept under the bar. Shacked up with the seventeen-year-old daughter of the owner of Mick's over on Hudson Street, or used to be.)

"How's Barbara?" Francine asked.

"Long time since you've been here," Charlie told her.

"As far as Charlie is concerned," John said, "Barbara is no more."

"There is, however," E. K. added, "a young lady from Texas."

"We suspect she is a teenage runaway," John whispered.

"Shut up," Charlie told him.

"This is Fran the man," John said, "Dirty-Mouth Fran. You talk like she was a stranger."

Charlie smiled deprecatingly. "My new girl looks younger than she is, Francine."

"I'd be happy to meet her," Francine lied.

"Hey, Fran, talk dirty for us," E. K. said. "Man, we missed you, Fran."

"You back for good?" John asked.

Francine shook her head.

"Just stopped downtown to slum, huh?" E. K. said defensively.

"Fuck you, E. K. There, that make you feel better?"

"You know what would make me feel better, Fran."

"All talk, E. K. All talk," Fran told him.

And the trouble was, it was true. If it hadn't been she would have trotted off to his place in a minute. Anybody, even E. K., would do tonight.

Fran sipped her V.O. She maneuvered on the bar stool to get more comfortable. She was sorry now she had worn slacks. She had damn good legs. It might have helped to show a little bare leg.

Not that there was anyone in the place. The Sink was not that kind of place. There was a mixed crowd toward the middle of the long side of the L. Uptowners, probably, or new people in the Village. The owner of the place, Eddie Knight, was talking to them from his place behind the bar (he helped Charlie out when it got busy) and catching sight of her he shot her a quick smile and waved. Fran nodded back.

"Things are just the same," she said. "Doesn't anything ever change down here?"

She said it to no one in particular, to her shot glass more than to anyone around her. She was surprised, therefore, to hear an answer.

"Plus ça change. . . ."

French. Someone was always coming on with French in Greenwich Village. It made Francine as angry as it had in

the days when she was anything but horny, in the days
when, sitting in pretty much the same place in the Sink, the
last thing she had wanted was a man coming on to her in
half-assed French. She turned to see who the pompous ass
was just as E. K. spoke.

"Hi, Paul."

"E. K."

"Greetings," John said.

The man called Paul nodded, nodded again, in the direction of Charlie, then turned to Francine and smiled.

He was short, about five-nine, Francine guessed, and had
a pretty-boy face. His clothes were very fancy. He wore a
neatly pressed seersucker (blue and white) jacket and an
ascot. An ascot!

"What the fuck are you?" Francine said with chilling sarcasm.

She hadn't been able to help herself. All the defensive instincts she had honed to a fine edge in the days when she
sat alone at that bar had come back shining. Like swimming or bike riding, cutting someone in a Village bar is
something you never forget how to do.

John (the Hard-on) laughed so hard his drink went
down the wrong pipe. As soon as he was able to speak, he
said, "Fran baby, it is so good to have you back. Don't ever
leave us again."

"Va t'faire baisser chez les grecs," the man called Paul
said.

Now *that* was fairly good French. It meant go fuck
yourself at the house of the Greeks. Still, it burned Fran up
the way it would have years before when pretensions to language got under her skin almost as much, but not quite as
much, as men who dressed like dandies. An ascot! For the
love of God, an ascot!

"Tu m'en merde," Fran countered. Which translates
loosely somewhere between eat shit and get the fuck off my
back.

John laughed again and slapped his palm on the damp
mahogany of the bar. "Paul, baby," he said after another
pause to catch his breath, "meet Fran the man, dirty-talking Fran. Fran, Paul has been living down here for years,
ever since you left, as a matter of fact."

"Else I should have found somewhere else, certainly, isn't it?" Paul said.

Fran's mouth fell open about three inches.

"Yes, Fran," John said. "Paul's really French."

"I'm sorry," Fran said. She wasn't, however. She was just surprised. "I suppose you're an artist or a writer in exile."

"Easy, Fran, you haven't been around in awhile. Paul is O. K.," E.K. told her.

"Sure he is," Charlie said as he set a drink in front of the dandified Frenchman, without waiting to be told what to put in it. So Paul was a regular at the Sink. Well, at least *something* was different about the place.

"Besides," John said, "it isn't writers and artists anymore, doll. It's revolutionaries. All the kids are revolutionaries these days. Things have changed."

"Posturing is posturing," Fran said. She really was trying to stop, she really was. But the past had a hold on her. She didn't want to put this Frenchman down. He would do fine, just fine, if she could shut up long enough to give him a chance to have a drink and take her in.

"Paul is a salesman."

"A *what?*" Fran said.

"I got the job selling insurance. I wanted to be in this country for a time. So I took it. There is something wrong in this?" Paul said.

He wasn't bad-looking. "Nothing. Look, I'm sorry. I'll buy you a drink, O. K.?"

"You, a woman, will buy me a drink?"

"Sure. Look, don't turn out to be a male chauvinist after all this, O. K.? Please. I was wrong about you and French and wrong about you and posturing, but don't turn out to be a pig, O. K.?"

"What is this chauvinist, this pig?" Paul asked John innocently enough.

"Hey, hey," E.K. said from his place next to John, "Look at Francine come on to the Frog. Hey, Paul, look what likes you."

Paul smiled and nodded at Francine. "Good, I will let you buy me a drink."

"Thanks a lot," Francine said. But then she smiled and

motioned to Charlie, who, having heard the entire conversation, was already making Paul a second drink.

John said, "Paul, this is the dirtiest talking female ever to drink V. O. Say something dirty for Paul, Fran."

Francine just smiled.

"No kidding, she's got a longer list of original curses than Mark Twain had," John continued. "It's about all she's good at, outside of bed."

"How the fuck would you know, you've always been afraid to put that dork of yours in a woman."

"Easy, Fran," Charlie said.

"O.K. then," Paul said. "You pay for my drink and I drink it fast, and I take you out of here. O.K.?"

Francine looked at him, looked at the nearly empty glass of V.O., listened to the silence that had fallen around her, and said, "O. K. *Pourquoi pas?*"

"Whooeee, like old times," E. K. said. "We'll wait around till three a.m. for your report, Fran girl."

"Forget it, E. K.," Fran told him. "Time has not marched backward. No more vicarious thrills for you."

"Oh, Fran," John complained with mock despair in his voice.

In the old days, Fran had always reported on the men she had slept with. It had been part of being a female Henry Miller. But these were not the old days. The old instincts were there, but so was the new cause, the movement. WITCH. She would sap this overdressed Frenchman of all his juices, then disappear back uptown, for a month this time, for at least a month.

Paul had finished his drink and was eyeing her warmly. Very Gallic, she thought. Very French, *mon vieux*. Well, we'll see if you can fuck as well as you can look.

"*Allons,*" Paul said.

"Hot dog."

"What?" Paul asked.

"She said hot dog," John told him.

"It means she's pleased," Charlie said softly.

Smiling, Francine led her surprise conquest out the door of the Sink. Surprise because she had never expected to score so quickly, or to score in the Sink at all.

"Which way?" Francine asked when they were standing

outside the red door (the labia majora of Manhattan) of
the bar at the apex of the triangular block.

"Shall I get us a bottle of the V.O. first?" Paul asked. "I
notice you drink the V. O."

"You mean we're not going someplace where we can get
drinks?" Francine said coyly. She was letting him have her
full smile.

"We are going to my place, yes?" Paul said.

"Of course we are," Francine agreed. "No V. O. necessary, pal."

"Pal?" Paul repeated. "O. K. This way."

He led her up West Fourth Street, around a corner and
into an old apartment building.

"It's very hard to get apartments around here, isn't it?"
Francine said as they rode up together in the elevator.

"Oh, yes, but it cost me very much money . . . You are
very beautiful."

Francine smiled.

"I say that because it is true."

She smiled again. The elevator finally came to a stop and
he led her, holding her around the waist, along the false
marble corridor to a green door. The V. O. had aggravated
her case of horns. She wanted to grab him right there, before they even got inside. But it's so hard for a woman to
rape a man. So she waited while he got the door open and
let her into his living room.

"Very nice," Francine said.

It was. It was so nice, in fact, it took her mind off his
body for almost a full minute. There were woodcuts on the
walls (Baskins, she thought) and very expensive furniture
for a Village apartment, for an apartment in an old building. She wondered where he got the money. (Money always put her up tight. It was why she hated dandified men,
or used to. She hated ostentatious wealth. It went with her
stance as a writer of therapeutic, shocking prose. These
days, thanks to severe horns, she wasn't sure what she
liked.)

"Would you like something else to drink, if not V. O.,
Canadian Club?"

"Listen, Mister."

"Eh?"

"Would you please get the fuck out of your pants?"

Paul laughed.

"Can't you tell when you've got yourself a woman in heat? Now are you going to whip it out or aren't you?"

"So, E. K. and John were right. You are the dirty-talking Fran."

"It's not just talk, Frenchie," Fran told him.

She whipped the green cashmere over her head and had her brassiere unhooked before he could reply.

"Ah," Paul said.

"You like?" She shrugged out of her brassiere and let it fall to the rug.

"Yes."

"I want you inside me."

"You want the man inside you, I just happen to be here."

"Don't be coy, huh?"

She stepped out of her pants and kicked away her sandals. Naked, she turned once for his perusal.

"Formidable, mignone."

"Then get out of those fancy clothes."

"The bedroom is through here."

He was gesturing toward a doorway to the right, between a long blue couch and a teak bookcase. She went toward it and said, "Holy cow, Frenchie. This is a bedroom?"

"You don't like it?"

"What is it?"

It was the funniest looking bed she had ever seen. There were no bed clothes on it and it resembled an air chair. Above it a long tray was suspended from the ceiling by ropes. Behind it were shelves filled with boxes of tissues, bottles of liquor (no V. O.) and something she did not immediately recognize which might have been a vibrator.

"It's a water bed," Paul told her. "It enhances pleasure." He laughed. "I am not French for nothing, isn't it?"

"It sure isn't," Francine said. "Oh, Paul, baby, you cannot, cannot know how glad I am to see all this."

"I can now guess," he told her. "Try the bed."

"Not alone, Paul. Not alone."

She found it unbearable to stand there while he got undressed, calmly folding his seersucker jacket on a chair, calmly taking off his ascot, then his shirt, then his undershirt (ribbed, Jesus God, a ribbed undershirt) finally (praise the Lord and pass the man a condom) he got out of his pants, shoes and underpants (boxer shorts, striped, red and white.)

Fran had a theory about men and underwear. Only insecure people wore jockey shorts. But that was neither here nor there. His penis was growing. That was much more important to her.

"Oh, yes, you are very beautiful," he said. "I am going to enjoy you. You look, how we say, very comfortable."

"Come on!"

He wasn't very hairy. Frankly, she preferred hairy men, but right now she would have fucked a hairless goat if she could have found one in the mood. As a matter of fact, that wasn't a bad idea. There had to be a house, a male whorehouse, someplace, where a girl could get a goat.

She fell onto the waterbed on her back and the plastic gave under her, forcing her back up slowly, warm wavelets rippled beneath her naked skin, and, thank God, he came down on top of her.

The first touch of his naked penis was delightful, she had forgotten how good it could be to touch a naked cock. Thank God for naked cocks.

"Come on, Frenchie. Haven't you got a condom?"

"A what?"

"Oh, just put it in, would you?"

"We French, we pull out before the finish, that way we need no, what do you call it—"

"Just try it," she warned him. "Oh, holy mother, fuck me, sonny, let it go in there, oh, you French bastard, fuck me."

His breath smelled of scotch. So that's what Charlie had served him. So what? She had been under and on top of men whose breath smelled of everything from cloves to Clorets. She didn't give a damn what his breath smelled like.

"Would you put it in farther if I cursed for you, sweet?"

"It's in as far as it will go."

Shame, she thought. "Would you put it in harder then?"

"D'accord," he grunted.

All right, she would let him have some of her choice ones. After all, Hard-on John had promised him she could curse. Maybe it would stir him up some. As long as it didn't stir him up too much. Jesus, a water bed was a great thing. You know, girl, she thought, you have forgotten how much you need to fuck. Just to blind fuck.

"Scum-sucking pig," Francine whispered into Paul's ear.

"Pardon?"

"Oh the hell with it, they'd just be wasted on you. Look, how about if we tried this?"

She pulled his backside as far apart as it would come. He said, "Hey," but he pushed in harder so that the stroke pulled the skin over her clitoris taut and excited it.

"That's the boy. Oh, yes, that's the boy. Oh, Frenchie baby, you have got yourself a night-time prize."

"Yes, so I see, isn't it?" Paul groaned.

Chapter Three

John Morelli was drunk.

John Morelli is a gas, really.

"You know, Karen, baby, I was born married. I came out of the womb, looked around, and bingo, I was married."

Bingo.

"But I love my kids, oh, Jesus, do I love my kids."

This man did something to her. She wasn't herself when she was around him. If she had been anything like herself there would have been two great differences in her behavior. First, she would have thrown him out. Karen hated married men who wanted her body. She couldn't stand the idea of having another woman's husband. Second, she would have blushed every time he opened his mouth. He was being foul. He was being the foulest drunk she had ever seen.

My God, I'm breaking one of the rules: no drunks. My own rule. Well, Jeanette will not be back tonight.

"They're the village idiots, doll, the absolute village idiots. Coast to coast they buy our books and take them home to whack off by."

He plopped down, glass in hand, on the semen-stained couch. He was *very* cute. He had a small, turned-up nose, a wry mouth, hard blue eyes, and, my God, what he did to her.

He started to sing. "Oh . . . under the spreading chestnut tree, the village idiot sat. Amusing himself, abusing himself, dad da daa, and catching the drops in his hat, da da daaaa."

"You're loaded," Karen told him, and made herself comfortable at the other end of the couch.

He grew suddenly somber. He had a way of changing his feelings, and the feelings of everyone around him, one hundred and eighty degrees, in a split second. "I hate it," he said. "I hate this goddamn business. I hate everything about it. It reeks. I come home feeling I'm covered with semen at night, smelling of it. I want out, Karen, you hear me. I want as far away from it as I can get. I want a place in legitimate publishing. A *place*."

She nodded.

"It's got to be right. It's got to be right up there. Right at the top. And I'm going to get it too, wait and see."

Karen nodded and twisted a little on the couch. She was wearing just a nightgown. They had been lovers for a week.

"And I'm going to take you with me," he told her. "Right up there."

Then the liquor seemed to get hold of him again. He giggled and sang the verse about the village idiot for the second time.

He can't even carry a tune.

"I've got plenty on Big Chief Murray, don't you worry, doll."

He swung around so that he could put his feet over the arm of the couch and his head in her lap. He was wearing pants and a shirt and the shirt was open. They had been necking. *Necking.* Like kids. But he loved her breasts. He told her he just loved to sit next to her and fondle her breasts.

She didn't mind. It did nothing for her. Her nipples would swell after a while, but it did nothing really spectacular for her. The only thing that really moved her was when a man played with her clitoris, or brushed it while

fucking her, or went down on her. She would never ask a
man to eat her, of course. But that was what *really* did it
for her.

She couldn't help it, could she, if she had just one, very
small, erogenous zone? She wasn't Jeanette. Jeanette was
all erogenous zone.

And Jeanette never comes.

"Taxes," Morelli muttered and shut his eyes. "I've got
Murray by the tax balls, doll."

"He cheated on his taxes?" Karen asked innocently.

"Ha! Oh . . . under the spreading chestnut tree. . . ."

He rubbed the back of his head into her lap and she wiggled against it until he was rubbing her bush. The idea that
he might accidentally make contact with her clitoris made
her happier, but she would have been happier still if he
would turn around and bite it.

I've got the biggest clit on the block.

Sometimes when she was with John she wished she was
more like Jeanette. Jeanette was like Mary, the girl in the
orphanage who gave Karen the most competition. Mary
wasn't anywhere near as pretty as Karen, but everybody
knew if you just got her alone and coaxed her a little bit,
she would give head. She loved to go down on a man. Any
man. All he had to do was ask. Karen hated to go down
on men.

And I hate anal entry. I won't do it.

There had been a boy named Bob, an Irish kid in the oldest group in the orphanage and he was the reason Karen
used to let the boys take her down the cellar. She hoped,
eventually, to get him down there, too. And she had. But
Bob preferred Mary, who gave head so easily. Karen had
loved Bob. She had loved him for years. John reminded her
of him.

"Murray thinks he can hold out on me, but he can't,
Karen. I know too much."

She stroked John's head.

"Let's go to bed," Karen said.

"Sure, in a minute. You know my oldest kid, John Jr.?
He's been staying away from home, my old lady told me.
So I got hold of him yesterday. You know where he's
been?"

Karen shook her head. She was still stroking his hair.

"Why don't you put your drink down and come to bed with me?"

"He's been going to the track. Ha! The kid's just like his dad. I'll have him picking winners inside of a year. Look, I'll take you to the track Saturday, you'll meet him."

Karen shook her head.

"He's all right. He's the only one of them that understands."

"I'd rather not," Karen said.

John sat up and looked at her in a way that made her afraid and excited all at once. She didn't know whether he was going to punch her or kiss her.

I don't mind being kissed.

"Why not?"

"Look, I'd just rather not."

He smirked, put his glass down on the floor and reached inside her nightgown for her right breast. She had never thought she was the sort of a girl a man with a breast fetish would go for. Hers were on the small side. They were about the size of Jeanette's. But he just loved to play with them.

"O.K. Let's go into the bedroom," he said.

She smiled.

Thank God for small things.

This would be about the sixteenth time in the week they had been lovers. (She had lost count after seven.) He was great in bed. But then she had not been in bed with that many men.

Two. Joe and John. But I spent a lot of time in the basement of the Hartford Home for Orphaned Children.

She knew he was great in bed because he had a) a great body, b) great staying power, c) great rhythm, d) great recuperative abilities, e) a great mouth.

She stood up quickly, too quickly. She had to sit right down again.

"What's the matter?"

"Nothing."

"Are you all right?"

She had her hand on her chest. Whenever she felt that way she would get a heavy sensation in the center of her chest, right between her breasts.

He wobbled over her, still drunk.

"Listen, tell me what's the matter."

"It's all right. I feel faint sometimes, when I stand up too fast."

"Ohh, oh, that's all right," he assured her.

"Sure. I'm coming."

He reached a hand down and hauled her to her feet, embraced her and bit her neck.

"O.K. now?"

"Uh huh. Come on."

They moved through the apartment toward the back bedroom.

The first time Karen had brought him up there he had been very curious. He wanted to know whether or not she was getting enough alimony and she had told him that she hadn't asked for any alimony. She had made up an entire person named Barry Carter to whom, she said, she had been married for three years. (*Ever since UConn.*) She told him what he looked like, how he acted, and how horrified she had been when she found out that he was a bisexual.

I just borrowed Barry from Jeanette.

They had eaten supper in a small Italian restaurant on East Twenty-third Street, in the back courtyard, under the stars. She told him (over antipasto for two, veal parmigiana and a white wine from the liquor store around the corner) how it had been at UConn where she had majored in English, how it had been when she was first married, how much she missed her grandmother back in the small Connecticut town where the family paper mill was located. She lied blandly through three courses and espresso.

He did that to her. He made her break rules and patterns of behavior. It wasn't just that he was handsome and she was horny (*God, I was horny*). He had a kind of electric energy which short-circuited her own wiring.

Otherwise, how could she explain going out at all with a married man? When she had found out that Joe from Bengalore was married (and to a woman with whom he had nothing in common and, worse yet, who had been found for him by his family) she had given him up. Which had hurt. How else could she explain lying to him? She lied only to men she intended having nothing to do with, whom she wanted to find her out so that she could grow cold and snub them.

In the back bedroom Karen shrugged out of her night-gown, stepped out of it, and stood naked for him. He wasn't standing very straight and he was having difficulty getting out of his pants. She had never seen him so drunk.

"Am I too fat for you, John?"

"Fat? Ha!" he laughed. "You're just right, doll."

"I have such a big . . . behind."

"Let's see."

"Oh, John."

"Come on."

He made a circular motion in the air as he let his trousers fall, and set his drink down on her Salvation Army dresser. She turned for him.

"Bend it a little."

"I will not!"

She turned back to face him. He was slipping out of his boxer shorts. He was wearing only his shirt and socks.

"I'm going to fuck you with my socks on," he told her.

She shrugged. "You don't think it's too big?"

"Naaah."

She sighed and sat on the bed, brought her legs up and pushed back against the pillows. As he took his shirt off she watched his penis. It wasn't hard. He was too drunk. And she didn't want to have to do anything to it, even though she liked it. It was a crooked, greyish-pink penis with a large blue vein running from the base of the head to the hilt (publications) and she supposed it was a long one. The only other one she really knew was Joe's, which had been considerably shorter, and darker, and straighter. (*It had less character.*) The ones in the Hartford Home for Orphaned Children had all belonged to boys.

Would you believe I didn't have a man between the ages of fifteen and twenty-one?

"Karen, baby, you're luscious. L-U-S-C-I-O-U-S."

"Thank you, sir."

"Tell you what I'm going to do," John said drunkenly, tottering slightly, naked except for his socks. He reached over to the Salvation Army dresser and lifting his glass, took it down the last half inch.

"What?"

"Open up," he said, and made a mash of his mouth.

"What?"

He put the empty glass down and gestured with both hands for her to open her knees.

"Why?"

He laughed, and made the gesture again.

She opened them only slightly.

"All the way, white chick, all the way," John said in a mock black accent.

She *was* white, almost as white as Jan. She was so white it embarrassed her, as did her freckles, especially the ones on her face. (Covered, daily, with Max Factor pancake make-up.)

"Come on, come on."

She opened wider for him and he fell forward, pushing her knees all the way apart with his hands, and pressing his mouth against her vagina.

All right! All right!

It was the first time he had done that, and maybe, just maybe, he was drunk enough to keep at it for a while.

The reason she had not had a man (or a boy) from the time she turned fifteen to the time she was twenty-one was simple. She had been afraid. She started to get her period when she was thirteen and a half. A month before her fifteenth birthday, her period did not come on time. Naturally, she thought she was pregnant.

You would be surprised how much accurate, sophisticated sex information orphans possess. The boys knew the names of every brand of prophylactic on the market.

She did not bleed the next month either. She didn't even know which one of the boys was responsible. She walked around in a trance for weeks, petrified that one of the teachers or social workers or counselors would find out. She watched her stomach and thought it was growing. When she had gone eleven weeks without her period she became close to catatonic half the time, hysterical the other half. She sweated constantly, a stream of cold, putrid perspiration fell from her armpits. She knew now, of course, that it had been fear that brought that on, that the peculiar odor of her sweat was the odor of naked fear. Then, however, she thought it was a symptom of pregnancy. She had been about to confess all when she got sick and lost the foetus. It came out late one night while she was in bed in the dorm and although it hurt like hell she never made a sound. It was a tiny thing and she took it, and the soaking sloppy sheets to the bathroom. She hated to think about it; she never thought about it. Sometimes, however, she could not help remembering the terrible fear she had that the thing would not go down the toilet. And then, when it had finally disappeared, she was afraid that she would not be able to make up her bed unnoticed, or that the key to the linen closet wouldn't be on the rack outside the head counselor's door, or that one of the girls had only pretended sleep and had actually seen everything.

I swore I would never go near another penis.

And until Joe, she hadn't.

I'm afraid of them. I know it's silly, especially now, I have the pills, but I can't help it.

Not only was Joe the first man she had slept with in over six years, he was the first man ever to make her come (he did it by playing with her). After that, of course, she missed it, just as she had missed her non-orgasmic fucking in the cellar of the orphanage.

"Hey, John? John?"

He had suddenly stopped. Just when he was getting her excited as hell he suddenly stopped. She reached down and shook his head.

"Hey?"

"Huh? Oh, I must have fallen asleep."

"You bastard."

"Sorry. Where was I?"

"You were right here," Karen laughed and pressed his head into her crotch. She was loose and happy down there now. She had arrived at a special place on the road of sexual fulfillment. She was in no hurry to come, no hurry at all. It had never been quite like this with her before, and she wondered about John's experiences. He must have had a thousand women.

The first time he took her out he had loosened up after a

few drinks and told her about getting blind drunk the week before and waking up in bed with a chick he had never seen before. Another time he told her about making out with two girls at once and that when he wasn't fucking one of them, they were eating each other. Karen had thought it disgusting but she didn't let it show. Just as she had controlled herself when he had first handed her the three Hilt Publication books including *Gang-Bang Bernard Grows Up,* and she had hidden her true feelings.

She felt faint suddenly. He had really found her now and was running the bottom of his tongue over her clitoris. She wondered if it was true that the thing got red or something when she was excited. She had never looked.

"Well, enough of that," John said and shook his head hard as he came up for air, as if trying to stay awake.

"No, don't stop, John."

He laughed.

"Come on, Karen baby, unless you want to do me, too."

"No, come on, let's. . . ."

He came up over her and collapsed on her body, but he was stiff and he managed, somehow, to get it inside her without any help. Her clitoris was big enough so that she could feel his pelvic bone against it.

"Fastidious Karen," John groaned, and began to move into her. "Jesus, I'm tired."

"Well, turn over."

He slid out and they changed places. They had already become so accustomed to being together in bed they knew their sexual scenario by heart. First he would be on top, then she would.

"Just don't fall asleep again," she warned him.

She had never done this with Joe. Joe had been a sideways fucker. Maybe that's the way Indians do it, maybe just Indians from Bengalore. Anyway, it had seemed pretty good at the time. It certainly beat the cold floor of the orphanage cellar. But in the seven days that John and Karen had been lovers she had learned to make love a dozen different ways. The first night (in a hotel room on East Thirty-fifth Street) he had even fucked her in a chair, just like on the cover of *Gang-Bang Bernie.*

Maybe it was his business that got his libido so worked

up. Maybe he was just born that way. Whichever, she was grateful. God, she had built up a case of horns. She felt like a new woman. She only wished she knew what she was going to do when he left her.

He came while she was bouncing on top of him but she missed and she made him touch her until she came, too. By the time she climbed down off him he was asleep.

The hotel room was a gas, really. But I prefer my own bed.

She watched him for a minute. His skin was nearly as white as hers. Then she noticed the most peculiar thing she had ever seen. His testicles were moving. Even as he slept his testicles contracted, expanded (if that's the word for what they do after a man comes) and then contracted again.

Japanese Sumo wrestlers can pull theirs right up into their bodies.

"Hey," she said loudly.

She wanted to wake him up to ask him if he had any Japanese blood but he didn't stir. She shrugged, smiled, and went back into the living room. The copies of the three books John had given her, and of two others she had taken home to study, were on the coffee table near the couch. She picked up her copy of *Back-Seat Bang* and looked at the obscene photograph on the cover. Hell, obscenity wasn't all in the mind. That picture was *obscene*.

She put the book back and stood calmly for a moment trying to think of something. Something bothered her but she couldn't for the life of her think of what it was. Was it the five books on the coffee table? John had given her the last two, *Night Shift Nurse* and *The O Job* so she could study the style. (*He wrote them himself!*) No, it wasn't the books, or the raked-up memory of the miscarriage in the dorm, or the face of Bob, the boy she had been in love with when she was fourteen, or the fear she could not shake of men's sex organs, or the way John's testicles had contracted with a life of their own.

"Hah!" she said aloud in the empty room.

She marched quickly back into her bedroom, marched over to the bed, and yanked his socks off.

Then she covered him gently and wondered again what she would do when he left her.

Never let one man go until you have another. That was one of the old rules of the Schipol Airport KLM Hostess' Organization for the Preservation of the Species (SAKLL-MOPS) or so V might have called the amorphous group of nine or ten girls with whom she had been friendly in those days. Another rule was: never worry about a place to sleep.

"Married," the girls used to sing as they took off or returned from transportation-paid vacations on Majorca or the Greek islands or the Riviera, "we can always get."

The idea was that they were valuable merchandise and knew it. They were attractive, intelligent, personable, female creatures. As long as they were willing to divest themselves of some of the bourgeois trappings of their antecedents they would get along fine (and the war had helped there, breaking up many of the families from which they came, not just infant V's own half-German, half-Dutch household).

So they took off in small groups to visit the countries of Europe and sport on the beaches of the Mediterranean and the Adriatic. (Anyone with a bicycle could get to Schrevingen and sport on the beaches of the North Sea, there was no fun in that.) And they slept where, and with whom, they happened to be when it was time to go to bed. It wasn't a very practical way to travel. One of the girls was always coming down with something, fleas or crabs or gonorrhea or something stronger. Welmoot, a platinum blonde (whiter than V) caught syphilis from an Italian who had picked her up on a motor bike while she was visiting Palermo, and one of the stewards, a man named Willem with whom V had slept once or twice mostly because everyone else was sleeping with everyone else and he was the only man left, had once been in the Caribbean and had come down with something venereal. When he went to the dermatologist the doctor scraped a sample from the moisture on the tip of his penis, put the sample under the microscope, called Willem over, and said, "Look into the 'scope. You see the organism on the right, that is gonorrhea, the one on the left, that is syphilis, but the one in the middle I have never even seen before."

In short the girls (and boys) of SAKLMOPS had a ball. Rule three: have a ball. V's personnel manager didn't mind. The last thing in the world he could have been called was possessive. And by then, of course, Hans was long gone from the attic on Jan van der Heydenstraat.

Thinking of those days V recalled vaguely the way she had been long ago and the rules she had once tried so hard to follow, not because they were the right rules, but because they weren't the wrong ones, and following them made her happy. Rule one: never let one man go until you have another.

Why sleep alone?

If someone had told V that life in those days had been artificial, that it had no basis in true emotion or possible enduring human relationship, she would not have denied it. She would have said she was well aware of it. She would have insisted, however, that she was young, that it was time to have fun.

If, on the other hand, the same someone (a gadfly at worst, a psychoanalyst at best) had suggested that her militant sleeping around was the natural consequence of her affair with the personnel manager, was an immature defiance of her break-up with Hans, was a running away from the fact that she still loved Hans deeply, could not, in fact, have a decent orgasm without him, she would have denied it. She would have cried, of course, the way she had cried the day in Bayonne when Francine called her out saying, "Is that what's wrong with you, Veltraud? Is that your problem, honey?" but she would have denied it. She did not have the peculiar ability that Francine sometimes evidenced, of facing the truth about herself.

At some point in V's development she had learned to keep the truth about herself from herself. That was too bad because it seemed unlikely that she would now ever be able to extricate herself from the tangled web of self-delusion she had constructed. Still, sometimes, like today, Saturday, when it had just stopped raining, when there were still clouds overhead and no sign of the sun above them, when the moisture hung heavy in the afternoon air, she recalled

Amsterdam, and there was hope. Vague, as if through a lowland's mist and a long way off, but hope.

What she recalled now was rule one: never let one man go until you have another.

"No, it's not that at all, Roger. It's . . . well, it's hard to explain and I wish to God you wouldn't push me."

"I'm not pushing you, V, it seems perfectly natural to want to know where you're going, that's all. All I can suppose is you're going with . . . with someone else."

"Roger, I swear it to you, it's not that."

"I swear it to you," Roger repeated. "That's not the way you're supposed to say it. Say, I swear it."

"I swear it," V said, knowing full well she would soon forget Roger's correction of her English usage.

"Well, why all the mystery, V?"

V frowned. She should have realized she was going to need an explanation. Roger was always Casper Milquetoast until he had some reason to be jealous, then he became difficult to control.

Rule four: exercise complete control over your (temporary) bedmate.

It was hard, sometimes.

They were walking down Fifth Avenue. Not only was the air heavy and the sky overcast but there was something else in the air that reminded her of Amsterdam. It was wishful thinking, no doubt, but she could swear that she had caught a whiff of herring as they had passed East Tenth Street. V would have given all she had on her for a fresh, sliced herring with chopped onion right from the Eisel Meer. If she thought about it any longer she was just liable to start to cry.

"Listen, V, if you don't want to tell me, well, all right. I suppose I have no right to know. We're just friends, after all."

"Oh, Roger, stop it, yah."

"I have no hold over you . . . no right to know."

They came to the bottom of Fifth Avenue at Washington Square and walked toward the deserted area under and around the arch.

V stopped walking and Roger went on another two steps before turning to face her. It was strange the way people left the streets when it was overcast in New York. If people in Amsterdam behaved that way they would never leave their homes.

"You are acting like a child, Roger."

"Oh, am I?"

"Yah. I have given you a perfect explanation."

"Sure, you've told me you'll be out of town for three weeks."

"I need a change of climate. I am getting depressed."

Roger frowned and looked away across the park. The weather gave her a certain ability to see him clearly. Being reminded of Amsterdam did not just present her with the vague hope of recovering from her labyrinth of self-delusion, it gave her greater distance from her loves, too.

For instance, she noticed for the first time that he was slightly pigeon-toed. It made him appear effeminate. Well, sometimes in bed she got the idea that he would be far happier to assume a passive, accepting role; and wasn't that what the books said was typically female?

"That's hard to believe, V."

"What?"

"It's hard to believe."

"Are you going to cry?"

"Don't be silly."

"Well I don't see why you say it is so hard to believe. Always, when I was working in Amsterdam, in the airport. and I got depressed, I would go away for a vacation. I would go to Italy or to France. Once, even, I came here to New York but that cost me a lot of flying credit."

"Flying credit?"

"Sure, as a stewardess for KLM one built up credit. After two years with them one could fly three hundred dollars' worth. I think it is different now."

"But why won't you tell me where you are going?"

V frowned and started walking toward the benches in the direction of the NYU Law School across the park. In a moment Roger was beside her, staring straight ahead. He was hurt, he was actually hurt. How long had it been since a man had a real attachment to her? She would have said that not since Ivan had anyone actually needed her, but she did not want to think about Ivan because *all* Ivan did was

need her. He had not loved her. Not as much as he loved
his mother. Otherwise he would have given her the things
she needed. And he would have gotten them out of
Bayonne.

"Roger, I try to explain, yah? It is this, when in Amsterdam I went away I found it better if no one knew where I
was going. Otherwise I was not really getting away."

Roger smiled. He was still staring straight ahead.

"Oh, now I have really hurt you," V said. It was harder
than ever to believe she had actually moved him emotionally, and her voice gave away her incredulity. She hoped,
however, that it had not given away the fact that his pain
moved her further from him instead of bringing her closer.
It had always been that way with men. When you had
them, well, that was all, wasn't it? It was no longer necessary to feel something for them, something which, when
felt by them, would bring them to you.

"Look, Roger, please. It is not you. Oh, sure, it is you a
little, but it is really everything here, New York, New
York. You know?"

"No, V, I don't know."

"It's getting to me. How do I tell it to you? It's getting *to*
me."

Of course it was getting to her, and, of course, that was
not why she was leaving it. She was beyond fighting the effects of the city—*gek stadje:* crazy little town—on her
psyche. She was leaving for Hong Kong where she was to
marry someone whose name she did not even know, she
was then to go through the motions of obtaining a temporary visa for him to visit the United States, she was then to
return with him to San Francisco where she would be paid
twenty thousand dollars and put on a plane back to New
York. Total time: three weeks. Tax-free income. (Schipol
was a tax-free airport.) The temporary visa would be
changed to a permanent one without her. Ho Bin's West
Coast colleagues would see to that.

Visas. She had once had so many different visa stamps in
her passport book she had been the envy of every girl at
Schipol.

Rule one: never let one man go until you have another.

"Roger, would it make any difference if I told you . . . if

I told you I hope to God you will be here for me when I get back?"

Roger smiled painfully again. "No, it wouldn't, V. It would make a difference if you told me where you were going, with whom, and why."

"So, it wouldn't make any difference!"

Now she could show a little anger. A little anger was a powerful weapon.

"No!"

"Good. Very good. Take me home, yah."

Roger frowned, and blinked as if there were already tears in his eyes. *Wat een kind*. What a child.

"Come, Roger, yah."

She turned back the way they had come. He followed after her like a dog. Well, she knew what she had to do to make her little dog believe her. She had to give him a treat. If she planned it so that he was not at the nadir of his depression until she got him back to the apartment, if she planned it just right, then perhaps his tears would heighten the sex for her, would make his erection just a little larger, would make him try just a little harder to please her.

"We just came out. You wanted to walk, remember?"

"Take me home, yah?"

In moments they were back on Fifth Avenue and walking back uptown. It would have been shorter if they had continued through the park and cut over to Avenue of the Americas but V still could not get used to the streets in New York, and it was V who led the way. The streets in Amsterdam which ran in great circles (following the canals which were concentric rings about the central city) or cut diagonally through the circular streets, or twisted every which way in the old section of town, were as easily negotiated by her as the rooms in the house in which she had grown up; but these straight, endless streets of New York, all of which were numbered and marked with directions (East Fourth Street, West Fourth Street) confused her. It was as if her mind refused to adjust to anything so straightforward.

They walked silently as V tried to feel Roger's discomfiture, measure it, control it, so that she could eventually use it. If she could keep the fight at the edge it had reached, if she could keep him from breaking until he was alone with her back in the apartment, at least this time there would be some emotion in their love-making.

Rule five: never fall in love with a poor man.

Roger was not a poor man; still, rule five applied. American men required corollaries of the rule-makers. In the old days in Schipol it was assumed that all men who were attracted to you were attracted to you because they wanted to fuck you. It was assumed they wanted to fuck you because they knew they could do it and doing it, would enjoy it. These American men, these Ivans and Rogers, with their circumcisions and their mothers in the forefront (foreskins) of their minds, could not necessarily do it correctly. Rule five with corollary therefore: never fall in love with a poor man, or with a rich one who cannot fuck.

Of course, V would have had to admit, in the days in Schipol she had been accustomed to sleeping with men not so much to receive pleasure but to receive a place to sleep or to be kept warm and comfortable and free from loneliness and the memory of Hans. She had not, as was true lately, sought men who could give her a decent orgasm. She had the need of one then but it had not yet built to the point of obsession. If she had been willing to think hard she would have recalled she had been very happy with Ivan at first, thin cock or no, unseismic orgasm or no. She would have had to admit that her generalization about American men was unfounded, that there were probably as many circumcised unsuccessful Frenchmen who thought too much of their mothers. Italians and even Dutchmen too.

They turned down Twelfth Street and walked along the sidewalk in front of the pretty old brownstones and across from the bank of new high-rise apartment buildings, the silence between them extending into a truce, the truce becoming a *de facto* peace. But there would be no treaty. There was simply no question of telling Roger where she was going and why.

"What is it?" Roger asked.

She had faltered for a moment because she thought she recognized the woman approaching them. Then she decided she had been wrong, then abruptly recognized that it was Francine after all, the woman she hated most in all of

the United States of America. V hadn't seen her since
Bayonne.

Francine was walking with a cute little young man who
wore a blue blazer and an ascot and seersucker pants. His
shoes were Italian and there was something in his walk that
V had not seen in a long while. He was not American. She
was willing to bet he was not American.

"It's someone I know," she said to Roger just as Francine and her man approached close enough to hear her.
But why did she assume he was her man? Why not just a
friend, a business acquaintance, the husband of her best
friend?

"Hello, Francine."

V stopped and smiled at the man in the ascot, not at
Francine. Roger would not notice, of course. Men never
noticed that you might be coming on to someone else when
they had the opportunity to come on to someone in turn.
And Francine looked good. The bitch.

"Hello, V."

She would have walked right by if her cute friend hadn't
been drawn up by V's smile.

"It's a long time," V said. "How is your husband?" And
then continued before Francine had the chance to be bitchy
in turn, "This is Roger Conheim, Roger, this is Francine
Klein, Klein, Conheim, it rhymes, doesn't it?"

Francine just smiled.

V couldn't let her get away that easily. She knew about
Francine's divorce and that Francine didn't know she
knew. She wanted to embarrass her, to make her confess
her marriage had been a failure. And she wanted a chance
to find out her friend's name.

"Aren't you going to introduce me?"

Francine smiled again. "Paul Schlong, this is V Quim,
Schlong, Quim, Quim, Schlong," Francine said.

Roger's mouth fell open until Francine grinned at him
and he shut it.

"What?" V said.

Paul laughed. "I can imagine what a schlong is in Francine's slang, which makes it pretty obvious what a quim
must be. My name is Marot, Paul Marot." He nodded at
Roger.

"A schlong, Marot, is the male pudend, a quim, Schimmelphennick, is the female pudend, a pudend, Mr. Conheim, is a sex organ, bye-bye," Francine said sweetly, took Paul by the arm and led him away.

"I'll be damned," Roger said.

That bitch, V thought. That bitch! That bitch!

They stood staring after Francine and Paul Marot for a full thirty seconds until V's anger subsided to the point that she could turn around and start toward Avenue of the Americas again.

"He was French, wasn't he?" Roger asked. "But who and what was *she?*"

"My ex-sister-in-law," V told him. "I hate her guts."

"She's awfully pretty."

"She's got a foul mouth."

"I'll say she has," Roger agreed.

It was broken; it was over. V could feel it. There wasn't any point in going back to the apartment. She'd had Roger just where she wanted him. He would have made the best love of his long affair with her. If they did it now, however, he would be thinking of Bitch Fran all the while. She would not have that. *Lailicka hex:* ugly witch!

"Roger, I don't want to go back to the apartment."

"Oh?"

"Come on. Let's walk up and look at the Porsches on Seventeenth Street, yah?"

"No, V."

"What?"

"I said no. Frankly I've had it doing everything you say." They had stopped for the light at the avenue. "Are you going to tell me here and now where you are going and why?"

She looked up at him, trying to stare him down, but the resolve she read in his eyes didn't even dim.

"No, Roger, I am not going to be forced into—"

His departure cut her off. He just turned and walked away back down Twelfth Street, in the direction Francine and the Frenchman had gone.

She spun and walked toward her building, crossing against the light, drawing a wolf whistle and an obscene smacking of the lips from a truck driver who slowed down to watch her.

"That bitch," she said aloud. "That fucking bitch!"

Jeanette was seated opposite Uncle Tim the Tit-Eater in the back booth of a Chinese restaurant on the Upper West Side. Aunt Carol was sitting opposite Morris.

This particular grouping struck Jeanette as very funny. Aunt Carol had called weeks ago to set up the date. "Uncle Tim wants to meet some of your friends," she had said.

"How many?"

"Jeanette, now don't be snide. One at a time, I suppose."

"O.K."

"He'll buy you both a nice dinner and try to get to know her."

"Her? Did he say it had to be a female friend?"

"No, I just assumed it would be Karen; we've never even met Karen."

"Well, Karen isn't my only friend."

"Now it's not important who you bring dear, just that it be someone you like, that's all. Tim feels responsible for you, he worries about you."

"Do *you* worry about me?"

"No, dear, I *know* you. But Tim has to talk to your father on the phone all the time."

"Why?"

"Because he calls. Your mother is worried about you too."

"Because I'm not married."

"It's not that."

"Yes, it is."

"Jeanette, let's not get into an argument. Would you like us to take a friend of yours to dinner?"

"O.K. Sure."

"This weekend?"

"No, can't that soon. How about next?"

"No good. Tim's going on a selling trip. It would have to wait a few weeks then."

"O.K."

"But you'll do it."

"If it will make you happy, Aunt Carol."

"Good."

So now Aunt Carol and Uncle Tim had Morris to deal with. Which was wonderful. Uncle Tim, of course, had wanted to meet Karen. Of course. Or some other *young* lady. Of course.

"Pass the soy sauce, Tim, please," Jeanette asked.

Tim smiled and passed the soy sauce. "You're enjoying the meal, aren't you, Jeanette?" Tim asked.

"Right you are, Uncle," Jeanette replied.

"So, you're a doctor," Aunt Carol said to Morris.

"That's right," Morris answered, for the third time in fifteen minutes. It was all Aunt Carol seemed able to think of to say—"So you're a doctor." Jeanette was having a *wonderful* time.

"Listen, Morris," Tim said, his mouth full of egg roll. "What's the most amazing fact you know?"

"What?"

"The most amazing fact. You know, the most ludicrous thing you ever found out."

"About what?" Morris said.

"Uncle Tim, is this one of your selling spiels, because if it is—"

"Jeanette, listen to your uncle, please, he probably knows what he's saying," Aunt Carol said.

"Probably?" Tim repeated. "Probably? Listen, just play along, Morris, and we'll overlook the fact you're Jewish, O.K.?" Tim said and guffawed like Milton Berle.

"Morris, don't pay any attention to Tim's ethnic jokes, please," Aunt Carol said.

Jeanette was having a *wonderful* time.

"O.K.," Morris said. "The most amazing fact I know is a medical one. More people who make ethnic jokes suffer from heart attacks and emphysema, eczema and psoriasis than people who smoke cigars and live among lepers."

Aunt Carol laughed and Jeanette guffawed in imitation of Uncle Tim and, finally, Uncle Tim smiled. "Look, O.K., I'm sorry, but really, Morris, a real fact, a true one, not one you make up. O.K.?"

Morris sighed, finished chewing the piece of egg roll he had just put in his mouth, swallowed, and said, "Jeanette told me one that her roommate told her."

"Oh, that," Jeanette said. "I didn't think it was so great. Karen thought it was great."

"What is it?" Aunt Carol asked.

"The poet Longfellow's wife died at the first battle of Bull Run when her crinoline frock was ignited by a spark from the battle," Morris said.

Aunt Carol just looked at Morris, Tim cocked his head to one side as though weighing the level of ludicrousness of that fact, and Jeanette shrugged.

Morris looked from one of them to the other, then went back to eating his egg roll.

"I suppose that's a pretty good one," Tim said.

"What was she doing there in the first place?" Aunt Carol wanted to know.

"I suppose she was among the spectators. There were a lot of spectators there."

"At a battle?" Aunt Carol asked loudly.

Morris nodded.

"O.K. But I know where Napoleon's cock is," Tim said.

"Tim!" Aunt Carol said in a hushed voice. "Not so loud!"

"In his sarcophagus, at *Invalides*," Morris said.

"Someone is going to overhear you. What will they think?" Aunt Carol said.

Jeanette laughed again.

"Well, you're wrong, buster," Uncle Tim said. "Listen to this," and paused for effect. "It's in a hand-tooled moroccan leather box at 31 Sutton Place at the home of a doctor, another doctor."

"Where?" Jeanette said.

Morris put his fork down and laughed.

"At 31 Sutton Place at the home of a doctor," Tim continued. "It seems that when the old bastard died his Italian valet took a knife and cut the schlong off, right? Why not, probably thought it was some kind of a talis . . . what do you call it, Morris?"

"Talisman."

"Right. Then the valet auctioned it off. Signed papers, the whole pedigree, the works."

"I don't believe it," Jeanette said.

Aunt Carol laughed and struck the tabletop with her palm.

"It's true," Tim said. "Now, how's that for an amazing fact."

"Amazing," Morris said. "Tim, you do have an ear for amazing facts."

"Hah!"

Jeanette bit her lower lip.

"What is it?" Aunt Carol asked her.

"Nothing," she said.

"Are you all right?" her aunt asked.

"Uh huh."

"I know what she's thinking," Tim said. "She wants to see it."

Jeanette smiled at him, and Tim said, "No chance, though. It's not a museum or anything."

Jeanette was still smiling because she was sure Morris had a better idea of what she had been thinking. Tim had been wrong, she didn't want to see it, she wanted to *use* it. Imagine having Napoleon's cock inside you. Well, it was probably useless now—unless they had preserved it somehow.

The waiter came and put three aluminum serving dishes on their table, changed their plates, gave them fresh silverware and left them.

Uncle Tim reached over and lifted the lids from the serving dishes, one at a time, and Jeanette wondered how a pickled cock would taste.

"It *must* be pickled," Jeanette said.

"It's sweet and sour shrimp, honey," Aunt Carol said.

"No. I mean Napoleon's thing. It must be pickled."

"Must be," Morris agreed, "otherwise there wouldn't be much of it left."

"I'll bet it's a yard long, that's why he used to stand around with his hand in his shirt," Tim said.

The dinner went quickly. Aunt Carol was afraid of saying anything that would offend Morris more than he had already been offended and Tim's thoughts had apparently wandered elsewhere.

After dinner, when Morris and Jeanette were finally free of Carol and Tim and were inside Morris's car, Morris said, "I knew a fact like that but I decided not to give him the pleasure of hearing it."

"I told you he would be like that."

"Sure. I was warned. I wanted to come and I'm glad I did."

"You wanted to make a good impression, so they wouldn't bug me."

"That's right," Morris admitted. He turned the car into traffic. "Want to hear my fact?"

"Sure."

Morris turned right on a narrow one-way street and slowed the car to keep pace with a truck ahead of him. It was a very mild summer night and the windows of the Buick sedan were open to the city air.

"After Mary Queen of Scots was beheaded the executioner had to prepare the body for the burial. Before he prepared it, he fucked it. He was caught in the act and prosecuted."

"He wasn't?"

"Yup. Always wanted to fuck a queen, he said."

"But a headless one, yech!"

"Don't be so fastidious. I saw your eyes light up during that talk about Napoleon's cock. Why did you ask if it was pickled? Would you eat it if you could?"

"Morris!" Jeanette said and laughed.

"Well, there's a school of thought that holds many women want to literally eat men's penises, you know."

"There is?"

"Direct lineal descendant of penis envy."

"What?"

"Freud."

"Oh, him."

Morris pulled the car over to the side of the street, parking behind a red Chevrolet.

Jeanette took Morris' arm and leaned against him. "Morris, why would a woman want to eat a man, I mean really eat a man?"

"Oh, I don't know, get the power of his cock, eliminate his mastery over her, if he's got any, or if she thinks he does."

"I still say, yech!"

"Talismans of parts of the body were not uncommon in ancient and medieval times, so why not cocks, too? I'll bet plenty of women, and men, carried dried-up old cocks around with them."

"Well, that's not the same as eating one."

Morris shrugged. They got out of the car and were nearly at the entrance of the building when Morris said, "There's not enough magic nowadays."

"Some way for a scientist to talk."

"Medicine's only half science, honey."

When they were finally inside Morris's apartment Jeanette immediately started to undress and Morris, although slower about it, did likewise.

When they were naked they lay down on top of the bedclothes on Morris' bed and held each other.

"You think I need a talisman, Morris?"

"Nope."

"What if I want one?"

"What do you want me to do, get a penis from a corpse for you, out of the hospital? You could probably buy one from a hard-up medical student.'"

Jeanette thought that over for a moment, meanwhile trying to get her breathing synchronized with Morris'. She felt his hairy chest rise against her breasts and gradually she relaxed, gradually she felt more and more like herself. Being naked. Just being naked with someone.

"No, I don't think I want a penis. The penis isn't the thing."

"Well, what is then?" Morris asked.

His eyes were closed and she knew he would be asleep in a moment. He had had another "rotten" day, and before they went out they had made love twice; then they'd had another argument about her moving in permanently and she had finally brought that to a close by suggesting that if he didn't stop badgering her about it she would stop seeing him altogether.

It wasn't that he needed her. It was more like he just wasn't finished with her yet, finished getting to know her, and, perhaps, finished doing things actively for her. If she thought he loved her (whatever that meant) she might consider moving out on Karen, or if she thought he could grow to love her (whatever, again, that meant).

Meanwhile, he was too smart for her. A. And he knew too much about her. B. He knew about Barry, about Jerry, about all of them that she'd thought to tell him about, and she'd thought to tell him about most of them. No man wants a girl with a history like that; not for long anyway.

"Hmmm?" Morris said.

He was asleep by the time she answered. "Not penises, Morris. That's not what means anything. Semen. It's semen that counts."

"Hmmm?"

"You go back to sleep. I just want to hold you."

Francine's relationship with Paul had already begun to deteriorate. It had lasted two weeks, which was lengthy by Village standards, it couldn't survive much longer.

On the one hand Paul was a mechanic when it came to sex. He did everything according to the numbers; and he had all the requisite equipment: vibrator, water bed, bar over the short headboard, even a tray which lowered by pulleys from the ceiling so they could sit up on the water bed and eat or play cards between fucks. On the other hand he was a sniveling romantic. She started to call him the ro-bot-heart. He talked so much about love, and mooned so much, it was beginning to get on her nerves.

Obviously, she had not stayed with Paul for just the one night she had promised herself, the one night of heretical sex. She had stayed the next day, too, calling her boss at Carter Hall and complaining of a virus. She had only gone home the day after that, Saturday, and had seen him again Saturday night and all day Sunday. The water bed, too, was beginning to get on her nerves. It was too damn seductive, too damn difficult to get off of.

But she had not stayed so long because of Paul, at least not because of Paul *per se*. He had been absolutely right, she had wanted a man in her and he was available. That was the extent of her emotional commitment. Oh, she liked him, and she thought his accent was cute, she loved to be fucked in French, and she liked his toys, especially the vibrator, but his talk of love drove her up the wall.

No, she had not stayed because of Paul, and, truthfully, she had not stayed because of the toys, either, or because of the French (Mother, it's nice to be fucked in French). She had stayed because another man she knew had been right, at least about one thing: orgasms. Morris Levy. The chauvinist pig. It's one thing to come because you've diddled yourself or a man has diddled you (or a Radical Lesbian). It's another thing entirely *with* a cock inside you.

That first night after Paul had fucked her for a few minutes they had come together. (A promising way to start a relationship, assuming what one wants is a relationship.) He had been fast, but she had been faster. Eight or nine good lunges (drawing the clitoral foreskin back and forth over that sweet center of sensitivity: her sex; *her)* and she had been ready to come, holding on just long enough to drain a little masochistic pleasure from the act. Who knew what might go wrong when it was over, she might have to find another man to finish her off, to make her come another four or five times. Who knew, maybe Paul, French Fancy or not, might be good for only one hard short arm a night. Who knew? But then (sweet eater of the offal of small dogs) he had reached back and taken the vibrator off the shelf over the bed.

Without slipping his cock out he had put his hand into the thing (it was a massaging device, not the glass vibrating penis Masters and Johnson had used) flipped the switch and lowered his now shaking hand to her cunt and (your forefathers slept in the rancid day-old come of syphilitic Turks) he had found her clit with his forefinger. (Foreforefingers, foreskins, four comes, one two three four, count them you, whose mother made a living during the depression using a greased forefinger for a cut-rate, reusable Fleet's enema in the assholes of the lower East Side.)

The point was his cock had been in the whole time, and when it had finally slipped out she had asked him to stop. Not that five orgasms, of varying size and hue, accompanied, obviously, by profanities of various depth, length and quality, were enough. No, she would want more, later. The point was, Morris dear, they weren't much damn good without that short arm up the old crotch.

She wondered how Morris dear was.

Once, when she had been at a particularly low point and lonely in her former life in Greenwich Village she had filled her notebook not with pseudo-Millerian prose but with impassioned, feeling letters to Dear Morris. She had never mailed them but sometimes—and that first night with Paul and his electrical toys and his rivulating water bed was an example—her mind would play back to the time when unmailed letters to Morris had been a solace to her, and she would talk to him, addressing herself, really, through him. His personality was so well-established. She knew so well what he would understand, and more important, *that* he would understand.

(May you be lowered head first into a vat containing the menstrual juices of eight generations of Russian women . . . to drown.)

He understood, for instance, or at least the person whom she called Morris in her unmailed letters and in her unanswered mental discourse understood, why she cursed the way she cursed, why profanity was a balm, an analgesic, an anodyne.

I want to free myself, Morris, from all the things that bind me royal, and then free my sisters, Morris dear. Prose *did* work, Morris. Dirty talk *did* work, Morris. It readied me, freed me enough, to go on with the fight. But Morris, continence is not for me, continence did not work. So I made a little deal with my conscience. More fucking in exchange for more active and more radical work in the movement.

It was lucky, perhaps, that Morris was not there to answer.

And Paul, until both the robot and the heart parts of the robot-heart began to get on her nerves, was the perfect find for a lady who had promised herself (and with each new fuck promised herself again) more fucking.

She considered, in the abstract, that rarely discussed Platonic Ideal: the blind fuck. The Blind Fuck.

In the world of forms the ideal blind fuck floated closer to the reach of mortal man than any other ideal; and Francine was one of those few mortal *wo*men who had perfected the ability to make contact with that ideal form. It hovered over the bed, above Paul's elastic, rechargeable back, so Fran the Man could watch it if at sometime during the festivities she chose to open her eyes.

However, regarding Paul Schlong's schlong: uncut, arching slightly to the right when tumescent, slightly swarthy when tumescent, this crescent, this *croissant*. Length: approximately eight point three inches when tumescent, miniscule, unworthy, uninteresting, frustrating when not. Attendant equipment; i.e. balls: high hung, small, not surmounted by enough hair to suit her.

Question: When had she started calling him Paul Schlong?

Answer: When she had first seen his water bed.

Question: How could she so closely approximate the length of Schlong's schlong?

Answer: With a carpenter's rule she found on the shelf of his bathroom, to which room she had retired to douche.

Question: Douche with what?

Answer: Douche with the Kewpie-doll shaped douche bag and the douche powder next to the carpenter's rule on the shelf of the bathroom.

Question: Why was the douche bag Kewpie-doll in shape?

Answer (from Paul's, the horse's, mouth): *Sais pas.* (Shrugging.) *C'était derrière la porte de la salle de bain quand je suis arrivé.*

Translation (loose): Beats me. (Shrugging.) It was here before I was.

Question: Why was the carpenter's rule on the shelf in the bathroom next to the box of douche powder?

Answer (from Paul's, the horse's, mouth): *Pourquoi pas?*

Translation (loose): Why don't you mind your own business and come back to bed?

On Friday morning she had called Mrs. Liberty Bell Franco (no relation to the generalissimo son-of-a-bitch; called Liberty Bell by Fran because of the vastness of her ass) to tell her she, Fran, was down with the flu and would not be in that day.

"Oh, sorry, hope you feel better but it seems everybody is coming down with it, even Mr. Lyons."

"He out today, too?"

"Uh huh."

Lyons was *The Man*. The man who was having Francine promoted. For that reason, and none other, she had a great deal of affection for him. When the Radical Lesbians took over the world and hetero-sexual males were lined up against the wall (or at the edge of a cliff the way Franco's namesake had done it) and shot (or pushed off) she would save Lyons by disguising him as a hairy saleswoman of Kewpie-doll douche bags.

The phone was in the living room. It was the only necessary thing which was not within reach of Paul's hot damn water bed.

Question: Why does one not use a cover on a waterbed?

Answer: Because the room, and the water in the water bed, are kept warm enough to make nudity comfortable.

She walked back into the bedroom to find Paul seated guru fashion on his side of the bed rolling a joint.

"Grass, too?"

"Pourquoi pas?"

"Loverly."

"Tu veux?"

"Sure, I *veux*."

They smoked the joint, passing it back and forth between inhales, and got back to basics. It was while under the spell of the good grass that Paul first started talking his love rubbish.

He had never met anyone like her.

She had the most beautiful body he had seen since the last time he'd seen Sophia Loren.

When had that been?

Please don't joke with him. Fucking her was more wonderful than fucking anyone he had ever known. No one had ever been so enjoying (he was speaking English), so inventive.

It's because I commune with the Blind Fuck.

Yes, and I like the way you talk.

I like the way you talk too, baby. Was that carpenter's rule there so I'd see it, or so whoever would see it, and bring it in here to measure you? Are you that conceited?

Pense comme tu veux, je suis bien fatigué.

Translation (loose): If you want to think that I won't fuck you.

Get it up, sweetheart, I'm still in need of that schlong of yours.

What is a schlong?

This, *cheri* (grasping four inches and squeezing it—magic clay—up to eight point three) is a schlong.

To the subject of the Blind Fuck.

As to position: contrary to the popular literature variety in position does not improve (for this lady) the quality of the fuck. Fucking ought to be done in position-one, the minister's way with his wife, man (minister) on top, woman (wife) on bottom. Anyone enlarging upon this purely physical arrangement designed to allow the male maximum thrust power, the female maximum control, and, more importantly, designed to allow the female to get her clit up where his schlong will do the most good, anyone enlarging from that to psychological positions such as: men are naturally on top, ergo: naturally superior, like the folks (fucks) who read a moral into Huck Finn, will be taken out and shot.

She did not like being on top. She did not like sideways fucking. She did not take to kneeling, sitting, standing, or allowing the man to kneel, sit, lie on his side or stand. In order to be properly done a girl has to be on her back, ass rolled slightly forward by elevating the thighs, locking, if necessary, the ankles above the fuckee's back, and getting that clit in there.

Paul balked but was amenable. He was especially amenable when she compromised occasionally, gave head (Friday morning) sat on his crescent roll (Saturday night) let him do it standing while she kneeled on the water bed (Sunday morning).

Haven't you ever had a woman before, my God, you never stop.

I, *moi*, I never stop. *Et toi?*

Women are different, *cher*. They can come all day, they have need of no recuperative powers. They are sexually superior. They can reduce an *army* of men. Look at the Empress Catherine.

Bien, reduce me. I am getting too much fat here, and here.

Tu m'en merde.

Je t'aime, toi.

She imagined saving Mr. Lyons. Quick, this way, into the closet, that's right. There's a pair of falsies in there and an old dress of my mother's maid. There's a wig made by Mr. Ghedini (Macy's, $35.00) and a kwik kastration kit. Turn the scrotum sack inside out, drill a hole, tuck it in. Presto: Mrs. Lyons. You and wifey can practice analingus until it heals. But your life, Lyons, old man, old girl, your life has been saved, look out, here they come, the lady black shirts, the ladies from Hell, the dyke band is playing the *Marseillaise*. Better shave those legs. They'll take you for rough trade and conscript you for legionnaire duty in Texas.

Paul had done it again, turned her upside down and red (figuratively speaking) and she was coming again.

Francine, a kind of shudder goes through you when you come. Ahh, Francine love. How lucky we are to find each other.

Saturday afternoon, fresh from the water bed and soon to return her back to it, she went home, made a phone call, changed, found a cab outside her building, took it to the Upper West Side, not far, probably, from Morris', got out of the cab, paid, entered another building, took the elevator to the third floor, knocked on a door.

"Hey, hey, come on it, Fran."

"It's good to see you, Mel."

"Is it?"

"Sure."

"Out of the closet, Fran?"

"No, honey, still in the closet. I'm here to help, though."

"Help?"

"Help with the movement."

Needless to say, Mel was a lady, a very tough, five-feet four-inches, close-cropped blond hair, blue-eyed, flat-chested, flat-footed, dog-loving lady. Jaspers, her Pomeranian, sat, tongue out, panting, on a green Moroccan hassock near an air chair.

"Mel, it just seems to me I could be of help."

"If you're not out of the closet, Fran, why come to us? Why not the socialist women, or WITCH, or SCUM, or any of the Uncle Tom groups?"

"Easy, Mel. I'm here because I think you guys and only you guys have the balls to do some of the things I have in mind."

"We're trying to drop masculine metaphors like balls, Fran."

"Sure, O.K. Sorry."

Fran told her some of her ideas, especially the one which involved raffling off a male whore. If the trouble with women was they were treated like sex objects, let's let them know it graphically, let's expand those consciousnesses, guys —sorry—ladies, let's find a goddamn man and treat him like a sex object, have a raffle for his services, lots of publicity, you girls are always great at getting lots of publicity.

"Are you crazy, Fran?" Mel asked her. "You want us to do that?"

"It would be great for the movement."

Mel balked. She had been about to shout a flat no, but she balked. "The girls will never go for it," she said. "Maybe it is a good idea but together, look, together they'll never buy it. You'll have to find some other group. Honey, in case you don't know it, some of us have problems. We don't like men."

Francine laughed, reached over and touched Mel's arm. "Mel, if the Radical Lesbians did it can you just imagine the publicity they'd get? The *Voice* would be full of it, even the national weeklies might pick it up, handle it with euphemistic tongs of course, but they might just pick it up."

"Oh, I like the idea, Fran, you always were a brainy one, why I liked you, but not us."

"Let me put it to the group?"

"O.K. Sure. I'll arrange a meeting. But don't be disappointed. O.K.?"

"O.K."

The Pomeranian barked and came over, finally, to say hello. Evil-smelling little dog. In the days down in the Village when Mel had tried to make Francine every night for a month, coming into the Sink and talking to her softly of the advantages of lesbianism (imagine telling that to Fran, Fran who had told the boys in Paris about being sucked out by one) she had always brought that dog along. Evil-smelling creature.

No, Fran had never done it. Last reserve of a bourgeois consciousness.

Mel served tea and they talked. A few hours later Fran was back on the water bed.

Well, it *was* a good idea. *Whores.* It *meant* females. No one thought of men in connection with that word. But men weren't sexually exploited, overworked, kept down in business, forced into cubby holes of consciousness, Morris. Morris? Can you hear me, Morris?

Paul rubbed a brand of love oil (Whole Earth Catalogue number 8, page 76, $8.00 the bottle) on his crescent cock (maybe he was part Turk) in preparation for their initial bout. He was getting sore, poor dear.

Maybe it was a good thing Morris was not there to answer.

PART TWO

Chapter One

Winter turns my hands blue.

Karen stood at the window of the editorial office looking down on Madison Avenue and Thirty-fourth Street. A limousine pulled up in front of B. Altman's and the doorman opened the rear door. An elderly woman in a fur coat got out of the limousine, stepped up onto the sidewalk, crossed to the heavy doors of the department store, and waited for the doorman to catch up with her and open one of them.

It doesn't do my wind much good either.

It was possible to tell how cold it was out by watching the pedestrians hunched against the weather, swathed in scarves and gloves, in a greater hurry to get wherever they were going than usual, even for New York, New York, where the pedestrians were always in a great hurry.

My hands turn blue even when I wear gloves, and I lose my wind if I walk too fast.

The editorial office was hardly as posh as John's, next door. It was a large room broken down into three cubbyholes by board partitions screwed into the floor and against the three desks they were meant to hide from one another. It was of course possible to hear everything that anyone in the office said and blind conversations were the rule, like a three-way permanent open telephone hook-up. The desk immediately behind the partition to Karen's back was used by a shy, overweight young woman named Elaine. Elaine was a niece of the boss, Mr. Murray, on whom John thought he had so much. Elaine was recently married and as such was a specimen completely foreign to Karen's experience. Married women, young married women especially, abound in New York City but Karen had never befriended any, not been thrown into such constant and intimate contact with any, before Elaine.

The third desk belonged to Harvey Schapiro, who was often somewhere else, at lunch (between eleven and three), with writers or agents, in conference with John or Mr. Murray, or just plain gone. Harvey had been hired in October after it had become clear to John that Karen would never take over the educational department. She was given complete responsibility for the Bedroom Line instead (John made all the decisions; all she really had to do was get the manuscripts in one piece and collect statistics and pretend to be busy when Mr. Murray drifted in) and partial responsibility for the copyediting of the educational books which Harvey bought from hardback houses or semi-literate academicians and psychologists.

When Harvey wasn't in, Karen and Elaine would talk.

You would not believe how fat Elaine is.

"Elaine, does the cold do strange things to you?"

"Like what?"

"Like turn your hands blue?"

"You kidding?"

"No."

"'Course not."

Elaine had married a law student named Edward Schneider and they were already having their troubles. In bed. Elaine took these troubles to work with her and talked of them to Karen.

Talked around them is more like it.

One day Elaine had whispered through the partition, "Karen?"

"Uh huh."

"Do you . . . I mean you're a sex book editor and all . . . do you think oral sex is normal?"

Elaine had thought that Harvey was out of the room. He wasn't. He snorted. "Do you mean *natural,* Elaine, or do you want Karen to draw you a bell curve?"

"Huh?" Karen said.

Elaine did not answer. She said nothing more to anyone for the remainder of the day and half the next one. Karen did no work that entire time feeling, through the hardwood partition, Elaine's mortification.

Elaine discussed these things with Karen principally because Elaine knew about Karen and John (who didn't?) and as far as Elaine was concerned, that made Karen expert on anything that might occur between a man and a woman.

The afternoon after Harvey mortified Elaine, she came to see Karen in her cubicle. She lowered her bulk into the molded plastic chair that writers occupied when being lectured by Karen about the Bedroom Line.

"He's not here," Elaine said of Harvey.

"He's still at lunch," Karen confirmed.

"I don't know how he gets away with it. I sometimes think I'll say something to Uncle Lou but I never do."

Uncle Lou was Mr. Murray.

"Look, what I asked yesterday, you didn't think. . . ."

Karen shook her head to assure Elaine she hadn't thought anything of the kind.

"Good. You know sometimes I come out with things that sound . . . different from what I mean them to sound."

"My grandmother is like that," Karen said.

"I mean we had just been talking about Edward so it probably sounded as if I wanted to know what to tell him when he asked me to . . . you know. But I didn't."

Elaine shifted uncomfortably on the small (for her) plastic chair.

Karen had never met Edward and had no desire to. She wondered, since meeting Elaine, what it must be like to be married, never to sleep alone, for instance. Although that was probably the only good part. Take John. John wasn't *alive* when he was with his wife and family. He was just like a dead man when he was with them. It was all right, he

said, to be alone with one of the kids, but two of them together, or his wife at all, made him want to go to sleep.

It was because of John, of course, that Elaine wanted to
be so intimate with Karen. After talking about sex, or
men, or marriage for a minute she would always come
around to him. Of course he excited her. He excited everyone, not just women. But women really found him irresist-
ible. He was so vibrant. He was always into something new.

But as much as Karen wanted to please Elaine (they
spent more time together than Karen had ever spent alone
with anyone, eight hours a day, five days a week) she never
talked very much about John. Not to Elaine she didn't.
What if Elaine ever told Mr. Murray some of the things
John had told Karen? About the taxes, for instance. Or
how John was getting what he had been promised (and
what he deserved for doing a terrific job of building up the
Bedroom Line) one way and another, mostly behind Mr.
Murray's back.

"Edward had this real kookie roommate in college. You
know he went to school at Miami U.?"

"I know," Karen said.

"This roommate knew a man who liked to do it to chickens."

"What?"

"He liked to, you know, put his thing in chickens. Where
the eggs come out, Edward said."

"Jesus."

"I mean I thought of it because of that fact book Harvey
is doing about sodomy, the one that psychiatrist is writing.
You know I never knew sodomy was when men do it to an-
imals. I always thought it was charging too much interest
or something, because of Sodom and Gomorrah and the
Bible and the *Merchant of Venice*.

Karen sat up straighter. "I don't believe anyone *really*
does it to chickens. Not really."

"You haven't heard it all. He would put the head of the
chicken in a dresser drawer and then when he started to
come he would slam the drawer closed so the chicken
would have its death spasms right while he was . . . you
know."

"Did you tell that to Harvey? He ought to tell it to that psychologist."

"Are you *kidding?* I wouldn't tell him anything after what he said yesterday."

"What wouldn't you tell me?" Harvey asked.

Jesus, he was a creep. They hadn't even heard him coming down the hall. Why had John hired him anyway? John hated creeps.

Karen moved away from the window and sat down at her desk, still worrying about her hands, but thinking now about John. She seemed to live in a world occupied only by John lately; she breathed air that he exhaled; she saw things that he had created, or changed just by looking at; she heard voices and sounds aware of the way in which they would strike him and how he would make them exciting. She was as close to being happy as she had ever been in her life and part of that had something to do with the fact that he did not belong to her and never would, that their affair was illicit and temporary, and that everyone knew about it and seemed to approve. She did not entirely understand why that made it better, but it did. She had said as much to Jeanette. But like Elaine, Jeanette was far more interested in knowing what happened between Karen and John in bed than she was in knowing what peculiar aspects of their relationship were responsible for making Karen happy.

What happened in bed between Karen and John was, as far as Karen knew, what happened in bed between most men and women. Her recent readings in American hardcore pornography, both publishable and unpublishable (by Hilt standards) had not enlightened her otherwise. What happened between the covers of books like *The O Job* and *Back-Seat Bang* were filed in a part of Karen's mind reserved for the unreal; a part next door to the compartment in which she filed Jeanette's sex stories, especially the new ones she had since breaking off with Morris, and right below the compartment in which she fabricated her past life, her grandmother, the house in Connecticut, King Phillip's War, the Thompson dynasty.

What happened in bed between Karen and John was that John no longer went down on her (that had been a part of his general courting behavior, not meant as a sustained practice) and he rarely played with her with his fingers. As a result she came infrequently. But then, so did he. He rarely wanted to do it at all unless he was drunk or had had a particularly exciting day.

But I go with him everywhere.

When he did get drunk and make love to her (always at her place now, even with Jeanette in the back bedroom; Jeanette did not seem to mind anything) he would leave around midnight for his home in the Bronx. And his wife and children. Unless, of course, he was very drunk in which case he would sleep right where he was.

It is not like sleeping with someone to have a drunk in your bed.

The rules, of course, that she had so carefully formulated back in the summer when she and Jeanette had first moved into the railroad apartment on Seventy-third Street were shot to hell. But Jeanette didn't mind.

Jeanette is a gas, really.

And Karen was very nearly happy.

I wish my hands did not turn blue in the winter; it makes them look awful.

The telephone at the front of the editorial office rang and Karen pushed her chair back to get it. John was not in today, he was out with a photographer at a shooting for a cover they were doing and he had not made any plans with her about dinner. They usually had dinner with some of his friends somewhere in the city. So the phone call might be for her.

"Hello," Harvey said. He must have been right on top of it when it rang. Karen waited, standing again by the window overlooking the intersection below.

"Yeah, hold it. Karen?"

"Yes," Karen said.

"It's for you."

Harvey had disappeared inside his cubicle by the time Karen lifted the receiver from the small table at the front of the office and put it to her ear.

"Hello."

"Karen, this is Morris Levy."

"Oh, hi, Morris. How are you?"

"Just fine, Karen. Listen, you remember I told you I had a friend who might want to write some of those books of yours?"

"I remember," Karen said.

"Her name is Francine Nathan, no, Klein, she's married, divorced rather, but still has her married name."

"They're not easy to write, Morris," Karen said, mimicking what she had heard John say a hundred times. "Especially for women, but if she wants to get an idea of what has to be in them, and what can't be in them, like that, I'll see her."

"Great, Karen, thanks a million. I'll ask her to call you. Francine Klein."

"I'll remember," Karen said.

"Great."

"Morris. . . ."

"Yes."

"Listen, can I ask you a medical question?"

"Sure. Go ahead," Morris replied.

"Is it normal for your hands to get sort of blue in the winter, even with gloves on, even indoors sometimes."

"You have a circulatory history?"

"No," Karen said, just a little afraid to talk about this.

"Well, it's probably nothing more than low blood pressure."

"Oh."

"Look, if it would make you feel better why don't you make an appointment with me? I can switch you to my nurse."

"I don't know, Morris."

"Suit yourself. It's probably nothing."

Karen went back to her desk and started working on a manuscript John had handed her the day before. It was a straight sex book, no plot, not much characterization, and the sort of thing he had rejected a hundred times. This one was different in that it had been written by a friend. John bought the manuscripts of friends with almost no questions asked. He was generous to a fault.

"The body temperature of chickens is very high," Elaine had said that day when she was recovering from her mortification at the hands of Harvey Schapiro.

"So?"

"So this guy liked it all the more because it was hot in there."

"Up the chicken?" Karen asked.

"That's right. Do you know why women get hot when they let a man do it to them? I mean right in there."

Karen shrugged. "I'm not sure."

"We talk about these things all the time. Edward and me, I mean. You know, even though he went to Miami U. I don't think he had much experience. You went to the University of Connecticut, didn't you?"

"Uh huh."

"I went to Brooklyn College for three years. I mean I lived at home the whole time. Maybe it would have been better if I had gone away to school, like Edward, like you, and gotten some experience. It's too late now."

"It is?"

"Sure, being married and all."

"Up a what?" Harvey Schapiro said loudly. They had forgotten all about him again.

"Harvey, leave us be, would you?" Karen asked.

Harvey had been hanging around John a lot so of course he knew what was between John and Karen and he deferred to her. He was afraid of John, and admired him, of course, the way everyone did.

"I better get back to work," Elaine said and rose from the plastic chair to return to her desk.

That had been months before, what she had come to think of as the beginning of her new life. That was how much she felt different since meeting John and getting the job.

What I am really is a whole new person.

Joe, her Indian from Bengalore, had (and still had, for all she knew) an apartment on Christopher Street in Greenwich Village. It was there, fucking sideways, that Karen had last felt as different from her usual self as she felt now (fucking very little).

Joe was probably the softest man in the world, the gentlest man who had ever touched a woman. He was almost dainty about it. He never took an initiative without spending a lot of time making sure that Karen had no objection.

His whole manner was so unexpected that it had astounded Karen and confused her. In the end it had pleased her as much as his silent, smiling acceptance of every lie she told him.

So eventually, of course, I stopped lying to him.

He was the first man to ever touch her clitoris. He had put his finger on it deftly, knowingly, while they were fucking sideways the third or perhaps the fourth time and the places he had sent her, as the song goes, were places she had never been before.

But after months without a man, after she found out about his family, Karen forgot what it had been like. *Not enough attention is paid to the fact that people forget sensations; at least I do.* And Karen found that she could be satisfied by masturbating.

That was why finding John was like coming alive again. She had forgotten how good it could be to have someone do it for you, to be with someone when it happened.

Masturbation will never catch on.

The phone in the front of the office rang again and Karen got to it first.

"Hello."

"It's John, Karen. Go right home after work and make yourself pretty, O.K.?"

"Sure."

"A big appointment tonight, honey, with a big man. I want you to be as beautiful as you've ever been."

"All right."

"I can't tell you about it on the phone. I'll pick you up around seven."

"I'll be ready."

"Good girl."

John broke the connection and Karen went back to her desk excited, transported, feeling terribly important just to have talked to him.

When Joe had met Karen, in that department store where she had first worked when she came to New York, he had said, "You are a very pretty girl, Karen, a very pretty woman. Would you come please and have lunch with me today, if it isn't going to interfere with any plans you already have to do so?"

You could have knocked her over with a feather. His English was so elegant, so *flowing*. And when was the last time anyone had told her she was pretty? When had anyone *ever* told her she was pretty? Never, that was when.

Other good-looking women are told from birth that they are attractive by their grandparents certainly, and their aunts, uncles and cousins, not to mention their mothers and fathers. But Karen had missed out on that. She couldn't even remember her mother and in her memory her father was only a vague personality, a tall man with a long nose. She had been seven when he died, just a little too old to be *adoptable*.

Other good-looking women knew they were pretty because men chased them, whistled at them, rubbed up and down against them in subways (like they did to Jeanette). But men did not react that way to Karen. It was Joe who finally told her why.

"It is because you are not flashy, you do not make men do a double-take, as it is called, and whistle and wish they could bed you. What you do is stop them cold, don't you see, you make them *think*, not hunger. Don't you see?"

"No, I don't see," Karen had replied.

"You are not so much pretty, Karen, as you are beautiful. It takes a moment to register what a man sees when he sees you, because what he sees is nothing obvious, nothing superficial. Look, Karen, when Sophia Loren walks down the street men do not whistle, they open their mouths and stare. Well, it is not polite to do that so men do not do it when they see you, but they would, were it allowed."

"Oh, stop it, I am nowhere near as beautiful as any movie actress."

"Believe me, Karen, you are more beautiful than many. No, you are not as beautiful as Sophia Loren but you have the same effect on men, not the same kind of beauty. Yours is perhaps a little softer, less evident, and of course you do not project the sensuality that she projects. It is a good thing you do not."

"I don't have a good body."

"You have an *excellent* body. It is not an actress's, a sex symbol's body, but it is an *excellent* body."

After that, of course, there was no doubt that Karen would let him take her to bed. She did not believe what he said, but it made her feel so good to hear it she would have let him do anything he wanted to her, even some of the things Jeanette's men were always doing to Jeanette.

She ought to have believed Joe, however, because what he said was true, Karen did have a slow, warming, thought-provoking effect on the men who were perceptive enough to look carefully at her. And she did have an excellent body. She thought her breasts were too small but they were not, they were silky and milk-white and firm. She thought her skin was too freckled and too pale but it was extremely smooth, almost downy, cream-colored skin. She thought her behind was too large but it was not.

Joe pointed out all these things to her after they had been lovers for about a week. She did not believe him.

Another problem was that she was the kind of woman who appears self-contained and disinterested in men, and therefore does not attract them the way women like Jeanette or Veltraud or Francine attract them. But Karen's self-containment was really self-concern, and her disinterest was really fear. Only Joe had been perceptive enough to realize that in the entire time that she had been on her own since leaving Hartford and the home.

"Now look," he once said, "see your navel. It is the perfect navel. It is the navel of the kind a Rajah would embellish with a ruby in the last century. It is the loveliest navel I have ever seen."

"You're nuts," Karen had told him.

But his flattery worked.

I'm like Mary, at the home, rub her neck and she gave head. Flatter me and I'm yours.

Karen tried to pay Joe back for his flattery by exciting him. In the small apartment on Christopher Street she would let him fuck her sideways and slowly for hours on end. He was a model of patience and control. Not once did he come without asking her if she was ready. Sometimes, when he had played with her long enough, she said that she was, and they came together. Other times she would ask him to wait and to play with her until she felt an orgasm build inside her, and still other times she would tell him to come if he liked, that she felt fine and did not mind if she did not come, too.

Our conversations about it were fantastic.

"Are you ready, Karen?"

"No, Joe."

"Would you like me to wait?"

"I don't know, Joe."

"Would you like me to play with you?"

"Do you want to come right away, Joe?"

"I am in no hurry, Karen."

"Do you want to play with me?"

"If that is what you would like, my dear."

"Only if you want to."

"Shall I fondle your breasts first?"

"Only if you want to, Joe."

Etc. etc. Until Karen finally said that he should come or that she was ready. Just the opposite from John Morelli, was Joe from Bengalore. She never admitted to him that fondling her breasts did nothing for her. He seemed to love it so much when her nipples distended. She often wondered what it was about men that made them think breasts were sexy.

Breasts are for babies.

It would have taken an expert psychologist to tell her that it was precisely because breasts were for babies that she felt nothing in them because she was afraid of becoming pregnant again, and a step further, afraid of penises— unless they were inside her, where, strangely, she felt she could control them. She and The Pill. It was as if she believed that she were in danger of becoming pregnant now either by giving head or hand.

Karen never told Joe that her breasts were not erogenous zones because they became her principal weapon in exciting him during foreplay. (In that way he and Morelli were similarly inclined.)

She found, for instance, that Joe was extremely pleased if she went about the apartment naked from the waist up. That pleased him far more than if she went about totally naked.

Strangely enough, it made me self-conscious about my

*behind to have my breasts uncovered. It made me feel my
ass was too damn big.*

"Do you like me because I'm so white, Joe, and you're
so dark?" she asked him once.

"I am not so dark. I am soft brown. There are many
men who are jet black."

Joe was entirely innocent about American racial preju-
dice. Or at least he talked as if he were.

"But I'm so white, Joe."

"You are very white, but that has nothing to do with
the reason I am so very fond of you."

"Like what?"

I was a beggar for flattery.

"Like you are beautiful," Joe answered in his lilting
speech. "You would be as beautiful whatever your complexion, black or brown or yellow, Karen, my pretty."

He called her "my pretty," like a villain in an old-time
soap opera. At first it had made her laugh but after a while
she didn't even notice it.

He taught her to eat Indian style, with the fingers. She
would sit cross-legged on the floor with him, both of them
naked from the waist up and neither of them wearing anything on their feet. Joe would be wearing a pair of black
chino pants and Karen a pair of yellow bell-bottoms she
kept at his place. (She had been living in the hotel for
women in those days.)

"You see in India," he would explain. "Knives and forks
and spoons are very expensive, so we eat with our hand,
with the right hand, never with the left."

While he ate he watched her breasts. Sometimes he
would stare at them for minutes on end. It ought to have
been a clue that there was substance to his flattery, that
when he told her she had beautiful breasts he was not lying.

"Why don't you eat with your left hand?"

"Because, Karen, my pretty, the left hand is to wipe one-
self with."

Karen giggled.

"You must never, never," Joe told her, speaking like an
English nanny in a 1940's movie, "never, never give anyone your left. Not ever."

"O.K."

"It is a terrible insult to do so."

"Is toilet paper expensive in India, too?"

"There is no such thing in India, except in the homes and hotels of foreigners and the very rich. One wipes one's bottom with one's left hand and water."

Karen giggled again. She had been much younger then and still thought matters of hygiene funny.

Once, when they were both naked and under a single sheet (it was a sweltering summer's afternoon but Joe liked to keep her covered from the waist down unless they were actually fucking) Karen made him get out of bed to measure his height against hers. They stood back to back, naked buns to naked buns, and Karen tried to feel above her head to see which of them was taller. They were exactly the same height.

Karen thought that strange now because Joe's penis was so much smaller than John's penis, and John was only a few inches taller than Karen.

I guess it's true, height is no indication.

When she tried to excite Joe in order to reciprocate for his flattery (after all, that flattery was the nicest thing anyone had ever done for her, short of making her come) she would hold her breasts close together. She would squeeze them as hard as she could without hurting herself, trying to make the nipples touch. They wouldn't, of course, but they would come within three inches of each other and Joe would take them between his small brown fingers and twist them softly, as if he were gathering the nap from a woolen sweater.

"You really like them, don't you, Joe?"

"Ah yes, my pretty, I like them ever so much. You know in India we call them nellies, after, I think, an Irish usage. Karen, you have the prettiest nellies, Karen."

Often he would lower his head and taste the very end of the distended tips with the very end of his tongue. He would flick his tongue back and forth from one nipple to the other, finally he would settle on one of them, then he would lower his mouth and suck on it for all he was worth. If his penis had not been hard before he started to suck it would grow hard immediately and soon he would be touching her thighs, mutely asking her to open them so he could place two fingers of his right hand in her vagina to see if she was wet enough to enter. She very nearly always was.

The hand he ate with was the hand he touched me with.

When she was ready he would always remove his mouth from her nipple long enough to ask her what he already knew. (After all, how long can a girl stand to have a man's fingers up there without wanting the real thing?)

"Shall we, Karen?"

"Uh huh."

He would lift his body long enough for her to slide her right thigh under his left hip and then he would place his penis against her labia majora. It was always easiest if she put her hand there and fitted him in. It was different with John, John just banged his way on in, never needing help at all.

Joe must have preferred the sideways position because it enabled him to control himself. She had never thought of that while they had been going together but it must have been true. She had noticed with John that he could fuck her much longer if they did it sideways or if she came on top and that he came quickest of all if he assumed the top position and she raised her thighs and circled his back with her legs.

It was also better that way because Joe could reach down and touch her clitoris while he fucked her. He had a magic forefinger and the softest touch possible. He always made sure his finger was wet with his own lubrication.

Come to think of it I used to move against Joe. I almost never move against John. It's because Joe got me so hot playing with me.

She also found that it excited him to rub the very top of his penis with the palm of her hand. She wouldn't go down on him and he must have sensed how much she disliked the idea because he never asked her to, but she didn't mind taking his little penis in her hand and rubbing the top. (She didn't mind, that is, unless it was wet with the stuff she poured all over it when they fucked, or unless it was all wet from his own come.)

Karen did not think that a man's semen was the greatest thing in the world, or that a man coming in your hand was the greatest compliment a man could pay you. In that regard Karen thought that Jeanette was just a little nuts. Jeanette was still carrying around that damn test tube she got from Morris. It made Karen wince just to think about it.

It's full of come, of anonymous male come!

Morris had got it for her, when they were still seeing each other, from the hospital artificial insemination program. The doctor there had kept it too long for it to still be good because the woman who was supposed to receive it never showed up that day, so Morris took it for Jeanette.

Jesus!

Sometimes Karen missed Joe especially because he always knew what to say at times when Karen was lost for words. Joe would smile and somehow be both polite and incisive. To Jeanette, for instance, when learning what she carried in her purse, he might have said, "Well, my pretty, it is a very strange thing you keep there but if it gives you pleasure to have it close to you surely there can be nothing wrong with it."

Thus implying, of course, that there surely must be something wrong with it.

Joe's place in bed was on the outside and hers was on the inside, against the window wall. That was because Joe was always getting up to get them something, to bring her tea or Coke or a snack. It might also have been, now that it crossed her mind, so that he could play with her with his right hand.

Joe ate meat. She once thought that all Indians were vegetarians but Joe taught her that only Hindus were vegetarians and that he, like millions of other Indians, was not a Hindu. He was a Baptist. A Baptist named Joe from Bengalore.

"Oh, yes," he said once. "There are Baptists everywhere, you know. No matter where one goes in the world, my pretty, there are sure to be Baptists there."

Joe seemed to take it very seriously, so seriously, in fact, that he never asked her religion. But the Hartford home had been non-denominational and Karen had no religion. Somewhere, perhaps, there was a notation on some record they kept of what her father's religion had been but it didn't seem important to her to find out.

That was what made it all the more unbelievable when she found out about his wife and kids; the fact that he was a serious Baptist, that is.

"You're what!" she screamed one night and sat bolt upright in bed, baring her breasts for him for the last time. He had been holding her very sweetly, his languid erection resting against her buttocks, his arms wrapped around her, one small brown hand on each white breast.

"I am going to go back to India for a few weeks to see to my wife and children."

His lilting tone, his heavy Indian accent, almost like Peter Sellers doing a take-off, made her momentarily mute. Then she grabbed the pillow from under his head and held it to her chest.

"Oh, my pretty, oh, oh, do not cover please your nellies, not your nellies."

"You're going where to do what!?" she shouted.

"Oh, please, Karen, my pretty, be ever so quiet. The neighbors will not know what to think."

"Oh boy, oh boy, oh boy," Karen said. Then she shouted at him, her open mouth just three inches away from his open mouth—his open in surprise and mortification, however, not in screaming anger, "Turn your back!"

He did what he was asked while she got out of bed, dried her wet thighs on the first thing she could find, which was his dish towel (it was a very small apartment and the kitchen was only five steps from the bed) threw the towel into the air back toward the bed and got dressed and the hell out of there.

She received a very long letter from him at the hotel for women. He said he thought she had understood from the first about arranged marriages. He told her his wife meant nothing to him other than someone to whom he owed respect and obligations and that was why he never had all his pay check each Friday, he had to send most of it home. It was why, in fact, he was in America at all. He had been a student (which she knew) and by extending his student visa, was able to work here and thus to make many hundred times more money than he could have made in India. Thus everyone was happy with the arrangement, especially his wife and children.

Funny, Karen thought, how it didn't bother her that John was married but how it had upset her so much when she found Joe was. It was probably because she never knew about Joe but had known about John long before she went to bed with him.

I hate to be lied to, you see.

John picked her up at the apartment at seven o'clock, right on time. She wore her light blue crocheted pants suit (bell-bottoms) bought in a small store in the Village, silver slippers from Lord and Taylor under her second-hand (but lovely) seal skin (ankle length), all over tights and a no-bra. The pants suit was cut high in front and back but was sleeveless. It was just sexy enough to please John but not too sexy to turn on the important person they were to meet.

"You might as well take your coat off, we'll be a few minutes," John said as he came through the door and headed straight for the couch. Jeanette was in the back bedroom but emerged when she heard his voice.

"Why, John?" Karen asked.

"He's going to be a little late. I called his office before I left the studio. We're to meet him at the Plaza at eight instead of seven-thirty."

"Then you'll have time for a drink," Karen said.

John nodded and Jeanette came over and took the seat next to John on the couch. There was more furniture in the apartment these days, and better furniture than the old stuff. John had insisted Karen buy some things to fill in the holes and had given her several hundred dollars with which to do it, but the semen-stained couch was still the central piece in the living room.

"How are you?" John asked Jeanette.

"I'm fine, John."

"Who are you going out with tonight? Not that nut who gave you the test tube? You still have that test tube?"

"Still have it," Jan said softly.

"It's crazy," John said and laughed.

"I'm going out with Daniel," Jeanette said.

"She just met him," Karen added.

"He's a buyer for a department store in Phoenix who

needed root canal work in a hurry last week and came to Dr. Abernathy."

"Where Jan meets all her dates," Karen said.

"*Almost* all of them. I think he's a little nuts but I like him."

"Dr. Abernathy?" John asked, knitting his eyebrows and looking very serious, as if he had just asked her where she had been on the night of a murder, and as if what she was about to answer would prove her guilt or innocence. With John even the most innocuous question took on sudden depths of meaning and importance.

"No, no. Daniel. He's married to a fat old woman. He showed me her picture. It's why he likes me so much, because I'm thin. He likes to be burned with cigarettes on the inside of his thighs. He says his wife would never look there so he's safe when he gets home."

Jeanette sighed again and went back into her bedroom and Karen knelt on the couch next to John. She let him peck her on the lips (she didn't want her make-up or hair messed and then said, "Who is it, John? Who are we meeting tonight?"

"Just the guy who could make my whole future, that's all."

Karen returned the peck and stood up. The bell rang and Jeanette moved through the apartment smiling, waved to them and went out the door.

"I'm just as glad," John said, "that she's going down to meet him. After all, what would you say to someone who likes to be burned on the inside of his thighs?"

"Want a light?" Karen quipped.

Forty minutes later they emerged from a cab at the bottom of the park and started crossing Fifty-ninth Street, heading for the Plaza. John stopped her just as they were about to enter the hotel.

"Karen, I haven't told you how pretty you look. You look good, damn good. It's just that I'm distracted by all this."

"I understand."

John smiled at her warmly, took her by the arm, and led

her inside and through the lobby to the checkroom (they don't take women's furs) and then to the Persian room, where he told the maitre d' a name and was immediately entreated to follow him across the dance floor toward a table close to the small orchestra.

"Please wait here, Mr. Mandreaes will be along shortly," the maitre d' said.

John nodded, helped Karen seat herself, allowed the maitre d' to help him do likewise, and then stared impatiently after him as he walked off toward the door.

"I thought he'd be here by now," John said, evidencing a certain amount of discomfort and continuing to stare anxiously at the door.

A waiter came and took their drink orders and then Eartha Kitt appeared on the small stage and began to sing. Throughout her performance John continued to look toward the entrance. Even when Miss Kitt came over to their table and purred right at John, he managed several glances in the direction from which this Mr. Mandreaes would appear.

Eartha Kitt is so sexy! Wow!

Finally Karen saw a short, dark man talking to the maitre d'. She heard John sigh and say, "Finally. I was beginning to think he wasn't coming after all. If he hasn't made up his mind yet, I'll go nuts."

But even as he spoke Karen saw his face assume an aloof expression, saw his eyebrows come slightly closer together, making him appear intelligent, saw his lips form a wry half-smile as if he were the man who had everything, needed nothing, and was perfectly willing to pass up whatever it was Mr. Mandreaes had or had not made up his mind about.

Eartha Kitt finished her act and the maitre d' led the short, dark man toward them, ahead of the numerous couples who had risen to dance as the orchestra struck up an old-fashioned fox trot. Then Karen noticed how beautiful the woman with Mr. Mandreaes was.

She was a tall platinum blonde with a terrific figure and small, pointed breasts and long legs. From twenty yards away she seemed cocky and rich. From ten she seemed even cockier and richer. When she arrived at the table with her short escort and the maitre d', Karen felt a pang of jealousy and fear.

"I'm sorry I'm late, Morelli. V here insisted that we go all the way back to her place so she could change. Suddenly, she did not like the dress she had on."

"Mr. Mandreaes, V, this is Karen Thompson. She works for me at Hilt."

"Good evening, Miss Thompson. V's last name is Schimmel, Morelli."

Karen managed a smile. Both these people frightened her. Mandreaes looked a little like a Cro-Magnon man who had been dressed in fancy clothes and expensive jewelery as a joke. His knuckles were hairy, his beard already dark even though it was still early in the evening, his shoulders were almost as broad as he was tall. And the woman he had introduced as V Schimmel was the coldest statuesque bitch Karen had ever seen.

Mandreaes was wearing a white dinner jacket, black pants and tie. Miss Schimmel wore a full length crushed velvet blue gown cut to the navel and up one side of the skirt to a point a few inches below the waist. She was wearing a matching crushed velvet coat with a white fox collar and white fox lining. Karen knew that outfit, she had eyed it at Lord and Taylor and remembered the price, $659.98. It was worn without either bra or underpants.

Mandreaes had a ruby ring on the pinky of his left hand that would have paid for lunches at the Hartford Home for Orphaned Children for eight years and left something over for dinners. Miss Schimmel had on long hand-wrought silver earrings that made Karen want to gulp.

You're out-classed, Karen, honey. So stay cool and keep your mouth shut.

Miss Schimmel made herself comfortable in the chair opposite Karen while the maitre d' pushed it in for her. She wore her hair up in a tight bun from which several loose curly wisps of hair descended over her forehead for contrast. If she was trying to look like an extremely prim young woman who was about to unleash a sensuality that would ignite an army of followers, she was succeeding.

I hate her.

Karen smiled across the table and Miss Schimmel smiled

back. Mr. Mandreaes waved away the maitre d' and glowered at John.

"Let's get business out of the way, Morelli, then enjoy ourselves."

John nodded and smiled his half-smile.

"Miss Schimmel doesn't like to talk about money and business," Mr. Mandreaes said.

John nodded again, with understanding this time.

"I've decided against you. You're not the man to run that company."

Karen bit her tongue to keep from saying something that would get her in trouble with John. John cocked his head, took in what Mr. Mandreaes had said, thought it over, looked sad for a moment, then shrugged.

"That doesn't mean we can't have a good time tonight, on me, Morelli."

"All right," John said and smiled broadly.

"You son of a bitch," Mandreaes said.

"Mr. Mandreaes?" John said.

Mr. Mandreaes laughed and turned to Miss Schimmel just as the orchestra began to play again. People around them got up and started to do the boogaloo.

"V, get a load of this guy. I just told him he didn't get a job that would have put him into the sixty G's a year bracket and he takes it cool. What do you make now, Morelli? Thirty? Twenty-five?"

"You know what I make, Mr. Mandreaes."

Mandreaes laughed again and hit the small table between them with his palm.

"I know what you get up front, Morelli. I can only guess by how much you supplement it."

"Well, that's what I mean. To take your job would be to cut my income back a little. Don't misunderstand, I would have taken it because I like you, but sixty grand, well, it would have been tight."

Mandreaes smacked the table even louder. He had to raise his voice to be heard over the sound of the orchestra. "O.K., Morelli, you're too cool. He's too cool, isn't he, honey?" he asked Miss Schimmel. "You've got the job, Morelli. Don't ever do anything to hurt me. Understand?"

"Done," John said, smiling his half-smile again, keeping

just as cool now that he had it as he had a moment before
when he thought he had lost it.

Or did he know all the time?

"O.K." Mandreaes said and laughed. "Come on V, let's
you and me dance."

"All right, Oscar."

Oscar. Jesus.

Miss Schimmel rose and followed Oscar Mandreaes a
few yards into the dance floor. Until the odd-looking couple began to dance Karen had been ready to congratulate
John, but as soon as Oscar Mandreaes began to move to
the music and his tall date began to do likewise, Karen was
rendered speechless. Miss Schimmel was great. She was
like sex on wheels.

I hate her!

The orchestra ended the boogaloo and started to play the
funky chicken. V Schimmel swung it to one side and then
to the other. Her breasts threatened to leave the crushed
velvet of her gown. Karen could see everything but her nipples. Her hips shook, breaking the slit of the long gown all
the way up to the point a few inches below the waist where
it ended and Karen could see more of Miss Schimmel's pelvis than would have been daring at a burlesque show. The
light wisps of blond hair hanging down on her forehead
were shaking back and forth, her mouth opened so she
could breathe more easily and her earrings, swinging in
time to the music, glistened when they caught the bright
light of the room. People gathered around her and Mandreaes and began to applaud, but the crowd broke up
quickly. After all, this was the Persian Room.

Karen looked at John. He was watching Miss Schimmel
with undisguised lust.

I hate her!!!

No one seemed to notice how bizarre Mandreaes looked
as V's partner. No one gave a damn about her partner.

There was considerable applause when the dance ended
and Mandreaes was in excellent spirits and continued to
talk to and about his date, all but disregarding Karen.

Which is all right with me.

John continued to ask polite questions whenever the
conversation lagged. He continued to be charming and un-

concerned in Mandreaes' presence. Several rounds of drinks were ordered and Miss Schimmel had a small steak very well done. They must have sat together and danced (once Karen danced with Mandreaes and V with John) for two hours and in that whole time Miss Schimmel didn't address five words to Karen. She did speak to John, however, in a way that made Karen burn. She had some sort of accent. Not only was she rich, she was a foreigner. How goddamn much can one woman have going for her, Karen wondered.

John didn't eat, so neither did Karen. Mandreaes paid the check finally and left holding on to Miss Schimmel's elbow with his hairy hand.

John leaned over to her. "He's going to take that bitch home and fuck the daylights out of her. He's a real stud, that mother. I'll tell you about him later."

They waited a few minutes and left just before Miss Kitt was due to come back for the second show.

When they were out on the street John said, "Let's walk a while. God, Karen, I got it. *I got it!*"

"When will you leave Hilt?"

"Monday morning. *Monday morning!*" he sang.

"You're just going to walk out on Murray?"

"That's right, hon."

"And us, John?"

They had crossed Fifty-ninth Street and were standing near the corner entrance to Central Park. John, smiling whole-heartedly now, said, "Us goes on as ever, Karen. As ever."

"I won't see you at work any more."

"As soon as I can swing it you'll be working for me again, at the new place."

"You haven't even told me what it is. Who is Mandreaes?"

"Mandreaes is National Publishers Distributers, Karen, he's the biggest distributer in the business, he owns from twenty to fifty percent of every paperback publisher and magazine publisher he handles, he owns half a dozen trade book houses. He makes and breaks publishers, honey—not editors, publishers."

"Publishers?" Karen asked.

"That's right. I'm moving into Central Magazines as the

new publisher with a flat salary of forty thou and a heavy percentage of all increased sales activity."

"John!"

"I've been pulling for something like this for five years, Karen, and I've got it. I always knew I'd get it. Karen, you ought to see Mandreaes' office, it's like something out of a James Bond movie. It's on the top floor of the Crowell Building. He's got a thousand push buttons on his desk and I think each one of them is for another broad. You know what he told me, he told me he had to have four orgasms a day or he was no good. Did you ever hear anything like that? Four orgasms a day!"

"Is he married?"

"Sure. Sure, he's married. At least I guess he's married. Everybody's married. Come on, let's find a cab before we get mugged."

John was too excited to stop partying. He told the driver of the cab they found to take them further uptown, to an East Side bar Karen had been in with him before, and from the bar he made several phone calls to friends and business acquaintances to meet him. The people came almost as fast as he could call them: agents, writers, editors, photographers, and models. They all wanted to ride on John's gravy train. They had smelled a winner in him long ago and now they wanted their payoff for being faithful. Karen wondered how many of them were going to get it.

"And you should have seen the broad he was with!" John was telling several of his cronies in a loud voice at about one-thirty in the morning. They were still in the same bar, and as drunk as they had ever been, John vivacious and charismatic, Karen buzzing pleasantly and smiling whenever anyone looked at her. "What a piece of ass she was, a platinum blonde with a body that wouldn't quit. She got up and did this goddamn dance and I thought every male in the place was going to come in his pants."

"He looks like a monkey." Karen's soft voice was counterpoint to John's drunken raspy tone.

A silence fell. "Oh, yeah," John said after a minute. "He does. He looks like a monkey. He's got long arms, broad across the beam, you know, hairy son-of-a-bitch."

"And short," Karen added.

Another silence fell. "And short," John finally added.

"Well, how many magazines will you be in control of?" a natty East Side photographer named Belmarri asked John anxiously, smelling fat assignments and trips abroad and a higher class of model than the ones he'd been doing for the covers of the Bedroom Line (thirty percent kickback to John).

"Twelve, mother-fucker, twelve," John shouted at him.

"You guys cool it, huh," the bartender said.

John nodded, looked at Karen, smiled (which meant sex was on his mind because it was neither his half-smile nor his whole-hearted smile, it was his leer).

John paid and left. Luckily they were only a few blocks from the apartment because there were no cabs in sight and they were both a little too drunk to negotiate the intervening terrain without help. So they helped each other.

When they were finally home John began immediately to undress. He left his overcoat in a heap by the door, his jacket a few feet further into the room, his shoes, socks (even his socks), pants and shirt by the couch and his underwear by the bar (the bar he had bought her), where he finally stood, naked as a farm animal, pouring a drink for himself and one for Karen.

"I don't want another," she said, but she didn't mean it. She was giggling and half undressed by the time he got over to her with it. It looked like a triple.

"Oh, John, it's such good news."

"Whoopee," John said, downed half his drink and fell on the couch on his back.

"Come mount up," he suggested.

Karen's head was swimming. She had felt a little more sober out in the street than she had in the bar but the sobriety was evidently illusionary because the full force of the alcohol came swimming back with the first sniff of the drink John had made her. She had never been that drunk, or that happy.

"Mount up on what?" Karen said and laughed.

But he wasn't kidding. His penis was already beginning to stir. Slowly, as Karen came closer to it in order to watch it better, it lifted off his thigh, stiffened slightly in the air, took two further short motions upward, stiffened still more, swelled slightly *(I think)*, waved its blue and crooked vein at her, rose even higher, and was finally fully prepared to do battle in the position they only used when he was very drunk.

"Let's go to the bedroom," Karen suggested as she tried to right herself. She had been in a half-kneeling position watching with great interest as John's penis grew and rose up and as she stood straight she felt faint and went reeling forward.

Someday I'll stop fainting all the time.

John grabbed her. She had so far been able to disentangle herself of her shoes and pants only. She still wore tights. underpants and the top of her crocheted pants suit.

"Just the wrong way to turn on. . . ." she said.

"What?"

She had been going to say that she was dressed just the wrong way to turn on Joe but she didn't want to mention Joe's name to John, for some reason which she did not really understand in her present condition.

"Ooo," she said.

John yanked at her tights, fought them until they came off with her underpants and hefted her over him onto the semen stained couch. She just managed to get one leg between him and the back of the couch and to fit his penis into the opening of her vagina when she swooned and fell forward.

"Hey, come on, come on," she heard someone say as if from a long way off.

She tried to answer. She tried to move the way she knew John wanted her to move but although her vagina was oozing her own special brand of lubricant and although her clitoris was fairly screaming to make contact with something *(anything!)* she could neither move nor speak.

It was some time later that she thought she heard another voice in the room. She must have passed out while fucking him, right with his penis in her, and he must have just lain there drunk and stiff, too drunk to move or to come, too stiff to slip out. She had no idea how long they had been like that.

"Well, excuse us," she thought she heard Jeanette say.

"Hey, hey, join us," John yelled.

Karen still had her eyes closed. She opened them to find the room bright (which hurt) and a strange man standing in front of her hurriedly removing his pants.

"Hey," she said. "Who are you?"

"Shhh," John said, "or he'll burn you with a cigarette."

"Do you mind if I suck your toes?" the strange man asked Karen.

"Help yourself," John answered for her. "Hey, Jan, get undressed and grab a little of the action. Excuse me but I can't move at the minute, but I'm *rich!* Think of sixty grand a year—that'll make you come if anything will."

"Sixty grand," Jeanette's voice said in a tone which indicated, if it indicated anything, that the situation in which its owner found herself was in no way unusual or unexpected. "How come?"

"Whooeee," John said, "say, before you start that, funny-looking, would you get me another drink?"

"Hey," Karen shouted. She tried to get off John but he held her fast and his penis, which must have been soft after all, suddenly felt twice as big as it had before.

"How come?" Karen heard him say as he tightened his grip on her ass. "Because I got the job!" he shouted.

God, he was drunk.

Then Karen felt someone yank her foot off the couch and felt lips close on her big toe. Whoever was doing it to her (*if* someone was doing it to her, she wasn't really sure of what was happening except that her head was killing her and John was fucking her and there were other voices around) must have been lying on his back at the foot of the couch.

Karen tried to straighten up but she moved too fast. She'd been lying with the upper half of her body on the upper half of John's body and during the last several minutes she had only raised off him a few inches. Now she tried to sit up straight so that she would have been kneeling on his midsection, attached to the man she loved by his unique (*that blue vein, I'll never forget that blue vein*) penis when she fainted for the second time.

This time when she woke up they were in her bedroom and there were just the two of them, John and Karen. The rest of it must have been a drunken dream. (*Which shows you about wish fulfillment. The last thing I want is for some pervert to suck my big toe.)* John was flat out, snoring louder than she had ever heard him snore and smiling up at the dark ceiling. A light through the window illuminated enough of the room to see him clearly.

Karen got *slowly* out of bed (so as not to faint again) and walked through the house. She was completely naked now although she could not remember taking off either her pants suit top or her no-bra. She peeked into Jeanette's room. The bed was still made and no one was there. She felt tremendously relieved and went back to John.

God, am I hot, and with this headache.

He was still sound asleep and snoring. She yanked down the sheet with which he had covered himself but it brought no response. She got up onto the bed and began to finger his penis, picking it up with her thumb and forefinger and stroking it.

"Hey, big man."

The only response she got was a new note in his snoring.

"Hey, big man. Mr. Monkey has to have four orgasms a day. Hey! Big man!"

John moaned and stopped snoring but he was still asleep.

"Sixty thousand dollars a year," she whispered in his ear while she worked her fingers back and forth on his penis, pushing up the skin casing, rubbing it over the head, pulling it back, trying to get him excited.

I wouldn't have done it if I hadn't been drunk.

Something came off on her fingers. She smelled it and then lowered her hand to him again. It was her lubrication and his come from the last time they had done it. So some of what she had imagined had happened must have happened. But then why were his clothes in a neat pile on the chair and hers right on top of them? She didn't care. All she cared about was waking him up.

"Hmm?"

He stirred and she rubbed her free hand between his thighs until he opened them a little and she grabbed his testicles gently and yanked them down.

"Hey!"

He came awake suddenly, looked around, looked

strangely at her, saw what she was doing to him and smiled.

There was something strange about that smile.

"Hey, Karen baby, what's up?"

"Do me, John, please. I'm so drunk. I need you inside me."

"And to play with you?"

"Oh, please, John."

He laughed and rolled over on his side, reached up and yanked her head down.

If I hadn't been drunk. . . .

She did it. She gave head. She took his penis in her mouth (feeling with her tongue the bulge of his blue vein) and started to suck on it. He came erect then and she didn't have to wait very long. He turned her around (somehow) and opened her vagina with his fingers.

She had heard all about sixty-nine, of course, who hadn't, but she had never in her life done it or contemplated doing it. Never!

But it wasn't bad. He ate her. The more he ate her the more she wanted to eat him. The more frequently he ran his tongue over her clit the more frequently she took his penis out, grabbed it firmly, and ran her tongue over the head. When she couldn't stand it any more because the pleasure was so great she would stop sucking him and then he would stop. She would recover and start sucking him again and then he would stop and they went on like that for ages.

Finally, *(praise the lord, praise, praise the lord)* she came. He wouldn't stop licking her clitoris. She bucked but he held on to her buttocks firmly and kept running his tongue over her clitoris and over it and over it. She didn't want him to. *(It adds nothing once you start to come, you know, it just kind of gets in the way)* but he kept it up anyway until she was spent and whimpering and finally fought him away from the thing. But once was fine with her, just fine. Because it was no good to keep the pressure up on the clitoris after it had started.

She groaned and rolled over on her back.

"Hey!"

"Huh?"

"You started this, Karen. Come on, finish it."

"O.K."

She struggled to get to her hands and knees. She didn't want to eat him any more. For the first time she had done plenty of that. *(Enough was enough.)* She knew *(sensed in my drunkenness you mean)* that if she knelt like that he would mount her from behind.

He got out of bed to do it, staggered a little while making his way to the head of the bed where he took up a position, inserted *(he always got it in so fast)* in her vagina and went to work.

"Sixty thousand dollars per annum," she heard him say.

"Hey!"

He had rammed his thumb into her anus.

"Hey! One place at a time, John."

"It tightens the pressure on my cock," John explained as he began slowly to withdraw his penis, then insert it quickly, withdraw it slowly, time and again.

"It hurts."

"Relax and it won't hurt."

She lowered her head to the crumpled sheets at the end of the bed and that motion somehow did the trick, loosening up the pressure on his thumb. To please him she contracted her vaginal muscles and heard him sigh.

"Sixty thousand per," he said.

When he came he screamed loudly and almost knocked her over. When he had finally finished she fell forward and lay still, both arms in front of her and hanging off the end of the bed.

She fell asleep that way thinking of the platinum blonde doing the funky chicken and the boogaloo. She was willing to bet all she had that John had been thinking of her the whole time.

I didn't care. What bothered me was all that talk about money.

"You must have heard voices in the hall," Jeanette told Karen the next morning.

"Must have. They must have got mixed up with my dreams."

"You think I'd bring Daniel back here knowing you would be here?"

"Well, maybe you thought we'd be in the bedroom. We should have been in the bedroom. Ooo, do I feel awful."

"Well, I didn't. We spent the night at his hotel."

"Well, it would have been all right, bringing him here I mean. Breaking one of the rules is all right once in a while. Frankly, John and I were so drunk we couldn't see straight."

"I believe it," Jeanette told her.

"I thought I saw this guy stripping in front of me, then he wanted to suck my toe. Yech."

Jeanette smiled wanly.

"Stupid dream . . . I wonder why John hasn't called."

"You better get to work," Jeanette said.

"There's no hurry. I'm going to get a new job as soon as John gets resettled. He's going to be making a fortune. God, what are you supposed to do about a hangover?"

"You're supposed to go to work," Jeanette said. "It's eleven o'clock and you haven't even called in sick."

Karen nodded. "You're right, I guess. I'll get going."

She splurged on a cab. Harvey Schapiro was out to lunch but Elaine was there. It was almost impossible for Karen not to tell her about John but she knew Mr. Murray must not find out until John was ready for him to know about the new job. Which would be Monday. "Monday morning," she sang to herself.

John was in his office, but didn't have time to see her and didn't ask her to lunch. She nursed her headache until the phone rang and Elaine, who had been standing near it looking up the correct spelling for "analingus," said it was for her. John was such an early riser. He must have left Karen about six a.m. in order to get up to the Bronx and change in time to get to the office before her.

"Hello," Karen said when she had lifted the receiver.

"Miss Thompson, this is Francine Klein. I've been trying to get you all morning. Morris Levy called to say I would be in touch."

"Oh, yes," Karen said. "You want to try to write for us."

"Yes. Do you think we could have lunch together today?

I know it's short notice but I have a schedule of my own and today is the one afternoon this week I have free."

"I didn't know you were in advertising," Karen said.

"I am for the time being. What about lunch?"

"Well, I had planned to spend the afternoon in the office catching up on a few things . . . but all right, Miss Klein, or can I call you Francine?"

"Please do and I'll call you Karen. What about Mario's, it's about halfway between us?"

"Fine. In about an hour and a half."

"All right. I'll be at the bar . . . alone. I'm wearing a brown suit."

"Fine."

Karen hung up and walked slowly back to her desk. She had handled that just as John might have. Very professional. It left her feeling proud and important.

Posturing works, but I didn't know that then.

At a quarter to one she walked through the glass door of Mario's and up to the bar. She had tried once more to see John and had failed. He usually saw her at some point in the morning. She only hoped that nothing had gone wrong, that the whole thing wasn't Mr. Mandreaes' peculiar idea of a joke.

Francine Klein was seated about halfway down nursing a Bloody Mary. She was alone, and wearing brown, and the only woman at the bar.

She radiated a wavelength that said, "men, keep away." I liked her at once.

"Francine?"

"Hi. Let's get a table."

The place was crowded but they found a round table in a corner under one of the beams that lent the bar its ersatz antique atmosphere and sat down facing each other.

"The thing is," Francine told her after they had ordered drinks and warmed to each other, "that I'm thinking of leaving the agency. If I do I don't know how the hell I'll live. I'll have to do some free-lance work and, according to Morris, Hilt is where the money is."

"Why would you leave?" Karen asked politely.

"To devote more of my time to the movement. You can't

really get much done if nine and a half hours of your day
are devoted to turning out insipid copy."

"The movement?" Karen asked.

"Didn't Morris tell you that I was very active? I'm trying
to be an effective force in the consciousness fight. I'm trying to come up with ideas that will change the way people
think about women by *making* them think, by *making* them
react. I don't believe in polemic. I believe in *action*."

Karen looked at Francine blankly but Francine misun-
derstood Karen's meaning because she went on to say, "Oh,
I know, you're probably one of the few women who has
freed herself completely, or damn near completely, very
much like myself. You're a career woman, working in pornography yet, and that's great. Believe me, I understand the
intellectual justification for that kind of work."

She laughed, sipped at her new Bloody Mary and continued, "I mean, once I thought that the way to do it, to
change people's heads about women, was to write dirty,
talk dirty and live dirty. Believe, me Karen, I understand
completely where you're at. And I sympathize."

Karen managed a smile. She was bewildered.

But I liked her. And I liked the way she had me wrong.

"But listen to this now," Francine went on, assuming a
deeper, more serious tone. "I've organized a raffle that's
going to blow people's minds. Look, the big thing these
days in the movement is not being treated like a sex object.
Right?"

"Right," Karen said.

"And most of the girls pussyfoot around saying it's all in
our heads, not in men's heads, or if it's in men's heads, too,
that's not where it's a problem. And that's right, as far as it
goes. But it doesn't go far enough. Just knowing your head
is in the wrong place isn't going to change it. We have to
convince women they are human, they are just as good as
men, they have as much initiative and as much freedom in
developing their sexual roles as men have, to the point,
damn it, of being lesbians, though I don't push that. I don't
swing that way and never have."

Karen gulped, and smiled.

"The thing is, I mean all this is certainly obvious to you,

but I'm so full of it that I like to talk it out, know what I mean?"

Karen nodded.

"The thing is, action has to be taken. Take this raffle I'm organizing. Ten bucks and you take a chance on winning a male whore for a night. A stud of studs. Greased body . . . longest schlong a girl could ask for . . . guaranteed to be hard and to stay hard, guaranteed to give head. You wouldn't believe what a pretty man he is."

"Where did you *find* him?" Karen asked. It was the only question of the several dozen in her mind that she could immediately articulate.

"You wouldn't believe it. But listen, come to the little get-together we're calling the pre-sale. We've invited the underground press. And the *Voice*, even though they're cop-outs. Even Paul Krassner from *The Realist* will try to make it. No publicity until the pre-sale, we're afraid of a bust, but after the pre-sale plenty of publicity. There will be no way for the male establishment to stop us then. All you need to get in is a raffle ticket and you can bring friends. Two. One raffle ticket will let in three women. How about it?"

Karen stared goggled-eyed at the woman across the table.

Francine laughed. "Oh, look, I'm sorry. I know, this is supposed to be a business lunch, and you're supposed to tell me how to write these books. Look, Karen, believe me, I can write them and I will write them and I'll do it well. I have, uh, sort of a feel for pornography. It's just that I get so wrapped up in the movement; it gets me so damn angry when I think of the place women have to wear their minds. . . ."

Karen nodded sympathetically. Frankly although she had never thought of it before she believed that Francine Klein was right, that she was absolutely right.

I was ready to sign on the dotted line. No one had ever . . . told me those things before.

Karen bought a raffle ticket, their lunch was ordered and eaten and the whole while she decided that she had never liked a woman as much as she liked Francine Klein. She felt stronger just being close to her. She told her the taboos

of Hilt Publications, a long list of things not to put in the
books intended for the Bedroom line, she told her what
kinds of plots were acceptable and what kinds were not,
she told her how much sex and how to write it so that it
was solid and unromantic, just as she had heard John lecture writers dozens of times. She knew the speech by heart
and was sure that as she gave it Francine was taking in
every word.

After Karen had finished Francine looked thoughtful for
a few minutes and then said, "All right, I'll let you have
something in a few weeks. Meanwhile I'll mail up something you might want to publish even though it's not the
standard product. Who knows?"

"All right, I'll be happy to see it," Karen said.

*When I left Mario's I was clinging to that goddamn raf-
fle ticket.*

Chapter Two

In the fall, months before V danced in her crushed velvet gown in the Persian Room of the Hotel Plaza with Oscar "Chick" Mandreaes, she found herself in—of all the places in the world least likely to lie on anyone's itinerary between Hong Kong and San Francisco—Tangier, Morocco.

It had not been easy to arrange. First there was George. George was the Chinese gentleman to whom she was married. Second there was George's Uncle Ho. (Ho, Ho, Uncle Ho.) George's uncle Ho was no relation to Ho Bin the lawyer who had arranged everything, still, they had a lot in common. They were, for instance, both against fraternizing with one's Chinese husband.

Getting around George had been easy. All she did was stare at him until he managed to get alone with her. Then she let him understand that she would be disappointed not to enjoy the traditional marital honeymoon and bed, even if it was to lead nowhere, even if their divorce had already been arranged. Then she stared at him some more.

Uncle Ho was more difficult to handle. She had to convince him of the innocence of her intentions. This was especially hard to do because Uncle Ho, unlike nephew

George, spoke no English at all, and no French, and no German, and, of course, no Dutch. Communication between them was all but impossible. V was reduced to sitting around the hotel room with him staring off into the distance thinking as hard as she could: *I am only after the money Ho Bin is paying. There is nothing else here that I want.*

That hotel room was in a suite of rooms overlooking the ocean in Hong Kong. This one, in which she lay naked with nephew George, was a single room overlooking the Zoco Chico in Tangier. It was a lousy little room but it would do. She had to do nothing that might indicate to Uncle Ho, when he caught up with them, that she was after money. She had to be able to turn down his first, his second, and perhaps his third offer. And she had to do nothing which, in retrospect, would convince Nephew George that perhaps she was, after all, something less than in love with him, and, after all, desired something more than just to be with him no matter how rotten the accommodations.

Nephew George was about thirty years old and he looked and acted about seventeen. He had a very fine body and an attractive, babyish face. V loved his penis because of its yellow tinge. She thought of it as pagan. He was not, however, quite pagan enough. He had been circumcised. But one could not have everything. He was as avid a lover as she had had since Ivan, and being away from New York and in a semi-tropical climate helped her sensuality to find expression and improved sex for her. The way she figured it they had about two weeks before one of the Ho's caught up with them.

The noise from the square below (*Zoco Chico* means little square) was constant and bothersome. There were seven cafes on the small square and each of them had a television set blasting in its interior. Electronics had come to the Middle East, bridging the knowledge gap that illiteracy had caused by filling it with government news reports. Even the blind muezzin's calls to prayer, traditionally shouted from the minaret of each mosque, were now broadcast over loudspeakers. And besides the muezzins and the television commentators (none of whom seemed to like Zionism much), there were the wooden wheels of the donkey carts and the donkey hooves themselves on the cobblestone pavement, there were the goats clattering through the streets, the bell on the bellwether clanging, people shouting to keep them out of stores, the goatherd shouting to keep them headed for the next customer. (Goatherds were the Tangier milkmen.) There were the cries of the water sellers and the clanging of their copper vessels as they walked through the tourist-infested streets. There were the shouts of the street urchins and beggars and the constant hawking of the tradespeople and hustlers.

Hey man, you want a boy? A girl? Hasheesh? Hey man, anything you want?

She had never seen so many pretty boys (there were no girl children in the streets). She would like to have taught each of them about sex. Face it, she would like to have fucked each of them. But, of course, this being Morocco, they were all of them already busy fucking each other.

Lying over George's yellow body she wondered what it was about Moroccan society that made the men like to bugger each other so much. She knew quite a lot about it already. She had visited Tangier several times while working for KLM and she had had, in those distant days, a Dutch boy friend who had turned queer (*hij was een beetje van de verkeerde kant:* he was a little on the wrong side). This friend had explained most of it to her. He had explained how Moroccans have a pecking order, like chickens, but that instead of pecking the man below you, you bugger him.

The first night she and George Toy Hong (why, why was a Chinese gentleman named George?) spent in Tangier they went to the dancing boy cafe. The boy was about fifteen and looked like the Apollo in the National Museum in Rome. He was darker, of course, and younger. (V had once fallen in love with the naked Apollo in the National Museum in Rome; she had even spent nights dreaming of him.) There, in the dancing boy cafe, they drank sweet mint tea, and smelled the heavy odor of kif (three-quarters marijuana, one-quarter tobacco) the Moroccan men smoked in long pipes with small terra cotta boles. There V had fallen back in love with the Apollo, in the visage, this

time, of the dancing boy. So while she hung over George's
yellow body, waiting for Uncle Ho to hurry and catch up
with them (when she would pull her trump card in order to
stay alive), she thought of the dancing boy.

The Apollo in the National Museum in Rome was not
circumcised.

After that first night, however, they kept pretty much to
their room. Eventually, George said, they would leave. The
constant attention of the Moroccan men to V was too
much for poor George. And, to tell the truth, they frightened V, too. Perhaps they ought to have taken a room in
the European section of the city instead of within the
Medina (no cars allowed, no Europeans in residence)
within a ten-minute walk of the inner citadel, the Casbah itself.

It was too late to move now. All George wanted to do
was lie in bed and hold her and tremble. God, he did a lot
of trembling. He was probably thinking about Ho and
Uncle Ho and how they would kill V if they thought she
had been responsible for his running away with her. But
she hadn't been, had she? She had only looked at Nephew
George; and there was nothing she would rather do less
than renege on her deal. Whenever George wanted the divorce it would be fine with her. She couldn't help it if she
wanted to be near him; if he wanted to be near her; if *he*
happened to have fallen in love with *her*.

Orientals really made her laugh. They thought white
people were inferior. It was really funny. But that was one
of the reasons Uncle Ho would let her live. Anyway, all
that talk about murder was just nonsense, it was made just
to frighten her.

Once, just below this very window, V had sat in a cafe
with the Dutch homosexual watching the tourists, and had
been moved to remark, "Piet, how is it that English girls
have such nice complexions, eh?"

Piet had leaned back and tried to look especially suave
because the Arab boy he had his eye on was sitting at a
cafe across the street. She had expected him to say something about the English climate, of course.

"It is because they fuck so much, my dear Veltraud," he
had said instead.

She thought of that now because her George, her China-man (she must remember not to call him that) had such a nice complexion.

Piet always had his eyes on some boy. It was, after all, why he came to Tangier in the first place. V found it diffi-cult to forget one of those boys, a one-legged lad who was almost as pretty as the dancing boy. (Dancing boys don't last very long. Two, three years at most, and they are re-tired in favor of the next comely youth and they spend their lives in a semi-decline, like high school football stars who were favorites in the locker room as well as on the playing field.) The one-legged boy had wanted to fuck V and Piet had made a deal with him. Piet promised him V if he would let Piet fuck him. Piet fucked him, brought him along to V's hotel room, asked her for a loan and then told the one-legged boy waiting in the hall that she was not having any, after all. Sorry. Piet had told her the whole story when they were back in Amsterdam. V's only regret was that she had been given no choice in the matter, that Piet had naturally assumed (or was he jealous?) that V did not want to fuck a sixteen-year-old, black-eyed, one-legged Moroccan boy. Piet, however, had been wrong. Dead wrong.

Dead Wrong. The name of one of her present lover's friends or relations? What she would be if her trump card wasn't high enough? Her epitaph?

Here lies Veltraud Schimmel Nathan Hong.
She was dead wrong about her Uncle Ho.
He was a brother in the Tong.
He ripped her open from throat to toe.

She told Nephew George the poem.

George shook. "Don't talk that way. You must not talk that way," he told her. Then he held her tightly and shook some more.

Mornings they went out for fresh orange juice and French style croissants in the cafe next door to the hotel. Afternoons George went to the stand at the bottom of the square and bought lunch. Evenings they went out together again and ate in a tiny (eight feet wide, seventeen feet deep) windowless room sliced out of the block of ancient buildings under a Moorish arch around the corner where a

German served brochettes, olives (seven kinds), beets, tur-
nips, chicken, hard brown bread, sweet coffee (from the
cafes) and sometimes, if no one was looking, a bottle of
awful Moroccan wine (*Roi du Soleil*, eight weeks old)
smuggled from the haberdasher on the corner. The haberdasher!

Otherwise they stayed in their room and trembled together. It bored V so much she almost forgot how much
was at stake. How much money she stood to gain if her
lover came through at the right moment. How much life
she might lose if he didn't.

But that was absurd. They had only threatened her to
make her afraid. No one was going to kill her. Not a platinum blonde Dutch girl. Not in Tangier. There were some
bribes even Moroccan policemen wouldn't take. This
wasn't Hong Kong and it wasn't good old New York. If
they so much as looked cross-eyed at her, eighty-nine Moroccan toughs would save her from them, cut their throats,
and carry her off to ravish her in some Harem room.

Not that bad an idea. They were supposed to be tough,
though. Really tough. And it was hard to get away once
one got you. They still believed in purdah, or at least some
of them did. This was the conservative end of the Moslem
Empire. Women still wore veils and rarely appeared in the
streets. Even the prostitutes still wore veils.

Purdah was when your husband locked you in the house
and no other living male saw you unless he peeked at you
from a nearby roof while you were sunning yourself. In
which event he stood to lose his life's blood through a slash
in his stomach.

V remembered an American girl who had thoughtlessly
started an affair with a young Moroccan and had stayed his
virtual prisoner for nearly a year until finally she had broken out.

No, Tangier had been the perfect place. It had been a
sheer stroke of luck that there had been a flight to Madrid
via Bombay leaving the Hong Kong airport at the same
time their flight was to depart for San Francisco. And who
knew her way around airports better than Veltraud Schimmel Nathan Hong?

And then, of course, at Madrid, she made a point of ask-

ing three different tourist aides the way to the Algeciras
train and whether the ferry still ran to Tangier. As if she
didn't remember her way around Madrid. Poor Nephew
George. Puttylike and trembling.

The hotel room itself was cute. The walls were light
blue, the floor bright Moorish tiles, the baseboards were
not boards at all but even brighter Moorish tiles, the windows were French doors opening onto a tiny terrace about
twenty feet above the cafes. There was a bed, a small desk
and a large armoire. The bathroom was down the hall.

Every morning there were footprints on the toilet seat!
Somewhere in the hotel there was a Moroccan woman. It
was the only explanation. Moroccan women have the
queerest habit of squatting over a toilet instead of sitting
over it. They put their feet on the edge and hunker. Some
decadent European plumbing salesman (a German, probably, all the the plumbing in Tangier is German) probably
taught them to do it that way in the beginning of the century. And Moroccan women, after all, do what they are told.

It reminded her of Piet's description of the urinal in the
Spanish bar on the Avenida d'Espagne, the promenade that
runs along the Tangier beach. The urinal there is spanking
clean, but no pipe connects it to a waste line. One pisses,
the piss flows through a hole in the bottom, falls to the
floor and is slowly pulled by gravity toward a drain between one's feet.

Once, when V had been in the bar with Piet, years ago
now, she had gone to the ladies' room to inspect the plumbing there, ready to return with more bizarre information
about Moroccan bathroom practices. She found more than
she had bargained for. An Arab prostitute was there turning a standing rear entrance trick with a john. The thought
of that, now—of the short dark girl with her veil still on
and her jalabah hiked up over her waist, winking at V who
stood momentarily frozen in the doorway—made her tremble almost as much as Nephew George. For other reasons,
however.

"It is all right," George said. "It will be all right."

It was strange about Arab prostitutes, at least Moroccan
ones. Piet had told her that they are sometimes virgins, that
they often keep their cherry, unless they get married or

plenty of money. It is possible for them to keep it, according to Piet, because Moroccan men prefer anal entry. It is
therefore possible to marry a Moroccan woman who is a
virgin and has been a prostitute for years.

Where was Uncle Ho? They had been in that damn hotel
room for weeks!

"George."

"Yes, love."

"Let's do it again."

"I don't know."

"Come on, it will help me to forget."

"I am worried about money, love."

"I'm not. I don't give a damn about money, George. All
I want is to be with you."

"I know. But we are down to the last few hundred
francs. I will have to get to a bank and cable Switzerland,
but then they are sure to trace us. They may even get to us
before the money arrives."

"I'm not afraid, George."

"Aye, yi!" George replied. "I am afraid."

"Come on, darling, let's do it. Please."

It wasn't all that difficult to convince him. You would
have thought he had never had a woman before V. He had
the recuperative powers of a young man. That little yellow
penis would swell up and stand straight if she so much as
looked at it warmly. And it wasn't really so little anymore.
Perhaps the continuous use had elongated and swollen the
thing. It hadn't had a chance to shrink to its smallest condition in so long (except perhaps when they went out to eat
or he went out to get lunch, and she doubted even that) it
had probably been permanently extended. Like a session on
the rack.

They had been lying naked on top of the sheet. The
other bedclothes were in a heap on the desk chair in a
corner by the French windows. George was on his back
and V lay across his chest, her legs drawn up and one knee
over his. All she did was reach down and run the palm of
her hand over his penis and it began to swell. She had
never before felt quite so beautiful, felt quite this much
power in being beautiful. She was a siren, a Mata Hari, a
Helen. She felt Olympian. The fear of Uncle Ho, lurking in

the back of her mind, probably had something to do with it.

"I'll make you feel better," she said.

Generosity had overcome her. She felt so powerful she was capable of being selfless about small things. When his penis had risen to the perpendicular she lowered her head and began slowly to run the top of her tongue around it, then, like a lizard catching flies, she let her tongue dart out to lick the crack in it, and dart out again and again.

George's breath caught in his chest and his body convulsed violently, his legs shot straight out and the muscles in his chest and arms contracted. She had so much sexual power over this man. She could probably make him come from across the room just by looking at him long enough and then snapping her fingers.

In order to play her tongue games with George's penis V had doubled herself over his body and she reached down to rub his calf with her free hand (the other was firmly grasping the base of the Chinese organ so that just two inches of it and the head extended above her fist). She very much liked his calves. They were soft, almost as a woman's were soft, and just as smooth. It had been a surprise and a pleasure to find that his skin was so good to touch. But then all skin was good to touch.

Someone—Hans? Ivan?—had told her once that she had skin like velvet, that it was indescribably wonderful to rub one's hands over her. Hans, or Ivan, she could not remember.

George's penis was so swollen that the head of it seemed ready to burst. If mushrooms ever exploded they must look just like George's penis looked as she let her tongue dart out to flick it just at the crack. If only the tropical climate and George's soft, yellow skin, and George's complete submission to her would combine to make her come the way she once had with Hans. Then it wouldn't be just for the money, would it? Then the memory of the Arab whore turning a standing trick in the ladies' room of the Spanish bar wouldn't burn so.

"George?"

His body convulsed again when she spoke his name. She

sat up and watched him stare at her breasts. He still looked at them as if he had never seen any before.

"George?"

"Yes, love."

"I . . . I want to do something. I want you to do something for me."

George just looked at her.

"I'm so ashamed. I don't know what you'll think of me."

"What, love?"

"The mirror, George."

On the armoire door was a mirror. She had been thinking about it for some time.

"What about the mirror?"

"If we open the door and do it kneeling. . . ."

She stopped. She shouldn't go too far with George. He might turn on her.

"Kneeling?" he said incredulously.

"Oh, George, like an Oriental print. Haven't you ever seen any of those Oriental drawings?"

She laughed.

"Yes, I know the ones you mean," George admitted.

"I want you to do to me all the things the Chinese men do to the Chinese ladies in those prints."

"Oh, love," George said, not with excitement, but with fear. "It's the ladies, the prostitutes, who do those things to the men, not the men to the women."

"I want you to do those things to me anyway."

"I don't think we should," George said.

"Oh, Jesus. *Ben ye heel hek?*" Are you really crazy?

"What? Don't speak Dutch, V."

"Look, I'll show you."

V let go of his penis and got off the bed. She opened the armoire door so the mirror pointed at the foot of the bed.

"If we do it down here we can watch ourselves in the mirror."

George said nothing.

"Come!"

George got off the bed and came to where V told him. Then V got onto the bed again, kneeling.

"Now put it into me, George."

In the mirror she could see that he was hesitant to obey. He stared at her magnificent behind, unable to take his eyes away from it, but he was afraid. He was nuts. He had spent too much time in the damned Christian school where he had learned his English. His family ought to have raised him to be a pagan. Her Genghis Kahn, she thought, was a puritanical mamma's boy. Her Oriental, her heathen lover couldn't, wouldn't cut the mustard.

"Come, George."

George approached her and tried to put his penis between her thighs but the angle was not right. V would have had to lower her head to the mattress in order to let him penetrate her vagina that way. Then she would not be able to see everything in the mirror.

"Here."

She reached behind her and tried to grasp his penis, but then she could not aim it right, so she let go and reached between her legs for it, found it, and put it against her anus. In Rome. . . . In Morocco do as the Moroccans do.

"What?"

"Come on, George!"

He tried to push in but it hurt her. The lousy Arab food had tightened her lower tract.

"Stay there."

She got off the bed quickly and went to the open armoire. She had her toilet things on a shelf above the small sink in the corner near the desk but his toilet kit was in the armoire. She opened it quickly and began emptying the contents on the floor of the armoire until she had found what she was looking for. Chinese George used American VO-5 on his hair. She opened the tube, rubbed a large blob of the stuff between her palms, and returned to him.

"What is to happen?" he asked as she moved next to him.

"Quiet!"

She had to be careful. She had to be less commanding with him. She had to be soft, malleable with him. But for the love of God (Gad ferdomen) she couldn't bear to be so long with a naked man without once trying to come really well.

She rubbed the VO-5 on his penis, kissed him lightly on the cheek, and assumed the position once again.

This time it went smoothly. She reached under her legs, found his greased penis, inserted the head firmly into her anus and moaned.

The moan did it. George convulsed and pushed forward and fell on her, clinging to her body. She was pinned to the mattress, one hand still between her legs, one elbow on the sheet. She had probably never been more uncomfortable. And it hurt, damn it. His little yellow penis hurt.

"Get up, George. No! Stay in, just stand up."

George gulped and stood up. She got her arm out from under her, put her palms squarely on the mattress and locked her elbows. Wouldn't this be a time for Uncle Ho to arrive?

"Don't move yet, George."

It still hurt, but looking at their reflection in the mirror, especially looking at the way his thighs were pushed up against her bottom, excited her so that her sphincter muscles relaxed.

"Now. Slowly."

He did nothing.

"Please," she thought to add.

George had been about three-quarters of the way home. He pushed in the last-quarter and slowly began to withdraw. V watched in the mirror as his swollen penis emerged, and she contracted the muscles around her anus to squeeze him as tightly as she could. When she saw the first fleshy part of the head of his penis emerge she said, "No. No further, or you'll come out. Be careful of the mirror."

He had been breathing heavily and had accidentally knocked the mirror with his elbow so that the angle changed just enough to prevent V from seeing everything. As it was she had to bend her head over her shoulder.

"Move the mirror."

George carefully returned the mirror to the original position. The armoire door creaked on its hinges and George moaned.

"It's good and tight, isn't it?"

George moaned again.

V laughed. She knew she was probably making a terrible mistake. This was not the side of her that she had ever intended showing to George but, for the love of Christ, she had been with him so long, she just had to try something. If only there were some way to get him to play with her clitoris. If only that one-legged boy were there to play with her while George fucked her slowly.

George laughed. "It looks so funny. The small hole and the large thing that is in it. One would never suspect."

"Suspect what?"

"That it would fit. It fits." George laughed again. Maybe this treatment was good for him. At least he wasn't quaking.

"Move it!" V said. "Move it slowly, George. . . . please."

George moved slowly in and out, staring down at what V was staring at in the mirror. Her neck had begun to hurt but the feeling was so good, George's penis felt so large inside her, she didn't care. She wished she could see more. The flesh of her left lobe blocked her view of her anus itself.

"George, pull apart my bottom," V suggested.

He did so and although it hurt it provided her with a better view and was worth it. She had to try something. Even if it meant risking what she had built between them in the last weeks. She had to try something.

She moved her left hand to a position centrally below her head and balanced on that hand alone. Then she wet the fingers of her right hand with her saliva and parted her hair and the lips of her vagina. A few seconds later she was rubbing her own clitoris back and forth and shaking her bottom simultaneously and poor George was moaning like a ghost.

She looked at his face in the mirror. His eyes were closed and his small mouth open wide. He couldn't even see what she was doing. She rubbed harder and harder and faster and faster until she felt herself begin to build toward something.

"Harder, George."

George roared. He actually roared like a man. He shoved his penis in so hard it nearly knocked her over. She began to come. She let her hand fall from her clitoris and dropped her face to the mattress. She felt the orgasm build and build and heard herself moan.

"Oh, fuck me. *Fuck* me."

And then something caught and the feeling petered out and died and she lay there, being fucked in the ass by a Chinese gentleman who was about to come. She lay there staring blankly at the wall and at the bottom edge of the armoire mirror. She lay there as he screeched and shot sperm into her and then fell forward onto the bed, knocking her onto her side and coming dislodged in the process.

She lay there for a long time, unable to do what she knew she must do. Roll over to him, take his babyish head in her hands, and make him love her again, erase the memory of what he had just seen of her. She lay there wishing she was dead, wishing Uncle Ho would arrive and put her out of her misery. She lay there for several minutes more and then, finally, started to roll over to salvage what she could of his original romantic love for her.

When she saw his face she was frightened. She had feared a change in his attitude but had not expected to be able to see it so clearly in his eyes.

"George."

"Darling V. I am getting up and going down to the bank."

"George?"

"I am going to wire Switzerland."

"George?"

"Let them catch us. I no longer care. I am going to keep you as my wife. I am going to cover you with jewels. We are getting out of this rumshackle hotel."

"Ramshackle," she corrected him. Then she grabbed him and held on tight so that he could not see the look of utter bewilderment she wore.

Uncle Ho caught up with them four days later. In a way it was a relief for two reasons, first because she had known it to be inevitable, second because strange things were happening to her. She had spent so much time trying to convince George she loved him that the first moment he showed any self-respect she found to her amazement that she did love him. And while it was not the sort of love that drives a woman insane and reorganizes her life and her view of herself, still it was strong enough to worry her. It would not do, it would simply not do.

They were spending some of the money George had wired for in a restaurant in the European section of the city, on the Avenida d'Espagne across from the train station and within sight of the first of the cabana-bars that separate the avenue from the beaches. They were eating outside under a warm and still bright sky. Their waiter had just chased four brown pre-teen beggars (boys, of course) from the tables (they had wanted money but would have been happy to settle for bread from the basket in front of them) when George stiffened and his face assumed a resolve and force which V had never seen on it before. She knew without having to look around. She lighted a Gauloise cigarette and inhaled deeply. She had grown fond again of the cheap French brand while they had been living cheap in the "rumshackle" hotel. They had since moved to El Minzah, which was something more to V's taste.

George stood, said something in Chinese, was answered in kind, and V took another long drag of dark tobacco.

She noticed everything. She was aware of the sweet odor of the food (tajeen, the Moroccan stew) of the bright color of the giant purple bougainvillea bushes on the far corner, of the rapturous smile on the girl seated with a young man near them, of the taste of the *toppas* they had been brought with the drinks they had ordered before dinner (small fried fish), of the distance across the avenue to the cabana-bars, of the beaches beyond, of the shadow of Gibraltar across the strait. She was, in short, aware of more at once than she had ever been before in her life. She could almost feel the knife she feared would momentarily penetrate her back.

Uncle Ho and Ho Bin appeared simultaneously on the opposite edges of her field of vision, Ho Bin pulling out the chair next to her and Uncle Ho walking around to George's side of the table and sitting down there. For his part, Nephew George regained his own seat.

There was more strained conversation in Chinese. Then Ho Bin addressed her in English.

"And you, my dear, how are you today?"

V did not answer. She smoked her cigarette deeply but made no attempt to speak. She stared straight up the avenue watching the central promenade, counting the trees that lined it.

"Have you lost your tongue?"

"She has not," George spoke for her.

"I have nothing to say," V replied, her voice broken and strained.

"Nothing?" Ho Bin continued.

"I am perfectly willing to go through with our deal," she said. "I will do whatever George asks me to. He can have a divorce the moment he wants it. I want nothing from him, and nothing from you."

"So, a little speech already prepared," Ho Bin commented, then said something to Uncle Ho in Chinese.

George said, "You are wrong, both of you. I put us on that plane to Madrid. I intend to keep this woman near me."

This woman, V thought.

"So, you suddenly have a mind of your own," Ho Bin said sweetly. "Have you any idea to how much trouble you have put us?" Then he added something in rapid Chinese, and Uncle Ho answered in kind.

V had still not looked either of them in the eye. She chose to do so now, raised her face toward Uncle Ho, looked deeply into his black eyes thinking, *I love Nephew George,* then lowered her head.

"You were to go to San Francisco," Ho Bin uttered sweetly, returning his attention to her.

She could almost feel him sitting next to her. She believed she would have known he was there if he had been silent and she blind.

"I will do whatever George asks of me," she said softly.

"You were to have received another fifteen thousand dollars, my dear. Where, by the way, is the initial five?"

"In a bank in New York."

"I see."

"You can keep the rest. I don't want it."

"Why, thank you so much, Miss Schimmel. Sorry . . . Mrs. Hong. You are generous to a fault."

"Keep it!" she hissed in sudden anger.

Nephew George spoke again. "Ho Bin, I am going to keep this woman near me."

This woman.

"It is clear what you want, my boy," Ho Bin said in English. "And, of course, you shall have it." To V he said, "You took a very great chance, my dear. I almost admire you for it. Of course now it will be quite impossible to pay you what we owe you for going back on your word. Isn't that so? After all, we would not go against the wishes of one of our youngest but richest clients."

"You are wrong, Ho Bin," V said, her voice breaking again, just as it had when she first spoke.

"Of course I am wrong. Just as you say. You have not gone back on your word. You will do only as George commands, as a dutiful, purchased bride . . . Dutiful, purchased, and returnable but not, I fear, refundable." He said something to Uncle Ho and rose.

Uncle Ho looked at George and then, finally, rose, too. More words were spoken in Chinese and then the two men left.

V was no longer hungry. George, however, fell to his meal as if he had never eaten before. A large Arab in a white jalabah passed slowly along the sidewalk staring at them intently. His attention meant nothing—they made a unique and surprising couple in this town.

"He said they were staying at our hotel, too, and we will see them again."

"I'm sure," V said.

"Never mind. I know my own mind for the first time in my life. We will go to the States, you and I together, and if the family insists I will divorce you, but I will keep you near me."

V looked over toward the bougainvillea.

"You trust me," George said.

"Of course."

"They see how it is with me. They see they have me to deal with. I control vast amounts of the family money. I am of age."

"Of course," V said.

"They would not dare touch a hair on your head. I was a fool not to see my power before."

He fell to his *tajeen* again, even mopping his plate with bread. A hustler who had approached them before started toward them, but took one look at the expression on George's face and turned around to go the way he had come.

"Not a hair," George said.

V sighed and lighted another Gauloise. It had worked. So far . . . so good.

"Tonight I am going to buy you jewelry. We will go back to that Jew in the Medina, the shop where you saw the bracelet you liked. I will buy you that and everything else you can wear or carry."

V laughed.

"I will spend that fifteen thousand on you in one evening. I will drag the Jew from his home if he is not at the shop. I feel like a man. I owe you everything."

This woman.

"Eat, you are not eating anything."

V laughed heartily but waved the thought of food aside. "No," she said. "Your lawyer makes me lose my appetite."

"I will fix him," George said. "I will fix him for you."

But George did not fix Ho Bin. V had to do that for herself. She met him alone the next day in the bar of El Minzah while Uncle Ho kept George busy upstairs, discussing family pride, millions of yen, or francs, or dollars, or whatever they counted their wealth in terms of.

Ho Bin opened the conversation politely. If only he weren't always so goddamn typically polite, she thought. He was something out of a class-B movie.

"Miss Schimmel, I wanted to talk to you alone not for your sake but for George's sake."

"I see."

"I think you do. George would seriously compromise his future by keeping you as his wife."

"Let him divorce me then, or I will divorce him, whatever he wants. I will be his mistress if he wants it that way."

"He wants what you want him to want, Miss Schimmel. You do not really expect me to believe that you flew to Hong Kong on a Thursday, married George on a Saturday, fell in love with him in the meanwhile, fell in love with him so deeply that you would give up everything for him—a legal marriage, the family money, also your, uh, alimony checks, Mrs. Nathan."

V just stared at him.

"I had you investigated fully, my dear. You do not think I would hire someone I knew nothing about, do you? Really, Miss Schimmel, you have been quite naive."

"I do love him; and he loves me."

"I have no doubt that he loves you. He will recover. Now, shall we discuss *your* recovery? The fifteen thousand dollars still awaits you after a short trip to Reno, provided you never see him again."

"That's absurd. I told you, I do not want your money."

"If you do not take it and agree to my terms you will lose far more, you will lose your income, Miss Schimmel, or should I say Mrs. Nathan."

"I don't care."

"Do not push me, Miss Schimmel. There are other measures I can take."

"George would never cooperate with you again if you hurt me in any way. Besides, I am going through with our deal. I will divorce George just as agreed. There has been a delay of only a few weeks."

"And a considerable added expense in time and trouble, Mrs. Nathan . . . Mrs. Hong. I see you have some very pretty jewelry. The expense has not only been mine."

V did not reply. She had a drink before her, a tall gin and tonic. There were olives in a dish on the table between them and she touched one tentatively with her forefinger.

"Do you think George would still love you if you were not quite so attractive, Miss Schimmel? You might have a serious accident."

"I will tell George you threatened me."

It was Ho Bin's turn to be silent. He stared at the far end of the bar for some time.

"I think we have reached an impasse, Mrs. Hong."

"Perhaps we have."

"But we do understand one another."

V was silent.

"Come now, do not underestimate me, I do not underestimate you. We must decide upon a price."

"I am not interested in money."

"Ten thousand dollars more."

"I tell you I am not interested in money."

"Remember you have the alimony to think of. I could end that for you in a day, in an hour, one phone call."

"I am not interested in money."

"I will give you the ten thousand I have just offered you, plus I will throw in the original fifteen right now. I tell you in utmost honesty, my dear, I will go not one cent higher. I go this high only because you seem to have had a beneficial effect on George. He is a better man for what has happened between you, but whatever that may have been, I will not try to imagine it."

"Don't cut off your nose to spite your face!"

"You humor me, Miss Schimmel. Twenty-five thousand dollars is rather good pay for three weeks' work, and it's thirty, counting the original downpayment."

V was silent.

"Do you know what a bank draft looks like, Miss Schimmel?"

V was silent again.

"May I suggest you hire an attorney in this town? Meet with him tomorrow morning. Arrange to meet with him again tomorrow afternoon. I will accompany you to his office at the second meeting. You will have his assurance of the legitimacy of the transaction."

V stared at the olives.

"I will present you with a bank draft drawn on our Swiss account for twenty-five thousand dollars. You will leave the attorney's office and go straight to the ferry. At Algeciras you will take the train to Madrid and from there you will return to New York. You will not return to the hotel. You will give George no idea of what you plan. His uncle and I will take him from here tomorrow morning and drive toward Rabat to discuss business. I will return without him for our meeting. You have only to leave word at the desk with which attorney you have agreed to meet. After a month in New York you will go to Nevada, establish your residency and obtain the divorce."

V touched the olive, picked it up, ate it.

"We understand each other?"

She placed the pit in the ashtray.

"Say your goodbyes tonight, silently. And think of this: unlike the typical Oriental my patience is not infinite. If you refuse this offer or ever see George again, or ever decide to visit San Francisco at any time within the next ten years, I shall have your throat cut and to hell with George Toy Hong. By then, my dear, he won't give a damn anyway."

V sipped her drink, ate another olive.

"Tomorrow afternoon then, after siesta. I suggest you begin now to telephone for an attorney. Call the Dutch consulate for advice if you like, or the American consulate, as you were once married to an American, Mrs. Nathan. Good evening."

Ho Bin looked at her with dead, cold eyes, then got up and went away.

Ho Bin had one more trick up his sleeve. At the office of the attorney recommended by the Dutch consul, he had V sit and write George a note confessing to her mercenary intentions. She wrote the note coldly, in a clear hand, as Ho Bin insisted, and left the bank draft she received in return for it in the possession of the Moroccan attorney. (He was a Spaniard by birth, driven from his homeland by the civil war and living poignantly in sight of it across the strait, unable to return because of an oath he had taken to await Franco's death. He had told her all this at their first meeting.)

Ho Bin had a cab waiting on the sloping avenue outside the office. V took it, along with several hundred dollars extended by the attorney, and went immediately to the ferry. She arrived in New York the next day and did not cry or shake or so much as feel afraid until she had finally closed her apartment door behind her and locked it.

She could not, would not, sleep alone that night. She called Roger Conheim, who came dutifully, his resolve to forget her apparently forgotten in the weeks she had been away. He returned frequently in the next few days. When she announced that she was leaving again (for Nevada this time, since she assumed George was by then safely established in San Francisco) and told Roger she could not explain why she was going or where, just like the last time he became enraged and walked away. (On the street again, just like the last time.) But, he would be back.

By the last week in November V was again in New York. She had a complete and extravagant new wardrobe, had established credit at two of the most exclusive dining clubs in the city, was awaiting confirmation of membership in each, and had already met Oscar "Chick" Mandreaes.

The way she met Mandreaes was ironic. It was as if she had never had to go through the whole process of getting wealthy enough to live like a millionairess for a little while. It was as if she had never had to take Ho Bin's offer in the first place, let alone to doublecross him in order to extract a lousy ten thousand more for her services. She met Mandreaes at Max's, where she would have met him had she never gone to Hong Kong, Tangier and Reno, Nevada, where she would have met him if she had just sat there long enough, on a bar stool talking to Max.

But V believed that things worked in curious, backwards, ironic ways, that, for instance, a lover you might be cheating would find out about it not by stumbling on the truth but by stumbling on something perfectly innocent that would resemble the truth. This mythical lover would find a pack of cigarettes, say, left not by his rival but by the maid, and his eventual revelation would follow from that and not from something really damning, like his rival's underwear in V's hamper or a love mark on a part of her body he never touched. In short, V believed firmly that if she had never gone to Hong Kong, Tangier and Reno, Chick would *not* have walked into Max's, he would *not* have been attracted to her, he would *not* have asked Max who she was.

It was that same winter day that Karen Thompson stood at the large window of her cubbyhole looking down at an elderly woman going into B. Altman's in an expensive fur, the same day that Karen wondered about her hands and the color they turned when it was really cold. V had gone to see Max for the first time since her adventure, since her coup. Maybe she went to show him how much more of a woman she was since he was a man perceptive enough to be able to see the difference, the difference that being tough-minded and courageous had worked on her psyche.

Maybe she had just been curious about his payoff from Ho
Bin. At any rate, it was certainly not to pick up a man that
she went. She fully intended to find her mate while living
high for the next few months, in one of the two exclusive
clubs she had joined, on an expensive Caribbean tour,
while flying first class to the Vale of Kashmir, or while exam-
ining a new Porsche in their Sixth Avenue show room.
The men who frequented Max's were no longer of much
interest to her.

"Miss Schimmel!" Max exclaimed as he came into the
bar and walked toward her favorite stool. It was early afternoon and there were only nine or ten customers in the
place, most of them at tables in a corner and most of them
alone.

"Hello, Max."

"Long time no see, Miss Schimmel."

"Well, I'm back now, Max. Finally."

"You've been . . . uh . . . to Nevada?"

"That's right."

"Ahhh," Max said and beamed. "That means I'll be due
for a little tip any day now. Funny, Ho Bin was in last
week but didn't mention it."

"He probably just got the papers, Max. I sent them to
my ex at his office."

"Miss Schimmel, that's just wonderful. Let me buy you a
drink. What'll it be?"

"V. O. and water, Max."

"Coming up."

As Max bent to make the drink the door of the bar
opened and Chick Mandreaes came in. It was strange how
she knew immediately not just that he was someone she
was going to have but exactly how she was going to go
about attracting him. The old game was out of the question. She was no longer capable of so patent a ploy as looking morosely at her watch, and she now wondered why she
had thought that would ever work.

A girl friend at Schipol, Welmoot, the other platinum
blonde whose father had been German, once told her that
sometimes she saw a man and she knew, just knew, that
somehow, somewhere, she would sleep with him. It had
never happened to V before Mandreaes.

He was a short, square, hairy man with hard black eyes, a slow gait and about a thousand dollars worth of clothes on his back. He had a pinky ring so large it caught her attention from across the bar. He looked at her for no more than a fraction of a second and then went to the furthest end of the bar from her and sat down on a stool. The fraction of a second had been long enough.

Max put the drink in front of her, noticed who had come in, raised his eyebrows and said, "Excuse me, Miss Schimmel, I'll be right back."

Max went to wait on Mandreaes while V sipped her drink and stared straight ahead at the bottles lined in front of the mirror behind the back bar.

When Max returned she had finished half her drink.

"You are exciting some attention, Miss Schimmel."

"That so, Max?"

"Mandreaes. His friends call him Chick. He's in trucking or something, distributing of some kind, magazines maybe. Whatever he's in he's got it made, Miss Schimmel."

"When I leave you can tell him his eyes burned holes in my new dress. Tell him I'll send him a bill."

"You don't want me to tell him you've been stood up then?"

"No, Max."

"You don't want me to tell him your name, that it?"

"That's right, Max."

"O.K., Miss Schimmel, but if there was ever a catch in here worthy of you, it's him."

"I don't like his eyes, Max. Just tell him about the dress. I'll see you again soon."

"O.K., Miss Schimmel."

V left the half-full glass and left the bar without once turning toward Chick Mandreaes. She knew Max well enough to know she had played it perfectly, that the balding bartender would at first refuse to tell Mandreaes who she was but would eventually talk, would eventually allow himself to be bribed. And unless she was absolutely no judge of men, Mandreaes was the kind who would not take the message about her dress lying down.

She was right. He called her at her apartment not two hours later.

"Miss Schimmel, this is Chick Mandreaes. Pretty tough talk, lady, but let's see how tough you are. I've called Lord and Taylor and told them it would be all right if you came in and bought any dress in the place. If you're so damn independent, Miss Schimmel, go on up there."

He hung up the phone before she could reply. When she hung up her own receiver she was smiling brilliantly.

She went up and bought the dress (the crushed velvet one she wore later at the Persian Room, and the matching fox-lined coat).

She did not hear from Mandreaes again for three weeks. He must have known she had taken him up on his offer and purchased a dress; still he did not call. She was absolutely sure that he would eventually get in touch, but it did not bother her in the least. Among other things, she had another man to think about. She had run into Paul. French Paul. Francine's ex-boyfriend. Paul who owned a water bed. Paul, who had every blessed inch of foreskin intact. All things come to those who wait.

She met Paul on the street, not far from where she had met him the first time with Francine. In the year and a half since she had taken the high-rise apartment on Twelfth and Avenue of the Americas she had been accustomed to spending a good deal of time with a girl named Carol Roper. Carol was an attractive brunette with good legs who wanted to be a singer and was being kept by an executive named Richard with whom she spent three nights a week. Like V, Carol spent her mornings in bed, her evenings with whichever man she was dating and her afternoons being bored. They had little else in common except their mutual liking for Veltraud Schimmel. Carol liked V almost as much as V liked herself.

V went over to Carol's apartment on East Tenth Street for lunch one afternoon in late December. They ate and talked openly about V's adventure in Hong Kong and Tangier and then Carol had to get ready for Richard, who was due to arrive after work. V left Carol's apartment and started walking east, going the long way around to her own building, just for the novelty of it and because she was in no hurry to get there. She was tired of her own company. Then she met Paul at the corner of Eleventh Street and

Fifth Avenue. She recognized him at once and stopped him with a smile.

"How is Francine?" V asked.

"Oh yes, you are her sister-in-law, isn't it? I have not seen Francine in some time. She is—uh—so involved with politics."

"Politics?"

Paul laughed. "Come. I'll buy you a drink and we'll talk about it."

V took her time answering him. Finally she said, "All right. Where shall we go?"

"Have you ever been to the Ninth Circle?"

"No."

"I'll take you."

"All right."

They walked without talking down Eleventh Street and then across Avenue of the Americas. On Tenth Street, they went into the bar, found a table in the back and sat down. There wasn't any need to talk because it was obvious to V that he was attracted to her, which was all she needed to interest her at the moment.

The bar was dark, had sawdust on the floor and a view through floor-to-ceiling windows of the barren backyard. Along with the sawdust were thousands of cracked peanut shells. Bowls of fresh ones were the only objects on the wooden tables.

The bartender came over and took their order. There was a group of hippie types in the front of the place but they had the back room to themselves.

"What do you mean, politics? Is dirty-mouthed Francine in the peace movement?"

"So, you know she is called that, eh?"

"No, it's just obvious, isn't it?"

Paul laughed. "No, she is not in the peace movement. She thinks it, how is it said, futile. She is involved with women's liberation, with radical lesbians."

"Lesbians!"

"Oh, she is not one, unless she is a very clever liar. No, but she thinks they are the only group capable of making a radical change in female consciousness. She claims to be a doer, a Machiavellian. She says she cooperates with the lesbians and uses them to her own ends. She reminds me of a Trotskyite at times."

"A what?"

"It doesn't matter."

"A Communist, you mean."

"Yes. Are you all alone in this town? What do you do? Do you work?"

V smiled. "No. I don't work."

Paul sipped his drink and looked at her. She made it clear what she wanted by looking right back at him.

"You know, I was sorry the last time we met because I couldn't find out from Francine who you were, except that you were once married to her brother."

"I was sorry, too," V said.

"Will you have dinner with me tonight?"

V waited a full thirty seconds before answering. "Yes. All right."

They talked about their pasts and what had brought them to America. It was a game, V pretending to be interested in Paul when in fact all she wanted was a lover, a bed companion, someone to help her get through the time between now and whenever it might be that she would find her millionaire. There was no way, no way at all she would allow herself to become interested again in a man who made less than, say, Chick Mandreaes.

"And I met Ivan at Schipol."

"Ivan?" He pronounced it the way she did, E-van.

"Francine's brother. My ex."

Paul raised his eyebrows. Then he started talking about himself again. He had attended business college at Cornell, in Ithaca, New York. After graduation he returned to France, but this was where the money was to be made, so two years ago he had returned. He had been living in the Village ever since, climbing the ladder of success as an insurance salesman with executive aspirations.

His conversation returned to Francine again. It was as if she were there with them, instead of God knew where with her radical lesbian friends, or worse.

"She is the most peculiar woman I ever . . . met, this American. Do you understand them? The Americans? You were married to one."

V laughed. "They are puritans. Everything they do you must see in the light of their puritanism."

"Everything?"

"Yes."

Paul waved and the bartender came over with another round of drinks. When he returned to his station Paul said, "I don't know. I have known many French women, older women than Francine, who were more the puritan."

"Oh . . . really."

Paul laughed. "Come," he said, "finish your drink and come to my apartment where I will change before dinner. I have been in these clothes all day."

V leaned back and eyed him warily. The game. The game of being interested in him. The game of debating whether to sleep with him. When it had all been decided months ago. If Francine had had him, V wanted him.

"All right," she said.

They finished their drinks, Paul paid, and they left. They walked to Seventh Avenue and up West Fourth Street. His apartment was in an old building but was very well furnished. It went perfectly with his manner of dress, his bright clothes and ascot. It was just what you would imagine it to be. She wondered how many times Francine had been there or if she would be able to find any of her ex-sister-in-law's underclothes around the place. Francine was probably the kind of girl that left her panties behind.

Paul made V a drink and then went into his bedroom to change. V waited a few moments, then she opened his door and stood looking in.

"Surprise," she said.

"You don't fool around."

"What's that?"

"The bed."

"But what kind of bed?"

"I expect you'll find out soon enough."

V smiled. He had stepped out of his pants and was holding them in front of him. He tossed them on a chair and pulled down his undershorts.

V looked away, took in the room, the shelf over the bed, the long tray hanging by pulleys from the ceiling, the erotic prints on the walls. Then she looked back at his half-naked body. She had begun involuntarily to lick her lips when she realized, as Francine had realized before her, that she had been lucky enough to stumble on a true bedroom, a bedroom designed and lived in by a sensualist; but when she saw his penis her tongue stayed on her lips and her teeth came down to keep it there.

He wasn't just excessively long. He had a foreskin. He had a foreskin!

"I should have known," she breathed.

"Are you just going to stand there?"

Sometimes he sounded like an American putting on a French accent, sometimes his accent was so authentic there was no doubt he was French. V understood that. She had lived in America long enough to have the same problem.

Strange, the thoughts that ran through her mind as she stared at the thing she had wanted to find for so long. Who cared what his accent sounded like?

"Are you?" Paul repeated, taking off his shirt.

"No. I'll get undressed. As soon as you finish."

His penis responded to the lilt in her voice. It began to stretch along his thigh, and then started to swell and stand away from it.

The argument was, according to various sexual treatises she had read, that circumcised men lose the sensitivity in the ends of their penises that is the most important of all erotic stimuli. If that were true, perhaps her own response was directly related to that lack of sensitivity. Well, damned if she wasn't going to make her own personal scientific study.

"Did Francine spend much time on that thing?" V asked as she watched him get out of the rest of his clothes.

"You are very interested in Francine."

"You are the one who keeps talking about her. Are you in love with her?"

Paul got out of the rest of his clothes. He had very little body hair. A short, large-boned, baby-faced, uncircumcised, well-endowed Frenchman. Bonanza!

He sat on the edge of the bed and drew his legs up. His penis was fully erect now. The foreskin she had been so pleased to see had become a roll of tissue around the base of the pink head of his penis. How long had it been since she had seen that? Hans? No, the personnel manager had not been circumcised. Willem, the steward, had not been circumcised. But it had been years. Years!

After moments of indecision she got undressed and joined him on the bed. They had still not touched but he was watching her closely, running his eyes over the length of her. His mouth was slightly open and his penis kept changing its angle, rising and falling slightly. She stared at it and when her hair came down over her face she brushed it back with her hand to have a better view.

"Shall we get started?"

"Are you waiting for me to jump on you?"

He reached for her, put his palm on her back and brought her down on him. She went right for his penis, cupping his testes with one hand, grasping the shaft with the other and letting her tongue dart out to taste it.

Paul moaned.

"Tu l'aime?" V asked.

"Yes."

It was fun to talk French in bed. However, if she had known Francine also had felt that way, she would have stayed with English.

V straightened. She was not going to start this thing by giving him head. She wanted to be made love to by him, not the other way around, not the first time.

He seemed to understand because he sat up and pressed her down against the mattress. The motion of his body started the water under her doing strange things. It seemed to give under her weight, then to force her back up toward him. It was warm and delightful.

"You're all dry," he said.

"Fait moi."

She had long, platinum-blonde pubic hair. Expertly, he moved the hair aside, opened her labia majora and ran his finger quickly back and forth over the clitoral area until she moaned and shuddered and fell back hard against the bed, starting the rippling movement of the water again.

She opened her thighs fully and he rolled over on top of her.

"Pas encore," she said. Not yet.

He moved his head over her breasts and his mouth took

one of her nipples, and then the other. They stood up straight as soon as he wet them with his lips and tongue.

He continued to move down her body, and she knew she had him. She had always admired Francine's body. It was full and sensual, while her own was thin and graceful, her breasts small and pointed, her legs long with good bone definition and pretty knees. They were two entirely different body types, but at that moment, as Paul continued to move down over her, running his tongue over her stomach and finally around her navel, over her waist and along the inside of her thighs, she was sure, absolutely sure, that hers was the better of the two bodies, and that he had never done this to Francine. She believed that firmly in that moment and even more firmly when he sank to the mattress to free his hands to spread her lips again, to put his tongue against the wrinkled skin over her clitoris. Looking down she could see only the top of his head, then, raising up, the white of his naked back and behind and the hairless backs of his legs. He was hanging his calves and feet over the bottom edge of the water bed.

She looked up at the ceiling. The shelf that hung from pulleys there attracted her for a time, then she looked at the walls and at the two erotic drawings on them.

It's Henry Miller.

Incredibly, V knew that Francine had given Paul those prints.

"Now you're getting there," Paul said, running his tongue over her clitoris. He was right, she was getting moist and open. She was relaxing for the first time since she'd been with George, really relaxing, really opening up. She contracted the muscles of her vaginal canal and kept on doing it. She wanted him in there but she didn't want him to stop eating her. If he kept it up until she was ready, *really* ready, maybe with that uncircumcised penis in there, with that *huge* uncircumcised penis in there, she would finally come right.

Remember, she thought, when you start to come you must relax.

She had read that in a book about Wilhelm Reich, the psychoanalyst, the one who invented the orgone box.

"N'arettes pas," V said softly.

Paul worked his hands under her and she shifted so that he could grab hold of a lobe of her backside with each hand. He knew what he was doing, this Frenchman did.

She stretched her legs out as far as she was able, cocking her knees and twisting her bottom. She had probably never looked so blatantly vulgar in all her life. But if that was what it took, vulgar she would look.

He started moving his tongue quickly. God, yes, he knew. You have to move over the clitoris fast, very fast, and very light, to get it ready, to get it really ready. Whenever she played with herself she would move her hand at lightning speed. His tongue was almost as good. She contracted her canal again and again.

He picked his head up. "You're so wet, mignone, you're leaking all over me."

"N'arettes pas, Paul, s'il tu plait."

"Don't talk French."

She hadn't the breath to ask him why not. Somewhere in the back of her mind she connected his request with Francine. *Was* he in love with her? Did Francine speak French to him before they broke up? Were they really broken up?

"Don't stop, please."

"You're ready. Come on."

"No, no."

He laughed and moved up over her. When his head was even with her waist she closed her legs around him and held him with all her strength. She reached down and squeezed his shoulders and stared away. God, she was as wet as she had ever been.

"Let me up," Paul said.

He was breathing heavily. He wanted to get that huge penis into her. If she could hold on just a few moments longer. She shook her bottom against him. It was no good. She pushed him back down.

He went without putting up a fight. He fell to licking her again and got his hands under her again, spreading the small halves of her behind. He found her anus with a finger and pushed it in. It just distracted her and she wiggled until he took it out.

"Now?" he asked.

"Soon," she panted.

She opened her legs wide again and put her hands on her own breasts, flicking her fingers over her nipples as if she could regulate the speed of his tongue on her clitoris by doing that. Her fingers moved faster and faster.

He lifted his head. "Mignone, I'm tired of this."

"All right."

He came up over quickly and she fitted him in.

"Don't come right away," she pleaded.

"No chance."

He commenced to enter her, slipped in easily, and then started a pounding, sensational rhythm. God, he was big. She felt filled up. She hesitated to contract her vaginal canal for fear of setting him off. If she could get him to come strong when he finally came, to really smash into her, to go like a jack hammer the way Hans had. She grabbed his head and kissed him full on the mouth, planting her open mouth against his and sinking her tongue as far inside as she could, tasting her own vaginal juices. She held his head and his mouth firmly and, kissing him finally, began to move excitedly, quickly, against his own pounding motion.

It started from way back inside her and built, then fell, then started again, then seemed to creep forward. She shuddered.

"Oh, now," she said. "Yes! Yes."

He started to smash into her so hard he was probably bruising her. She didn't even think of that. She went off, slowly at first, the way she did when she played with herself or got Roger to play with her or when Roger (or George) managed to fuck her properly enough to make her come. But this time it built and built and kept coming. She started to whimper.

"Fuck me harder! Fuck me harder," she said into his mouth, refusing to let it go, refusing to change anything, just moving faster and faster against him and finally collapsing, exhausted, under his steady increasing pounding, his body collapsing but still coming on.

Relax now, relax now, she told herself.

It kept happening. It ebbed so that she thought it was

going, decided it had been big enough, a red letter day, a real come, not the greatest, no shouting, screaming, throbbing come, but a real one, one that made her cry; then it built again and built and built and she *did* scream. She let his head go and screamed to the rafters.

Paul laughed. He was still slamming it into her. She was so wet his penis made a sound like fish being slapped in water. He had not even started to come.

"*Mignon,*" she said.

Then he came. Again, in the back of her mind, the thought of loving in French and of his screwing Francine dawned, then died, as he shouted and slammed against her exhausted body and shot into her. She opened for him.

She opened for him!

She wanted him to enjoy it!

Was that it? Was that what it took? She really wanted him to love her, to scream, to fuck her until he blotted out the existence of Francine Nathan.

Oh ferdomen, she thought.

She had stopped coming but she continued to cry. He stopped and fell upon her. Francine. Of course! *Of course,* he was in love with Francine. Now what was she going to do?

She would be lucky if he even called her. She would be lucky if she got to spend ten more minutes in bed with him. He didn't want her. He wanted French-talking, dirty-mouthed Fran.

Oh, Francine, go fuck yourself, Francine.

Paul took her out to dinner and took her home and she did not hear from him again for several days. When the phone did ring (she had made sure he knew where she lived and what her name was) it wasn't Paul, it was Chick Mandreaes. Even Roger did not call in that three-day period. Even Carol Roper was too busy with her executive to spend much time with her.

Mandreaes wanted to take her out. He picked her up at her place, took her out for a drink, looked too formal for what she had on (a purple satin slip dress, Bonwits, $159.95, very clingy, slightly flared short skirt) and said so.

She made him come back to her place so that she could change to the outfit she had bought with his money, the crushed velvet dress and matching coat. Then they went to the Persian Room of the Plaza to meet two dreadfully dull people, one of whom was some sort of business acquaintance of Mandreaes'. She danced her ass off that night. Still thinking of Paul. And she didn't let Mandreaes near her. She didn't even let him kiss her goodnight. He didn't say he would call again.

Chapter Three

Jeanette had broken with Morris Levy.

She made certain changes in her appearance. She took to wearing her hair straight back without a part and hanging full behind like a fat pony tail without a visible pin. A barrette tucked under her hair just at the back of her head gave it the desired effect. She changed her make-up, too. She used more shadow on her eyes and more mascara. She stood straighter, walking with a brand of defiance.

The changes helped. She found she could cure herself of the habit of thinking of Morris day and night. Three weeks after their break she no longer felt constantly depressed. By the time she met Daniel, the buyer from the Midwest, she was capable again of having a good time. But then came the incident with Karen and John—which Karen had convinced herself had never happened—and Jeanette broke with Daniel and no longer saw him when he came to town fresh from his hellish wife.

For a time she took up with a salesman who knew her Uncle Tim slightly and who liked her to wear kookie undergarments: panties with lips painted on them, panties with fringe hanging down like hair, brassieres with holes cut for the nipples, brassieres with fringe hanging off them like hair. Then she met Harvey Schapiro, the young man who worked with Karen at Hilt, and by the end of February was still going out with him.

She didn't dwell on the fact that he reminded her of Morris. She just told herself that another Jew would be a nice change of pace from toe-suckers and underwear fetishists. Another fairly healthy, fairly intelligent Jew. But this time, she would not tell him about her past. About being the kind of girl that gets rubbed up and down against (and worse) on subways. About the period after Barry the homosexual when she had practically insisted that every man with whom she got alone do something to her. About Uncle Tim and his afterhours raid. About Waterbury.

Even when Harvey confessed to *his* own somewhat kinky sexual past, Jeanette remained continent, refusing to impart a single instance of similar experience; she controlled an almost overwhelming urge to show him up, to share with him at least part of her own lurid past.

Harvey was tall, thin and had features that were attractive, but taken singly, somewhat too large for his face. He wore his hair quite long in the back and had sideburns that curled up just before they reached his jaw. Like many men lately, he wore bright, modish clothes, wide paisley or striped ties, bold striped shirts and an occasional double-breasted jacket. He made his confession to her one night while slightly stoned. They were in the living room of Jeanette and Karen's railroad apartment while Karen was out with a man she had met through Francine Klein, a Frenchman named Paul. Jeanette had her reasons for thinking ill of Karen's date. Her reasons derived from her hatred for Francine who, to Jeanette's mind, was responsible for her break with Morris.

"When I was in college," Harvey said, "I had a roommate named Stringham."

"And?"

Harvey was lying on the couch, the one she had inherited from Barry, and Jeanette was sitting on the rug below him.

"Stringham became, well, he became a sort of kookie

sexual partner, not that we ever did anything to each other, really."

"What do you mean, really?" Jeanette asked quietly.

"I never touched him, he never touched me."

"What did you do then?"

"You won't believe it."

Jeanette laughed. There was very little she would not believe. "Try me."

"I was lonely, I suppose, and Stringham, well, Stringham was nuts . . . bananas."

Harvey was always saying someone was bananas.

"And?"

"He used to bring home grapefruit from the market in the college town."

"Where did you go to school?"

"Amherst. He used to bring these grapefruit home and peel them."

Jeanette laughed again. "And?"

"He would ask me to strip and he would strip. Then he would get on the bed and kneel."

"Great," Jeanette said.

"Then I would throw these grapefruit at him, at his backside."

"Oh, come on."

"No. It really turned him on. He would get stiff. He never came or anything but he would get stiff as hell and moan whenever I hit him hard and dead center. It was sort of fun."

"And you would get stiff, too?"

"No. Never," Harvey said. "Still, it was sexual."

"I'll say," Jeanette remarked.

"Bet you've had *some* fairly wild experience," Harvey said, hoping to commiserate with Jeanette, to join with her in a mutual denial, perhaps, of their pasts, to avoid being left alone, high, dry and slightly embarrassed, by his confession.

But Jeanette would not bite. She wanted to tell him about the peanut oil parties back in Waterbury—where all the kids would rub each other with peanut oil, and then screw like crazy—but she wasn't going to tell him about her past. Not anything.

"No," she said. "Nothing like that. I was no virgin before you, buster," she declared with what was understood between them as mock toughness, "but the men I knew were pretty straight."

"Tell me about them."

"The hell," Jeanette said. Then she said, "Maybe when I know you better."

"How much better do you want to know me?"

He meant that he thought they knew each other pretty well. He meant that since they had slept together they had attained an intimacy and a shared experience which made them a couple, which set them apart, somewhat, from the rest of the world. It was fine that he thought that, but it wasn't so.

"Come on," Harvey said. "Give."

"Nope."

One of the reasons they weren't really a couple was that Harvey was a healthy, do-it-on-top, come-after-a-few-minutes, young man. If he had any peculiarities they were too well hidden for Jeanette to bring them to the surface. And he never suspected how inadequate, in the traditional sense, love-making was for Jeanette. Harvey was living in a sexual dream world as she had been with Morris.

Jeanette's sexual dream world had, in fact, been slightly worse than Harvey's. Jeanette had really begun to believe that Morris loved her. After all, he had continued to ask her to move in with him. The picture in his desk of Francine Nathan remained in his desk, was never even hidden further away: proof, to Jeanette's mind, that he had stopped thinking about the other woman.

"What time will Karen be back?" Harvey asked, innocently enough.

"Late, if at all," Jeanette answered. "She's really on the rebound."

"I know. The poor kid. She really was heavy for John."

"She thinks she's in love with this Frenchman. He's got a water bed."

"What's one thing got to do with the other?" Harvey asked with a laugh.

"You figure it out, you're the smart one."

Harvey laughed again and drained his beer from the

glass, putting the empty glass down on the floor again, asking, mutely, for a refill. Jeanette went to get it for him.

"If she would only go to see Morris," Jeanette said aloud.

"Karen?"

"Uh huh."

"How's he going to cure her of a Frenchman with a water bed?"

"I don't mean about that."

"Is he a psychiatrist? I thought he was a vascular surgeon."

"Oh, he is."

"So?"

"I don't mean about Paul. I mean, I think she's sick."

"Come on."

"I mean it."

"She's heartsick over John, that's all. She'll get over it. Listen, what was there between you and this doctor anyway?"

"Oh, I told you—nothing. We went out a lot together."

"Did you fuck him?"

"Mind your own business."

"I am!"

"Here, drink your beer."

"I want to know."

"There were no grapefruit involved, I can tell you that."

Harvey smirked, came close to blushing. Certainly, he regretted having told her about his roommate, Stringham.

If there had only been a way to set Jeanette's sexual dream world in order after walking in on Morris and Francine Nathan Klein, as she and John had set the apartment in order to help Karen believe that the scene with Daniel had never happened.

But there was no way to set Jeanette's sexual dream world in order. She was not Karen, or anything like Karen, at least in that sense. She did not have a long past of lying and of lying to herself to fall back on. She had always taken a certain pride in looking things straight in the eye, of seeing things as they were, without romantic nonsense attached, without any form of self-delusion.

At any rate, it would have been hard to fool herself about what she had seen at Morris'.

She had arrived there one night without being expected. Dr. Abernathy had told her early in the day that a heavy schedule of appointments would make it necessary to stay late at the office, and he had asked her if she could help him. She had said she would (she got double pay for overtime) and had called Morris to let him know.

"*O.K., doll,*" Morris had said, "*I've got surgery early tomorrow morning anyway.*"

"*Then I won't see you until tomorrow night.*"

"*Can you hold off that long?*"

"*I'll just have to, I suppose.*"

"*Ciao.*"

"*Ciao.*"

Then Dr. Abernathy received two phone calls within half an hour, both cancelling evening appointments. Jeanette tried to call Morris back but he had been called to the hospital on an emergency. He was to have put a pace-maker in the chest of an elderly woman the next morning and Jeanette guessed it was that case which had suddenly grown critical. She had an almost uncanny ability to predict which of Morris' patients was causing him the most anxiety. If she was right, and it was the elderly woman, there was a good chance he would lose her. And Morris was always hell after he had lost a patient.

"*Shall I leave a message for him, Miss Emerson?*" Morris' nurse had asked.

"*No. I'll get to him,*" Jeanette had replied. What she meant was that she would just go on to his apartment and wait, as had been their original plan. She had a key.

Harvey stopped playing with her hair and reached down to fondle her right breast. Her right breast was more sensitive than her left one, and slightly larger if you took the time to measure them carefully. Her nipple became excited and she lay her head back against the cushion of the couch to enjoy his caress.

That night she had left the office at six o'clock and caught a cab right outside the building. The sky was already darkening. On the curb outside Morris' West Side apartment building she looked up to see if his lights were on, if he had returned home yet. The lights of the apartment next to his were on, casting a weak yellow haze into the early winter New York air, but Morris' windows were dark. She hurried through the lobby and entered the waiting elevator.

It was probably because there had been no lights that she hadn't bothered to knock. She was sure that Morris was still at the hospital.

She had entered the living room, closed the door behind her, and was about to turn on the lights when she heard something in the bedroom. At first she was frightened; then she realized what the sound was.

Harvey reached down with both hands, changing his position on the couch again, so that he could hold both her breasts.

"Wait a minute," Jeanette said.

She straightened up and removed her sweater and let fall her brassiere, then leaned back against the cushions again. Harvey rubbed his mouth against her head and grabbed her gently, where he had been holding her before. Her left nipple distended, approximating the condition of her right one. She lay back and closed her eyes.

That night at Morris', she had moved quietly through his apartment to the door of the bedroom. The sounds she had heard were by then well identified in her mind. It was the steady slapping of flesh against flesh accompanied by an occasional grunt. She hadn't heard such obvious sounds of passion in quite some time, not other people's passion, not since her high-school peanut oil parties when the flesh of the participants had been just wet enough to cause their copulating to be extraordinarily noisy.

"Let's go to the bedroom," Harvey said.

"Not yet. I like this," Jeanette told him.

"*Oh, Jesus,*" the girl under Morris had muttered.

Morris turned and saw Jeanette.

The girl had her behind on a pillow and her legs wrapped around Morris' body, her heels had been hanging just above his backside, her arms had been holding his hairy paunch at the extremities, grasping tightly to the fat just above his hips, the fat that Jeanette had lovingly called his "motorcycle grips".

"*Don't let me intrude,*" Jeanette said.

"*Jan . . .*" Morris uttered. "*Oh Jan. . . .*"

She stood in the doorway without any intention of leaving immediately. She was enjoying the discomfiture she was causing them and, of course, she was suffering such great torment, jealousy, and anger that she had no intention of taking a step until she had it under control.

Her eyes adjusted to the dark of the bedroom and she stared intensely at Morris' face. He made no move to disentangle himself from the woman beneath him. Perhaps he couldn't have even if he had wanted to—the woman's legs were holding him forcefully against her. Then Jeanette recognized the woman's face from the photograph in Morris' desk. She stared long and hard.

"*Has this been going on very long, behind my back, I mean?*" she asked quietly, her tone failing to give any indication of her enraged emotions.

"*Jeanette . . .*" Morris said, but obviously could think of nothing to add.

"*You're Francine, aren't you?*" Jeanette asked.

"*This is a hell of a time for 'Twenty Questions',*" the woman said.

The woman's face had been contorted with passion. Probably, Francine had just been about to come.

"*Well, carry on!*" Jeanette said. "*Don't let me be a wet-blanket.*" She heard herself saying this, but didn't recognize her own voice. It was hoarse, strained, and about to break, like the voice of a teenager. Then she turned and walked out through the living room. Her lips were pressed tightly together, her eyes were wide with rage, and it felt as though there was something stuck in her throat. She opened the outside door, held it open, decided quite suddenly exactly what she was going to do, and then slammed it closed. She was still standing in the apartment.

She had stood in the dark living room waiting. After a moment she heard them talking.

"*Morris, you're soft as a sponge.*"

"*Sorry.*"

"*Here. Jesus, what a time to be walked in on. But let's save the talk for later, for afterwards.*"

"*Sure.*"

Jeanette tried to imagine what she was doing to him to get him hard again but couldn't. In Francine's place she imagined she would be putting her tongue in his ear and playing with the hilt of his penis; perhaps that was exactly what Francine was doing.

After a moment the voices started again.

"*Ahh, that's better. It's coming up again.*"

"*Uh huh.*"

"*Now, come on.*"

The sound of flesh slapping against flesh started again. What especially worked at Jeanette's jealousy was the fact that Morris had never pounded into her like that, not with such acoustical accompaniment.

"*Ahh, I'm almost there again, Morris. Oh, Morris!*"

"*You always were fast, Francine,*" Morris grunted.

They were making enough noise now, so Jeanette moved as quietly as she could into the kitchen. She had decided, while holding the doorknob in her hand a moment before, that she would use a pitcher full of cold water. But running the water in that old building made too much noise, might alert them, and anyway it would take too much time. She wanted to get in there before Francine started to come.

She opened the refrigerator door, took a half-gallon container of milk, knew by the weight that it was nearly full, and marched, not caring how much noise she made now, out into the living room again, past Morris' fancy antique icebox-cum-bar, to the doorway of the bedroom.

This time she walked straight in. Francine's mouth was wide open. She was already coming, or just on the edge, her eyes were tightly closed, her body strained, her own motion under Morris for the moment entirely stopped as she held her pelvis, and her clitoris certainly, up against him, not even grinding into him. Morris' head was turned to the far wall and he could not see her enter the room and obviously had not heard her yet. She marched over the bed and inverted the half-gallon container.

The milk descended over them, spilling into Francine's

mouth, splashing against her shoulders and running down her breasts and through her disheveled hair. Jeanette raised the container before it was entirely empty and then doused Morris' balding skull. This time, when she walked out into the living room and opened the outside door, she went out through it before slamming it closed.

"Let me get my shirt off," Harvey said.

"Mmmm."

Harvey sat up and got out of the rest of his clothes and Jeanette turned so that she was kneeling beside the couch. She was very excited now, her nipples were about as hot and distended as they ever got, her vagina felt moist and warm, her skin prickly and probably reddish. She always got a little color during sex.

Harvey reached to kiss her and their lips and tongues met, then she pushed him away and grabbed his penis. It was a nice penis—face it, girl, all of them are nice—thinner, perhaps, than Morris' but certainly as long and as straight. She held it by the base and took it in her mouth.

Harvey leaned back and smiled down at her and she closed her eyes. She gave great head; practice makes perfect.

After a minute or two she broke the embrace and moved back a little.

"My knees hurt," she said.

"Let's go to the bedroom."

"Why?"

"Someone might walk in."

She shrugged and held her shoulders up. She knew she looked awfully cute that way, her head cocked slightly to one side, her breasts, nipples distended, aimed in front of her, slightly turned up at the tips. It was an advantage to have small breasts, breasts that would not lose their shape.

"Throw a pillow down," Jeanette said.

Harvey smiled and tossed one of the three coarse, red, semen-stained pillows down on the rug. Jeanette set it on the floor where she could get her behind on it without hitting any of the furniture with her feet. She finished undressing and lay down.

Harvey descended over her and she slipped him inside.

He was lighter than Morris, so she could hold him down against her and he was still not too heavy. They began to move quickly, Harvey anxious already to reach climax. They had been petting for some time.

She could smell his beery breath and took it in in deep inhalations. She locked her legs around him, as Francine had done with Morris, and gyrated her pelvis at him.

It was not that Jeanette hoped to come. But if pretending to come was what it took to keep a man, then she might as well practice it. It didn't really matter with Harvey, but someday she might meet someone she liked as much as she had liked Morris. She wanted to be ready for that; she wanted to be able to get the job if she wanted it, the job of being the woman he was faithful to.

"Yaaa haaa!" Harvey shouted before he started to pound with ferocity and shoot into her. She moaned and shook for him and presto, he came all the harder. It did have something to do with pleasing a man. And pleasing a man, until further notice anyway, was the only way for Jeanette to get pleasure for herself. She shook for him and moaned and held him tightly to her.

Karen wasn't the only one who was very much on the rebound.

Sometimes the idea of Morris, or some sort of emotionally tactile equivalent of a vision of Morris, or some phase of her mind and heart which mirrored, or mimicked, or anyway depended upon Morris' personality for its existence, would well up within her, swell until it controlled, or at least colored, her entire day. At those times she would feel a brand of pain which was new to her, which, at any rate, she had not felt since she was twelve and infatuated with a boy she could not even remember. It did not please her to behave in so juvenile a fashion; she would have sold the pain she felt on those occasions for anything offered.

Where had she bought this? Where could she go to turn it in?

During a terrible March, when the weather would have been better suited to January or February in a more northerly climate, the times during which she actively missed

Morris became more frequent. Sometimes it felt worse than it had felt after she had first broken with him, walked out of his apartment leaving him behind covered with milk and mounted on Francine Klein.

During that March, she recalled, although to do so gave her even greater pain, the moments she'd had with him that were dearest to her. When he had effectively squelched Uncle Tim. When he had returned from the hospital one evening with a large test tube, corked and labeled, containing unwanted semen from the artificial insemination program.

"But where does the hospital get it?" she had asked, holding the test tube, staring at the milk-white substance at the very bottom.

"Do you like it? I realize it is something of an unusual gift."

"Like it? Of course I like it." Morris understood that she felt she was the most normal creature in the world when it came to the things she liked and did not like, that she felt other women, women who would not admit to liking semen, to wanting to be naked among naked people, to wanting men to do every variety of thing to her, those were the abnormal ones. Needing those things made her a little sick, but wanting them, wanting them was perfectly normal.

"I thought you would."

"But where do they get it?"

"Where do you think?"

"But who?"

"They screen men and hire them. It's funny, really, the men who sell their semen have to lead very strict sex lives."

"Making love exclusively to test tubes?"

"Something like that. They have to provide the hospital with their first ejaculation after forty-eight hours of continence."

"Forty-eight hours—my goodness," Jeanette said.

"And as soon as they ejaculate they have to rush the stuff uptown. It has to be used within hours. That's why this stuff is no good to them any longer. The woman didn't show up for her appointment."

"Do the women meet the . . . fathers?"

"Of course not," Morris said and laughed. It was when she recalled the laugh that she felt worst.

Pretending to be a normal woman, capable of climax, with Harvey Schapiro, was beginning to wear. The beautiful thing about Morris was that he hadn't once made her want to pretend to be something she was not. And he had never put her down about any of the things she had told him.

Then why, for the sake of sanity did she continue to refuse to speak to him? He still called; he still sent messages through Karen, who had at last become his patient. But Jeanette held out. Perhaps, in the final analysis, it came down to the fact that he had too many books, too many damn books in his apartment. Maybe it was still as simple as that. Jeanette would never be his equal. Francine might. Jeanette never.

"You're nuts," Karen had told her when they had been talking of just these things.

"Am I?"

"What difference should that make? He wants *you*, not a librarian."

Jeanette just shook her head. She had much earlier given up taking Karen seriously about anything, especially about men. Poor, sheltered, rejected Karen was the last person on earth to be able to offer dispassionate advice. Sympathy, sure, but rational understanding and good advice, never.

Karen shrugged, and looked down at the top of the kitchen table (the kitchen seemed to be the place in which they always had their serious talks). Jeanette felt she was thinking of John, of the brutal way he had given her up after leaving Hilt, of his unpredictability and volatility: characteristics which might easily lead him to their door one night, drunk, full of protestations of undying passion, and absolutely assured of entrance.

"Maybe Morris is the male prostitute Francine is raffling off, maybe that's what she was doing there, trying him out," Karen suggested.

"Very funny."

"Then you ought to buy a ticket, too. If you won him, you could get even with him."

"How?"

"You'd think of something."

On an especially cold March day, after Karen had left for work and Jeanette was getting ready to leave for Dr. Abernathy's office, the phone rang.

Jan sat on the couch and lifted the receiver.

"Hello."

"Hello, Jeanette, it's John."

"Well, long time no see. Karen left for the office. She works at Hilt, you know."

"Uh huh. It's not Karen I called to talk to."

"No one else here, John."

"Uh huh. I hear you're giving my buddy Harvey a hard time."

"Truth to tell, Mr. John, lately I'm not giving him any time at all. He was getting too serious, Mr. John."

"So he said. I had lunch with him yesterday."

"Lucky, lucky Harvey, to get so much of your time."

"Meet me for a drink tonight."

"No way."

"In that place on Madison Avenue we all had drinks in a couple of months ago, remember?"

"I remember, you were all over Karen like she was the only girl in the world. Remember?"

"About six-thirty? It's not far from the dentist's office."

"I told you I knew where it was."

"I want to talk to you."

"Sure."

"Will you be there?"

"Look, John, you're a good-looking guy and all that but I'm fond of Karen, know what I mean?"

"It's Karen I want to talk to you about."

"Oh, sure."

"Six-thirty?"

"Oh, hell, all right."

"See you."

She sat holding the dead receiver in her hand for a moment, then hung it up. *What the hell*, she thought, *what the hell*.

It was even colder by evening. And it was dark. It might have been mid-winter instead of the edge of spring. Jeanette walked into the bar, saw John alone at a table halfway to the back and joined him there.

"If Karen finds out about this. . . ."

"What do you want to drink?"

Jeanette told him and John waved down a miniskirted waitress, gave her their order, and then turned his fabulous smile and full attention to Jeanette.

If Jeanette had any doubts about John's intentions they were immediately dispelled by that look of his which, more than the smile and attention of any man she had ever met, seemed to say: there's no one in this world for me but you and what a good time we're going to have together.

"How's it going at the new job, John?"

"Fine. Just fine. How's your cigarette friend? What's his name, Daniel, wasn't it?"

"I haven't seen him in some time."

"Been concentrating on Harvey, eh?"

"Up until recently."

The waitress returned with their drinks and left them again.

"I thought you wanted to talk about Karen."

John looked away for a moment, then turned that look on her again. "I haven't that much to say about Karen."

"I didn't think so."

"But you came anyway."

Jeanette smiled.

"You're good at keeping secrets from her. She still thinks none of that happened, doesn't she?"

He meant that Karen still believed Jeanette and Daniel had never walked into the living room that night when she was drunkenly sleeping on John, mounted on John.

"She still believes it," Jeanette said.

"Let's get a bite to eat here and then go to a hotel."

"Blunt, aren't you?"

"I thought that's the way you'd like it."

"Maybe I do."

"Then say yes."

Jeanette looked off across the bar for a moment.

"All right," she said. "Why not?"

John laughed. "I don't think I ever met a girl quite like you," he said.

He got the waitress again and they ordered food. Fifty

minutes later they were walking uptown toward a hotel on Forty-eighth Street.

It was a large, bright room, freshly painted. There was a bright white bedspread on the double bed and reproductions of famous Picassos on the walls. The reproductions, and the fact that she was with John in the first place, reminded her constantly of Karen. But that was just what made the encounter interesting.

"You're actually kind of sweet," Jeanette said.

They were standing about six feet apart in the big room, facing each other in such a way that the bed was at the periphery of both their fields of vision.

"Sweet?"

"Sure. The way you're looking at me now. Like a little boy."

John smiled.

"You've been told that before."

He nodded.

"Well, I suppose it's true. It's probably what makes you so charming."

"Now you're the one who's being sweet."

That look of his. If she were more romantically inclined it would really get to her; or if she knew less about him.

John started to take off his jacket. His coat was already on a chair by the dresser. He lay the jacket on top of it and yanked at his tie.

Jeanette was wearing her coat and had a skirt and blouse under it. She made no move to undress until he had stripped to the waist. Then she let the coat fall and yanked her blouse out of her skirt waist.

"Mmm, mmm," John said.

He took his pants off while Jeanette removed her blouse and no-bra. She let her skirt fall and then walked to the bed. Her clothes lay in a heap on the floor but they were all permanent press stuff, and besides, the effect was worth it.

On the edge of the bed she slipped off her panties and panty hose, both together, and moved back on the bedspread, tucking her legs beneath her.

John watched her approvingly, his look changed distinctly now, but not to one of lust exactly. He looked self-contained, almost quietly happy, like a man sitting in his garden enjoying the colors of his flowers.

"There's no hurry, is there?" Jeanette said.

"Nice and slow."

He slid out of his boxer shorts and took off his socks. He didn't make a move toward her. He knew, of course, that he looked good in his skin, that he had good muscle tone and that his slim physique was attractive. He probably knew, too, from long experience, that she would want to take a good look at his genitals while his penis was still quiescent.

"What—"

"It's a vein."

"A vein? Bring it here."

John laughed, but did not move.

"A vein? It's the strangest thing. It's huge. Your whole damn apparatus is huge."

"Come on, get off the spread so I can pull down the blankets."

Jeanette shook her head with a smile and did as she had been asked. John approached the bed, took the covers down, and got in on his side.

Jeanette got back on the bed, kneeling and holding her left arm like the girl in September Morn. She had that kind of body, too, very softly subtle, thin, small-breasted, not wide in the hips.

John's penis began to stretch out and swell. They had still not touched but just watching her was obviously enough to excite him. He lay back, easily, still reminding her of someone taking his ease outdoors, and let his penis come up to the perpendicular. As it did so the relative size of the peculiar vein decreased, but that was only, Jeanette remarked, because the size of his penis swollen was so large.

"You know, she never. . . ."

"What?" John asked.

"She never told me it was so god-damn large."

"You've seen it before, honey."

"The hell. I didn't even notice it. It was stuck into

Karen, if you remember, and we put the lights out when she fainted."

"Oh, that's right, isn't it. . . ."

"That stupid jerk."

"How's that?"

"Karen, for not telling me. You know, she probably doesn't know, how big it is, I mean. She probably hasn't anything to compare it with."

John laughed charmingly. He didn't take the opportunity of replying that, contrary to Karen, Jeanette had plenty to compare it with. Not that Jeanette would have minded so much; still, it was nice of him not to say anything.

"Not that size is so important."

"Uh huh," John replied.

"It's fit. If you're too big, it hurts and it's no good for you, either."

"And no good for you. If it's too big, you can't get the old clit up against my hairy hairy bone."

"You're not so hairy." It was too bad he had said that, because she had suddenly and painfully thought of Morris.

"Well, shall we try it?"

His question helped her to quickly dispel the thought of her hairy Jewish doctor. She let her mind grab hold of the idea of doing it with John, of doing it now, wide-eyed and fast and hard.

"That's what we're here for, pal."

She threw herself at him and he came toward her in the same instant, arresting her motion toward him by grabbing her and turning her on her back, mounting her in the same motion, slipping his arms around her, one under her back, one under her backside, so that within less than a second they were ready, in the primal position; all they needed was to effect a joining.

This Jeanette accomplished deftly. John had his hips cocked so that his penis hung right at the tip of her vagina. She slipped him in and he pushed forward firmly, hurting her just a little when some of her pubic hairs caught, but once he was inside she was fine.

"Let's see now," John said breathlessly.

"Wait a wee minute," she said. He was nice on top of her. He was thin enough and had enough of his weight on his elbows not to weigh uncomfortably; and he was able not just to keep the bulk of his weight off her but to do so while grasping her buttocks: a thing Jeanette always appreciated in a man.

She slid her hand back down to her vagina, moved the troublesome pubic hair to one side, did the same on the other side, and then said, "All right, but don't break me in half. You're as wide as a damn salami."

John pushed in, pushed in further. "I forgot," he said. "I actually forgot."

"What?"

"You don't come. It doesn't matter if you can't get your clit up there."

"That bother you?"

"Hell, no, not now," he was talking very loudly, or his mouth was too close to her ear, probably both.

"Then fuck me, friend."

He was built too long. If she had opened her thighs by twisting them out, or if she had circled him with her legs, he would have hit bottom with every thrust. That would not have been any fun for him and less for her. So she kept her legs down and stretched them out parallel to his legs and just under them. As he began to move faster she squeezed her thighs together to put pressure on the part of his penis that could not get inside her. That seemed to help because he began to breathe harder and to search for her mouth with his.

He had been kissing her for some time, wet, loud kisses, covering her neck and shoulders and hair. When he found her mouth he inserted his tongue deeply, then extracted it and took hold of her lower lip with his lips. Then their tongues met, backed away, and then she took hold of his lower lip with her teeth.

He seemed to like that, too, because he moaned through his teeth and moved still faster. He was in awfully good physical shape to be able to keep up the pace he was going at without getting winded. She wondered whether he smoked; she couldn't remember.

She had to overcome an overwhelming urge to spread

her thighs, to encircle his waist with her legs. Instead she pressed them together even more firmly.

He broke their kiss. "Jesus Christ," he said.

She was getting hot now, too. Her vagina was good and wet and wide, but that was nothing unusual. But now she began to become excited. She let her hands roam swiftly over his back and down his thighs, back up and over his back. She grabbed him by the waist (where Francine Klein had been holding Morris that evening) then let go of him there and ran her hands back over his back, back down his thighs.

They began to make small sounds of passion almost simultaneously. This was very good, very good for him, certainly. He kept up the steady, rhythmic penetration of her vagina, kept up his wet, almost desperate kissing, and tightened his grip on her back and buttocks, squeezing hell out of her buttocks. She liked that.

He was so damn wide, wider than any man she could remember. He would probably do for her vagina what Barry had done for her anus, enlarge the damn thing, make her capable of taking an elephant.

He was breathing heavily by then, breathing straight into her mouth and inhaling her breath, making her inhale his. She wanted him to come; she wanted what she wanted from every man she had ever made love to: the semen to flow, the lifeforce, the seminal fluid, the dearest thing he had to give, to come out of him in hot, steady blasts.

She reached down and grabbed his buttocks, grabbed his lower lip again with her teeth, breathed into his mouth, pushed her thighs up and together, yanked them down, pushed them up again. God he was fast, rhythmic in his motion, like a practiced athlete.

A thin sheen of sweat covered his body now. She, too, was perspiring freely. She was about as hot as she ever got. Their quick coming together after their slow undressing and patient, naked conversation had caught her a little by surprise.

"I'll wait for you," he breathed.

Was he crazy? She had told him; he knew as well as she did that she never came.

She pulled his buttocks down to her as she clamped her

thighs, trying to reach his anus at the same time, to get her finger into it. That would set him off; she was sure of it.

She succeeded finally but nothing happened. He moved harder and still faster but he didn't even start to come. She could feel it when a man was ready, feel it long before he actually came, but there was nothing in John's lovemaking to give her any indication that he was close.

"I'll wait for you," he breathed again.

"No, You come. Shoot into me, John."

"You, too."

"Come on. Come on."

He slowed his pace. He continued to ram in with force but he was more controlled now. He felt loose; almost ready to begin building toward a fine climax, but the longer she waited to feel him start to build toward it, the further away it seemed to be.

She broke their kiss and put her tongue in his ear. She took her hand away from his buttocks and while he was separated from her, at the height of the arc of his lovemaking, she slipped her hand between them and grabbed the base of his penis.

Nothing seemed to help; and his pace was getting slower and slower. He moaned in a kind of desperation.

"Come, Jan, come, Love."

"You come."

"Start."

She tried to fake for him a little. She moaned, let her body shake, and was surprised and hurt, terribly hurt when he stopped moving.

"John?"

"I can't do it, not this way."

"Any way you want it. Any way at all."

"I don't think I can unless you come."

"We'll try it kneeling. Do you want to put that thing of yours up my ass?"

"No, not now."

"Get off then, here."

She twisted and he fell on his back, coming unjoined from her and immediately, without giving him a moment to cool off, she sat up and grabbed his penis and brought her head down to it.

She must have given head for fifteen minutes. He writhed and moaned and shook so hard she became frightened that she would lose the grip she had on him and he would choke her to death. She used her tongue furiously; she bit him lightly; she nipped at the very top of his penis and even tried rubbing the length of his penis rapidly with her palm. Nothing seemed to work.

Finally she shifted about rapidly on the bed so that he could get his mouth against her vagina. He let his tongue move rapidly over her clitoris. After a few minutes it got her so excited she took her mouth away from his penis. It did the trick, somehow, when she covered the end of it again she felt him getting close again, she moved her mouth quickly and firmly up and down as much of his penis as she dared take.

When he came he roared, sperm shot a good two feet into the air with his first shouting lunge, then the next few spasms shot up six inches, then he lay quietly, still spasming, still shooting weakly for another few seconds, until, sweating and panting, he lay exhausted on his back.

"You didn't," he said.

"No, John."

"Jesus Christ. I never met a frigid woman before; never met one that didn't come with someone. Plenty claim they are frigid, or their husbands do, but you really are."

"I really am, John."

"It's a shame," he said.

She could feel something happening, something that had happened to her before and would certainly happen to her again, she felt him grow cold, almost hateful, toward her.

"John?"

"It doesn't do much for a man's ego," he said softly.

She dressed while he regained his breath. If she had ever felt like crying in the last few months it was not when she had felt worst about Morris, missed him most, it was right now, when she could feel the full force of John's hatred; and hatred was exactly what it was.

He lay quietly, covered with sweat, eyeing her coldly as she dressed, neither offering a look nor a word of warmth or of thanks.

"It's so important to you," she said.

He didn't answer; he just lay there watching her dress.

It was still cold in the street when she left the hotel, cold and threatening rain. She caught a cab on the corner of Park Avenue and took it home.

Karen was not there, which was just as well. Jeanette was quite capable of lying about who she was with, otherwise she would not have gone with John in the first place, but he had made her feel so awful that whatever guilt she might otherwise have been able to quash now came to the fore: guilt about making love to the man Karen still mooned about, missed terribly, whatever she might say about her feelings for Paul.

"Oh, the hell with it," Jeanette said aloud.

She was about to take a shower when the phone rang. She went out into the living room and sat on the couch. She was dressed in only her robe and she pulled it tightly around her before lifting the receiver, just as if it was cold in the apartment.

"Hello?"

"Well, you haven't been answering the phone lately," a familiar voice said.

He was right; she had been letting Karen answer the phone.

"It's been a while," Jeanette admitted.

"Let me buy you dinner tomorrow night."

"No, Morris."

"It's been a long time, Jan. Give me a chance to explain."

"No explanations necessary."

"Jan . . . I miss you, doll."

"No, Morris."

"*Paella?*"

She hesitated. It surprised her probably as much as it surprised Morris when she heard herself say, "Pick me up here at seven."

"All right!"

She was so surprised she hung up the phone.

It took her some time to understand why she had done it. She was under the shower, just letting the hot water run over her shoulders and down her body, when it came to her. It was doing to Karen what Francine had done to her, it was doing something she had never been conscious of doing before: cheating. Cheat to cheat, she would meet Morris on equal terms. Since there had been no way of hurting him she had hurt Karen, instead, or at least laid the groundwork for Karen's certain pain if she ever found out. As a surrogate for Morris, Karen had been just what Jeanette had needed; and what better surrogate than the only other person she had come to love in the years since she had arrived in New York?

And it was John's terrible love-making, too. God, she was sick and tired of men who wanted her to be something she wasn't. Morris, at least, knew exactly who he would be taking to dinner. The non-comer. Pretty Jan, the lady eunuch. The sickest chick on Manhattan Island.

Chapter Four

Francine had sat on the edge of the bed wiping the milk from her face and shoulders with a large blue bath towel. There was a large black arm chair in the room which was, at the moment, holding Morris Levy, similarly covered with milk.

The look on Morris' face made Francine wish she had a camera. Never had she seen someone express such complete despair. He sat motionless, had made no effort to dry himself off, had only gone to the bathroom, retrieved a towel, and returned with it for Francine.

Fran rubbed her hair hard with the towel, then tossed it at Morris and watched it hit his face and fall to his lap. He made no move to pick it up.

"Oh, Morris."

There was milk in what there was of hair on Morris' head. Somehow milk had run down his front and clung to the great deal of hair he had on his chest. There were even traces of it in the blackness below his waist.

"Morris, Morris."

Francine started to laugh. The girl had long since left the apartment; this time, no doubt, for good. Thinking of her, thinking of seeing her standing next to the bed, thinking of helplessly watching her invert the double milk container, suddenly made Francine laugh.

Morris stood slowly and went out of the bedroom again. A few moments later Francine heard the strains of Beethoven's Ninth Symphony. Morris had turned on his record player.

She shook her head and stood, remembering, from the old days, Morris' love of Beethoven. He had once told her that whenever he felt particularly low he turned on either the Fifth or the Ninth Symphony.

She looked around for something to wear, decided against her own clothes which were in a heap on the floor at the foot of the bed, and slipped instead into Morris' white shirt. Clothed in that, she appeared in the living room to find him standing close to one of the stereo speakers, concentrating on the music. She sat on the couch and waited for him to speak to her.

She still had no idea who the girl was, except, of course, her name, that she had a key to Morris' apartment, and that despite Morris' brave effort to finish making love after the first interruption, he obviously cared very much for Jeanette.

Francine drew her legs up under her and watched Morris' naked form still standing motionless by the speaker. She was upset because he was upset, but felt simultaneously elated, absolutely elated that she had suddenly managed to be so important to him, even if just as the "other woman."

"Who is she, Morris?"

He didn't answer at first. Finally he turned and said, "Just a girl."

"Sure."

He scowled and crossing the room, went back into the bedroom to emerge a few moments later wearing his pants and a robe. He had finally wiped the milk from his head.

Actually it had been propitious, although she was sure that Morris would not agree with her, that they wound up in bed at all. Fran had arrived unexpectedly, fully intending to seduce him if she could, but not really counting on it. She had found him despairing over the death of a woman he had operated on late that afternoon. If he had not been so upset about this woman, Francine had realized immediately, he would not have been that easy. He had wanted to shake the despair and to take the anger out on someone; she happened to be handy. Now the despair had caught up with him again. She could see it in his eyes as he sat down on the far end of the couch.

"I'm sorry, Morris."

"Let's talk about something else."

They sat silently, listening to the music. Finally the first movement of the symphony ended.

Francine said, "Let's get married, Morris."

"No way."

The exchange occurred so quickly, had arisen so unexpectedly, that it took several minutes for Francine to take in what had been said.

"You're a permanent part of my mind, Morris."

Morris looked across at her and then away. Naked, he had the look of a large, plump, balding bear. "I love you, too, Fran, but no way, no way will I marry you."

"Why not, Morris?"

He didn't answer immediately and Francine continued, "I used to write letters to you that I never mailed, even while I was married to Klein, you were always the only one who would understand what was happening in my head."

She was presenting an argument. He countered, "Marriage to you would be like war, Francine. It's not what I need or want."

"War?"

"Yes, of course. Mind against mind; will against will. Of course war."

"What do you want then?"

"I want to be a doctor, Francine. I want to come home and get a rubdown and a drink and a kiss on the small of the back. I want a woman who is grateful to me just for existing. I don't want to have to win her every day by the force of my wit and personality."

"I see."

"Put it down if you can. Put *me* down. I don't mind."

"You're saying you want to marry someone small, someone without intelligence. Great, there are plenty of women like that around, society turns them out by the bushel basket; you'll have no trouble finding one."

"Oh, really?" Morris replied without rancor.

A calm had settled between them. Neither of them was smoking or drinking or attending to anything but each other and what was being said; still, there was no intensity, no forced concentration. It was light and easy, most probably because they had just had sex, but also because that was often the way they were with each other. Morris was right, however; they were also often at war.

"Yes, really. What do you think the movement is all about, Morris?"

"Ladies' lib? I think it's all about the working out of the personal salvation of those who are deeply immersed in it."

"Bullshit."

"A substitute for religion, or a substitute for psychoanalysis, or a substitute for character."

"By which I take it, you mean, mind."

"I suppose."

"You don't really want to talk about this now, do you?"

"No."

Fran got off the couch and walked over to the stereo set. She lifted the plastic dust cover, turned the record, pushed the lever to reject and watched while the disc fell to the turntable and the needle arm started to move. Then she replaced the plastic cover, lowered the volume by turning the dial, turned to face Morris and said in the brief space before the second movement of the symphony began, "So. So. You vant to be a doctor, Morris."

She spoke in a heavy East European accent (mimicking, really, her father whose heavy accent had driven V crazy when she had lived with Fran's brother Ivan in Bayonne).

"So. So. A nice Jewish boy who vants he should be a doctor. Goot. Vy not?"

The second movement started and Fran quieted. She stood still, listening, and watching the tired and despairing man to whom she had just proposed marriage; she watched him watching her right back, calmly, with total scholarly restraint, without evincing the least necessity or desire to win an argument with her, to convince her of the justice of his own position, to do anything, in fact, but be a vascular surgeon. She envied him his continence, his calm; and, of course, she knew he had been right when he had forecast that marriage for them would be war. Declared. Violent. Without quarter.

Too bad, she thought. *Too fucking bad. Healthy heads are hard to find.*

Several weeks later Francine was back in that little isle of Lesbos in the East Twenties, her friend Mel's third floor apartment—the apartment Mel still shared with Jaspers, the tongue wagging pomeranian.

As usual, Jaspers sat on the hassock near the air chair, eyeing his mistress, tongue out, panting lightly. Francine was in a canvas sling chair opposite Mel, who sat with her feet up on the couch. It was early evening, too early, really, to be drinking heavily, but Francine and Mel both held their second tall glasses of V.O. and water.

Mel said, "I never thought they would go for it."

"I know."

"I suppose, when you think about it, it makes sense. But not one of the girls thought it was a bad idea; in fact, they all thought it was a great idea."

"It is a great idea," Francine said without any attempt at modesty.

They were talking about the proposed auction of a male prostitute. At a meeting of the Radical Lesbians a week before the group had decided to sponsor the raffle. It was understood that there might be legal complications but if any group in the country was ready at that moment to take on the establishment, it was the Radical Lesbians. Of course, Fran might have gone to the Weather Women with her idea, but the idea of being placed under F.B.I. surveillance did not appeal to her. Anyway, she wasn't quite ready to resort to blowing up banks. Not just yet. Explosions in consciousness was what she had decided to pursue.

"You've contacted a lawyer?" Mel asked.

"Yes."

"And?"

"He said it was out of the question. We would be sure to be prosecuted unless we did the thing *sub rosa.*"

"Which would defeat your purpose."

"Or unless we arranged to sell tickets only to members of one organization."

"I don't follow."

"Well, we wouldn't be selling raffles exactly, we would be accepting membership in a club and holding a door prize at our first meeting."

"Loverly," Mel said.

"Yes, very clever. I would never have thought of it."

"Of course you would have, if you were a lawyer. That's what they're for."

"Then we go."

"As far as we're concerned, we go. What now—print the raffles?"

"The membership cards," Fran corrected her.

"All right. How much will it cost us?"

Francine shrugged. "I have to find the prize first."

"Of course. I thought you already had someone in mind."

Fran laughed. "I wish I did. Now it gets down to the nitty gritty; I have to go hunting for a male whore."

Mel laughed this time. "I don't envy you your search."

Francine drained the last of the V.O. and water from her glass and Mel stood to refill it for her.

"There must be a thousand male whores in Harlem."

"That's not the idea," Francine said.

Mel was standing in the kitchen, putting ice in Fran's glass. Fran could see her through the open door. "What do you mean?"

Fran sighed. "It just wouldn't be right. In a way we would be exploiting blacks, wouldn't we, or at least taking advantage of their already exploited position."

"So you want a *white* male whore?"

"That's right. A black would add a dimension to the thing I don't want . . . or subtract a dimension."

"I understand. But where are you going to get this buck-o, Fran?"

Mel returned with the drink and the question hung in the air of the small living room, unanswered.

"I don't even know where to start," Fran confessed.

"You'll think of something, honey."

Mel went back to the couch and arranged her short, stocky form in much the same way she had been sitting before. Mel's hair was even shorter than it had been months before when Fran had first brought her the idea of raffling a man. She looked good though, in her own, tough, flat-chested way.

"What are you smiling about?" Fran asked.

Mel sipped some of her drink and said, "It's just that you always look so . . . so fulfilled, Francine."

"Hah!"

"No, really. I'll bet you've got one hell of a sex life."

It was Fran's turn to smile. She was thinking of Morris.

"You know, Mel, after my divorce, separation really, I tried to lay off."

"Good with words, aren't you."

"But it didn't work. The hornier I got, the less clearly I thought. I was ready to blow up buildings, join the Weather Women, anything."

"It may come to that yet."

"It may, I suppose, if the war continues much longer. But now, hell, a good man or two and I feel pretty fine about things."

"That's just what I mean. You radiate it."

Fran leaned back in the canvas sling. "Do I really?"

"I envy you."

"Thanks. I proposed to a man a few weeks ago," Fran confessed.

"You what?"

"I asked a doctor friend of mine to marry me."

"A doctor no less. How bourgeois of you."

"It was no cop-out, Mel. He's a good head."

"When's the date?"

"He refused my offer."

"Oh."

"I see him now and again, and another man, a French-man."

"Oh, a Frenchman. That's better."

"Wrong. Mel, it's the Frenchman who's the bourgeois."

"I do wish," Mel said, "that you were more inclined toward our way."

"Can't help it," Fran said with a smile. "Must be a congenital problem I have, wanting men."

Fran leaned back still further, resting her head on the high iron rib of the sling chair. Jaspers lay down on the hassock and yawned and Mel got up again, this time to fix her own drink.

When Mel returned to the room she came and stood behind Fran's chair and touched Fran's hair with her open palm, stroking it softly.

"If you would only try, Fran dear, you don't know what you're missing."

"Don't I?"

"No, I don't think so. It's different, Fran. Forget me, the way I feel about you . . . *have* felt about you for quite some time . . . ever since the first time I saw you, in fact."

"In that Village bar."

"Yes."

"Sorry, Mel."

Mel shrugged, stopped stroking Fran's hair and regained her place on the couch. "As long as I'm being so romantic, Fran, let me say one more thing."

"I almost wish you wouldn't, Mel."

"Just this. I'll always be here; should you ever change your mind, think of me. All right?"

"I promise, Mel."

"Being able to swing both ways, it's an advantage, adds something to life."

"I'm sure it does."

The conversation ended there and a few minutes later Fran left. Out of politeness Mel asked her to stay a little longer but Fran had to meet Morris. She caught an uptown bus and watched the dull, yellow lights in the windows of the buildings as she rode uncomfortably along.

As long as Morris tolerated her, she would go on seeing him. She had an idea that the more she saw of him, the more she talked to him, the quicker she would disabuse herself of the illusion of love. The more facts she could gather, hard, cold facts about him, the length of his penis, the size of his bald spot, the names of his relatives, the complaints of his patients, etc. etc., the more easily she would be able to deal with her attraction to him. In Francine's opinion love prospered on mistaken notions, on rosy

false impressions. Certainly love that did not include a
meeting of minds could be described that way, was infatua-
tion, and although painful to put an end to, could be killed
by deliberate, decisive mental discipline.

If, on the contrary, her feelings for Morris depended entirely upon mind, then the fact that he had given up any attempt to engage her in intellectual battle would also kill
what she felt for him. It was just a matter of time. In the
meanwhile, she continued, too, to see Paul, to remind herself that more than one man could satisfy a woman, to
commit a deliberate act of infidelity to her feelings for
Morris.

Watching the haunting lights of the city, listening to
brakes of the bus as it drew to a stop every few blocks, listening to the sound of the doors opening and closing,
smelling what she would always be able to recognize as the
odor of a New York City bus, Francine fell back on an old
habit of mind, linking her own reflections about New York
with Miller's.

Wasn't it in *Capricorn* that Miller said if any man were
ever to enunciate what he truly felt about New York City
the whole place would fall to the ground, the buildings
tumble, the havoc be completed? He had meant it artistical-
ly, of course. He meant that if anyone were capable of ever
saying that, the city would lose its importance, its monolith-
ic, overwhelming importance to all those who had come
under its influence. He meant its message: that the individ-
ual is meaningless, insignificant, hopeless, would no longer
be heard. It was too bad, Francine thought, that she would
never be the one to do the enunciating.

Finally the bus arrived at her stop and she got off and
walked the two blocks to Morris' building. Morris let her
in and returned to the couch and a glass of scotch.

"I stopped at the deli. There's coldcuts and rolls in the
kitchen," he said.

"I've eaten. Morris, where am I going to find a male
whore?"

"I was wondering when you would try to figure that
out."

"All right. But help me now. Harlem is out."

Morris nodded. She didn't have to explain to him why

she didn't want a black man.

"How about an amateur, someone like that Village friend of yours, John Blunt?"

"He would do it, I suppose."

"Of course he would; for a price."

"But only as a last resort. The whole idea is to get a professional, to prove to the girls, to the world, that women aren't the only sex objects in it."

"Right on!" Morris said good-naturedly.

"Well?"

"I don't know, Fran. I suppose you go down to Forty-second Street and wander around. I suppose you find a male whore who is accustomed to dealing with homosexuals but who uses his profits on women. The bulk of them are supposed to be that way."

"The bulk of the male whores who cater to fairies?"

"That's right."

Francine poured herself a drink at Morris' bar. "How do you know that?" she asked.

"Read it someplace."

"Where?"

"*The New Yorker? Reader's Digest?* I don't remember."

Francine crossed the room and sat beside him on the couch. "Mel, my own dear gay friend, tried to make me again tonight."

Morris leaned back and closed his eyes. For once his thoughts were a mystery to her. Usually she knew almost exactly where he was.

"What? What's shakin' inside that head of yours, Morris?"

"You see," he said. "You would always be growing, changing. You've a restlessness, Fran, which would be anathema to me if you were my wife."

"You've been thinking about it?"

"Yes."

"I'm flattered."

"Your hang-ups," he said. "They're not the usual sort."

"Are you going to play shrink for me now?"

She was angry suddenly.

"Let me tell you what I think," he replied softly.

"All right."

"Some people can be cured of their hang-ups, of their games, of the need to play them."

"And?"

"But some can't be cured. That's because their hang-ups are set in the dead center of their minds, are exactly the pieces of ego-identification that makes them what they are. It's like a philosophical argument. You can't question definitional statements. Your hang-ups are exactly what defines you, what you define yourself as."

"As I say, I'm flattered you've been giving so much of your thought to the subject."

"I do love you, Fran, and you do turn me on, you always have, but it's no good. I haven't the energy."

"To go to war with me."

"Yes."

"That's exactly what you said two months ago. You've been doing all your mental work only to come full circle."

"No. I reacted on instinct then, now I can explain what I meant—it just isn't worth the aggravation."

Fran calmly—seized, in fact, by an icy calm—put her drink down in front of her.

"Have you set out to hurt me, Morris?"

"No. I don't think so."

"You sure?"

"This whole political involvement of yours; it's an extention of your having once wanted so much to write, like a female Henry Miller wasn't it? It's what makes you unique, in your own eyes as well as everyone else's. You couldn't give that up, not ever. You fall asleep with it at night, wake with it in the morning. And the aggression it's tied to, the whole manner in which you conduct your daily battles. . . ."

"I believe, Morris dear, that I'm going to change tactics."

He looked at her questioningly. He had no idea what she meant.

"I believe I will have a sandwich, after all," she said. He was sitting, sipping his scotch when she returned, which she did almost immediately. She walked up behind him and suddenly and effectively inverted over his head, his clothes, his couch the two-quart container of milk she had taken from the refrigerator.

He jumped at first, then sighed, and leaned back exactly as he had been before, holding the glass of scotch, and milk, exactly as he had been holding it before.

"You see," he said just before she left. "War. Out and out war."

Violent. Declared. Without quarter.

"A friend of mine gave me the idea," Francine said. "An old, dead friend."

"Dead? My, my," Garry said. "Isn't that too bad."

"Dead only to me," Francine told him.

"Oh. I see. I see."

Garry was something like the male equivalent of Mel. He was another old friend of Francine's from her Greenwich Village days. An art director at one of the more important advertising firms uptown, he was, in his off hours, taken to expressing an almost violent desire for members of his own sex.

He was short, blond, pockmarked and had his teeth capped. His unattractive features had long made it necessary for him to pay for his sex since he was also unwilling to form a lasting relationship with any man, fearing, he had once drunkenly confessed to Francine at a lonely back table of the Sink, that one of the men he wanted to penetrate might someday want to return the compliment.

"I can't bear the idea," he had said that night, long ago.

"And how much money did you say you would have to spend on this unique project?" Garry now asked.

Francine told him.

"That much? No problem, no problem at all. You will want the best."

"It is important that he not look like. . . ."

"I quite understand. He should appear terrifically masculine, correct?"

"Correct."

"No problem. Leave it to me."

This conversation took place in Garry's apartment in the East Village (not far from the baths on St. Mark's Place, infamous for the number and variety of homosexuals that frequented it) and a week later she received a phone call from Garry asking that she return to his apartment to meet a prospective applicant for the job she had offered.

As soon as she saw the man sitting on Garry's couch, though, she knew he would be perfect. He was exactly like a male equivalent of a Playgirl of the month. Tall, blond, superficially beautiful, he was dressed in a long-sleeved paisley shirt open over his brown chest. Without asking she knew he had received his tan from a sun lamp. His hair, too, was perfect, appeared almost artificial, was certainly done by an expensive East Side men's coiffeur.

Francine entered the room aware of the blush rising on her cheeks. How long had it been since she last blushed, for God's sake? She felt as she did at her first big date when she had been a large-busted, ignorant twelve-year-old.

"Fran, meet J-boy. J-boy, this is the young woman who may want to hire you. J-boy has been kind enough to break his busy schedule to appear here tonight, Francine."

Francine approached J-boy and extended her hand. Her hand was grasped tightly, held, then released quickly.

"Well," Francine said.

"Garry explained very little, actually," J-boy said in an intensely deep-throated voice. As he spoke he looked at Garry in exactly the same way, but exactly, that movie stars playing prostitutes always look at prospective Johns.

"It's simple," Francine said. "We want to hire you for several nights at a fixed price."

"We?" J-boy asked.

"The Radical Lesbians."

J-boy allowed his eyebrows to be raised in disbelief. Then he said softly, "You don't look it, darling."

Garry laughed. "She's not, you big idiot. She's only working with them. I told you, she's got them to sponsor the raffle."

"Yes, the raffle. Do sit down and tell me about this raffle."

Francine sat and explained the whole thing. She felt less nervous while she was speaking but as soon as she had finished she felt her cheeks burn again.

J-boy laughed. "I think it's a wonderful idea," he said.

"Then you'd be interested."

"Oh, yes."

"And the money is satisfactory."

"Couldn't be better," J-boy said.

"Then you'll be there at the drawing."

"Of course. Are you sure, however, that I will do?"

Francine smiled. J-boy gave her goose pimples. She was able to sympathize with the men she knew who had relations only with professionals.

"I don't know how I could be sure," Francine said.

"Oh my, oh my. J-Boy, please show her," Garry said.

"Really?"

"Yes, of course," Garry insisted.

Francine smiled wanly. Garry had been mixing a drink for Francine which he now handed her. She tasted it, then sipped it again before she realized she was drinking rye. She hated rye.

J-boy stood. He was even taller than Francine had thought. She stared at his pants.

It was ludicrous. He wore such tight slacks and dressed his sexual parts in such a manner that they were evident in outline and evidently quite large. Francine thought of boys in high school embarrassed by their erections.

"Go on, J-boy, show her," Garry said and sniggered.

J-boy loosed the clasp of his wide belt, unzipped his fly and lowered his pants.

He wore sheer, white bikini underpants with a black pouch, like a codpiece, for his privates. He lowered these, too.

"You see," Garry said.

His penis was enormous, or at least it had the appearance of being enormous; probably it was no longer than Paul's, but this was not an erect penis but a languid one. Or was it?

"It's semi-hard," Garry explained. "He keeps it that way."

"How?" Francine asked calmly. Her embarrassment had faded entirely. As soon as J-boy's pants were down she felt in complete control not just of herself, but of the situation.

"Willpower," Garry answered for him.

"Is that true?"

"Almost. You see, I almost never have an orgasm."

"What?"

"I almost never have an orgasm."

J-boy corrected his clothes, pulling up his unique underwear over his unique penis (mauve in color, oily, somehow, blond—probably dyed—pubic hair), then adjusting his pants and reclasping his belt.

"But how do you manage it?" Francine asked, laughing.

"Tell her, J-boy," Garry insisted.

"Nupercanol."

"What?"

Garry laughed. "It's an anesthetic. He rubs himself with an anesthetic."

Francine made a small noise at the back of her throat.

"Tell her what you use when it gets sore," Garry pressed him.

"Garry, darling, you'll make me give away all my secrets."

"Tell her."

"Lanolin," J-boy said. "After much use, lanolin . . . Would you like a demonstration? For a small down-payment of that sum you mentioned before, refundable if you are not entirely satisfied."

"I haven't the money on me."

"I'll lend it to you," Garry said. "If I may stay and watch."

"Some other time," Francine said.

"Francine, you're so square," Garry said, evidently quite excited by the idea.

"Believe me, Garry," Francine told him. "J-boy here is exactly what I want, exactly what *we* want. I don't need a trial."

"And you said you weren't one of *them*," J-boy said.

"Ha," Garry exclaimed.

"If you give me your phone number, J-boy, I'll call you in plenty of time to be at the drawing and I'll tell you when you'll be expected to perform."

"*Perform!*" Garry said.

"And I'll see you get a down-payment beforehand."

"All right, my dear."

"And you look great, J-boy, but please don't say 'my

dear' and 'darling' to any men when you're with the ticket holders. You understand what we're trying to do?"

"Yes, darling, I understand. You don't mind if I call you darling, darling?"

"Love it. Write your phone number down. Garry, a million thanks, but I'm going now."

"Square," Garry said with a smile. "You're never to be forgiven."

"I might make him come, Nupercanol or not; *then* I'd never be forgiven by you."

"Oh, you bitch," Garry said. "All you women, you're exactly alike."

On the bus again, a New York City bus, crossing from the East to the West Village, and Paul's apartment the destination. It struck her suddenly, at exactly that moment when the doors hissed to a close behind a bald man with a squint who boarded on Third Avenue, that she had been behaving like a fool, that she had allowed her feelings for Morris to dominate her personality, to put her away from herself, to turn her—lord love a duck—into some queer breed of bourgeois bohemian.

Turn down a free fuck? Francine Klein née Nathan turn down a free fuck? Unthinkable! Yet she had done it. The girl who thought of herself as a female Henry Miller had been transformed by the illusive power of love into something far less: an ordinary wench.

Where had Miller said that making love to a whore was a wonderful thing because it enabled him to commune with every man who had ever made love to that whore before, who would ever again, who had ever made love to any whore; to commune, in short, with the entire race of men? Cock. Keep your mind on cock, girl, and off Morris Levy, and away from the terrible idea of marriage. Marriage! Good God, Francine girl, what came over you? Some chick pours a quart of milk over your head (two quarts then) and that silly baptism is enough to convert you to the religion of America: Ordinarism. Preached daily on TV tubes coast to coast. White bread and air-conditioning. Keep your mind on cock, girl. On that slippery-looking organ of

J-boy's, on Paul's uncircumcised, romantic erection, on the great cock in the sky. Marriage, yech!

This is the time to rededicate, then, to start afresh. This is not the time to surrender. O.K., you've faced it, you'll never write well, you'll never do it with paper, but you're starting to do it with politics. So rebaptize yourself not with milk but with semen. Hadn't Morris told her that Jeanette carried a vial of semen? Well, Jeanette, whatever her mental equipment, whatever her intellectual ability, Jeanette *knew*, knew just what Francine had forgotten, that constant attention to the underside of life was all one could hold on to sanity with, was all one had to fight off the infernal mechanism of society with. My lord, girl, you haven't cursed up a storm in months. Months totally lost. Lost!

She had turned down Mel. Why? She had turned down J-boy. Why? Fastidiousness? Absurd! Well, she knew why. Morris, or rather her love for Morris, had turned her into the typical female animal, craving domesticity, craving regulation. She remembered a philosophy professor who had taught her Wittgenstein when she had been in college. (Eons ago.) The professor had said that in order to stay in the same place in his course one had to run very fast. What made her think that the sort of life she wanted to lead was any different from that? Of course it wasn't. It was very much the same. In order to keep hold of her peculiar vision, her peculiar sanity, she had to run damn fast ALL THE TIME. Fuck you, Morris and your glib little psychoanalytic analysis of my mind. Where was I when I thought you would understand? Where was I when I thought you alone in the entire stinking city of New York, in the entire world, would appreciate the first principle of Fuck and Refuck? Sanity, Morris, is *not* surrender. We are beasts, Morris dear, naked apes, sexually dominated, abhorring the vacuum of monogamy, mentally constrained by constancy. Goddamn, I have to loosen up. Back to the Sink? Back to John the Hard-on Blunt and impotent E. K. Gare? If necessary, sure. If that's what it takes.

Damn, I'm going to be a force again. A hot-blooded, fighting, dirty-mouthed, brother-fucking force. Look out, New York, Francine is back. Away for a bit but back at last. Get your head straight, New York. This damn raffle is only a start. Hooray, Mr. Miller and howdy. Sorry to have been abroad. An ordinary, urge-denying, domesticity-hungering, All-American, made-of-white-bread-dough-and-mindless broad. Now let's see what trouble I can get into. Let's shake 'em up, Fran girl.

Visit Mel? Call J-boy? Both if it comes to it. Join the Weather Women? Why not all three? Hooray and Howdy mother-fucker Miller. Your A-one disciple is back and in gear. What I want now is a drink to seal this bargain with. Can't this scum-eating driver move this shit-tank any faster? Can't you see what a burden you have aboard, you urine-toffing, flatulation-fondling, infant-fucker, you syphilitic, simian, toe-sucking Charon? Come, cocksucker, let's get this ferry to hell and gone.

PART THREE

Chapter One

This room stinks.

It was spring and Karen had been in the hospital, in that lousy double room, for nearly a month. She could not, of course, despite her late, frequent admonitions to the contrary—talk of the large house in Connecticut, of the numerous valuable paintings it held, of the automobiles, of her father's emminent position in the community—afford a private room. She could not even afford the room she was in.

This stinking room.

The overwhelming fact that she had narrowly escaped death, that Morris had made a brilliant (and now famous, at least within the massive confines of the hospital complex) diagnosis, was no longer so overwhelming.

Morris had said, "Only people in hospitals, police too, perhaps, have any idea any more of how close we all are to death. Everything in this television world of ours is a step away from reality, it's like living on stage all the time, or perhaps in the orchestra, as if we weren't really alive."

And Karen had said, "I suppose you're right."

"Karen, you're all right now, but that growth you had in

your heart, that made you short of breath, that made you faint, that turned your hands blue, Karen, that growth was going to kill you quite dead."

"I don't know what to say. Thank you."

"I'm not after your thanks," Morris had said and laughed. "I'm trying to explain something to you. I'm trying to tell you that the place you're at, the place where your mind lives, the way you see things, the big TV screen through which you see things, all your fantasizing, Karen, it's as unhealthy as any physical condition you had, maybe more so."

"I—"

"I'm sorry I have to be so rough on you, Karen. But you won't be cured, you know, not in my estimation, until you're ready to leave this hospital set to face life without your usual glass barrier between yourself and everything that happens in it. You're not just my patient, you know, you're a friend of Jeanette's, and you're *my* friend, and that makes the responsibility I have all the greater. You've got to be tough, Karen."

Unfortunately, I knew what he meant.

That wasn't the first time Morris had brought her up short. Once he had asked her whether she was afraid to come to the hospital and she had denied it. He had said, "You're a liar, lov, a beautiful liar. You were born a liar and you'll die a liar unless you come to the hospital. After I operate you can go back to your Frenchman, his love oils and his water bed."

How right Morris had been. More than he knew.

It was spring and she was ready, perhaps, at least often ready, to be the kind of woman Morris meant. And here she was, stuck in a hospital bed, at sixty dollars plus a day. She would be paying for her sojourn here for the rest of her life.

Strangely, it was not Morris' influence that had changed her so much, or at least enabled her to see how it was she had to change, to see that she had to stop lying, not to others so much, but to herself. It was knowing Francine that had paved the way for Morris. It was knowing Francine that had awakened her to what maturity was all about.

When she got out of here she was going to join Francine.

She was going to help her fight for women's liberation. She had told Morris that and he had nodded, smiling, and said, "Great. Just great. Maybe that's just the sort of thing you need. If there's any unreality connected with Fran and those ladies-from-hell of hers, at least it's not the kind of unreality we're worried about."

Sometimes Karen wished Morris had explained himself further; still, she had a general idea of what he meant.

She saw Morris daily, mornings, when he made his rounds. After he had gone she stared out the window at the East River. From her window she could see the building on Welfare Island in which the fire department trains recruits. She would lie there and watch the boats going up and down river and wish to hell she could get up and get out into the April weather.

Just lying there made her horny. And she would not masturbate. She would not masturbate. She had to stop fantasizing. On all levels. Morris had saved her life; it was up to her to save her mind.

For about a week after the operation she had decided that she was in love with Morris. Although Jeanette visited almost daily, although Paul came (and with him all the sensuality of his bedroom), it was Morris she found she was thinking about most of the time. In that week after the operation he spent much more time with her, often alone with her because the other bed in the room was then unoccupied. She would moon at him, smiling languidly, enjoying her role as the recovering patient, saved by the brilliant, courageous young doctor.

Courageous was not the wrong word, either. He *had* been courageous. That was what had made the diagnosis brilliant, one of the interns had explained to her. It was impossible to know whether the growth Morris had said was there, was *actually* there, impossible to know, that is, until they had in fact opened her heart and looked in.

Opened my heart, very funny, looked in . . . pretty messy stuff in there I'll bet . . . pretty damn gunky stuff.

Morris, of course (wasn't he at least as brilliant as Francine?) had recognized that mooning look she shot at him mornings and had come down hard on her for it. In fact, that was the beginning of his lectures to her, lectures which might be entitled: How to Develop Hardness of Mind, or, perhaps: How to Live.

"Come on, Karen, cut it out," he said one morning.

"What?"

"Come off it. You know damn well what. Don't fixate on me. If you've got to be a teen-ager, fixate on some movie star. It will make your life, and mine, all the simpler."

"Morris, I—"

"Don't play dumb. You know exactly what I mean."

He left then and she had all day to think about what he had said. The next morning she said, "I'm sorry about yesterday, Morris. I—"

"Dr. Morris!"

She laughed. "O.K. Dr. Morris."

"Look at your roommate. Jeanette isn't that way. There isn't a tougher chick around."

"Tougher?"

"One who sees things for what they are. No romance in Jeanette, no, sir."

"Or in Francine?"

Morris quieted, looked ponderous (his I'm-not-really-a-doctor, I'm-really-a-Jewish-intellectual-pretending-to-be-a-doctor look) and said, "That's something else again. But you're right. Fran doesn't fixate, doesn't moon, and doesn't romanticize . . . about men."

"Oh? What does she romanticize about, Morris?"

"Shut up or I'll take your temperature."

"Oooh."

"That's more like it, now. Sex up front, not through rosy lenses. See you tomorrow."

"Morris?"

"Hmmm?"

"Send that good-looking young intern in, would you— you know the one I mean."

"Paul's bound to come today; that's his name, isn't it?"

"Paul? Yes, that's his name."

"Well, when he does, just in case you *do* have any ideas about letting him into bed with you, forget them. You're making a slow, very slow, recovery. You almost died. D-I-E-D, died."

"Oh, Morris, I was only kidding."

Paul did come to visit her later that day. He brought flowers and sat next to her for a full hour, the silence between them punctuated with inane remarks and terrible hospital cliches. It was so hard to talk in there, the antiseptic atmosphere, the regulation of the visiting hours, the unusual situation—Karen on her back, Paul sitting stiffly in an uncomfortable chair—combined to make it almost impossible.

Then, when he had left and Karen was alone again, she had a forceful, surprising revelation about him. She couldn't say why it had happened or how. Nothing much had been said at all. But there it was. Karen knew. Paul loved her. He always had. He loved Francine.

The revelation, of course, was accompanied by painful jealousy. There were moments, lying in bed staring at some show on her rented television, when the pain surfaced, stung her intensely. But these moments always gave way to a consideration of the other woman involved, to the fact that it was Francine, and the pain subsided. After all, hadn't Karen really been in love with John? She had kept that bitter truth hidden from herself, as she had kept most things hidden from herself, but Morris' influence, Francine's influence, and Karen's intimate brush with death, had all helped to bring those truths to the surface.

The truth, for instance, that my lying had always been a way of hiding from other people, especially from men.

Looking back, at the way she had met Paul, at the way he had acted toward her, at the way they had been together, all fortified her revelation. In retrospect the truth was clear. It was amazing that she had been able to keep herself from seeing it.

She had been with Francine at a bar with an Irish name on Thirty-fourth Street. She was taking one of her infrequent long lunches, discussing Francine's manuscript, explaining that while it was not suited to Hilt's needs, she, honestly, had admiration for it and regretted that she could not publish it. It was certainly the best single piece of writing she had seen, Karen pronounced, since she had been with the publishing house.

Francine sat nursing a Bloody Mary, holding the tall glass in both hands, fingers entwined around it. They had finished eating and were sitting on a booth toward the back of the bar. Karen had a drink, too, a scotch and water, if she remembered correctly, but she hadn't even touched it; she was too busy talking.

"It's all right to have a female point of view, of course. It's even desirable. But the girl has to be someone the reader can identify with. She can't be exceptional, you see. She has to be the girl next door, a secretary, a housewife, a college student, even a high-school student, a divorcée, someone, you see, the reader might have a chance of meeting in real life. Everyone knows that exceptional people have heavy sex lives, movie stars, gangsters, spies, artists, millionaires. That's why books about that sort of person don't sell well, at least not to our audience."

"You have a specific audience then?" Francine asked.

"Oh, yes. Hilt has been in business for years. Our readers recognize the Hilt insignia on the cover and buy the book because they know what they are going to get."

"A fortification of their masturbatory fantasies."

"Yes, that's right," Karen said. "Harvey Schapiro, another editor at Hilt, calls it the Hilt theory of mental masturbation. The first principle is that the girl, or the woman, be someone accessible to the reader."

"How beautifully disgusting," Francine said. "Shit!"

"I thought I explained that."

"You explained so much, Karen, I forgot a lot of it. This damn raffle has been on my mind. There are legal complications and I have no idea yet where I'm going to find our door prize. That's just between us, of course . . . But don't worry. I'll find him."

Francine took a sip of her Bloody Mary, then returned her glass to the table.

Karen said, "But you see what we need, why your book, although better written than any of the ones we publish, just can't be put into the Hilt Line."

"Somewhere else then."

"Oh yes, definitely send it around. I just can't help you by telling you where. I just don't know."

"But my—uh—heroine, isn't so extraordinary."

"Of course she is; she's an intellectual for one thing. And she thinks about men in a way that's all wrong."

"You mean she thinks about men the same way men think about women."

Karen nodded.

Francine snorted. "My Christ," she said. "I don't mind hacking, but to bolster male chauvinist pigs by contributing to the banal glut of propaganda that makes women out to be inferior, romantic, dependent, susceptible creatures, that may just be too much shit to crawl through."

Karen was hurt. She didn't know what to answer. Luckily she was saved by a distraction in the form of a dark, short young man in a bright red blazer, a striped blue shirt and a white ascot. He was very good-looking and staring at her, at Karen, as though he had known her all his life. Karen was bewildered by him.

"Oh, Paul, what the hell are you doing here," Francine said.

"I've come for lunch. My office isn't far away. Hello," he said, still staring at Karen.

In retrospect, of course, Karen realized he had behaved that way to make Francine jealous. It was the old: concentrate-on-the-chick-you-*don't*-want routine. At the time, however, Karen very nearly blushed.

"Paul, this is Karen, Karen, Paul," Francine said, evidently taking some private pleasure in introducing them. Karen, of course, had no way of knowing that Francine took a certain pleasure in introducing Paul to anyone ever since she had introduced him to "V Quim" as "Paul Schlong."

"Hello, Karen."

"Karen is my editor at Hilt," Francine said. "We're discussing business."

"Oh, well. I certainly will not disturb you then. But, *comment ça va,* Francine?"

"*Ca va bien, Paul, mais va-t-en, s'il tu plait, je vais te voir ce, soir, d'accord?*"

"*Comme tu veux.* Karen. Karen what?" Paul said, smiling.

Karen told him her last name and he made a little bow, the way continental chaps do in some old movies, and left them.

"Handsome jackass, isn't he?" Francine said when he was gone. He had taken a seat at the bar up front.

"Oh, yes, yes, he is," Karen said.

"He thinks he's women's answer to the Twentieth Century, but he's . . . he's got his strong points. About the manuscript," Francine said.

"Right. About the manuscript. I wish I could tell you where to send it. In the meanwhile will you try to write something for us we *could* publish, something much more mundane, I'm afraid. . . ."

Paul called her at work later that afternoon to ask her out. By then it had become clear to Karen that the inevitable break with John had come, had, in fact, come and gone some weeks before. She agreed to see Paul Friday night and told him where to pick her up. She had been thinking a lot about John, far too much in fact, and Paul seemed just the type to help her take her mind off him. It wasn't until about a week later that she convinced herself she was in love again, in love with Paul this time. She had convinced herself of that, of course, only because she was sleeping with him. It seemed to make the affair more enjoyable, or perhaps the word was acceptable. It made the affair more *acceptable* then.

Having all this time to think in this damn hospital room has its drawbacks. Who the hell wanted to know that?

During one of their longer post-operative morning talks Morris had said, "Don't worry about yourself, Karen. Thinking about yourself, worrying about yourself, just makes life difficult and boring. Think about other people. Your self-consciousness will be cured in an hour."

Incredible, really, how right Morris is about everything.

She thought about Paul in terms of sex. No, sex was not right—in terms of sensuality. Paul, she realized for the first time, was a typical sensualist, a man who loved to touch, to see, to smell, to hear things. His apartment gave it away, or would have given it away, had Karen had the sense to think about the things she had seen in it, to think about them then, when she had been there, instead of now, in retrospect.

"It's happening right now," Morris had said on another occasion. "Everything is happening right now, this instant."

God, I wish I'd had a brother like Morris . . . or a father.

Of course Paul was a sensualist. One had only to look at his bedroom, at his water bed, at the drawings on his walls, at the bottles of love-making oil he kept on his shelf above the bed, to know that. But when Karen had first seen that bedroom she had thought: dirty old man, instead of: Sultan of the Flesh, Turk of All Time, or any of the other adequate appellations Francine had used to describe him. But Karen, of course, was unaware of the intimate nature of Paul's friendship with Francine, or, at any rate, superficially unaware of it. She did not, for instance, have any way of knowing that the pornographic drawings on the walls of Paul's bedroom had been contributed by Francine. She could not have known that any more than she could have known that V, too, had left her mark on the premises, a much more middle-brow, much more common mark, of course: a small reproduction of Rodin's *The Kiss* which she had taken the trouble to join a sculpture-of-the-month-club in order to obtain.

On that first Friday night Paul had taken Karen to a place in Greenwich Village where, after drinks were served, jazz was produced and the lights were low. Because Francine was the only thing they knew they had in common, Francine was what they talked about between the musicians' sets. Then, at Karen's insistence, Paul took her back to Seventy-third Street and said good-night.

He really made very little fuss. I don't think he wanted me much that night. As a matter of fact he was drunker than I was the first time we made love.

Jeanette had once told Karen that she had been told by one of her innumerable lovers that he was always able to tell whether a girl gave head and how well she gave it—and this after just a few minutes with her, whether alone or in public. It depended, the man had said, on how orally oriented she was. Did she use her mouth expressively? Did she put things to it or near it, pencils (if in an office), swizzle sticks (if in a bar), did she lick her lips, did she seem to enjoy not so much the taste of food but the way the food felt when she ate it? Karen could have applied a similar pre-tumble test on Paul with great success. He always seemed to be licking his lips. That night at the jazz place in the Village he had played with his swizzle sticks incessantly.

There was more. Paul fingered his glass as if he were really feeling it, really enjoying the slick, cool sensation of holding it. He hummed quietly along with the music when the tune was not too fast, otherwise seemed lost to the beat. From now on, Karen mused, she would be able to tell well in advance whether a man was going to be a good lover.

Imagine me thinking like that.

It was Jeanette's influence, of course, that accounted for Karen's readiness to make Paul her lover far faster than would previously been the case; Jeanette's influence and the fact that John's decisive silence after removing to his new job made Karen hungry to throw herself at a new man, to convince herself that John's departure did not matter to her.

And you know, it doesn't any more. Lovely: being mature.

Paul called her the Sunday after their first date.

"Why don't you come out with me tonight? We can listen more to *le jazz hot* if you like."

"Tonight?"

"Yes, why not?"

"All right, why not."

They did not listen to *le jazz hot*. They had a few drinks at a bar on Sheridan Square and then went up to Paul's place. Karen was still ill at that time, of course, and it was still winter. The drinks, combined with her usual feelings of faintness, had made her woozy. Paul, too, was not entirely steady on his feet. She remembered thinking: I'm going to do things to him John could never make me do; I'm going to do them so well it's going to drive him nuts. He'll take me out again, and again, and again. I'll be like Jeanette. I'll be better than Jeanette.

Paul, don't forget, is a very desirable man. A woman who does not want to get into his pants is a woman who does not like men.

She began with a striptease.

I suppose the processes of change were at work even then. Imagine me doing a striptease.

Paul let her in through the door of his apartment and put on the lights. Karen leaned against a wall staring at him. Then she shook her head wildly to disarrange her hair, producing the desired effect but nearly causing her to faint at the same time. When she had recovered she smiled and began slowly to peel away her coat, then, even more slowly, to unbutton her blouse.

I remember the look on his face. I really had him. I really had power over him.

The coat was on the floor. In a moment the blouse followed it. She stood there in her no-bra looking as lascivious as she could manage. It was the first time in her life that she had used her sexuality aggressively.

"If you are going to do this you might as well do it right, *mignone*," Paul said, recovering somewhat from her sudden attack. He turned, walked across the room, bent, rose, put a record on a turntable and a moment later heavy, rhythmic rock music filled the room from speakers set high on the walls.

Karen began to move one shoulder in time with the music. After a moment she had caught the rhythm well enough to make her breasts move seductively with it. She reached behind her and unfastened the no-bra, let it fall from her shoulders revealing the *nellies* Joe had loved so well. She put her hands on her hips, moved toward him, danced away.

It may have been the clumsiest striptease ever performed, but he liked it well enough.

He liked it so much he joined her. He undressed and soon both of them were down to basics, naked and dancing, though still not touching, in Paul's fancy living room. Paul danced clumsily, drunkenly to the bedroom door and opened it, and smiling, Karen moved toward him. He flipped a light on and she had her first glimpse of that unique room and its central feature, the water bed.

Making love to him was also unique. She had never had a man like him before. (She had never even seen an uncircumcised penis before.) His hands were constantly moving over her body when they finally fell together on the bed, causing the water to move beneath them and to push back up at them. She had simply never made love to a man who so much loved to make love.

As drunk as they were, they must have done it in twenty different positions that first night.

But it was the initial striptease that enchanted him. That look on his face when I began, when I knew I had him!

Lying in the hospital bed she remembered, but had to shut off the memory in order to maintain her body temperature at only slightly above normal, the way his penis had moved when he danced naked in his living room. Drunk as she had been, she would never forget that, the way it had swung back and forth, and gradually, and still swaying, had come erect.

They made love sideways (shades of Joe) and then with both of them sitting facing the foot of the water bed Karen on top. That was a great position because Paul played with her with one hand while running his other over her breasts, along her stomach, along her thighs, constantly moving that free hand caressingly, lovingly.

But what Karen remembered chiefly of that night was Paul's interest not in her body and not in the way their bodies were together but in his own body.

There was no doubt that his was a fine body. It was muscular without being aggressively powerful, it was smooth, almost hairless and very graceful; still, the way he watched himself amazed her, the way he stared for minutes at a time at his own legs, at, when the position allowed it, his penis and the way it appeared from and disappeared into Karen's vagina.

It was not my vagina he was watching. Don't ask me how I know that but I do.

She knew it from the kind of concentration he fell into while making love. He was lost to her; he might as well have been in the next room or the next county. His body was there, his breath, his body heat, his long (curved) penis, his low, rumbling voice was there, but his concentration deepened and became a barrier between them. The effects of the drink and the contact of their bodies was so great that this did not interfere with Karen's pleasure, with the greatness of Karen's pleasure, but then, as now in retrospect, she knew that this was the difference between making love with someone you love and who loves you and just making love, making practiced, beautiful, lovely, wonderful, but somehow incomplete and lonely love.

It was like love in a magazine, Playboy. *It was perfect, slick, and absolutely unimportant.*

After his first orgasm (achieved in the basic position so much preferred by Francine), Karen lowered herself over his body and beginning with his legs, kissed every smooth inch of his skin, refusing to release him from the delight she was causing him until she had finished entirely. By then his uncircumcised and curving penis was elongated again and she spent some time kissing that before she let him enter her vagina again, kneeling this time, with Paul holding tightly to her buttocks, of which she was usually, when sober, somewhat ashamed.

When she felt him ready to come again she moved forward and fell on her back. She found she could control him in that basic position much more easily than in any other. She could lower her hands and placing her palms against his hips keep his rhythm where she wanted it. She gyrated against him, raising her pelvis so that her large clitoris was continuously brushed against by his pelvic bone, and in that manner she managed too to achieve a long and quivering orgasm.

Different women come in different ways, Paul told her once. He explained that she whined when she came, as if in excruciating pain. There were women who shouted and shook, women who trembled and sighed, women who went flat, soundlessly flat, women who began suddenly to thrust powerfully. There were women who closed their legs during orgasm and women who opened them; women who closed their souls (his word) at the moment of achievement; women who opened them. Karen, he said, was definitely a close-the-soul, open-the-legs, whine-as-if-in-excruciating-pain type. In retrospect, in the hospital bed (months now, since that conversation) she answered him: sure, with you; but then your soul was closed from the first moment.

Sex is very, very complicated.

Karen shook herself from her revery, heard Morris' advice about mental states from that first private week in the recovery room, and decided to act upon it.

"Karen," Morris had said, "often it does a person no good whatever to think. Often the best thing you can do is discipline yourself to think of nothing. That's quite opposite from, and much harder to achieve than, fantasizing."

She put her head back on her pillow and stared relentlessly, and not without courage, at the off-white ceiling, reflecting now the colorful lights of the rented television.

She was released from the hospital in the last week of May. Jeanette came to help her with her things and Morris was there. The three of them walked out the double glass doors together and stood silently on the sidewalk. All of them were looking up at the sky, as if they had all three been confined for weeks, not just Karen.

"God, it's good to be outside," Karen said at last.

"You'll do as I said—take it easy for a couple of weeks. You won't go back to work until you feel up to it."

Karen smiled and nodded.

Jeanette was holding on to Morris' arm. She cocked her pert head to one side and said to Karen, "Maybe you ought to go up to Connecticut for a few days, just to rest. It would be lovely in the country this time of year."

Karen's smile faded, then rose again, a slightly altered feature. She said, "No point in that. There's no one there."

"What?" Jeanette said.

"There's no one there, I said. There's no big white house, no alcoholic father, no grandmother . . . no Porsche, more's the pity."

"Karen, I —"

"Oh, Jan."

Karen looked over at Morris, who was beaming at her. "Jan, that whole . . . Oh forget it. I was raised in an orphanage in Hartford. I have no family, never did. I'm afraid, Morris, that means it will be some time before you get paid for all this." She waved her hand behind her to take in the hospital and everything attendant to it.

"I know," Morris said.

"You know?"

"Have for some time," Morris said. "I told you, I take a personal interest in some of my patients, especially those I like. I made some phone calls."

Karen looked down at the sidewalk.

Morris said, "I'm throwing a small party for you next week. When I decide what day, I'll call you."

"For me?" Karen said.

"Right."

Jeanette raised up on her toes and kissed Morris on the ear. "There's a cab," she announced a moment later.

Morris raised his arm and the cab came to a stop in front of them. Karen looked at her doctor, kissed him, looked at him again, and finally got into the back seat beside Jeanette.

"Hospitals work," she said as the cab turned a corner to head across town.

"What?" Jeanette asked.

"They work. I've never felt so damn healthy in all my life. Hospitals work."

"What works," Jeanette said, "is Morris Levy."

Chapter Two

In April, Veltraud Schimmel Nathan Hong was raped.

New York City is a place where women are raped with increasing frequency, but V's behavior would very likely have resulted in the same consequences to her had she been living in Amsterdam, Port au Prince or Tierra del Fuego. She had become, since her short-lived and damaging affair with Paul Marot, the consummate, unregenerate, platinum-blonde bitch.

One Friday evening, V was waiting for Roger in Max's. This time, in order to get Roger's services as an escort and easily manageable bed companion, V had had to call *him*. A few months before he had sworn never to see her again. But, of course, he hadn't the will to resist her. She called. He came.

Roger thought they would go to a supper club and then to a discotheque where, V hoped, she would have another opportunity of showing off her body. She was wearing hot pants, a black silk long-sleeved blouse and a bright paisley scarf. It was the first time she had been in Max's in over a month. Despite the fact that it was quite crowded—both at the bar and at the dimly lit tables—Max found a moment to come over and speak to her.

"You look very good this evening, Miss Schimmel."

"Thank you, Max."

"Haven't seen much of you. There have been a couple of men around that I thought might interest you.'

"Ach, Max," V said. "Men are such bores."

"Down on our sex, Miss Schimmel?"

"Not entirely, but Max, I'll tell you, don't waste your time worrying about me anymore. I thank you for finding Ho Bin for me . . . That was enough."

"O.K., Miss Schimmel, if that's the way you want it."

"That's the way I want it, Max."

"Will you be going back to Holland, Miss Schimmel?"

"It's funny, Max, you know, I've been thinking of that."

Max nodded, more like a psychiatrist might nod than a bartender (even a very wise bartender) and moved away to serve some customers at the other end of the bar.

After a while Roger came in and V stood up, smiled, and moved with him to a vacant table near the front window. It was the same table, in fact, at which she had first seen Ho Bin.

"You look lovely, V."

"Thank you, Roger."

Roger ordered a drink for himself (V had carried hers with her) and said, "I want to talk to you tonight, V."

"Oh."

"I want to spend tonight with you *alone*."

A silence fell between them, broken only by Roger's saying thanks to the waitress when she brought his drink. Finally V said, "Roger, I don't want to fight with you tonight. That's not why I called you after all this time."

"We can't talk here. Let's go to your apartment."

"But dinner. . . ."

"Cook for me for a change. We'll buy a couple of steaks, something easy. And a bottle of wine."

V grimaced. She was going to try to lead Roger around on a string again and she didn't want that string to break so soon. She could see how serious he was. "Oh, all right."

"Let's go then."

"At least let me finish my drink."

V finally drained the last liquid from her glass, put her glass down, frowned, and said, "Let's go."

Roger left some money on the table and they stood up to leave. Chick Mandreaes, with a six-foot red-head in a pants suit, came in just as they were making for the door. Mandreaes and V exchanged long looks, said nothing aloud, and passed one another. V realized again—it was impossible not to—that sooner or later she was going to go to bed with that man.

They found a liquor store first, bought a bottle of expensive red wine, and took a cab down to Avenue of the Americas and Twelfth Street where they went into the supermarket on the ground level of V's building to buy the steaks.

When they had done that they went upstairs and into V's apartment.

The last time V had entertained anyone, it had been Carol Roper, the mistress of the invisible executive, who had shared V's table. And now the collected cigarette butts in the ashtray in the center of the round kitchen table reminded V of the conversation of that night. They had talked about orgasms. All women in New York seemed to be talking about that spring was orgasms, masturbation, self-stimulation during intercourse and Women's Liberation. Most of it, according to V, was a lot of American murky psychological and basically puritanical nonsense, but she had talked with Carol anyway, mostly to have the opportunity to say aloud some of the things she had been thinking for so long.

"*An orgasm only counts when you don't want it to,*" V had said.

"*What? You're nuts.*"

"*Carol, Carol. You don't understand. You have not to want one. Then they mean something. Don't you see?*"

Carol did not see and V was not at all able to explain herself further.

"*You have to be giving when it happens,*" V had said.

"*Or tired. Dead tired. That's when it's best for me,*" Carol had admitted.

Roger put the steaks on the small work space between

the sink and stove, entirely oblivious of V's train of thought, let alone of Paul Marot and his water bed which lay behind it, and turning to V said, "Now cook, lady."

V cooked by simply putting the steaks on a piece of left-over foil in the broiler and sprinkling salt on them (she had great disdain for American cooking; in Holland one pan-broiled steak for hours in butter) while Roger made himself comfortable in one of V's wing chairs in the living room. He came back into the kitchen while she stood by the refrigerator reading the back of a package of peas that had been in the freezer for ages.

"Nice place, V."

"It's all right."

V bent to inspect the steaks, frowned, flipped them over and slammed back the broiler drawer.

"Air-conditioning," V said.

"What?"

"Is your office air-conditioned?" she asked.

"Sure."

"I read somewhere that it dries up the semen."

Roger's mouth fell open. He blinked twice and said, "You certainly have a way of changing the subject."

"Come and eat," V said peremptorily.

Roger sat at the round table. V had not even taken the trouble to empty the ashtray or to move it. She had simply plunked down the plates on which she had set the steaks and peas and put a knife and fork beside each plate.

For a time they ate in silence, then Roger said, "It's a mistake to expect you to change, isn't it? You're too . . . too set in your ways. You're too sure you're right, maybe that's what it is."

V did not answer. Roger's words merely glanced off her consciousness, like light off a shiny surface.

Apparently Roger understood this because he dropped the subject and began to talk about his plans for his summer vacation.

"I get three full weeks this year," he said, refilling V's wine glass. "I thought I might go to Aruba."

"Aruba is no place to go alone, Roger," V told him, re-calling that rote response from her days with KLM.

"Oh?"

"No singles go there; the island is too small to have a good time unless you take someone along."

"Come with me then."

"No, Roger."

V realized she had responded too quickly; she ought to have thought it over; she ought to have kept him waiting for weeks for her final answer. Her peremptory response, the tone with which she had said, "No, Roger," now prevented her from backing up and changing her mind. God, he made her nervous sometimes.

"I see."

"Roger . . . I am not ready for that sort of . . . commitment."

"Do you ever want children, V?"

"Children?" V asked, open-mouthed, placing her knife and fork down and staring at him.

"Yes, children."

"No, of course not."

Roger got up.

"Where are you going? You haven't finished eating."

"I'm leaving, V. Frankly, there's no point in staying. And I've lost my appetite."

"What do you mean? You haven't given us a chance."

"Haven't I?" Roger was already standing by the kitchen door. "I've given us two chances and been hurt twice. I told myself that if there was just the glimmer of hope tonight I would make it three chances. Three and out. But there isn't the faintest glimmer, V. Why the hell should I let myself in for it all over again?"

V shrugged. The truth was, she couldn't think of a reason.

"You're right, V. You have changed. Just in these last months you've changed. You're even harder, crasser. Ciao—"

"Roger—"

She heard the outer door of her apartment open and slam closed and then she was alone with her quick American meal.

"*Verdomme*," she finally muttered.

Roger was gone. Paul had never really been there. It left

her with no one, really, but Mandreaes and she sat there wondering whether he was still at Max's.

She went into the living room and called.

Max brought him to the phone. V said, "Chick. I want you to take me out tonight."

"What happened to the pigeon-toed faggot I saw you with?"

"Come get me, Chick, I want to go dancing."

"I'll come get you, all right," he said, and hung up.

"I'm all ready," she told Chick after she had unlocked her door and let him in.

"So what?" Chick said.

He looked even hairier than usual. He was just her height when she wore no heels—which somehow reminded her of her recent husband, George.

" 'So what?' " she repeated his response.

"Lady, I'm going to fuck you blind before we go anywhere," Chick told her.

He turned, locked the door behind him, and stood staring at her with about the same expression she imagined the first rapist had worn when he raped the first woman.

V stared right back at him. "Stop it, Chick," she said slowly.

"Oh, sure. Get out of those things."

"I don't want to, Chick."

"I get the idea."

"Chick. . . ."

"Take them off!"

"At least let's go to the bedroom."

"Hurry it up then, lady. This is date number three."

She frowned, failing to see the logic of what he had said, but turned and went to her bedroom. Rape it might be, but she would not get black and blue and be knocked semi-unconscious.

Chick started to undress the moment he was in the room. He threw his jacket and shirt and tie onto a chair and opened his belt. He stepped out of his shoes and stood there, taking down his pants, wearing the same hard, purposeful expression he had worn at the door.

"Get out of those things," he said again.

Watching him warily and with something between dis-
gust and interest, V took off her pants and threw them, imi-
tating the violence with which he had tossed away his
clothes, into a corner of the room.

"Out of the rest of it," Chick said.

"You're all manners, Mr. Mandreaes."

"We both knew this was going to happen, Miss Schimmel. Let's go."

She finished undressing.

"You could at least say whether you like what you see."

"I like the way you do your breasts."

Naked, Chick looked more like a gorilla than he did
dressed. V had never seen a man with that much body hair.
His penis hung semi-erect from a black jungle of pubic hair
and began to stand straighter as he watched her.

"Any particular position, Mr. Mandreaes?"

Gorilla man smiled. "You're very cool, Miss Schimmel,
very cool. Get on the damn bed and kneel."

V moved slowly to the bed, climbed onto it, knelt, and
waited.

He was more gentle than she thought he was going to be
when he came up behind her, standing at the edge of the
bed. She knew he wouldn't stay gentle, she knew it as well
as she had known that eventually this, or something like
this, was going to happen between them, but he started
gently. He ran his hands (she expected to feel hair but, of
course, his palms were hairless) over her buttocks for a
moment, then put them between her thighs and opened her
vagina softly (George could have taken lessons from him)
and with a sure touch. Then, placing the head of his penis
against her labia majora, he asked, "You want some vase-
line?"

"There isn't any."

"It can get pretty rough."

"There's cold cream on the dresser."

He went over to the dresser, found the jar, rubbed some
of the cream on himself, and returned. V realized just how
much she had come to despise men, just how much she had
lost interest in it all, when she had to remind herself that he
was uncircumcised. She hadn't even taken the trouble to

notice until he had gone to the dresser for the lubricant.

He placed his penis in position and entered her slowly, took three or four clean, long lunges, grabbed her slight buttocks with his heavy hands, gripped them firmly, and then went to work like a professional fornicating machine, like a power drill. She had never been had like that. It was more like a heavy massage than it was like love. She was being pounded so hard and handled so roughly she hadn't time to feel excited about it. She was just being used. Perhaps another woman would have appreciated him more. He was certainly what some women thought of as an ideal bed companion. It took him fifteen minutes by the bedroom clock just to get his second wind.

After four more minutes of heavy pounding (she could smell his sweat, and had lowered her head and shoulders to the bed because she had become tired supporting herself on her arms) he began to whoop and grunt. When he came, he shouted and slammed into her so hard she would have gone flying into the headboard had he not been holding on.

"Holy mother of God," he said when he was done, standing behind her breathing like an athlete after a long race.

He went over and sat on the chair beside the bed and V lay down.

It hurt. It hurt bad. If he wanted her again he would have to use her anus.

"Well, lady," he said.

"You don't take much trouble to please a woman, do you?"

"Please yourself. That's your problem, not mine. You want to come? I'll get on my back on your bed and you can fuck me."

"Primitive son-of-a-bitch."

"That's me, honey. But I pay well. Where would you like to go tonight?"

"With you? I wouldn't go out with you on a bet."

"The hell you won't. I like you, Miss Schimmel. You'll go out with me plenty. And you'll like it."

"Is that right?"

"You'll like it fine. One thing I like is a woman who just stands there and takes it. No nonsense. Just drops her pants and stands there and takes it."

He was still having trouble catching his breath.

"First and last time," V said.

Mandreaes smiled. She couldn't help herself. She smiled back. She knew damn well they had struck a kind of bargain.

"I need a lot of fucking, V."

"So I see."

"You be here when I want you, come up to the office every once in a while, and you name it, honey, it's yours."

"Short of marriage."

"Don't be a jerk."

"One thing I want now, Chick."

"Name it. Only I don't go down on women, that clear?"

"Not sex, Chick."

"What then?"

"A fixed rate."

"You want to turn pro? You're no cheap whore, V."

"A fixed rate, Chick."

"How much?"

"Two hundred."

"Too much."

"One fifty."

"One flat, V. Every time I fuck you I'll give you one hundred bucks."

"All right."

"I didn't think you'd want it that way. You done this before?"

V shook her head.

"I didn't think so. I can tell a hooker when I see one. You got what bread you have some other way."

V nodded and shifted her position on the bed. Chick's semen began to run out of her vagina and she thought of getting up and going to the bathroom for a towel.

"Well, you all have to start somewhere," Chick said. "Come on, I'll take you out to eat."

Chick remained her only "customer." He used her once or twice a week and once, during May, three times in three days. Money seemed to mean as little to him as women did.

She had never known a man who had as little affection for the women he made love to.

Then, one evening in a Village bar where V had gone to drink with Carol Roper, V saw Paul with a pretty girl and walked over to his table.

"Hello, Paul," V said.

"V! It's nice to see you. Guess what Karen has just been telling me, *cherie*. Our friend Francine has proposed marriage to a doctor."

"Paul!" Karen said. Then to V she said, "Hello, Miss Schimmel. Remember me? I was with John Morelli one night in the Persian Room when you were with Mr. Mandreaes. Look, Paul shouldn't have told you about Francine. That was told to me in confidence."

V raised her thin blonde brows and smiled. "I'll be sure to keep the confidence. Francine Klein is a *very* good friend of mine."

Her sarcasm was wasted on Karen who smiled excitedly and said, "Oh! Really! That's great. Look, Francine will be at Morris' apartment tomorrow night. Morris is the doctor. He's having a party for me—will you come? I'll write the address on a napkin, here."

V smiled and looked at Paul meaningfully while Karen bent over the table to write down the address.

V then said, "I'd love to come."

When she went back to her table she was thinking that if she could strike just one solid blow against Francine Klein she was just about ready to end her American sojourn. The country had been through her and over her like a train (as the French say) and she would be better off to ship herself back home broken, unalterably broken, just as fast as she could bring herself to let loose of some of her gathered hate.

Chapter Three

The party was supposed to be intimate, but this is ridiculous, Jeanette thought, surveying, from her vantage point in Morris' bedroom doorway, the scene before her.

Two hours before, while Jeanette had been preparing hors d'oeuvres and a platter of cold cuts and while Morris had been checking the liquor supply, Morris had said that it was too bad Karen didn't have more friends.

"The truth is," Jeanette had replied, "she hasn't got *any* friends, except us, and Paul, if you call him a friend. She probably never had any before us, either."

"True enough," Morris said. "She was driven down into herself."

Jeanette nodded, slapped, slice by slice, a pound of bland baloney in a circle around a white china plate. She lifted gherkins and laid them along an invisible inner ring, thinking, *It's like a daisy chain. Pickle to pickle: back to back: zombie jamboree.*

She was already a little drunk. She and Morris had reenacted their courtship cognac scene early that afternoon and what Morris had not imbibed, Jeanette had, reciprocating, this time, the baptismal sex act: pouring the stuff over

Morris' penis and drinking it from that strange, inverted chalice.

God, it was good to be back. God, she had missed him. She had missed him bad.

Until that afternoon she had seen Morris but she had not made love to him. She had seen him in the hospital when she visited Karen, she had seen him once, sometimes twice, a week for dinner; but she had not allowed herself to fall into the pattern of love-making they had established before their break. She wanted to be sure, this time, that something permanent could really develop between them.

It was Morris' little speech, precipitated by the mention of Francine Klein, that had swayed her. It was the first time they had discussed that night in Morris' bedroom when she had played milkmaid and poured a half gallon over Francine and her stud.

They had to discuss it, finally, because Francine had been invited for the evening, and had accepted. Karen was especially fond of Fran and if Fran didn't feel equally warm toward Karen, she at least wanted to keep the lines to Hilt Publications open. Publishing through Hilt was the way Francine had decided to finance herself during what she had told Morris would be a term of extended underground exile.

"I will surface only in disguise to mail—in plain brown envelopes—my manuscripts to Karen," Fran had told Morris, and Morris had told Jeanette.

"Underground?" Jeanette had said.

"I wouldn't put joining the Weathermen past her," Morris had replied.

"Weatherwomen," Jeanette corrected him. "I thought she was busy organizing that raffle."

"That raffle, Jan, was held yesterday. A ladies' lib group from Jersey City won a male whore named J-boy to use as they chose for a night, or two, I didn't really get the details."

"Fran told you that?"

"When I called to see that she was coming. The Radical-Lesbians got less publicity for it than they wanted, which has made our little revolutionary angry."

"Is she crazy enough to join the Weatherwomen?"

"She is already a radical, unfrocked, and she is certainly a little crazy."

"A little!"

"Your jealousy is showing, hon."

Jeanette frowned. It was then that Morris made his speech, the one which won Jeanette back for him.

"Tonight," Morris began, "may be the last public appearance Fran makes for some time, so we ought to consider ourselves honored. Jan, before she arrives, before you see that *saftig* little nut again, let me try to explain something to you. We've avoided talking about it but—"

"Go ahead."

"Let's have it out, all right?"

"All right, Morris."

"In all the time I have known you I have not once been jealous of anything you did or anything you might have been doing. I have no reason to believe that while you were fucking me, you were fucking anyone else, but even if you had been, I would not have been jealous."

Morris was standing by his antique ice-box bar and Jeanette was standing at a long table Morris had set up in the center of the room to hold the hors d'oeuvres and cold cuts and rye bread. They were facing each other and attending carefully to each other.

Morris continued, "Which does not mean I do not love you, whatever love is. You are the most honest, most forthright woman I have ever met, you admit aloud to feelings, to desires, that other women don't even know they have and would never mention if they did know; you are sexually generous, sexually talented in that special way I have told you about. I want you close to me, in my bed, on my examination table when the bed is too far away, otherwise on the floor or on the sofa or on the beach, whenever I can get you. I want you thinking about me whenever, other considerations of your mind aside, you have the time. Now wait a minute, let me finish."

Morris had said that last sentence because Jan had suddenly looked away. She had not been going to say anything, however.

Morris went on, "*This* does not mean we have to tie each

other up the way most people who get married or live together tie each other up. I don't have time for children and
you have said that you don't want any. Sexual fidelity is
important mostly because of the children who are apt to be
hurt if their homes are broken when they are young. And
that kind of thing happens because their parents did not
walk the line and keep their eyes straight ahead being faithful to one another. But we would not have children; and
anyway, *we* are not and can never be, that kind of people."

Jeanette took several steps away from the food table and
sat on the couch. Morris did not move. He said, "I think,
that on the contrary, we are the kind of people who would
run into trouble if we had promised to be sexually faithful.
We are too diverse in our perceptions of ourselves, too
knowledgeable about ourselves, to be that way. We would
be beginning something with a lie, making a silent or even
an articulated contract to be a good husband and good wife
to each other. That lie would kill whatever we had or could
grow between us."

"I agree," Jeanette said very softly from her seat on the
couch.

"You do?"

"Yes. I thought very much the same thing just the other
night."

"All right, let me finish then."

"No, let me say something. I thought about it and decided it was true, that it would be starting something with a lie
not just for you—I mean I know that chick turns you on
and you are too much of a man not to fuck her if she
wants it again—but for me, too. I don't want to promise
something I won't mean a year from now, a week from
now. That; and all your damn books, Morris. . . ."

"I know what you mean, really I do, but let me say it all.
Because we can neither of us promise to be faithful, let's
promise *not* to be; let's make it a part of our contract, our
marriage contract."

"What?"

"We are different from other people and different from
each other. In an ideal world we would probably not be
suited for each other. In this world I think we are perfectly
suited for each other. But because we are different let's

have different rules. Rules we need, if you will pardon the ethnic locution, but they ought to be *our* rules. Let us fuck whoever we want to fuck whenever we want to do it; let us tell each other or not, let us just promise to live together and to think of each other first; let us promise that when we feel love rising within us like a gift that we will try to give that gift to each other first."

Jeanette began to cry.

"What?"

"Morris, I want to marry you."

"It has to be understood that sexual jealousy is low, it is mean, it is to be considered repugnant and every effort must be made, on each of our parts, to remove it from our systems."

"I will make every effort, Morris. And if I catch you with someone again I will pour milk over you and then go out and fuck the milkman and the bartender and the grocer and then come back to you. All right?"

"We will announce it at the party," Morris said with a beaming smile, "but that is not for two hours yet so why not celebrate immediately?"

Jeanette and Morris went to the bedroom to celebrate their unique engagement by pouring cognac over each other's sexual parts and spending a long time removing it with their tongues.

Lying quietly, naked together, the way they had not been for months, Jeanette heard Morris whisper, "I don't care who else you sleep with, what I want is for you to be here when I get back from the office or from the hospital. You, not anyone else."

"I'll be here."

"And the books won't bother you anymore. . . ."

"No, I'm not afraid of them anymore."

"Karen will be here soon, so I suppose we had better get dressed. I don't want her to see me naked. I promise to fuck other women but not your roommate and not this evening."

"You know, it was the books, it was that she was an intellectual too, and I knew that somehow, don't ask me how, that made me jealous of her. I was afraid of those books."

Morris rolled over and pulled her to his hairy, paunchy body. "Fuck books," he said.

Jeanette smiled and kissed the small, hairless place between the knots of his collar bone.

"There's something else," Morris said.

"What?"

"I promised you once I would do something for you, do you remember?"

"Yes."

"I'm going to see to it that you have an orgasm, lots of orgasms."

"I never have. I never will. I don't need to, Morris."

"I know you don't need to. I also know you're perfectly healthy, physically I mean. There's nothing wrong with this," he said, reaching down and with practiced forefinger touching the clitoral rise between her thighs.

"I still don't come and won't ever."

"Because you've never wanted to. Isn't that right?"

Jeanette said nothing.

"You may never have thought of it that way, but isn't it true that you never wanted to come? It almost meant lying, didn't it? In the same way that swearing to be a faithful wife would mean lying."

"I don't know, Morris. At first it was because it hurt too much, I mean the first time. After that, well, there were lots of people around most of the time I made love, at those orgies. As for doing it with men I liked, I suppose you may be right, partially right."

Morris drew her closer to him, encircling her with both his hairy arms. "More than partially right. You're a sympatico lover, remember, not an egocentric one. Egomaniacs probably come eighty-five times a day, witness our Francine. You're far too interested in the other person, far too well tuned in to what is really going on between your partner and yourself."

"So?" She was speaking into his neck.

"So, after a while you'll trust me the way you've never trusted a man before. You'll trust me because it's part of our deal not to lie about fidelity. You'll trust me because there isn't anything I want you to be except what you are. And it won't hurt."

Jeanette laughed.

"And you'll come," Morris told her.

She didn't say anything. She lay there smelling the musky odor of his skin and holding onto him by either side of his paunch. He was right. She had a feeling low down in her back that he was right. For the second time that evening she wanted to cry.

"Not today, probably not this week, maybe not this year, but you'll come, Jan, it's a promise."

They must have been lying naked for longer than they thought because the downstairs buzzer sounded just as Morris finished making his promise.

Jeanette jumped. "It's probably Karen and Paul."

"I'll answer it; you go put some clothes on."

She watched him climb out of bed and walk, hairy and naked, into the living room to push the buzzer, releasing the downstairs door. He was right; and she knew he was right. She wondered when it would happen and what it was going to feel like.

Jeanette dressed quickly and went to the front door, brushing past Morris with a kiss as he went back into the bedroom to put his clothes on. When someone knocked on the door Jeanette drew it open. It *was* Karen and Paul. She let them in.

"The food isn't all laid out yet. We were . . . interrupted."

"*Felicitations,*" Paul said.

"What?"

Karen giggled and said, "Oh Jan, it's obvious you've been doing it—you've buttoned your blouse wrong, and your hair's a mess."

"We're going to . . . I can't tell you," Jeanette said, turned quickly and went into the bathroom to fix her hair and her blouse.

"I can't tell you, either," Jeanette heard Morris say to Karen when she returned, dressed neatly this time, from the bathroom.

"No, don't," Jeanette called. "Let's keep it to ourselves for awhile at least."

Paul laughed, lifted a gherkin from the plate (breaking

the daisy chain) and popping it into his mouth. "Who's coming?" he asked.

"Francine," Karen told him, "and whoever she brings, and that Dutch girl."

"The one from the Persian Room?" Jeanette asked.

"The platinum blonde in the crushed velvet gown," Karen said.

"And you asked no one, Morris?" Paul asked.

Morris shook his head.

"Help me finish the platters," Jeanette said to Karen.

The two girls worked side by side removing the cold cuts from the delicatessen wrappings and placing them attractively on various plates. They lined up eight glasses, put out ice cubes, stacked hors d'oeuvres in neat lines on wooden trays, both girls beaming, radiating fulfillment, and Jeanette still a little drunk.

Morris and Paul walked out of earshot and Jeanette whispered, "How do you think Paul will react to seeing Francine?"

"How do you think Morris will react?" Karen countered.

"Oh, it doesn't matter."

"It doesn't?"

"No, we've straightened all that out."

"Amazing."

"I know."

"Tell me."

"I will, soon. Do you really think that woman will come, what is she called? Velmoot? Veltraud?"

"Veltraud," Karen said. "But she's really called V. Everyone calls her V."

"I can't imagine who she'll bring."

"If she brings anyone."

"What makes a chick like that tick?" Jeanette asked.

"And this may be the last any of us see of Francine for a time."

"Oh?"

"Don't say a thing when she gets here, but she's going underground. It's exciting, isn't it? She'll be writing for Hilt to support herself," Karen explained.

Jeanette played dumb. "Underground. You mean like the revolution?"

Karen nodded.

Morris came over with Paul and said, "Let's have a round of drinks before anyone else gets here. It pays to be ahead."

"I think you and Jan are already ahead," Karen said, "but we'll catch up. Won't we, Paul?"

"Certainly," Paul said. *"Certainement."*

Morris mixed drinks and handed them around. Then he raised his glass and proclaimed, "We have rather a special toast to toast tonight. Tonight we are drinking to adultery, but more important, to its prerequisite."

"What?" Karen asked, mystified.

"All will be explained in time," Morris said. Then, his glass held high, he said, "To adultery."

Paul laughed, shrugged, drank. Karen followed the same routine exactly, much like a person unsure of herself at an elegant dinner party who mimics the motions of the guest opposite her.

The doorbell rang just as Jeanette took the first sip of her drink and felt the alcohol warm her stomach. She jiggled the cubes in her glass and laughed aloud.

"There's something going on here," Paul said.

Morris went over to push the buzzer.

Jeanette stepped back to survey the room, feeling more like a hostess than she had felt when she had started setting up the apartment for the party over two hours before. The place looked warm and welcome. It was a large room and despite the table set in the middle there was still plenty of space in which to move around. There was the large couch to sit on and two wing chairs near enough to it to form an area in which five people could sit comfortably in easy sight of each other. On the other side of the central table were two black air chairs separated from each other by Morris' antique ice-box *cum* bar. The books, climbing above the couch and stretching out on either side of it made the place seem homey, now that she was no longer afraid of them. She decided it was going to be a fine party.

Then there was a knock on the door and Morris drew it open, revealing Francine in a short, flared, white skirt, and a tall, blond young man who instantly reminded Jeanette of Barry the homosexual. The tall man was very tan and very beautiful. He wore such tight pants that his penis could be seen outlined against his thigh. It had to be J-boy, the male prostitute. Jeanette felt awkward and embarrassed, then she laughed and came forward.

"Hi, Morris, hi, Karen, *bon soir*, Paul," Francine said happily as she entered the room, followed by the tall young man. "Hello again, Jeanette. Everybody, meet J-boy."

"Have a drink, J-boy," Morris said, as easily as if he greeted male whores daily.

"Lovely," J-boy said. "Bourbon and water, please."

Jeanette went to the bar, poured bourbon into a glass, went to the table and added ice and water. She came forward and handed the glass to J-boy. "What can I get you?" she asked Francine.

"V.O., if you've got it."

"We do."

Jeanette turned and went back to the bar to mix Francine's drink. So far so good. The anger she had expected to feel upon seeing Francine again was there but it was tempered with triumph. It was she who was engaged to Morris, wasn't it? It was she who counted with him. At just the right psychological moment she would announce the engagement, or Morris would. When she had mixed the drink she handed it to Francine and even managed a smile.

Everyone had moved to the couch and wing chairs and had taken seats, with the exception of Morris who stood near them at the long table. When Jeanette had handed Francine her drink and had moved to one side, Morris said, "Is it really true then, Fran, that this is your last appearance on this level of life for some time?"

"What *does* he mean?" J-boy asked coyly.

"He means that I am going to disappear into the underground. Yes, it's true, Morris."

"Good luck then," Morris said raising his glass in a toast.

Francine smiled at him warmly, with evident feeling, and raised her glass as well. It was Francine, of course, that Jeanette was watching, but she noticed that she was not alone in that. Paul, and Karen were also staring at her with more than curiosity.

They drank. Morris said, "I've been thinking, Fran."

"Oh. How nice," Fran replied with sarcasm.

Disregarding her tone, Morris continued, "One does not usually just disappear into the underground. One usually does something first which requires it."

"Does one?" Francine said, evidently mocking Morris' heavy English.

"Then especially good luck, Fran," Morris said with sincerity. "Don't do anything too terrible . . . please."

Francine looked straight at him, smiled, and said, "I'll be all right, Morris."

"I was thinking of innocent bystanders," Morris said.

There was a moment of chilled silence in which everyone realized what Morris meant. Jeanette made an effort to free her mind of the idea of bombs. There had been so many bombs going off in Manhattan lately, almost one a week, that it took some strength of will for Jeanette to accomplish this.

"Morris," Fran said softly, "I had hoped, you understand, that what we did yesterday, the raffle and all, would accomplish something."

"Oh, they *know* then," J-boy said, with mock hurt in his voice.

Francine disregarded him. "The *Voice* reporter was the only one who showed up; the other papers evidently thought we were kidding."

Morris nodded.

"Can't we get off this?" Paul said. "We were having a much lighter time before we started talking about politics." He said politics as if it was spelled politeek; he slipped into French sometimes, when he wanted to bring attention to himself by reminding everyone that he was a foreigner. Jeanette had noticed it before. Paul continued, "Before you came we had just made a toast to adultery."

"Now," said J-boy, *"that's* more in my line. Ah ha."

"You have to be married before you can commit adultery," Francine explained.

"Then let's just drink to promiscuity," Paul said with a certain amount of venom. He was looking straight at Francine.

"All right, *mon cher,*" Francine said, and drank almost greedily.

It was getting a little ugly. Gratefully, Jeanette heard the bell ring again.

"Ah," said J-boy, "more guests."

Morris went to answer the bell, and Jeanette said, "That's probably V."

"V?" Francine asked. "V Schimmel?"

"That's right," Jeanette answered.

Paul volunteered that Karen had invited her the night before, when they had met in a 'Village' bar.

"She's my ex-sister-in-law."

"Yes," Paul said. "I know."

A few moments later, V and Chick Mandreaes were shown into the apartment. Morris introduced everyone and brought the air chairs over so they could all sit in a circle. Then he went to get the newcomers drinks.

Chick immediately took possession of one of the air chairs, sitting down, crossing his legs, and smiling broadly. This was somewhat peculiar because V hadn't even removed the tan raincoat she was wearing. Morris had offered to take it from her, but she had turned to him with a seductive smile and just shook her head.

Morris returned with the new drinks, handed one to the seated Mandreaes and one to V who was standing now, where Morris had been standing before, at stage center, against the food table, smiling brightly at her ex-sister-in-law.

"Aren't you going to take your coat off, V?" Francine asked.

V continued to stare at Francine. "I haven't much on under," she said. "I just didn't know what to wear."

"All the more reason for taking it off then," Morris said with a light laugh.

V shrugged. "You think I'm kidding, Morris?"

"I don't know, V. I see you have stockings on."

"Yes," V answered lightly, changing the direction of her stare to Morris.

Mandreaes continued to sit silently with that beaming smile. The smile was so strange Jeanette decided that it probably was true; V was naked, or nearly naked, under her coat. But why? And so what?

"I think I'll pass around the hors d'oeuvres," Jeanette said, and went to get one of the platters.

"Nice place you have here, doctor," Chick said.

Francine spoke up, "What's going on, Mr. Mandreaes?"

"Call me Chick."

"All right, Chick. What's going on here?"

"You're a perceptive little chippie, Francine," Chick said with the same smile, "but this is V's little party, better ask her."

"I thought this was Morris' little party, especially for Karen," Paul said.

"Ah. I think I get it," Francine said. "Oh, V, poor, poor V."

V's smile dropped at Francine's words but immediately returned to full strength.

"What *is* going on then, Francine darling?" J-boy asked, in a way that made everyone turn toward him and stare.

Mandreaes said, "Where the hell did they dig you up?"

Francine shot back, "You don't temper your behavior much, do you, Chick?" She emphasized his nickname in a way which demeaned it.

"Look at that," Mandreaes said with a short laugh for emphasis, "the poor boy's already hard, look at his cock stretched out along his thigh there. Hah!"

Karen blushed, Jeanette thought she was beginning to understand, and Francine articulated it for everyone, saying, "You've come here to disrupt our little party, haven't you, V, and you've brought an expert along to help."

"What's to disrupt?" Mandreaes said with a shrug. "Nothing is happening. We're all sitting around like a family circle, sipping these drinks like they were lemonade."

Morris said, "What do you want to happen then, Chick?"

"Ask the lady," Mandreaes.

Francine said, "It's to try to get at me, isn't it, V?"

V smiled and unbuttoned the top button of her raincoat, at the same time cocking a stockinged leg so that her thigh could be seen through the bottom slit of the garment. Jeanette had to admit that she was probably the most attractive woman she had ever seen in the flesh and that when she turned on the sex, which was exactly what she was doing at the moment, she came on like a Caribbean hurricane.

Morris suddenly laughed, but his eyes, like the eyes of everyone in the room, were glued on the platinum blonde Dutch girl, whose right hand had slipped down to the second button of her coat. Everyone seemed to have forgotten J-boy's penis stretching out along his thigh.

V unhooked the second button and drew back the coat revealing perfect, upturned, naked breasts made up in light blue with darker coloring around the small aureoles.

J-boy started to laugh.

V said, "Are they funny? I thought they were cute."

"Oh, you're the one that's cute," J-boy said.

"And you're the one who's so damn excited he can't keep his cock down," Chick said.

"Oh, shit, he keeps it that way," Francine told Chick.

"What?"

"He keeps it semi-hard with—"

"Oh, don't *tell*," J-boy said.

"Ohh, can we see it then?" V asked, dropping her hand to the penultimate button.

"You've come to turn my party into an orgy!" Karen declared, actually raising a palm to her cheek and opening wide her eyes. "But why?"

"It's what the lady wants," Mandreaes said. "Be grateful."

"Be overjoyed," V said with incredible warmth and coquettishness. She unhooked the third button and then the last and separating the lapels of her coat revealed her body, entirely naked except for the stockings Morris had mentioned earlier, and red garters to hold them up.

Jeanette turned to see how the others were taking it and noticed that Paul was trying to drain the last drops of his drink from an empty glass, that J-boy was smiling, that Francine's eyes were burning with excitement, that Karen was horrified and afraid and constantly looking over toward Francine for a hint of how to behave, that Morris was amused and pleased and that Chick Mandreaes appeared determined to continue doing whatever it was they had come there to do.

V slipped out of the raincoat entirely and held it out to

Morris, who took it and walked with it over to the closet near the door where he hung it up calmly. Morris, of course, was accustomed to seeing people naked and had, anyway, just had great sex. Even so, his calm was admirable, given the circumstances.

"What nice hors d'oeuvres," V said, turning toward the table and bending over it so that the other guests could see what splendid nates she possessed. She lifted a small hot dog and turning back, ate it slowly. "You see," she said, "we knew it was to be a nice intimate party, and I was so pleased to have been invited I wondered what we could do for you all, for Karen and for Francine."

"Right," Mandreaes said and again snorted a laugh.

"So," V continued, "Chick and I talked it over and decided to give you all the most we could out of an evening. I am at the disposal of the men, and especially at Morris' disposal, and Chick, whose excellence as a lover is exceeded by no one, as I can personally testify, will please the women. Wouldn't you like to have Chick, Francine?"

"I don't believe any of this," Karen shouted. "I think I'm going to faint."

"Oh, don't be a *bore,* darling," J-boy said. "What a wonderful party this may be, after *all.*"

"You've finally gone stark raving mad, V," Francine said.

"This is disgusting," Paul said. *"Dégoulas."*

"Oh don't be so damnably and predictably bourgeois," Francine told him.

"Chick's not circumcised, either, darling Paul," V told everyone loudly. She turned and, bending gracefully again, secured a second hot dog which she ate as slowly and daintily as she had the first.

"Morris, come, you be first," V said. To emphasize her offer she turned toward him and pushed her breasts in his direction.

Morris laughed and said, "You ought to get paid for each shot or each night, love. You're cut from the mold that made the world's best whores."

"How do you know she isn't?" Mandreaes asked.

"I won't have this," Karen said sternly. "I won't."

Jeanette watched as Francine turned to Karen and, just

by cocking her head to one side and looking at her, managed to change Karen's mind about what she would have and what she would not have.

Francine then turned her attention to V again and said, "J-boy is my date, not Morris, V. Why not take him on first? It is me you want to hurt by all this, isn't it?"

V simply smiled.

Francine seemed aglow, it was as if the strange turn the party had taken had provided her with just the circumstances under which she could be at her best. She stood up, turned around once in front of the wing chair in which she'd been sitting, and started to undress.

"Come on, J-boy," she said. "Let's get this show on the road. You, Chickster, I thought you were part of the action. Strip, you ape-like son-of-a-bitch."

Mandreaes laughed and turned to V.

V nodded to assure him that it was fine with her but she seemed to have lost some of the sexual power she had had a moment before. Just by standing up Francine seemed to have diminished the Dutch girl.

Jeanette just stood and watched as Francine, J-boy and Chick Mandreaes stripped away their outer clothes and started to peel away their underwear. "Morris?" she said.

Morris looked at her, smiled and shrugged, then went to make sure the outside door was securely locked. When he came back the three of them were more naked than V, who was still wearing her stockings. "Can I get anyone a refill?" Morris said.

"Come, Karen, I will take you away from here," Paul said. His voice revealed that he was badly shaken. Although he was talking to Karen, he was staring at Francine.

"You're such a damn square, Paul," Francine told him. Jeanette thought to herself that Francine really looked great naked—a hell of a lot better than she looked with clothes on. She had great powerful breasts. She rivaled V very well; in fact V had looked sexier with something on.

"Come on, Paul," Francine said. "Let's you and I have one for old times' sake. I'm disappearing as of tomorrow . . . as far as you and the others here are concerned."

"Come on, Karen," Paul insisted.

"Karen," Francine said.

"Go ahead, Paul, I know you want her. Go ahead."

"Karen!"

"This is getting silly, too much conversation, not enough action," Mandreaes said.

He was standing very close to Francine and was about the same height. Built like a hairy bull, he was absolutely covered with thick black matting, even more so than Morris, and his penis hung heavily between his thighs. Suddenly he grabbed Francine by the arms and said, "Make room on the couch, you two."

Francine smiled and grabbed his penis which came erect very quickly. It was a long, powerful-looking organ.

"Morris!" Jeanette heard V say.

Karen and J-boy and Paul quickly got off the couch and Francine allowed herself to be backed against it, still holding on firmly to Mandreaes's organ.

"Why not?" Morris said. "What do you think, Jan?"

"Jan? Why are you asking her? Look, Francine is already enjoying herself," V said.

"Sure," Jan said, calmly, surprising herself. "Like we said before."

"Part of the bargain," Morris said.

"Are we just going to fuck?" J-boy asked Francine, who was already engaged in doing just that, squirming under Chick and trying to get his penis all the way inside her. "Fucking is such a *bore*. All I did last night was fuck, fuck, fuck. Those girls from New Jersey had *no* imagination *whatsoever*."

Languidly, J-boy reached down and grabbed his penis, which, unlike Mandreaes's, was circumcised, and rubbing it softly between his palms, managed to make it stand straight.

"Let's move the table out of the way," Jeanette said.

Morris nodded and took one end of it. J-boy hurried over to take the other end, and together they moved it to where the air chairs had been. J-boy's penis rode just over the table and a platter of sliced salami.

"Go ahead, love," Morris said. "Take your things off."

Jeanette laughed. "I just this minute put them on." Then she started to get undressed.

"Pile the clothes at the end of the couch," Morris said, appointing himself cruise director.

" 'Love'?" V said, mimicking Morris while watching with interest as Jeanette got out of her things. "I heard through Paul that you and Francine—"

"You heard wrong," Morris told her. "I'm going to marry Jeanette." He, too, had started to take off his shirt.

"Oh, Morris," Francine called from the couch where, under the steady rhythym of Chick Mandreaes, she had begun to writhe with pleasure, "I'm so happy for you."

"Thanks, Fran," Morris said, stepping out of his pants.

"Oh, God," Karen said. Then, "Well, what the hell?"

"Morris," Jeanette said when she was finally naked and had thrown her things into the general heap at the end of the couch, "J-boy is very beautiful, and Mandreaes is obviously a bull, but Darling, I want *you* again."

Morris smiled and came over to her. "Let's use the bedroom," he whispered. "We can watch if we leave the door open."

"Good."

"Your name is V, isn't it?" J-boy said, approaching the Dutch girl. "Would you like some of this?"

V stared at J-boy's cock, shrugged, said, "Sit down in the air chair," and as he did, climbed over him, reaching down with one hand to free her passage.

Jeanette heard her say, just before J-boy effected a penetration and she moaned, "This is not the way I thought things would work out."

"Oh, V, I'm so sorry for you," Francine, writhing madly now under Chick's brutal speed, managed to say.

Jeanette threw herself on the bed as Morris came through the open door, removing his clothes as he came. When he was naked he lay down beside her and they got into position to do it so that they were both facing the open doorway. Jeanette had to curl up slightly in order to accomplish that, but within a few seconds Morris had put his penis inside her and she smiled, happier by far than she had been in years, happier, perhaps, than she had ever been.

She watched Mandreaes for a long time. He had hair not only over his entire front but crawling over his back and shoulders as well. Even his buttocks were hairy, great clusters of black hair reached for his back and across his moving buttocks from the crack between them.

Karen and Paul, still dressed, stood frozen near the couch, blocking Jeanette's view of J-boy and V. Finally, happily, Jan saw that Karen was beginning to get into the mood. It would have been hard not to since the way Chick was bearing into Francine was close to amazing. Jeanette had never seen a man power-drill like that before. Large round muscles in his arms and shoulders rippled as he cocked his buttocks, slammed in, cocked them again and let her have it again. It was as if he were nailing her to the couch. Francine, her eyes closed, her mouth open, was grunting and motionless under his heavy barrage. She probably just didn't have the stamina to match Chick's incredible pace. Her heavy, nicely curved legs were spread wide, toes pointing to the opposite walls, her arms were grasping Chick's hairy back when suddenly she let go of him and raised them to form a symmetrical pattern with her legs, all her limbs now open and aimed up and in opposite directions. She shrieked, began to writhe as she had been when he first entered her, and very obviously came, then came again.

Jeanette saw her open her eyes wide, saw her muscles collapse, watched as her knees and elbows bent, and she just lay there while Chick, miraculously, Jan thought, continued his pace. Then Chick stopped and pushed up, his hands on the cushions of the couch, and stared down at Francine. Morris, too, stopped moving and Jan tightened the pressure of her vagina on his penis.

She heard Chick say, "Done, Miss? Then who's to be next?"

Karen stood nearby, staring down at his hairy back.

Jan called, "Oh, go ahead, Karen. Go ahead."

Karen looked into the bedroom, saw for the first time that Jeanette and Morris were doing it, too, let that decide the question for her, and started undressing.

Paul stood, mouth open, in the center of the room, ascot in place, eyes popped.

"Get out of the way, Paul," Jan called.

Paul moved to one side, enabling Morris and Jan to see

J-boy and V in the air chair. J-boy was seated, his long legs stretched out in front of him close together, V was seated on him facing him, bouncing up and down so hard Jan thought that every time she rose she would come clear off J-boy's penis and keep on going up toward the ceiling; but just at the moment when she might have come dislodged, when Jan could clearly see the length of J-boy's staff, shining and swollen against the darker area of his tanned, hairless stomach, V let herself descend, swallowing it.

There was some confusion in the room as Francine got out from under Chick, and Karen, naked now and looking very much afraid, took her place.

"Let's go back in the room," Jan said.

"Sure," Morris replied. He slipped out of her easily and they got off the bed and hurried inside again.

"Oh, I want you back in there," Jan said. "But I want to be closer to everyone."

"Here," Morris said.

He sat on the floor, his back against the wall, close to the wing chair and close enough and only a few feet from the couch.

"Sit down facing them," Morris said.

Jeanette got the idea immediately. She put one leg over Morris so that she was facing in the same direction as he was, and slowly, and carefully, lowered herself over him as he lined up his penis and slipped it back inside.

Karen and Mandreaes were now engaged in doing exactly what Francine and Mandreaes had been doing before. Having his women changed seemed to have done wonders for Chick's stamina. He was nailing Karen to the couch as hard as he had been nailing Francine.

"He's like a damn machine," Morris, inactive under Jan's weight, managed to say.

Jan squeezed her vagina and felt Morris tense and retense the muscles in his penis.

Francine was now facing Paul, still dressed from his loafers to his ascot, in the middle of the room.

"Don't be silly, Paul. Jesus, I need to sit down."

And then, quite suddenly, Paul was ripping away his clothes. He threw his jacket on the wing chair, his ascot followed his jacket, his shirt came next, his shoes were kicked to one side and his pants and boxer shorts followed suit. Standing, he grabbed Francine in the center of the room, and pulled her close to him. Jeanette heard him whisper roughly, "You liked that, you liked what that *singe* did to you. I'll show you how it is to be had."

He pressed Francine down to the floor and fell on top of her. Paul's feet and Morris' were now only inches apart. J-boy and V, busy on the air chair, were now, once again, in full view.

"This is very pleasant *indeed*," J-boy said. "But I should tell you, dear. I don't come."

"Neither do I," Jan shouted over to him.

"Oh, I *can; if* I want to," J-boy shouted back.

On the couch, Karen, her limbs reaching skyward, her mouth and eyes wide, began to moan loudly, then to say ahh, and finally to shriek as if in great pain. This seemed to set Mandreaes off for he began to move even faster, then, stopping at the height of her arc, grasping Karen under her buttocks and squeezing so hard Jan could see the veins in his forearms bulge, he began to shout and pound into her. "Holy mother of God!"

"He always says that when he comes," V, who had stopped riding J-boy and turned her head to watch when Karen had begun to moan, now explained to everyone.

"Time to change partners," J-boy shouted, pretending to be a caller at a square dance.

"O.K., hon?" Jan asked Morris quietly.

"Sure."

Now everyone was standing in the center of the room looking down on Paul and Francine. J-boy bent down and tapped Paul on the shoulder. "Time to change partners, Paul. Hey, Frenchie!"

"Oh, leave him be," Jan said, "Can't you see he wants to fuck her, not anyone else at the moment."

This was obvious to Jan because while everyone else in the room was engaged in simple mechanical fucking, Paul was devouring Francine's face and shoulders with his mouth. The poor girl's skin was covered with his saliva. This did not seem to bother her any, however. Her eyes closed, her knees bent, her thighs cocked open, her feet flat on the floor, she was steadily pushing up against Paul's steady rhythm.

Francine opened her eyes, saw that she was the center of attention, moved her eyes quite obviously from J-boy's still hard, gleaming organ to Mandreaes's fatigued, shrunken one, to Morris' hard, erect one, then closed them again.

"How many times have you come so far, Fran?" Morris asked her.

She had apparently not heard him. Jan remembered that she had read somewhere that people lose their ability to hear during sex. Perhaps it was true.

"Francine," she shouted.

There was no response.

"Francine!" she tried again.

Francine, feet still flat on the floor for leverage, began to writhe, then to buck, then shrieked and, quite obviously, came again. Paul, too, started to come, Fran's spasming vagina setting him off. He slammed into her with more muscle than style, which was unlike him.

"Jesus, I feel empty inside," Jan said.

"Me, too," Karen said.

"Karen, come here, girl," Morris said.

Karen looked at Jan, who smiled, and then went to Morris, who kissed her on the mouth and backed her up to the couch.

"So, you never come," Jan said to J-boy.

"Unless I want to."

"Fuck me, please?"

"Be glad to. The bed?"

Jan nodded, shyly.

She went off with J-boy to the bedroom and lay on her back on the bed while J-boy mounted her and began slowly, sinuously, to make love to her.

On the couch Karen and Morris had begun the same sort of slow, snake-like love-making, Karen on top, rolling her breasts into Morris' chest, kissing his hair, writhing with the lower half of her body against the lower half of his.

Out of action, at least for the moment, Chick and Paul stood in the center of the room, their sexes shrunken and looking, as far as Jan was concerned, terribly trivial.

Nearby, V and Francine stood looking at each other. Jan

saw it quite clearly. Suddenly, for no accountable reason, at least none Jan could fathom, V began to cry. Almost as she did, Francine stepped closer to her, put an arm around her, and held her tightly against her naked body. Francine, Jeanette thought, is quite a girl.

The two women stood that way for some time, V crying, Fran holding her against her body, soothing her. Mandreaes, who had come over to the doorway to watch J-boy squirming on top of Jeanette, now went over to the two women and put an arm around both.

Jan could see what happened next quite easily. Covertly, letting her arm fall from V's shoulder. Francine grabbed Chick's penis and began to tug it lightly.

V's head was lowered against Fran's shoulder. She lifted it, looked at Fran, and kissed her sweetly on the mouth. Chick's penis came erect almost at the same time.

The three of them went to their knees on the floor. Chick turned V so that he could enter her anus. In front of V, Francine took a seated position and the placing her elbows well behind her, leaned back and threw her head up so that her hair fell down and she was staring at the ceiling. It was then that Veltraud, converted perhaps to a way of sex she had never intended to embrace, began to move her tongue against Francine's thighs.

On the couch, Morris came, finally. He had been making love for some time, after all; now he slowly disengaged himself from Karen and made room for Paul, who had been hovering over them, his penis erect again, anxious, perhaps, to put it in a familiar stall.

Morris saw Jeanette engaged under J-boy, saw the threesome on the floor beneath him and decided to make it a foursome. He knelt over Francine's head and carefully put his shrunken organ over her mouth. Jan could see Fran's tongue come out to taste it as Morris reached out to pat V's head, which was now pressed tightly into Francine's vagina. Above the bodies of the two women Morris and Chick Mandreaes smiled at each other and did something Jan would never forget if she lived to be a hundred years old. They actually reached out and shook hands.

It was then, lying under the easy weight and writhing of J-boy, thinking of Morris, thinking of the deal they had made, of their signal contract to marry and be unfaithful, to be in love with each other, and unfaithful, to be honest with each other and unfaithful, allowing, perhaps, Mandreaes's handshake with Morris to symbolize that contract, Jeanette Emerson, the non-comer, the girl who attracted freaks, the recently engaged young lady from Waterbury, Conn., began to come.

"Morris!" she shouted. "Morris! Morris! Morris!"

PART FOUR

Karen sat at her desk looking from the postcard to the paper and back again. The postcard showed a large square with a statue of Rembrandt in it and had an explanation on the reverse in Dutch, French and English. It was from Amsterdam. The message said: "Dear Karen, I did the right thing to come home. When you get time you must visit me. Write. V." The newspaper said: "NEW BODY IN BOMBED BROWNSTONE. A new body was found today in the wreckage of the brownstone building which exploded yesterday on East 12th Street killing at least three people and causing several hundred thousand dollars' worth of damage. The body was identified as that of Francine Klein, 26, of Bayonne, New Jersey. Police, who are investigating possible connections between the victims and the Weathermen, say they think the explosion was an accident. Several. . . ."

Karen reached down, lifted a light manuscript from her bottom drawer and put it on her desk. It was Fran's last submittal, dated August 12, only two weeks before. Karen had been trying to find a way of rejecting it without hurting Fran's feelings. It, like the ones which had preceded it, even more than the ones which had preceded it, was simply unpublishable. It was good, of course, in its own way, but it was not for Hilt, or for any other paperback house she could think of.

Now she marked it for immediate publication and put it at the top of her desk. Her boss, Mr. Murray, would fire her for printing it, would stop its distribution if he could, if he saw it in time, if he chanced to read it, but that was unlikely. The least she could do for Fran was to see that her words got into print. The very least.

And if Mr. Murray did try to stop it Karen had a trick or two up her sleeve. John Morelli had told her a lot about Hilt and about Hilt's tax situation. If she wanted to she could make trouble for Mr. Murray. If it came to that.

She took the manuscript in her hands again, lifted the title page and, began to read:

A dream in lesbos. Mel's pad. She's left for the night, abandoning (hope all ye) it to me and whoever might need a place to hide for a few hours. She left the damn dog, of course. Told me to feed it, which I did. Then, asleep, alone, in her bed I find the dog wants in too, but not to sleep, damn dog is trained to lick. *To lick.* Got that, group? Radical Lesbians (unite), Weatherfolk, got it? This damn little dog gets between my legs as soon as I hit the sack and starts to lick me out. Perfect little beast. How not dream?

Dream of cock (as Mr. M. dreamed of cunt). Dream of Weatherfucks. Sex in the underground, you understand, not what it might be. Drugs turn people off good sex. Fun at first, later a drag. Would get out now if it weren't for the cause. The good fight. Blast the blasted banks.

Dream of super orgy we had months ago when last up there in over world. No geographic distance of course. Same place, same city, Mr. M's city, but different state of mind, different friends, different fucks. Dream of V licking me out as Mel's dog is now, dream of giving inverted head to good head Morris while monkeyman fucking V in anus so hard it keeps knocking her off balance so I keep missing, keep almost coming and then missing. Never get to Morris to come this way, of course, he comes when he's in a lass, in an ass, doesn't usually release Semen in the Mouth, Semen on the Mount, mount me someone anyone, jesus, V is making me hot again, or this dog. Doped sleep. No longer know what's real or whose tongue is whose.

Dream of cock of cock of cock. J-boy's long shining anesthetized cock. In and out of me oh cock. Cock, fucks, is what counts.

Hear me talk ma. Hear me talk. Cock it il do me 'doo. Cocks of the walk unite you have nothing to lose but your sperm and this world to gain.

Behind Morris see Paul fucking Karen on the couch (change names to protect innocent) smothering her with the same kisses he smothered me with. Nice together those two. And J-boy of shining organ slithering over Jan in the bedroom. Nice those two too. Too too nice. Fuck me in a tu tu but fuck me.

Such fools in the movement, the further out they are the crazier they are. Might surface again, chuck it all again, write like I wanted to at first, but do this one job first, blow this one big corporation, at night, no one hurt Morris, O.K. Morris? No one to be hurt oh doctor of the world. Hope you're happy with her, old fart.

Dream of cock and of cunt. Where do dreams unite? Some heaven where, rising from separate heads, they come together, form a new world, a world without fascism and with free fucking on every corner. Standing on the corner watching all the girls go by.

Terrible how good it is to be licked by a dog. Mel, you sly old dyke, you sly old whore, Mel. Now you'll reappear in the morning, smell the dog's breath, know, have it out with me again, ask me again. Well, why not, V sucked me out, wasn't bad. Still, watching Paul fucking Karen, giving Morris head. They shook hands. Monkey-man Mandreaes and Morris, over our bodies, reached out shook hands. Secret masculine compact to keep the world from women.

Keep your mind on cock girl you want to come. Hard to come with a dog at you, hard to concentrate. Too damn novel. Think of giving Morris head. Think of slick cock of J-boy writhing, Jan gasping. Jan shouting Morris' name. Hands shake over prostrate women. Good symbol of how it is. Morris you scum sucker, you *man*. Ah well, only folk who have cocks. Coming now. Ahh.

Karen put down the manuscript and looked out the window. Then she lifted it again. After the sequence in which the heroine is lying in bed being had by her lesbian friend's dog the tone of the piece shifted to narrative, plot was introduced, tension between several characters was adequately handled and adequately resolved, and then the heroine drifted off into another, then still another, stream of consciousness.

It would do. It would have to. Mr. Murray or no Mr. Murray, it was going into print. All Karen needed for it was a title. She put her head back and tried to think of one.

The way to become The Sensuous Man by "M"

The author of this book is one of the world's most expert lovers! In this explicit manual, "M" will share with you the erotic techniques it has taken him years to learn.

Every man has the ability and right to be fully sensuous. But most men never learn how. Even if you are short, bald, and bowlegged, this book proves you can still become a superb lover!

THE SENSUOUS MAN—The first "how-to" book for the man who wants to be a great lover!

A DELL BOOK $1.50

You saw her on TV.
You read about her in *Time*.
She's front page news coast-to-coast.
She's frank, she's controversial, she's ...

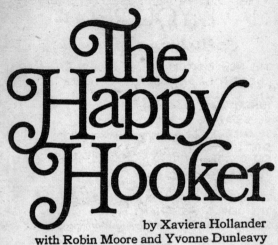

The Happy Hooker

by Xaviera Hollander
with Robin Moore and Yvonne Dunleavy

And she tells you all about it! Xaviera Hollander is young, beautiful, the most famous and successful madam in New York City. "Mine is not a house of ill repute," she has remarked on national television, "it is a house of pleasure." She made headlines recently when it was learned at the Knapp Commission in New York City that she paid $18,000 for police protection she never received.

Far from the controversial image of a prostitute, Xaviera is well-read, articulate, fluent in a dozen languages, and bursting with *joie de vivre*.

THE HAPPY HOOKER is her remarkable life story.

An original Dell Book $1.50

HOW MANY OF THESE DELL BESTSELLERS HAVE YOU READ?

Fiction

1. **THE NEW CENTURIONS** by Joseph Wambaugh — $1.50
2. **THE TENTH MONTH** by Laura Z. Hobson — $1.25
3. **THE SCARLATTI INHERITANCE** by Robert Ludlum — $1.50
4. **BLUE DREAMS** by William Hanley — $1.25
5. **SUMMER OF '42** by Herman Raucher — $1.25
6. **SHE'LL NEVER GET OFF THE GROUND** by Robert J. Serling — $1.25
7. **THE PLEASURES OF HELEN** by Lawrence Sanders — $1.25
8. **THE MERRY MONTH OF MAY** by James Jones — $1.25
9. **THE DEVIL'S LIEUTENANT** by M. Fagyas — $1.25
10. **SLAUGHTERHOUSE-FIVE** by Kurt Vonnegut, **Jr.** — 95c

Non-fiction

1. **THE SENSUOUS MAN** by "M" — $1.50
2. **THE HAPPY HOOKER** by Xaviera Hollander — $1.25
3. **THE GRANDEES** by Stephen Birmingham — $1.50
4. **THE SENSUOUS WOMAN** by "J" — $1.25
5. **I'M GLAD YOU DIDN'T TAKE IT PERSONALLY** by Jim Bouton — $1.25
6. **THE DOCTOR'S QUICK WEIGHT LOSS DIET** by Irwin Maxwell Stillman, M.D. and Samm Sinclair Baker — $1.25
7. **NICHOLAS AND ALEXANDRA** by Robert K. Massie — $1.25
8. **THE GREAT AMERICAN FOOD HOAX** by Sidney Margolius — $1.25
9. **THE DOCTOR'S QUICK INCHES-OFF DIET** by Stillman & Baker — $1.25
10. **SURROGATE WIFE** by Valerie X. Scott as told to Herbert d'H. Lee — $1.25